The Hyper... to ... M... ...sive hull.

The huge starship lurched and rolled, collapsing the giant guard rings that protected her Drive crystals. In moments, these disintegrated with catastrophic results, releasing tremendous free energy and turning the great starship into an inferno of deadly radiation fires.

Brim spun around just as the bulkhead split asunder and a wall of radiation fire burst into the corridor from the bridge, flooding toward him like a blazing cataract. Ahead was one of the ship's great security doors.

Smashing at an EMERGENCY CLOSE plate as he dove through the opening, he only just got himself to the other side before three massive blades dropped in place to bar the advance of the flames. As he gasped for breath, his mind's eye saw eight similar sets of blades that had fallen at the same instant on the other levels of the doomed starship.

He was now forever sealed off from the forward end of the ship . . .

■ ■ ■

ALSO BY BILL BALDWIN

THE DEFENDERS
GALACTIC CONVOY
THE HELMSMAN
THE MERCENARIES
THE TROPHY

Published by
Warner Books

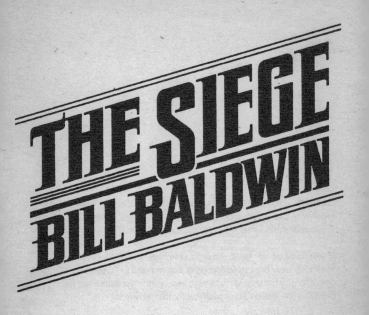

THE SIEGE

BILL BALDWIN

WARNER BOOKS

A Time Warner Company

Enjoy lively book discussions online with CompuServe. To become a
member of CompuServe call 1-800-848-8199 and ask for the Time Warner
Trade Publishing forum. (Current members GO:TWEP.)

WARNER BOOKS EDITION

Cover design by Don Puckey
Cover illustration by John Berkey

Questar® is a registered trademark of Warner Books, Inc.

Warner Books, Inc.
1271 Avenue of the Americas
New York, NY 10020

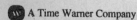 A Time Warner Company

Printed in the United States of America

First Printing: March, 1994

10 9 8 7 6 5 4 3 2 1

Imperial Standard Date: 32 Diad, 52013.

Prologue

Outfitted in snug, Bearish finery, complete with requisite egg-shaped hat to cover his ears and add at least an iral to his normal six-iral height, Rear Admiral Wilf Brim, Imperial Fleet, grinned with pure pleasure as the elegant troika sped him through a dazzling Sodeskayan blizzard. Traditionally known as a "love sleigh," the rare antique was drawn by three shaggy black droshkat thoroughbreds loping effortlessly over the powdery snow—the center 'kat trotting in shafts while the other two, loose save for long traces, padded along like ebony ghosts. The three great animals set hundreds of tiny bells to rhythmic jingling from their burnished harnesses, producing melodies from a thousand years in the Sodeskayan past. Only cloud-muted thunder from a lifting starship momentarily spoiled the illusion that the sleigh was racing through the planet's rural countryside. Tomoshenko Memorial Starport on artificially heated Lake Demyansk lay a mere thirty c'lenyts to spinward from the sprawling Borodov estate. And the capital of all Sodeskaya, "Holy" Gromcow, unfolded along a riverbank only twenty c'lenyts farther on.

To Brim's left, Grand Duke Anastas Alexi Borodov snapped his whip and joggled the reins with the exuberance of someone half his age. Driving a Sodeskayan troika was a special art, for the driver was required to stand—no mean feat for a Bear of Borodov's years. As a true *yamschik*, he was privileged to wear a special badge: two bright orange zavencock feathers protruding from the right side of his hat.

On Brim's right, massive General Nikolai Yanuarievich Ursis, galactic-class Drive engineer and (in rare years of peace) dean of the renowned Dytasburg Academy, puffed contentedly on an intricately carved Zempa pipe as chalky trunks of ancient, somnolent birches whizzed by on either side of the narrow rustic lane. Stumps of frost-burned azalea and skeletal dogwood protruded from the snow, half screening bare stands of oak and poplar behind them.

This was Sodeskayan winter at its old-fashioned best—if not its most genuine.

Despite the quiet tranquillity of the late afternoon, however, Brim found it all too easy to recall the savage conflict—now generally referred to as the Second Great War—that was spreading rapidly throughout the Galaxy. He'd personally had a hand in turning back the League's first barbarous assault against his own homeland.

Now, only a few thousand light-years from this great capital, Nergol Triannic's League of Dark Stars was assembling an even greater invasion force than the one he'd arrayed against the Imperial capital of Avalon. In the balance was the huge agglomeration of stars, planets—and wealth—that made up the colossal Sodeskayan heartland. Commanding the vast invasion force was none other than Field Marshal Rodef *nov* Vobok, with fat Admiral Hoth Orgoth—recently humbled during the Battle of Avalon—in charge of space operations. This time, the Leaguers meant to take no chances for failure. Brim knew—he'd literally had to fight his way to the Sodeskayan capital. . . .

Less than three Standard Days out of Gromcow and scarcely half a metacycle into a blustery morning watch, he had been sitting in a jump seat on the navigation bridge of the fast Sodeskayan liner *Alexasander Grobkin*, conversing—in Avalonian—with Captain Peter Nesterov and Chief Navigator T. P. Stefanovski. At a warning from their Helmsman, the three peered through the aft Hyperscreens toward three fast-approaching points of light that moved at an oblique angle to the normal rush of stars. Suddenly, an authenticator system filled the bridge with its mewling alarm— its coded KA'PPA challenge to the three mysterious ships had not been properly answered. To port, disruptors on their lone escort, a little 26,000-milston Smetlivy-class attack ship named *Gordi* began to index and swing like an athlete flexing his muscles.

"So," Nesterov remarked emotionlessly, "Leaguers again, eh?" Tall, ruddy-haired, and endowed with the huge, droopy whiskers common to natives of Sodeskaya's frigid Hargovian-Sector planets, the Bear was a *very* senior captain of the Sodeskayan flag carrier *AkroKahn*.

"League national industry is war, it seems, Captain," Stefanovski replied as flashes from the Leaguers' ranging shots sparkled brightly among the onrushing stars. A small, dark Bear from Gromcow proper, he had the nearsighted countenance of one who has spent most of his career staring into a display. Moments later, the Hyperscreens dimmed momentarily as six or eight closely spaced explosions rocked space nearly a c'lenyt to port. Stefanovski frowned into the wide-area star map of his display and shook his head. "At least they are no better shots than their predecessors in the last war," he said mordantly.

Brim chuckled grimly, thinking back on myriads of similar flashes in two separate wars over more than twenty Standard Years—so many, they failed to arouse much fear anymore. They'd simply become part of his existence. Only recently, he'd been one of a small band that repulsed the greatest siege ever mounted against a single star system. Not that war *ever* got to be old hat, really. One was too busy trying to stay alive for it to ever reach that status.

He looked around the bridge, watching tension mount among the starship's Helmsmen, navigators, systems officers, communicators, and the meager team of junior officers whose job was to command the forlorn batteries of disruptors jerry-rigged to the sleek liner for wartime travel. The light, rapid-firing 57-mmi twin-mounts were little more than child's toys against Leaguer attack ships, but if nothing else, they gave the feeling of hitting back, though even a direct hit was liable to do little damage.

"Bastards take their own sweet time," Stefanovski mumbled.

"Perhaps *you* are anxious for their arrival." Nesterov chuckled darkly. "For me, I could easily wait until end of time."

Brim felt the Drive winding up and glanced aft, watching the Drive plume expand as *Alexasander Grobkin* accelerated in preparation for the complicated, three-dimensional zigzag maneuvers that would help her survive the attack—or at least cause the nearly impotent crew to feel that they were doing *something* in their own defense. Outside, a blinding Hyper-Flare went off, sending dazzling incandescence through the great arch of Hyperscreens over the bridge. Groans came from everyone caught with their eyes open before the crystal panels automatically darkened. The Leaguer's scout ship—a Gantheisser GA 88, from its silhouette—actually eclipsed its own flare for a moment, then disappeared ahead into the confusion of rushing stars.

Even Brim's eyes—more or less accustomed to flashes of disruptor fire from Avalon's recent siege—ached, so powerful were the flares. Then the stars outside canted wildly as the ship abruptly climbed for her first zigzag, while their escort moved out to port for more fighting room. Brim clenched his fist, *hating* to be so xaxtdamned helpless!

As if that thought had somehow triggered it, every one of the transport's pitiful little 57-mmi's and the full complement of 130 mmi's aboard the *Gordi* opened up on two more greenish Drive plumes that were now heading their way from aft. Another turn—the stars slid down and to starboard. "Now comes attack," Nesterov said soberly as the plumes steadied on course toward the little attack ship. "Seems Leaguer bastards have orders for escorts this trip, eh?"

As the bridge crew yelled encouragement, Brim and Stefanovski soberly watched the battle unfold, uselessly grabbing their armrests as another violent turn angled the stars across the forward Hyperscreens. Now the three attackers were pressing home their attack on the *Gordi*, weaving violently in the face of her fierce disruptor fire. At the same moment, the first two released a HyperTorp each and turned away in a hail of roiling explosions. To Brim's eye, the deadly missiles appeared to be running true as they rapidly narrowed their distance from the ship.

"Universe," Stefanovski exclaimed, glancing at the escort, which as yet had made no attempt to dodge the torpedoes, "*Gordi*'s not doing anything."

"Ah, her captain waits for last torpedo," Nesterov observed as *Alexasander Grobkin* zigged again.

"Will soon be too late," Stefanovski whispered through tight lips.

At the last possible moment, *Gordi* launched a decoy and the three HyperTorps wavered momentarily, then changed course and exploded safely a half c'lenyt distant.

"Voof!" Nesterov gasped, glancing aft again. "Last Leaguer still on torpedo run, would you believe?"

"His last torpedo must have hung up," Brim guessed.

"Ah," Nesterov agreed, "that must be so!"

Someone called out in Sodeskayan as the bridge filled

with what had to be shouts of encouragement from the Sodeskayan gunners.

"Sweet mother of Voot!" Brim started. "The bastard Leaguer better break it off soon or—" Abruptly he stopped in the middle of his sentence as *Gordi* scored a direct hit at point-blank range and the enemy ship blew up in a roiling fireball that engulfed both attacker and defender.

"Is all over now." Nesterov groaned quietly.

When the *Gordi* emerged from the fireball, cries of horror filled the bridge. Two of her aft turrets were gone, with the whole bow section of the Leaguer attack ship embedded in their place. The wrecked escort slewed off course as a solid mass of radiation fire erupted from her hull and she began to slowly fall behind.

It was Brim's all-too-real introduction to contemporary Sodeskaya and the trouble that had befallen that great domain of planets since his peacetime visits there only a few years before the war.

The Second Great War existed only as a name. More accurately, it was a logical extension of an earlier, eleven-year struggle that had entered temporary hiatus thirteen years previously in 52000. That year, following a series of military reverses, the League's Emperor, Nergol Triannic, suddenly abdicated his throne for the lonely planet of Portoferria, then proposed a peace treaty and concomitant armistice until the treaty could be approved.

Shortly following these critical events, the victorious Empire found itself divided into hostile camps of war-weary reconciliationist groups and equally war-weary militants. Most reconciliationists coalesced rapidly into the politically powerful Congress for Intra-Galactic Accord (CIGA). Militants, however—comprising various military and veteran organizations—were still required to focus the bulk of their efforts on such workaday tasks as securing the far-flung bulwarks of

Empire. They therefore steadily lost political influence at all levels, and subsequently, after furious debate throughout the Imperial Parliament, the League's treaty—already signed by League Emperor Nergol Triannic—was pushed through by CIGA Chief Puvis Amherst. It was formally ratified on the neutral planet of Garak by then-Emperor Greyffin IV two days prior to the Year's End holiday in Avalon, 52001.

Amid vociferous Admiralty protests and resignations, Imperial Fleet reductions, with resultant base closings, began promptly in 52001 to rigid schedules prescribed in the new treaty. Each of the former antagonists chose referees to oversee the other's disarmament progress. After two successive Imperial Fleet reductions in 52002 and 52003, out-of-work veterans gathered for a "March on Avalon." Most departed peacefully after Parliament vetoed cash bonuses recommended by Greyffin IV; however, other, more adamant veterans were forcibly expelled by special detachments of Imperial Marines wearing the special CIGA flash on their uniforms and lead by CIGA-aligned officers.

A further reduction in Fleet strength during 52004 completed Imperial disarmament requirements and resulted in the smallest Fleet in the Empire's history. Half a galaxy away in Tarrott, Puvis Amherst personally confirmed similar reductions in League strength, but the scattering of starsailors who remained loyal to the Empire suspected the League's claims were little more than fabrications. Unfortunately, a clamor of pacifist emotion sweeping the Empire—though ultimately emotional and uninformed—was nevertheless politically unassailable. And while the League secretly built a new and much more powerful fleet, the Empire continued to sink into impotency.

In 52005, culmination of a three-year study by the blue-ribbon Interdominion Reparations Committee resulted in a report fixing League war liability at one hundred thirty-two billion credits, to be indemnified during the next ten Standard Years. Zoguard Grobermann, League Minister of State, promised that the Chancellery would "take the sum under advisement," but no further action was forthcoming.

In 52006, the anti-League president of Beta-Jago, Konrad Igno, was assassinated by an unknown murderer during the traditional midyear holiday interval in that dominion. League Minister for Public Consensus Hanna Notrom denied any knowledge of the act, and soon afterward the League's Supreme Council cynically enacted laws law forbidding assassination to prove once and for all their peaceful intentions.

Early in 52007, exiled Nergol Triannic published his semibiographical *Ughast Niefft* as a formal declaration of proper League objectives. By Avalonian midsummer, League sympathizers annexed all planets of the Gammil'lt star system at the request of the openly League-endorsing Chancellor I. B. Groenlj. At year's end, CIGA elements in the Imperial Parliament itself passed the Cavir-Wilvo Bill posing stringent limits on Imperial starship manufacture.

Soon after Standard Year 52008 began, exiled Nergol Triannic returned in triumph to Tarrott and resumed the reins of League Government wearing the then-outlawed black uniform of the Controllers, elite regiments of specially chosen soldiers from which he traditionally chose his personal guard. Less than one month later, Conrad Zorn, prominent intragalactic traveler and industrialist, was found murdered after accusing the League of secretly expanding its Deep Space Fleet. By midyear, Triannic repudiated the League's reparations debt and reintroduced compulsory military service for all League citizens. At the end of the League's Festival of Conquest holidays (Imperial Standard Date: 2 Nonad, 52008), Controller forces entered and occupied planets of The Torond, enthroned League sympathizer Rogan LaKarn as ruler, and proclaimed the "eternal" political union of League and Torond.

Midway through 52009, Zoguard Grobermann and Hanna Notrom jointly announced League incorporation of the Zathian planetary system, as the result of a plebiscite. Soon afterward, Nergol Triannic issued a stern warning to the Dominion of Fluvanna concerning treatment of League citizens dwelling on its planets.

Early in 52010, after CIGA-inspired frustration of numerous Imperial attempts to defend the important Dominion of Fluvanna (supplier of nearly one hundred percent of the Empire's Drive Crystals), Emperor Greyffin IV formed the Imperial Volunteer Group (IVG), "leasing" the first eleven Starfury starships and their crews to Fluvanna for a year. Shortly thereafter, League forces invaded and occupied the Dominion of Beta-Jago, ignoring protests from throughout the galaxy. Two months later—on trumped-up charges—Triannic also declared war on Fluvanna, thus supplying a spark that would eventually reignite war itself.

Until well into 52011, CIGAs throughout the Imperial Parliament prevented implementation of the Empire's mutual-assistance treaty with Fluvanna. However, with abdication of Greyffin IV, Onrad V became Emperor and declared war on the League even as IVG forces destroyed huge League space fortifications at Zonga'ar and set Triannic's timetable for conquest back nearly a Standard Year. Within a month, the new Imperial Emperor dissolved his IVG, ordering the battle-proven crews back home to be scattered throughout the newly expanding Imperial Fleet in preparation for the inevitable Battle of Avalon.

Wilf Brim—one of the first to join the IVG rolls and commander of the Zonga'ar raid—formed the vanguard of this historic migration. Assuming command of 30 Wing, 11 Group, Home Fleet Defense Command, on 205/52012, he hurled himself into a desperate effort to bring his crews and their ships into readiness. His efforts paid off more quickly than anyone expected, and his command played a key role in the defense of Avalon's five capital planets when the Leaguers prepared to invade only weeks after their lightning victory over the Dominion of Effer'wyck. During the next six months of desperate fighting, the badly outnumbered defenders managed to inflict such grievous casualties—in both crews and starships—to the Leaguers that Triannic postponed the whole invasion program.

Now, with renewed fleets—and huge land armies that had gone unused since the fall of Effer'wyck more than a year ago—Triannic was poised to launch his second campaign. And this time, he expected success.

CHAPTER 1
The Ugly Truth

"I can't believe I need a parade uniform," Brim groaned, glancing over the array of clothing Barbousse had laid out on the bed. "I'm supposed to be going on maneuvers in a battle crawler, not to a three-day banquet."

"Beggin' the Admiral's pardon," Barbousse replied, "but m' instructions from the Embassy say you may need that parade uniform a *couple* o' times before they bring you home."

"Hmm," Brim mused. Borodov had warned him of the same thing, and *he* was, after all, the Knez's brother. "When do you suppose that'll be?" he asked, peering through the morning dusk at an expanse of snow-covered gardens and statuary below.

"Couldn't get the times or the dates, Admiral," Barbousse replied. "But since the whole show's being put on for the Knez, they're pretty certain to be when *he* wants."

Brim nodded resignedly. Only in Sodeskaya. . . . "Pack it all," he said in resignation.

"Aye, Sir," Barbousse agreed, and set to loading the single grip that Brim would consent to take with him, despite the fact that many of the high-ranking Sodeskayan officers would be followed by at least three—each double the size of its predecessor.

Brim checked the time. Since his days as a Sublieutenant aboard the old Fleet destroyer I.F.S. *Truculent,* he had known both Borodov and Ursis to always be punctual, almost to a fault. "I'll be in the study," he said, opening the dark oaken door that separated his suite of rooms from the upstairs hallway. Descending the grand staircase two steps at a time, he presently emerged into the immense central arcade of Borodov Manor, the "Gallery," where a young Bear—Borodov's great-grandfather, Brim recalled—stared out from a portrait by Novar Sograve, arguably Sodeskaya's most revered portraitist of the last millennium.

He paused for a moment, contemplating the portrait and the young, aristocratic Bear it had frozen in time. Sograve's utter genius had captured the supreme confidence that characterized an age *long* gone by—bearing no resemblance to the last two hundred-odd years of almost constant war, in which lifetimes were frequently measured by how long one managed to avoid being killed. Brim's own daughter, Hope, was being raised by a nurse because her mother had been blasted to atoms by League disruptor fire only metacycles after she had given birth—in Avalon's Imperial Palace, no less. And Margot Effer'wyck, the one abiding love of his life and a Royal princess in her own right, was now a fugitive from her husband—Rogan LaKarn, Grand Baron of The Torond and a shameless League sympathizer. The galaxy wasn't a very nice place to live in, presently, and offered little promise of improvement, at least in the near term.

From the Gallery, he passed through another great hall and finally emerged into the vast library with its colossal fireplace, lofty ceiling (surfaced by a priceless forty-eighth-century Rhodorian trompe l'loeil painting), spiral staircase, and two-story bookcases filled by an enormous collection of ancient volumes, some with actual *paper* pages.

Ursis was already seated in one of the ample leather chairs, puffing thoughtfully on a huge Zempa pipe and filling the room with an aroma that most humans charitably compared with the redolence of burning yaggloz wool. Even seated, the Bear was a most imposing figure. He had small, gray eyes of enormous intensity, dark, reddish brown fur, a long, urbane muzzle that terminated in a huge wet nose, and delicate, though hirsute, six-fingered paws. When he smiled—as he was doing presently—fang jewels glistened in the warm light of the room. Tonight, he had dressed in the tan-and-crimson uniform of the Sodeskayan Surface Army with gold-trimmed peaked cap, gold-buttoned reefer jacket, white shirt, black tie, and black-leather ankle boots. Traditional Sodeskayan shoulder boards—in gold—on his jacket were decorated by the twin wreathed stars of a Lieutenant General, which were also applied to each cuff of his coat. Three rows of campaign ribbons beside his left lapel attested to long years of fighting the League. A curious, starburst-shaped badge on his right breast denoted onetime involvement in the Knez's Imperial Guard. "Voof," he said by way of greeting, and indicated a chair beside him. "Next few days, Wilfooshka, you receive first introduction to why Sodeskaya needs you so much."

"On maneuvers, Nik?" Brim asked with a frown. "But even Leaguers admit that Sodeskayan land forces are the best trained and equipped in the Galaxy. Everyone thinks they are unbeatable."

The Bear only nodded somberly. "Not everyone," he said.

"So you've been saying," Brim replied, "but I still don't understand."

"You will soon enough, Wilf Ansor," Borodov interposed, entering the room from a private passage. " 'Trees and Bear cubs shiver in rhythm during springtime frolic,' as they say."

He was dressed in a maroon version of Ursis's uniform, denoting the Sodeskayan Engineers, with *three* stars of a Colonel General on the black leather of his collars. More chestnut in color than his longtime friend Ursis, Borodov was much older and somewhat bowed by his years, standing only a little taller than Brim's six irals. His eyes, however, sparkled with youthful humor and prodigious wisdom behind a pair of old-fashioned horn-rimmed spectacles. And although his graying muzzle was not nearly so intimidating as that of his massive companion, enormous sideburns provided him with a most intellectual countenance. "Considerable numbers of us Sodeskayans believe . . ." He stopped in mid-sentence and walked to the bar, where he busied himself decanting three large goblets of clearly Logish Meem. "No doubt," he mused, "it will be better you make up your mind without our influence. You are, after all, big Fleet expert—not us. Eh, Nikolai Yanuarievich?"

Ursis nodded to Brim. "Fleet aspect of maneuvers is why you are here, Wilfooshka," he said, "—or more precisely, *lack* of a Fleet aspect." He shook his head sadly. " 'Only frozen mountains can howl at moons in dead of snow season,' as they say."

Brim narrowed his eyes. The human had yet to be born who could understand Bearish aphorisms—and the Bears seemed to *know* it. Yet they continued to quote from some clearly infinite source, as they had since the first interstellar Bears met early interstellar humans in their primitive space-ships. One simply learned to filter out the aphorisms and concentrate on discourse that *did* make sense. "That bad, eh?" he asked, accepting a goblet of Logish Meem from his host. "I suppose I *shall* have to see for myself."

"As you assuredly will," Borodov promised, handing a goblet to Ursis. "But for now, is time for civilized drinking, followed by much stick-to-ribs kind of sustenance necessary for surviving primitive life on maneuvers."

Ursis looked up and frowned. "Primitive life?" he asked. "Aboard a battle crawler?"

The older Bear shrugged and grinned with mock sheepishness. "Well," he conceded, "perhaps is not all that primitive. But one takes every excuse one can for hosting festive bash. Especially now," he said, suddenly becoming grave. "Who knows what tomorrow brings? Leaguers' coming invasion looms large, in my view—and with it, much, *much* change in way we live." He settled into a chair and stared into his goblet of meem. "*If* indeed we live," he added, nodding slowly.

"If indeed. . . ." Ursis seconded.

In the reddish half-light before dawn, a gigantic government limousine skimmer—escorted by four hulking troopers on gravcycles—thundered into the high portico of Borodov Hall and pulled to a stop in clouds of powdered snow. While the household staff gathered in the cold to make their farewells, the troopers dismounted and stood at rigid attention while both chauffeur and footman jumped out to open the passenger compartment and pack valises. Climbing into the giant skimmer's passenger compartment with Ursis, Brim watched butlers, cooks, gamekeepers, droshkat keepers, gardeners, and other principals of the manor file past Borodov, bowing, curtsying, and mumbling a few words before passing on. He had visited the great Sodeskayan villa numerous times over the years and had often seen the staff gather when Borodov went traveling. This morning, however, something was elusively different. The love these servants had for their master was very much in evidence, but overlaying it all was . . . what?

A sense of foreboding, perhaps?

Borodov would have been careful to put on a face of confidence with regard to the pending attack by the Leaguers; nevertheless, it was difficult to paint a bright picture under the circumstances. Although the home planet of Sodeskaya herself had not come under direct attack for some hundreds of Standard Years, and though no one would officially admit it now, a tremendous assault was clearly imminent. It darkened the comings and goings of Sodeskayans everywhere.

The farewells at last complete, Borodov climbed through the door, grasping a hamper of refreshments to keep them from starvation all the way to the spaceport, and the great limousine glided silently into the morning behind its gravcycle escort.

Little more than a metacycle later, they were thundering into space aboard one of the Fleet's NJH-26 star launches, a sleek Sodeskayan executive transport renowned throughout the Galaxy for both speed and elegance. In the warm, wood-paneled passenger cabin, deep-cushioned sofas lined the walls and four Bear-sized recliners occupied the corners. Soft, indirect lighting illuminated a sumptuous breakfast— their second since arising—set out in the ship's local gravity on a low table equipped with an expressing device that filled the air with the delicious aroma of fresh-brewed cvc'eese. Indifferently Brim passed time watching the Bearish Helmsmen as they broadcast messages via KA'PPA (instantaneous, character-only communications in which data arrives everywhere in the Universe simultaneously) to military route coordinators at various control stations orbiting the beacon stars that marked their route.

Glancing about the plush cabin, Brim paused to wonder what kind of reality he might expect to see in maneuvers that would be interrupted by formal banqueting and other ceremonies he associated with visits by royalty. Even the elegant starship in which they rode seemed out of place in an essentially military function. The refreshments, the cvc'eese, the luxurious appointments, all combined to make the trip more like a holiday outing than a purposeful military exercise. Old Borodov had already stretched out on a bulkhead divan and was fast asleep, even though Ursis appeared to be wide awake, peering thoughtfully out the Hyperscreen port at the stars rushing by.

As if sensing Brim's attention, the Bear turned and smiled grimly. "You have odd look in your eyes, Wilf Ansor," he said. "Will you share your thoughts?"

Brim pursed his lips. "I'm not certain I can, Nik," he replied, "—not that I don't want to; it's just that I'm not certain my thoughts are well formed enough." He looked down at his hands. "I suppose it comes down to something like . . . well . . . unreality, for lack of a better term." He gestured around the cabin. "It's as if we were flying off to attend some sort of staged event—a tableaux, if you will, with formal banquets to break up the weightiness of things. Certainly not serious maneuvers—or at least what I think of when people mention something like that—when armies practice warfare against one another."

"Very perceptive, my furless friend," Ursis said, nodding his head. "And yet, now is not the time to speak of it. Anastas Alexi and I predicted your reaction before you even landed in Sodeskaya." He frowned. "We also agreed that it was very necessary that you experience these maneuvers yourself early on, so that you would provide us your help knowing all aspects of job 'up front,' so to speak."

"Hmm," Brim mused. "Sounds a bit like my mother."

"Like your *mother*?" Ursis asked in surprise.

"Yeah," Brim said, breaking out in a grin. "You know. Mother Bears have got say the same things to cubs as human mothers do—like, um, 'This won't be pleasant, but it will increase your moral fiber.' "

Ursis smiled and nodded vigorously. "You understand, then."

"I still don't have to like it." Brim grumped with mock annoyance.

"True," Ursis agreed with a twinkle in his eye, "but think of the moral fiber you are building."

*　*　*

At length, the quiet rumble of the Drive was replaced by the thunder of high-powered gravity generators, and they came out of HyperSpeed, curving off toward the feeble light of a Category-19 star. Less than half a Standard Metacycle later, they were on a stormy final, bumping and juddering above the surface of Vorkuta, a frozen landscape that absolutely beggared the word *barren*. "Desolate, eh, Wilfooshka?" Borodov commented, peering through torn clouds and driving snow at a dreary underworld passing rapidly below.

Brim nodded, feeling a shudder pass along his back. "Makes Gimmas Haefdon look like a tropical paradise," he said grimly, making reference to the Empire's gigantic Gimmas starbase orbiting the dying star of Haefdon. "Except that Gimmas once knew life of *some* kind. Doesn't look like anything ever grew down there."

"Is mostly right, Wilf Ansor," Ursis growled with a little smile, "—except for growing Sodeskayan colony. Small city of Bears in other hemisphere contributes great wealth to economy." He gestured grandly out to port. "All Vorkuta is colossal field of gold and other more precious ores, would you believe?"

"Sounds as if it's worth defending, then," Brim quipped.

Ursis shrugged. "Only one of *many* like it, old friend," he said with a shrug. "And if Nergol Triannic and his Time-Weed-smoking Controllers get their hands on *this* kind of wealth, nothing in the Universe will stop them. 'Caves and darkness are no strangers to winter-weary crag wolves,' as they say."

"As they say," Brim replied with a nod. Unfortunately, what the Bear had just said was no secret at all—barring the aphorism, of course. Everyone who could travel faster than light knew about the Sodeskayan riches. Over the millennia, many others had tried to conquer the Bears' homeland. Ultimately, each had failed, but none had arrived with a war machine to rival the one Nergol Triannic and his League of Dark Stars was now assembling. *This* time, evidently, things could be different.

Brim had often seen battle crawlers from the air—as had any Helmsman associated with the military. At one time or another, he'd even sped over some of the Sodeskayan machines himself—but he'd never had time to pay much attention, concentrating instead on destroying crawlers that belonged to the Leaguers. *Those* he'd learned something about.

Even so, nothing in his experience had prepared him for his first close-up encounter with the big Sodeskayan machines. A staff skimmer had just delivered him and his two companions through five c'lenyts of driving sleet from the temporary starbase to a snow-filled basin at the edge of a massive escarpment five hundred irals high, at least. Through the storm, he could see thirty or more of the squat monoliths protruding through the snow in five neat ranks like rows of prodigious teeth, massive and sinister, dark-mirrored flanks reflecting what little of the weak daylight that managed to force its way through the storm clouds. "Voot's greasy beard," he whispered as the skimmer pulled to a stop some distance from what appeared to be an open entry port.

"Our latest," Ursis growled above the thunder of unmuffled gravity engines. "S-33 main battle crawlers. Big, eh?" Even inside a well-sealed staff skimmer, noise from the brooding, pyramid-shaped machines was almost deafening.

"Look like thraggling monuments," Brim replied at the top of his voice. Then attempts at further communication became useless as the driver opened the door and they got out into the frigid air, boots crunching in the dry, powdery snow. Brim augmented the heat in his Fleet Cloak, then looked up and shook his head in wonderment, blinking as wind-driven snowflakes—and the acrid stench of ozone—stung his eyes. The word *awesome* did little good as a description. These crawlers, if indeed something so large might be expected to move, even at a crawl, were more than seventy snow-draped irals square at the base with an overall height of some thirty-five irals. Angular and awkward-looking vehicles, they presented few flat planes upon which ground-based disruptor fire could score a direct hit. Each was painted with a bright blue flash to denote membership in the "Blue" army— "enemy" tanks would be painted with green flashes, Ursis had explained earlier. Midway between the base and what appeared to be control-room slits near the apex were two huge 350-mmi disruptors mounted on swiveling rings that provided the big vehicles with terrific firepower. Brim shook his head absently. They looked crude in comparison to the beautifully finished starships to which he was accustomed. The great mirrored plates from which they were fabricated had been cut with no obvious smoothing and were joined by jagged welding beads, some nearly an iral in thickness. Clearly, Sodeskayan battle crawlers were built for ruggedness and impregnability—with little regard whatsoever for weight or the ability to move without infringement of their surroundings. The sound they made at idle alone was enough to shake the ground. . . . Suddenly Brim realized that his two companions were grinning at him.

"Perhaps you wish to trade one of your starships for such a graceful beast," Borodov yelled out.

"We would intercede with Knez for you," Ursis roared with a look of mock dementia. "But perhaps you would like to ride in one first?"

Brim rolled his eyes. "I had to come halfway across a Galaxy for *this*," he groaned.

"Where else might you go?" Ursis quipped at the top of his voice. By this time, a number of guards had noticed them and were standing at rigid attention while one spoke into a mobile communicator. Moments later, a smartly dressed Sodeskayan Captain stepped from the S-33's side hatch and marched briskly toward them, coming to an abrupt halt in front of Borodov and saluting. "Generals, Admirals," she shouted. "I am Captain Olga Votov, commander of this crawler and leader of Formation One. General Vaslovich, our Squadron Commander, bids you welcome and asks that you will please join him inside."

Borodov smiled, returning the Captain's salute. "Thank you, Captain," he said. "Please lead us to the General." He nodded for Brim and Ursis to follow, then set off through the driving storm, boots crunching on the deepening snow.

Just inside the crawler's entry hatch was a small vestibule whose deck vibrated and trembled to the thunderous rumble of the crawler's power plant. Here, the reek of ozone was joined by the odors of hot lubricating oil, toasting electronics, sealants, polish, Hogge'Poa, and unwashed Bears—not unlike the odors Brim normally associated with starships. Votov motioned them up a precipitous companionway so steep it amounted to little more than a ladder. Beside it, an inner hatch provided Brim a fleeting glimpse onto the crawler's vast machinery spaces, where a number of Bears had gathered around what appeared to be a massive gravity generator fronted by reactors of some kind. At the next level, the captain led them into a narrow passageway hung with pipes, conduits, and wave guides, passing finally into a small cubic chamber Brim estimated to be nearly at the core of the vehicle's mass. In the center, another ladder passed through the metal ceiling. The noise moderated somewhat as they ascended this into what was clearly the vehicle's bustling control room. By the time Brim and his grip reached the landing, Borodov and a Sodeskayan Major General were greeting each other with traditional Bear hugs—which Ursis turned into a threesome as soon as he reached them. After the native compliments, Borodov turned and motioned with his head.

"Wilf Ansor," he called, "please come meet old family friend, Gregory Rufino Vaslovich." Dressed in a great tan OverCloak and padded helmet, the General was at least as large as Ursis—perhaps even larger—with light reddish hair and a single gem in his right fang.

Moments later, Brim felt himself engulfed in yet another Bear hug.

"Wilf Ansor," the Bear said, stepping back with a great smile, "but I have often heard of you." He laughed. "According to Anastas Alexi here, you should be Bear also, for he refers to you more as a son that furless human."

Returning the General's infectious grin, Brim glanced at old Borodov and nodded. "I am most honored," he said—and he meant it. In many ways, the old Bear *had* been like a father to him.

"So now you ride in battle crawler with us?" Vaslovich asked. "Will be much different than starship—lots bumpier."

"We have warned him, General," Ursis interjected, politely continuing in Brim's native Avalonian rather than the Sodeskayan tongue. "But is exceedingly important he gets best view possible of ground forces in action. He has important job to do here."

"With Marshal *nov* Vobok, 'the Hunter,' peering over collective shoulders," Vaslovich observed, "Fleet people from Avalon are important to our very existence." He nodded. "We Sodeskayans have always counted on Imperial Fleet to support our ground forces."

Brim took a deep breath. *This* time, the Fleet might not be so helpful as in the past. Its reserves had been decimated staving off nearly six Standard Months' worth of League attacks on its capital planets that were even now becoming known as the Battle of Avalon. "No doubt that Emperor Onrad will send all the support he can spare," he equivocated. "Meanwhile, I feel certain that the Knez has great fleets of his own."

"This you will observe for yourself," Vaslovich said. "Nothing has been held in reserve for this exercise. Knez Nikolai demands to see everything."

Brim was about to comment when Captain Votov hastened from the communications console and saluted. "The exercise begins," she interrupted impassively.

Vaslovich nodded, then turned to Brim and his companions. "Please find seats, my friends," he said. "We shall move out immediately." With this, he began an immediate dialogue in Sodeskayan with Votov.

"Sit here, Wilfooshka," Borodov said, patting the back of a jump seat between the Captain and what appeared to be a gunnery console, directly in the center of the forward viewing slit. "You will need good view if you are to grasp our . . . 'problems,' as it were."

Nodding, Brim wrapped his Fleet Cloak around him and slipped into the hard cushions. His two companions occupied chairs on either side of a special command recliner farther back in the control room that obviously had been rigged for General Vaslovich. Moments later, Votov handed him one of the helmets peculiar to crawler crews, then slipped into the left-hand seat and began the process of buckling herself in.

"Watch me, Brim," she rumbled, "and do not skip single buckle. Battle crawlers not equipped with local gravity."

"What was that?" Brim asked over the rumble of the power plant. "I couldn't hear you."

"Helmet, Admiral," Votov yelled with a glower. "Put *helmet* on."

Cheeks burning, Brim donned the helmet and was immediately rewarded with Sodeskayan crosstalk from at least a dozen conversations, but when he turned to Votov, these faded.

"You can hear now, Admiral?" the Sodeskayan asked dryly.

Brim nodded. "Perfectly," he said, wondering if the helmet would automatically transmit his voice directionally.

It did, for the Captain nodded, then began to speak as if she were giving a seven-year-old his first lessons in thermodynamics. "You will want to secure each of the seven belts on your seat," she said. "This one first," she continued, pointing to a red belt that passed across her lap. "Then two green and four blue." After this, she returned to her control panel without a comment.

Brim immediately set to buckling each in the order Votov prescribed until all seven were taut.

"Belts are comfortable?" Votov asked without looking up.

"Yes, thank you," Brim said, surprised that the brusque tank commander cared at all for his comfort.

"Then straps are not yet tight enough," Votov replied, starting what was clearly a check-out sequence of the crawler's systems.

Dutifully, Brim tightened the straps until they hurt. Soon afterward, a visage of the communications officer appeared in one of Votov's globular displays and said something in Sodeskayan.

"It begins now," Votov warned presently over her shoulder. "Brace yourself, spaceman." As her hands moved surely over her control console, the sound of the crawler's power plant doubled, then the whole control room canted dizzily to one side and rocked drunkenly for a moment, finally lurching to an uncomfortable sort of equilibrium. No local gravity aboard *these* monsters.

"Cruising elevation," Votov explained, without prompting. "Soon we move out."

Through the viewing slots, Brim could see clouds of snow erupting vertically from the bases of each crawler as one by one they raised themselves some few irals from the ground on shimmering columns of gravitons. The hovering behemoths had suddenly changed from rows of static fortifications to five ranks of dynamic power and malignancy. Somehow from the ground they looked a lot more potent than they did from the air. Presently a flurry of activity at the communications consoles hushed the normal crosstalk coming from Brim's helmet, the sound of the power plant increased, along with the vibrations of the deck, and with a single curt word from Votov, the crawler began to move forward—with all the deliberate acceleration of a battleship.

"Not quite what you are used to, eh?" Borodov's voice came from behind him.

Brim turned and grinned. "Not quite," he said, but the huge machines continued to accelerate until they were galloping over the rocky terrain at a quite acceptable clip— nearly takeoff seed for a number of starships Brim had flown. And, at least to all appearances, they were certainly unstoppable. The now-speeding lines of battle crawlers were pulverizing nearly everything in their paths, including boulders more than twice their size. "What now, General?" he heard Borodov ask, again in Avalonian.

"Line of low hills ahead," Vaslovich said, "—conceals 'enemy' base. Our job is locate and put out of action." He laughed. "Easy job for crawlers like these, except for one problem."

"Which is . . ." Borodov asked.

"Problem is that 'enemy' is set on putting *us* out of action first."

"Most intolerant," Ursis observed dryly.

"They will cooperate," Votov growled. She moved her hand slightly, and the big crawler began sidling to the left— with the first two ranks in tow. At the same time, the fourth and fifth ranks skittered to the right, leaving the center rank to continue alone on the original track—directly for the center of the hills.

Peering through the driving snow, Brim thought he saw something move in the distance ahead. Whatever it was, it quickly disappeared behind a curiously shaped pile of snow-covered rocks. "Were you expecting company out here?" he asked Votov.

"Company, Admiral?" Votov asked, clearly intent on achieving the hills in the shortest time possible.

"Off to the right," Brim said. "Behind that odd-looking pile of boulders."

"Where . . . ?" Votov began, then nodded. "Ah," she said. "I see, now. Truly, your reputation for sharp eyes is deserved, Admiral." She turned to Vaslovich and said something in Sodeskayan.

The general replied, also in Sodeskayan, then turned to Brim. "Congratulations, Admiral," he said, switching to the Avalonian tongue. "You have just spotted modern adaptation of old Sodeskayan battle ploy—from days before interstellar travel. Control station for anti-tank minefield."

As Brim watched, the two ranks of crawlers braked precipitously, then, as if controlled by a single driver, began to angle sideways to the right.

"We need to capture station you discovered if we are to get through without significant losses," Votov said quietly.

Brim frowned. "*Capture* a control station?" he asked. "Wouldn't it be easier if you just blew it up?"

"Soon you will see for yourself," Vaslovich said. "Carefully watch snow field where we were originally heading."

No sooner had Brim swung his glance to the left along what would have been their original direction of travel than nearly half a square c'lenyt of snow erupted with what looked like thousands of spiderlike machines—each apparently larger than a Bear—with circular bodies and six needle-thin, articulated legs, speeding wave-on-wave over the snow. "Voot's greasy beard!" he gasped under his breath. "Those are mines?"

"Powerful mines, Wilfooshka," Ursis's voice proclaimed

from Brim's rear. "Any one of them can disable a crawler—three can destroy one."

"Essentially, they are self-controlled," Borodov's voice broke in as waves of deadly, malevolent-looking machines surged toward the tanks. "But they can take orders from remote controllers such as one you spotted. Now we must capture controller technicians themselves or risk being overrun and shamefully put out of action early in game."

"Can't you just *shoot* the controller station?" Brim asked.

"Is beauty of mobile minefield," Ursis replied. "When under no control, mines steer for anything that moves. Only sure defense is capture control station, then command ugly little bastards go sleep. Otherwise, many, many casualties."

As he spoke, the din of the power plant rose to almost deafening heights and Votov led three other crawlers out ahead of the others and made straight for the rocks Brim had spotted only moments before. "They had thought to surprise us." The Captain's voice chuckled darkly in Brim's helmet. "Your eyes, Admiral, spared us much embarrassment. See!" He pointed to the left, where the first waves of mines had reached the leftmost crawlers. Bright flashes of light indicated machines being declared out of action by orbiting referees.

Moments later, Votov came to an abrupt halt beside the pile of rocks Brim had spotted. From this angle, Brim could see five Bears with green armbands huddled around a mobile console, now looking up at the crawler with surprise in their eyes. They were quickly marked dead by members of the crawler who jumped to the snow, then took over the strange-looking console and began to manipulate its controls. Soon afterward, the hoards of skittering spider-mines wobbled to a halt.

After much conversation in Sodeskayan, Vaslovich turned to Brim. "Even with our good fortune," he said in Avalonian, "the minefield cost us half our twelve machines. Without you, Admiral, things would have been *much* worse. Now," he said, pointing off to the low range of hills, "we have a few battle crawlers extra to fight *those*."

Brim looked up to see four ranks of five S-33s each had appeared over the hilltops and were now descending the icy slopes toward them, trailing clouds of billowing snow. And *these* crawlers were painted with bright green flashes that manifested "enemy." "Er . . . *interesting* odds," he observed.

"This time" Vaslovich replied, turning for a moment to face Brim, "in addition to your extraordinary vision, our side has been given a few secret weapons from home to even things." He grinned. "We think *you* especially will find these surprises interesting—perhaps as much as our colleagues among the 'Greens' will find them disconcerting." Nodding a command to the communications console, he returned his attention to the frozen panorama forward and put the great battle crawler into motion, directly toward the oncoming "enemy."

Brim grinned. The surprise would have to be something else, indeed, to surpass what he'd already experienced in the few cycles since the crawlers had started out on their mission. *And* it would have to arrive quickly to avert the disaster that was rushing headlong at the remnants of Vaslovich's left flank. Suddenly—long before the disruptors of either side could begin to bear—four dark shapes hurtled out of the snowstorm overhead on a course directly toward the approaching Green crawlers. A moment later, the "enemy" forces were peppered with the same bright flashes of light perpetrated by the spider mines, and a number of their S-33s stopped in their tracks, out of combat. As the flying shapes circled around for another pass, more flashes of "disruptor" hits sparkled among the surviving Green crawlers, that had by now begun ineffectually to return fire.

"Are those *starships*?" Brim blurted out in spite of himself. "I've never seen anything like them."

"We call them Ro'stoviks, or, in your tongue, 'Space Bastions,'" Vaslovich replied, with a decided inflection of smugness in his voice. "Military designation is JM-2—and officially you have never even heard of them. Existence of such attack ships is highly secret, but you among all non-Sodeskayan Imperials are cleared for nearly everything."

Awestruck, Brim continued to watch as the curious-looking—assuredly well-armored—starships made pass upon pass at the enemy crawlers, shouldering aside "hits" from the ground that would have utterly crippled a normal fighting starship. By the time Vaslovich arrived at the scene, all forty Green crawlers had been declared out of combat by the orbital referees, and the Blue squadron thundered past without firing a shot.

The incident, however, had started Brim from his bemusement and he frowned, wondering where the remainder of the Sodeskayans' combat space patrol was—for *either* side. Those four deadly ground-attack ships were the only evidence that the mock battle was even taking place during an age of interstellar flight. Certainly the Greens should have sent in a few attack ships to defend their crawlers against the Blue Ro'stoviks. But the ships had failed to appear—at least as far as could be seen from the view slits of a crawler. He frowned, tempted to question his hosts about the situation, but resistant to asking such an obvious—at least to himself—question so early in the maneuvers.

Still, a number of critical flags had been raised in his mind. And not all of them had to do with lack of a combat space patrol. For example, even though the new ships were clearly devastating against ground targets, could their specialized designs stand up in combat against Leaguer ships in space combat? He was still wrestling with his desire to ask questions when the cabin noise dropped precipitously and the crawler stopped just short of the hill's crest. Now the communications console became the center of attention, with

Vaslovich in a four-way talk with Votov and two other voices that Brim surmised were commanders of the other four formations. At length the conversations stopped and Borodov's voice sounded in his helmet.

"Probably you are wondering what that was all about," the Bear said.

"Hmm." Brim chuckled. "I suppose I *will* have to learn Sodeskayan before this is all over."

"For now, I shall gladly act as interpreter," the Bear said. "It seems that so-called 'enemy' camp is better equipped than we were led to believe. At least twenty crawlers more than intelligence estimated, even before unfortunate encounter with the minefield."

"Our other formations," Brim asked, "—they took some damage, too, then?"

"Smaller losses than our own, so far," Borodov replied. "But too few crawlers remain in our squadron to both nullify enemy and achieve day's objective."

Brim nodded. He could guess what was coming next. "What's the name of those starships—*Ro'stoviks*?" Brim asked.

"Correct." Borodov chuckled. " 'Space Bastions.' See, already you learn Sodeskayan."

Brim grinned. "Always was a quick study." He chuckled. "They'll be called in, too?"

"Even as we speak," Ursis replied, his voice suddenly drowned out by the thunder of what could only be spacegoing gravity generators. Soon afterward, the crawler's power plant rumbled and the big machine lurched over the brow of the hill—just in time to reveal four JM-2s soaring and plunging above what appeared to be an extensive collection of Green machines, sprinkling literally thousands of sparkling disruptor "hits" that would render crawlers and maintenance vehicles alike as "destroyed" in the eyes of the orbiting referees.

"Ought to keep the opposition busy down there," Brim commented as the crawler careened down the hill at great speed, its own disruptors firing in simulation mode with great, deep-throated cascades of sound that completely drowned out the noise of the traction engines. No more than thirty cycles later, the great "enemy" concentration was neutralized and Vaslovich was leading his abbreviated but still-powerful columns on to the next objective for the day.

Brim fretted silently as the frozen terrain flashed past the viewports. Not a single shot had been fired from the sky in defense of the Green army. Why? The lack of support raised troubling questions, and he resolved to begin seeking answers at the first opportunity. However, even though the JM-2s were much in evidence during the subsequent mock "battle," the remainder of the local day passed before he could begin his questions.

It was not until long after the last dim light faded from the horizon that the wearied crews—and their passengers—stopped for rest and sustenance. Through the viewports, Brim could see what appeared to be the lights from several hundred crawlers amid a multitude of glowing, hovering battle lanterns. Inside, Votov's control room was rapidly filling with the dreaded redolence of Hogge'Poa as nearly everyone in the crew lit up a Zempa pipe. Brim was tired as he could remember, and every muscle in his body seemed to ache—especially those near his shoulders, where the taut safety harnesses had nearly crushed his bones. Achingly, he released the catches, then groaned as he bent forward to get out of the seat. Amid the Bearish clatter behind him, he heard another grunt of protest and turned to see Borodov rise tortuously to his feet. The old Bear grinned.

"Ah, Wilf Ansor," he chuckled, "is good to see someone so much younger have same complaints after day in battle crawler." He nodded toward Ursis, who was standing nonchalantly by the control console in animated conversation with the General. "Perhaps elderly Bears and furless mortals like humans should seek occupations on starships instead."

Brim laughed ruefully. "No doubt about that, Doctor," he said. "Except that one can hardly call *you* elderly." Then he frowned. "And speaking of starships, my friend . . ."

Borodov smiled. "Yes?" he replied, with a meaningful look in his eye.

"Anastas Alexi," Brim began, glancing around the control room, "you must know that I could hardly have been more impressed with the performance of your new JM-2s. They appear to be capable ground-support ships, but . . ." He opened his hands palm up. "Well . . ."

"You wonder, perhaps, why Green forces had none?" the old Bear asked.

"That and a lot more," Brim replied.

Borodov nodded. "Also lack of combat space patrols, I'll bet," he said, "—ships that *should* have protected Greens from our Ro'stoviks, but didn't. Right?"

"Right," Brim replied earnestly. "Dr. Borodov—there was *nothing* valid about those maneuvers today, and you know it. Why . . ." he glanced around the control room again, "if those Greens had been Leaguers, our JM-2s would have had swarms of killer ships keeping them busy. They'd have been lucky to get off a tenth of the shots they managed." He frowned. "*Unless,*" he added, "those new ships are as good against first-line attack ships as they are fighting battle crawlers."

This time it was Borodov who glanced around the control room. "I suspect they are not," he said quietly. "They are too specialized—and of course I know the maneuvers are not valid for the very reason you named. So does Nikolai Yanuarievich. The fact is, we Sodeskayans have no *real* Fleet. At least none capable of the mission assigned to it."

"Voot's thraggling beard," Brim whispered. "I thought the Knez was supposed to see *everything*."

"He is," Borodov said, "and will, as the maneuvers continue."

"Then," Brim stammered, gesturing frustration with his hands, "he'll see the same things we saw."

Borodov nodded somberly. "As you point out, Wilf Ansor, he *will* see."

"Then . . ."

"What my brother will see is not as important as what he will *perceive*," the old Bear said.

"I don't understand," Brim said.

Borodov glanced about the room again. "We shall talk about this further in private—when Nikolai Yanuarievich can join is," he said. "Meanwhile, you can obtain others' answers to your questions about support from space—*judiciously*, of course—during the banquet tonight." He nodded. "You will be rubbing elbows with many political heavyweights in Army."

"*Banquet?*" Brim gasped. "Tonight? I was ready to cram down a few field rations and turn in."

Borodov looked stunned. "Wilf Ansor," he said in surprise, "day has just begun. Soon, big field bash for Knez commences. Much excellent food and Logish Meem! Not to be missed!" He glanced at the archaic mechanical timepiece he carried—reward for sponsoring an archaeological mission some few Standard Years back. "We have less than Standard Metacycle to change into dress uniforms for first banquet," he said.

Brim felt his jaw drop as a flock of enlisted crewmen suddenly appeared from below guiding lines of bobbing grips behind them. Soon the crawler's control level became a dressing room—for both sexes. Bears seemed to become libidinous only when females came "into season," as was the polite Sodeskayan term. From Brim's standpoint, it certainly made for a more peaceful—if somewhat boring—society.

"Forget aches and pains, Wilfooshka." Ursis chuckled from across the room. "*Little* bit meem is best lineament in known Universe—*lots* meem even better, eh?"

Brim grinned in spite of himself. Meem certainly did seem to be a certain cure for many aches and pains. And if he knew anything about Sodeskayan banquets, the Meem would be both plentiful and excellent. Breathing a short prayer of thanks to the powers that be—Barbousse *was* a bona fide miracle—he opened his grip and began to change uniforms.

The banqueting took place in what appeared to be a small city of ornate, colorful tents surrounded by two lines of battle crawlers from both Blue and Green armies. Brim and his two companions arrived at one of the larger, certainly more ornate tents in the midst of a worsening blizzard. At the entrance, a formation of at least fifty soldiers bowed while four footmen—dressed in white breeches, gold vests, and bright-red calotte hats—ceremoniously swung the tent flaps open to reveal a huge, ornate chamber under high, vaulted canopies of gold-embroidered fabric. The tent walls were resplendent with vivid tapestries that depicted what appeared to be heroic scenes from Sodeskaya's ancient past, all splendidly woven in kaleidoscopic hues and colors. Thousands of smoky, flickering candles—real, from what Brim could discern—both heated and lighted the elaborate setting from five huge cutglass chandeliers. The floor, however, had been given no preparation whatsoever and was little more than a damp slurry of ground rock and dust. Probably, thought Brim with a private chuckle, it was the Knez's one concession to "roughing it."

At least two hundred Sodeskayan officers were already gathered in the enormous tent, sipping deep-hued meem from vast crystal goblets, filling the already candle-hazed air with pungent smoke from Zempa pipes and wearing the diverse—often bizarre—parade dress that had developed while the Great Empire of the Bears evolved. As in the Imperial services of Avalon, most of the uniforms were based on Sodeskayan service dress—white, double-breasted tunic over white shirt and black tie; gray riding trousers or long gowns adorned by wide, red stripes on either side; and high, black riding boots—worn with by various configurations of aiguillete and dress belt, each seemingly more grand than the next. Aside from headdresses (some almost ridiculous in complexity), the primary means of rank identification were collar patches and shoulder straps, except that general officers seemed to be wearing gold buttons and badges. Here on the wastelands of a barren planet, after a wearisome day of simulated combat, Brim found the whole scene had an aspect of utter improbability. As if the circumstances of impending war, one that could be *lost* easily, had been reduced to little more than trivia.

A grandly outfitted majordomo—clearly some high-ranking court retainer—caught sight of Borodov, consulted a small note board, then bowed deeply and blew on a silver whistle before announcing their names amid a long discourse in Sodeskayan. The glittering crowd applauded politely and gave way, while high-booted footmen appeared from out of the crowd with trays of great crystal goblets, and—meem in hand—the three plunged into the noisy soiree.

For Brim, the next interlude passed in a confusion of trivial, wordy flourishes as Ursis and Borodov introduced him 'round the room. He had no opportunity at all for thoughtful discussions about anything military or otherwise. One elderly officer asked him in flawless Avalonian about Starfuries, but as he tried to describe the famous Imperial attack ships, he watched the old woman turn and carry on a conversation with someone else. After that, he kept his remarks short and meaningless, as was evidently expected.

Presently, off to one side of the room, near an extremely ornate entrance, the famous Sodeskayan Palace Guards—at least a hundred singularly dressed soldiers in glistening silver breastplates and plume-crested helmets—began to form on either side of the closed tent flaps. Brim had often seen holographs of the prestigious organization; in person, their fame was even more justified. He shook his head, trying futilely to understand how the Knez could justify the terrific expense of bringing them all the way to this remote outpost of the domain. Then Ursis introduced him to *still* another dignitary, and he returned to the evening's prevalent trivia.

At last a flurry of excitement near the ornate entrance—and a rush of bitterly cold air—claimed the attention of nearly everyone in the room. "Anastas Alexi's brother, Knez Nikolai," Ursis explained, peering over his spectacles.

"And royal retinue." Borodov sniffed with a slight, disapproving shake of his head. "One would think Nikolai could spend maybe one night alone in bed."

Brim glanced toward the entrance, where the Palace Guard was now formed into two formations on either side of the open tent flap. Suddenly, he caught sight of a dark, squat little Bear whose (clearly retouched) visage decorated the entrance of every public building in Sodeskaya—Knez Nikolai. His uniform carried the garland-and-star insignia of a Sodeskayan Field Marshal, but his headgear was simple: a small, eight-pointed crown starry with glittering stones.

He was accompanied by a number richly dressed civilians, clearly high-ranking members of the Court. Brim recognized lantern-jawed Ogon Rostov, the Minister of Finance, from the Bear's frequent visits to Avalon; Slovina Brz'mell, Foreign Minister, was likewise easy to identify from her large, black nose. A number of other officials also looked familiar, probably from his visits to Sodeskaya over the years, but he couldn't place any of their names.

On the heels of the officials came a second wave of lavishly dressed Bears, all female. They followed the imposing figure of Katerin, the Knezina, dressed in a flowing white gown studded with a collection of rare hallo-pearls that would have purchased a squadron of at least half a dozen Starfuries—and paid their crews for a Standard Year.

"Poor woman," Ursis whispered mockingly, raising his eyes heavenward. "One hates to see poverty displayed so openly."

"I shall try not to notice," Brim replied just as facetiously under his breath.

Near the entrance, some of the revelers launched into low bows of obeisance as the Royal Party started to circle the room. From time to time, the Knez stopped to exchange a few words with favored members of the Officer Corps. When he reached Borodov, he smiled and stopped to chat for a few moments, nodding to Ursis as he did so. Then, as he prepared to move on, his eyebrows raised and he stared Brim directly in the face. Turning to Borodov, he seemed to ask a question that included the word "Breem."

The Grand Duke's apparent reply added "Wylf" and "Ansor" to the "Breem."

At this, the Knez turned and again stared thoughtfully at the spaceman. "Admiral Brim . . ." he said in faultless Avalonian, "I have heard of you—and your heroic efforts during the Battle of Avalon."

Forbidden as an Imperial to bow to anyone, Brim could only nod that he had heard the accolade. "I am most honored, Your Highness," he said.

The Knez smiled. "Yes," he said, nodding thoughtfully. "You are, I suppose. As a Knez, I rarely speak to anyone below the rank of Baron." Then he smiled slightly. " 'After crag wolves skid on ice cap, it is already too late for rogue-snakes,' as they say." He nodded once more, as if pondering thoughts of some consequence. "We shall meet again, Admiral," he said quietly, and at length, as if he had reached some sort of decision, "when the proper moment arrives—as it will." With that, he turned and nodded to his brother, then strode off, the Royal Court following obediently in his wake—each turning to smile or nod at the Imperial guest from Avalon.

Immediately Brim was nearly mobbed as other partygoers quickly realized that the comparatively low-ranking Imperial Admiral was a person of some importance. Everyone began talking at once about the Imperial Fleet. And they talked in Avalonian. He had a difficult time indeed keeping his laughter under control while marveling (to himself) at how quickly these high-ranking Bears could pick up a fundamental understanding of a language when scant moments before they could speak *only* in Sodeskayan!

For the next half metacycle at least, he patiently answered every question he could until a grizzled old Admiral introduced himself as Gromos Boskei. Brim had been *waiting* for this opportunity.

"So, Admiral," the old Bear asked, "what did you think of first day on maneuvers?"

"Impressive, Admiral," Brim answered as casually as possible, "—especially the use of your new MJ-2s. They appear to be powerful starships."

"Ah, but they *are!*" Boskei stated proudly. "You saw what they did to best crawlers in known Universe." Around him others nodded wisely, as if the Admiral had uttered a mighty gem of wisdom.

"*Indeed* I saw," Brim agreed. "But could they have done as well had they, in turn, been forced to battle League killer ships?"

The Admiral stopped and frowned. "This I do not know," he said after a moment of thought. "But it matters little. We are assured that the necessary protection will be supplied when necessary."

"I see," Brim said. "But why wasn't it provided to the Green team today?"

"Not needed," the Admiral said with a great smile. "Is only maneuvers today."

"You mean—" Brim started, but the Admiral and his companions suddenly turned their attention to a number of footmen who were propelling long buffet tables crowded with gleaming whiteware vessels in fanciful arrangements, chafing dishes of all sizes, stacks of glittering plates, and burnished gold and silver serving suites. And the aroma wafting from the chafing dishes alone was enough to make Brim's mouth water. It seemed like days since he'd had something to eat! Suddenly, Ursis and Borodov were at his side.

"Is soon time to refill empty stomachs," Ursis said as the Admiral and his retinue drifted toward the buffet tables.

Brim nodded. The Admiral was beyond inquiry. And besides, the smell of food was tickling his considerably hungry palate. Off to one side of the tent, the Royal Party were seated in opulent, high-backed, brocaded chairs before an ornate table laid with exquisite golden plates and utensils. "Where are *we* supposed to sit?" he asked, glancing around the room.

Ursis smiled. "We do not sit," he said. "For now, only the Royal Family sits. Rest of us mortals eat standing up."

Brim frowned and looked at Borodov.

"Is true," the old Bear said. "But take heart. Food and meem at gatherings like this usually so good, nobody notices. Especially after few goblets of meem." He squinted at a footman who carried goblets and a huge, sweating bottle of white, unmistakably Logish Meem. "Over here," he signaled, snapping his fingers. "Come." He chuckled to Brim and Ursis. "First we drink toasts to friendship and like. After that, we can eat without notice of tormenting feet."

"Maybe I'll just eat a little, first," Brim said, popping a

mushroom cap filled with rich, pungent sausage into his mouth. "Wouldn't want to drink on an empty stomach."

"Here's to both meem *and* empty stomachs," toasted Borodov, thrusting a chilled goblet of white Logish Meem into Brim's hand. "The more empty the stomach, the faster one forgets sore feet—and missing starships, eh?"

"To sore feet!" Ursis toasted before Brim could even raise his goblet for the *first* toast.

After that, the banquet—at least for Brim—became much less focused. The cool, soothing Logish Meem was of a truly magnificent vintage, going down like a blessing from the mythological Gods of Logus. And the food was even better—if that were possible. Delicious soups and stews—some delicate, some robust—vied for favor with delicacies like sardines with green peppers, smoked salmon à la Sodesse in sour cream and tiny green buds, pâté of crag wolf, eggs and fish roe, game-fowl livers on tiny skewers, pungent cheeses, breads of every conceivable description, shape, and flavor. With nearly a Standard Day's fasting to fuel his appetite, Brim ate and drank ravenously, trading dirty dishes for clean ones at a furious pace and keeping up with the Bears easily—at least for a little while. As he grazed along the laden tables, Ursis joined him with a frown on his face. "Wilf Ansor," he said, "you are eating as though your stomach thought your throat had been cut."

Sluggish and somewhat tipsy from all the Logish Meem he had sampled, Brim smiled comfortably and chuckled. "It seemed that way a while ago," he admitted, "but I've thoroughly taken care of that now. What a feast! You Sodeskayans certainly know how to lay out a spread. Now, if I just had some cvc'eese—and maybe a place to sit. . . ."

"You think *this* is feast?" Ursis asked, nibbling what appeared to be a sautéed mushroom cap. "Wait till you see *main* course. Is not for nothing Knez Nikolai is famous all over Galaxy for field banquets."

"M-main course?" Brim started with something close to panic exploding somewhere low in his gut. "But . . ." At that moment, the back of the tent was ceremoniously opened, revealing the Palace Guard formed in two ranks on either side of a rich boulevard of carpets leading to another, still larger tent.

"They're serving more food in there, aren't they?" Brim gasped in a state of near panic.

"*Lots* more," Ursis said soberly as they started toward the new entrance.

"*WON*-der-ful," Brim pronounced slowly. "Just thraggling *WON*-der-ful."

"Come, Wilf Ansor," Borodov said cheerfully, joining the two at the entrance to the carpet. "Is more of great Sodeskayan repast—with even larger selection of Logish Meems, would you believe?"

"I think he believes," Ursis said dryly.

"He believes," Brim agreed. "He believes."

The second tent was even longer and more ornate than the first, though still lighted by thousands of authentic-looking candles in cut-crystal chandeliers. In addition to the candle haze, the air was already pungent with odors of spicy foods, though no buffet tables had yet been set out. However, it was fairly clear that this would be a sit-down meal for everyone—not just the Knez. Along the whole prodigious length of the tent ran a pair of parallel tables joined at the end nearest the entrance by a third that connected them. The Royal Party was already seated on their great, high-backed gilt-and-brocade chairs along the connector table, and behind all the two hundred or more remaining seats—still empty—stood enlisted soldiers dressed in special crimson parade uniforms with huge white plumes attached to their traditional tricorn hats.

Brim shut his eyes in hopeless defeat. He would now be

expected to eat again—with even more gusto than he had shown less than a metacycle previously. Swallowing hard, he followed down the long expanse of tables. Each place was marked by what appeared to be a heavy golden emblem, engraved with individual names. Brim had been seated with his two friends near the head of the outer portside table—high distinction indeed for a foreigner.

As the last guests took their seats, polite conversation began and the first course appeared—still another thick, spicy chowder accompanied by goblets of deliciously soothing, rose-hued Logish Meem. These were served *simultaneously* to each of the guests by individual servants standing at the rear of each chair. Somehow, Brim found additional room for the delightful fare and the meem, but wished to Voot someone had warned him about what was to follow. And between bites, both Borodov, on his left, and Ursis, on his right, introduced him to other guests sitting nearby. He met a gray, nearly deaf, bemonacled old General who mistook him first for an Imperial General. The ancient Sodeskayan soon lost interest, however, when he discovered that Brim knew next to nothing about ground fighting. Another General—one with the great muzzle and deep, brown fur indigenous to the remote Ragnar star cluster—had once shipped with Baxter Calhoun, Brim's mysterious mentor and fellow Carescrian. Still another had known Onrad personally when they were children together. However, no one near them said anything that would encourage talk about Fleet tactics. It was almost as if they had purposely been seated that way.

The chowder course was followed almost immediately by pungent slices of fowl—Borodov called it Grinovsh—thick with peppercorns and tangy fruits and served beneath a delightful sauce made from some sort of strongly flavored seafood. This culinary masterpiece was accompanied by a hearty red Logish Meem served in stout glass goblets and poured from large, unwieldy containers that looked as if they were made from leather—with the hair still attached. After this, another soup, thin and dark-hued, the color of an early dawn. Then small bowls of piquant-sweet ice, followed immediately by a delicate salad topped with rich, pungent spices in a thickened vinegar with overtones of more glen buds.

Through it all, Brim struggled to stay at least reasonably sober—and awake. Course followed course in a perfect iniquity of edibles, each more tasty than the last—and more filling. Finally, at least a thousand years from when he took his seat, toasts began somewhere out of sight at the main table. All were given in Sodeskayan, yet even to an Imperial, each sounded more heroic that the last. And between toasts, a huge, soldiers' chorus chanted lugubrious Sodeskayan hymns.

At last the Royal Party stood and exited, passing through a rear entrance amid great melancholic fanfare and chanting from the chorus. On this signal, the others also stood and began to gather into little groups, lighting up their dreaded Zempa pipes with abandon. Brim struggled to hoist the lorry's-load of food he had eaten along with a barrel of assorted meems. Now—while cvc'eese and cordials were passed around—there were even *more* high-ranking Sodeskayans for him to meet.

During the next metacycle or so, he discussed the day's maneuvers with a number of high-ranking Sodeskayans. And while he heard a number of views concerning the worth of the JM-2, nearly everyone accepted the doctrine that space support would be supplied when needed—when war actually came. Moreover, at least three of the Generals he spoke to felt that the introduction of killer ships would only add a factor of confusion into maneuvers meant to exercise ground forces and close-support equipment.

At some point, Brim noticed that he had been more or less

circulating among the Sodeskayans on his own, drawn here, introduced there, in a natural progression among these great affable denizens of the largest known civilization. Only after considerable searching did he locate his two friends. Borodov was deep in conversation with what Brim judged— by extremely furry ears and dainty boots—was a most handsome example of middle-aged Sodeskayan womanhood. On the far side of the tent, Ursis was surrounded by three furry-eared Bearesses who clearly had no greater interest in the known Universe than acquainting themselves with a large, handsome general officer.

Brim grinned. His friends had no further need of *his* company for the evening! He looked around the room again. Only a sprinkling of humans anywhere—from the diplomatic service, judging by their clannishness. One, a tall, handsome fellow with a sash of medals across his chest, appeared to be the Imperial Ambassador—Browning, or some such name. All were gathered in a small group; during the evening, none had bothered with a mere junior Admiral.

Suddenly the great tent felt excessively hot. Probably it was from the thousands of candles—or perhaps the huge banquet he had endured. Whatever it was, he felt a serious case of drowsiness coming on like an express train, both in speed and irrevocability. *And,* it occurred to him, he had no idea where he was supposed to spend the night, although he needed rest quickly.

Out of nowhere, a page appeared—*his* personal footman at the feast. "Is time, perhaps," the Bear asked, "to find resting place for Imperial Admiral?"

Brim smiled and nodded. "Is time, Sergeant," he said wearily.

The Sergeant bowed and started for the door. "Please to follow, Admiral," he said over his shoulder. Then, "Is probably advisable to turn up heat in Fleet Cloak," he added. "'Bear cubs and alba-pups cover noses carefully from the frost spider,' as they say."

Brim grinned in spite of himself. "As they say," he agreed, and followed the Bear into the frosty night. The snow had stopped, but the overcast remained, for not a star could be seen in the black sky overhead. "Where are we going?" he asked as they trudged along a seemingly endless row of crawlers, boots squeaking in the snow.

"To crawler," the Bear replied. "We have rigged cot for honored visitor."

Brim peered at an entry hatch—dimly lighted by a single battle lantern bobbing in the cold wind. The big machines were identical and—with exception of the green and blue team designations—carried no distinguishing imprint, at least none Brim could see. "How do you know which one we're heading for?" he asked.

"Ah—is easy matter, that," the Bear replied with a huge smile. "We go to crawler commanded by Captain Votov." He turned to Brim, who was now walking at his side. "Is right one. No?"

"Is right one, yes," Brim answered. "But *which* one?"

"*This* one," the Bear said, pointing proudly to the next crawler in the row. It looked for all the Universe like every crawler they had passed—except it *did* wear the Blue insignia.

"How do you *know*?" Brim demanded, drowsiness getting the better of his good nature.

"Not hard, Admiral," the Bear replied. "Is thirty-fifth in line."

"Universe . . ."

As Brim wearily dragged himself up the final ladder, he noticed—with no little relief—that at least a dozen cots had been rigged in the upper cabin; his grip was floating at the foot of one near the command console. The Bear-sized folding bed might have been cramped for a Sodeskayan, but it was huge for a man. And it was luxuriously appointed with huge quilts and a great plump bolster. He stripped to his underwear and dove inside the—*ICY!*—quilts in a matter of clicks.

"Can I bring Admiral Brim a nightcap?" the Sergeant asked from the hatch.

"N-no!" Brim stammered as his body slowly, agonizingly, warmed the frosty bedclothes. Even on the verge of freezing to death, he had imbibed enough meem for the remainder of his life—*if* he managed to survive.

Then there was nothing. . . .

CHAPTER 2

Hope For the Future—
In a Deadly Present

Next morning, Brim awoke with a terrible hangover and, if nothing else, a renewed appreciation—*awe* was perhaps a better term—for the internal capacities of Sodeskayans. In spite of his "early" retirement that morning, he was far from the first one up. Stretching his limbs—while attempting to ignore both a monumental headache and a tongue that seemed to have grown its own bushy pelt—he nodded to Borodov, who was sitting nearby on the side of his cot with a great smile on his face.

"'After long hibernation, Bears praise morning light,' as they say," the old Bear chuckled. "I take it you enjoyed banquet, my furless friend."

"*Then*, yes; *now*, no," Brim answered. "I may never eat again."

"Will make you very skinny, Wilf Ansor," Borodov replied, waving a mock-tutorial finger. "Come, my friend," he said, "we shall dress quickly, have mug of hot cvc'eese, and take walk in snow with Nikolai Yanuarievich. Is time-tested remedy for Bearish hangovers—probably will work for humans, too." He nodded to Ursis, who was peering at

47

them from across the room, then winked. "While treating hangover," he said under his breath, "we also talk about subjects on your mind from yesterday's maneuvers, eh?"

"In that case, I'll be ready in a click," Brim said.

"Is giving little bit longer than click," Borodov admonished wryly. "You are not only one in battle crawler with hangover."

Half a metacycle later, the three friends carried their steaming cups of cvc'eese out into a cold, dim morning, boots crunching in the dry, powdered snow while their breath billowed in the icy air. Behind them, the bivouac of colorful tents and great, pyramid-shaped machines rose from the snow-covered plain like the set from some fantastic stage play. Occasional shouts and the sharp, metallic clanking of machinery wafted across the snowdrifts, but for all practical purposes, the scene was silent as a wilderness ought be.

"Well, friend Brim," Ursis began, "now we talk about maneuvers. You have seen for yourself problems we face."

Brim frowned. "I assume you *don't* mean the lack of a space combat patrol, do you," he stated.

"That is correct," Ursis said flatly. "Our actual problem is everyone's *acceptance* of no combat space patrol." He looked at Borodov and shrugged. "Well," he added, "*nearly* everyone—certainly is all right by most graduates of Sodeskayan Military Academy."

"Avoid getting wrong concept, friend Brim," Borodov interjected in a cloud of condensation. "Not all Sodeskayan High Command is so much out of date." He sipped his cvc'eese. "Unfortunately, up-to-date ones—myself included, devil take it—are also least influential with Knez."

"So it's a political thing, then?" Brim asked.

"We think so," Ursis said, his brow wrinkled with concern, "though sometimes, seems as if Leaguers must be behind 'antiquarians,' as we call them behind their backs." He chuckled. "They are as much enemy to Sodeskaya's survival as Leaguers themselves."

Brim nodded, glancing back at the base. "Yeah," he said, "I know what you mean. We *still* have the Congress for Intra-Galactic Accord to contend with at home. But since they're openly funded by the Leaguers, they are a lot easier to counter—at least now that the war has started."

Ursis nodded. "In a way," he said, gesturing with his mug, "your CIGAs are at least more honest than our 'antiquarians.' At least majority of CIGAs are motivated by belief that they are bringing peace to Galaxy—even if they are really doing opposite. Antiquarians are driven only by desire to prevent others from sharing power in Gromcow."

"I don't understand," Brim replied.

"For most part Knez's High Command is made up of graduates from Sodeskayan Military Academy," Borodov explained. "I myself attended this school—as did brother Knez and most Sodeskayans with titles such as ours." He shrugged, glancing absently into the grayness above, where it had begun to snow again. "Is traditional," he declared.

"And . . . ?" Brim prompted.

"And," Borodov continued, "school teaches exclusively surface warfare. No one on faculty has experience with Fleet tactics—or anything else regarding nonsurface warfare."

"Mother of Voot," Brim swore under his breath, "now I'm beginning to understand."

"Upshot is, then," Ursis continued, "that although they maintain surface armies and interstellar supply systems without peer, their ascendancy at High Court in Gromcow has also allowed Fleet to sink into neglect, relegated to role of ground support only. And to maintain themselves in power, these Bears make certain Borodov's brother gets advice from nobody but themselves. Result: He feels confident that Sodeskaya is ready to fight Leaguers, when it reality opposite is true."

"Worst part of it is that many actually believe flawed logic they preach," Borodov added. "And they are literally paranoid about opposition. Good rumor has it they have actually murdered dissenters." He pursed his lips. "I have no proof, but certain individuals have . . . *disappeared,* shall we say."

"That explains why the two of you have been so circumspect lately," Brim said as snow began to sting his face.

"Only partially, Wilf Ansor," Borodov said. "It has also been important that you experience for yourself difficult problems we face here in Sodeskaya—with invasion not far over time horizon. Much needs to be done, and scant time remains in which to do it."

"Luckily," Ursis said, starting back to the camp through the worsening snowfall, "not everyone has head in pillows. Soon, as we make excuses to leave sham maneuvers here, we show you why we have some hope for future."

"Certain of us have been taking steps. . . ." Borodov said.

Brim smiled. "Why is it I suspected you two would be involved in something like that?"

"I have no idea," Borodov said, turning to Brim in mock horror. "Why, Nikolai Yanuarievich and I *always* go along with crowd. Is not so, my friend?"

"But of course, Anastas Alexi," Ursis said over his shoulder. "Virtual studies in conformity. . . ."

They were on the way to Gromcow before the Evening Watch.

Early the next Sodeskayan week, Brim found himself at the Imperial Embassy, filing his first regular report to Vice Admiral Baxter Calhoun, his mentor, onetime shipmate, and now commander. It was the second—highly secret—part of his mission, the part not even his longtime friends Ursis and Borodov knew about. His primary role in Sodeskaya *was* to act as an adviser assisting the Sodeskayans to rebuild their fleet. But he had also been sent to evaluate Sodeskayan chances of survival against the Leaguers' coming invasion. In its own war with the Leaguers, Emperor Onrad's Empire would have to spend its limited resources wisely; the days were long gone when it could afford aid to all its allies. Now only those with a fair chance for eventual survival would receive material aid. And this first report on the Sodeskayan outlook would not be very promising.

Comfortably dressed in mufti, he'd had Barbousse chauffeur him to Gromcow alone while Borodov and Ursis were attending to business in another part of the city. It was his first visit to the Embassy, and without a uniform, his arrival had been treated brusquely, to say the least—until he produced his military passport.

"Admiral Brim?" asked the clerk at the reception desk. "Yes, there's mail for you—sent by diplomatic pouch, no less."

"Thanks," Brim said, opening the sealed envelope. "Yeah!" he exclaimed. "Now, that's my idea of a beautiful young woman! Look't this, will you?"

The clerk wasted no time grabbing the stack of Holo-Grams Brim had already looked through. His eyebrows raised for a moment; then he smiled. "You're right, Admiral, she's beautiful, all right. What's her name?"

"Hope," Brim said.

"Your kid?" the clerk asked.

Brim thought about that for a moment. "In a way, I suppose," he said a little sadly. "I guess I'm some sort of 'uncle,' right now."

The clerk grinned. "I'll bet her mother's a knockout."

Brim nodded. "She was," he said, going through the stack for a second time.

"She *was*?"

"She didn't quite make it through the Battle of Avalon," Brim explained.

"Sorry," the clerk said.

"You needn't be," Brim said, putting the HoloGrams in his pocket. "I'm sorry enough for both of us."

The clerk suddenly frowned. "Admiral, you aren't *Wilf* Brim who used to fly in the Mitchell Trophy races, are you?"

Brim nodded, glad for the change of subject. "Didn't think people remembered things back that many years," he said facetiously.

The clerk smiled. "The last race *was* only a couple of years ago, Admiral," he said. "By Voot, I never thought I'd ever meet *you* face-to-face."

Brim felt his cheeks burn. Several years had passed since the final competition off Avalon when he permanently retired the Galaxy-famous Mitchell Trophy in Sherrington Ltd's great racing starship, the M-6B. Even so, he still found himself embarrassed by the celebrity status that had attached itself to his life during the races that prototyped not only the Empire's greatest attack starship, the Sherrington Starfury, but Sodeskaya's famed Krasni-Peytch Wizard Reflecting Drive. "Thanks," he said simply, "—a lot of people could have flown those ships and won. I was just lucky enough to be out of work at the right time to be hired."

The clerk smiled. "Right," he said with a chuckle. "And cows fly."

"Where's the KA'PPA room, friend?" Brim asked, attempting to change the subject again. "I need to transmit a message."

"I'll have a messenger take it immediately, Admiral," the clerk offered.

Brim smiled. "Thanks all the same," he said quietly, "but I'm required to send this one myself—in the code room."

"Sorry, Admiral," the clerk said, pointing toward a swinging gate, "only Embassy staff is permitted beyond—"

"Put this through your security machine," Brim interrupted, handing the clerk his military passport. "I think you'll find the permission I need."

Frowning, the clerk took Brim's passport and placed it in an interrogator box. Moments later, his eyebrows rose. "It's asking for my identification now," he said.

Brim only nodded.

The clerk placed all ten of his fingers on the box and waited. Presently, his eyebrows rose almost comically. "Mother of thraggling Voot!" he swore under his breath, then handed back Brim's passport. "According to this," he said, "I don't even have enough clearance to ask what clearances you've got—but you're allowed *anywhere*." Shaking his head, he returned to the console. "I'll notify all divisions."

Brim nodded again. "Thanks," he replied. "Now, where's the KA'PPA room?"

"T-that way, Admiral," the clerk said, still clearly dumbfounded by Brim's clearance. He pointed to a great marble staircase leading to the Embassy's second floor. "Turn right at the top of the stairs, take the third gallery to your left, and it'll be the last suite on the left. The security plate's right there beside you."

"Thanks again," Brim said, placing his fingers on a public interrogation plate.

"Access granted," the desk reported in a soft female voice.

Starting off across the bustling lobby, Brim took the staircase two at a time, then turned right along a wide, crowded mezzanine lined by huge carved doors in intricately scrolled frames. Top diplomats in *those* plush offices, he thought, striding rapidly over the thick carpet. The Foreign Office had always been the exclusive venue of wealthy Avalonian families, and plush posts were passed down through succeeding generations of school chums from the most prestigious institutions. The arrangement normally managed to produce enough competence to keep the system working well. But for every talented diplomat, at least ten affluent blockheads sat in high places to hobble their every move.

Brim turned at the second gallery leading to the left, then walked the length of the long hall, only to encounter a maintenance closet as the last door on the left. He frowned. It *was* the last door to the left, wasn't it? Opposite was a gravity-effects fire escape, so clearly neither door at this end of the hall were correct. Looking back the way he had come, none of the elaborate portals seemed right for a code room. He began to retrace his steps. The first real office suites he came to were administrative—ACCOUNTING and PERSONNEL. Both appeared busy, with both Bears and humans scurrying about their lobbies like swarms of insects. Farther along was an office suite marked EDUCATION, also surprisingly busy, then the TRADE MINISTRY.

At the SODESKAYAN-IMPERIAL CULTURAL EXCHANGE, however, a tall, attractive woman carrying a logic scriber stepped into his path and smiled. "You must be the Records Clerk they promised to send from the Museum Section across town," she said in a soft voice. "I'm Marsha Browning, Antiquities Section Chief; I saw you pass in the other direction looking rather lost."

"Oh?" Brim asked in surprise, glancing through the intricately scrolled doorway into still another busy foyer. "Well, I suppose I am lost," he said truthfully.

"Not anymore," Browning said with a smile. "You have no idea how glad I am to see you. They said they might not be able to spare someone today, and I really did need someone from Museum to verify the count."

"Glad to be here," Brim said—and he meant it. Neither young nor old, Browning was a damned good-looking woman—sexy, even dressed in a simple blue business suit, although it *did* have a very short skirt. She wore salt-and-pepper hair at an angle across her forehead and cut short above her ears. Wide-set, sensible brown eyes, full cheeks, a button nose, and sensual mouth—perhaps a little too wide— all blended into a most attractive, friendly sort of countenance. Tall and athletically built, she had small breasts, capable-looking hands, and long, shapely legs—a looker anywhere, especially on a planet where most of the occupants were Bears!

"Is something wrong?" she asked.

Brim felt his face flush—he *had* been staring. The woman radiated a sensuousness that would pride a woman half her age. Unfortunately, she also wore a wedding ring. "Er, no," he said lamely. "You . . . ah, look like someone I know."

"I see," she said with a little smile—she'd noticed, all right! "Well, come along, then, we've a great deal of work to do this afternoon, and very little time to do it."

Brim started to protest, but before he could utter a word, the woman started off across the lobby. He shrugged and followed, smiling to himself. Somehow, he felt little compulsion to correct her mistake. Besides, he was in no particular hurry to file his report, and the woman seemed as pleasant as she was pretty. Lucky husband, he mused as they passed through a suite of smaller offices and into a long corridor.

"Here we are," she said as he caught up at double doors leading into what appeared to be a small storage room. She pointed to a series of shipping boxes inside. "The Bershankaya collection, back from the Imperial Museum in Avalon. I'm sure you're relieved to see them returned in one piece."

"Well . . ." Brim started.

"By the way," she said, "I didn't catch your name."

"Brim, ma'am—Wilf Brim."

Browning frowned. "Are you new at Records?" she asked. "I don't remember any Brims there."

"*Quite* new," Brim replied, giving in to the unintended charade.

"Well, to work, then," Browning said, "and do call me Marsha."

"If you'll call me Wilf," Brim replied.

"A good arrangement," Browning said. "Now, we'll start with the top box."

"All right," Brim said. "What would you like me to do?"

"You don't know?" Browning asked.

"Afraid not," Brim replied, "—but I'm certainly willing to learn."

Browning shook her head. "I guess every section's a little discombobulated these days, what with the Leaguers ready to invade, and everything." She glanced into the storeroom and nodded toward the boxes. "We've got to inventory this, then ship it to the caves outside of town for safekeeping."

"Sounds like a good idea to me," Brim said. "Since you've got the logic scriber, you record while I open boxes and count."

"You've a deal, Wilf," she said, and they went to work.

As things turned out, the records clerk originally promised from the Museum Section never did show up. Brim and his new, accidental acquaintance worked until nightfall, cataloging more than a thousand small artifacts that composed the valuable collection. And while they worked, they found they had a great deal to talk and laugh about—except an opportunity for Brim to gracefully end the masquerade that was becoming more an more embarrassing as time went on. They finished just as lights began to glow in the streets below. "Thanks so much, Wilf," Browning said as he sealed the last box for transit. "You're a hard worker and a lot of fun besides. I can't remember when I've so enjoyed an afternoon's work."

"The same certainly goes for me," Brim said. In truth, he'd quickly become fond of this gentle-spoken, statuesque woman. During the metacycles they'd worked together, a certain chemistry had quietly asserted itself, and had it not been for her wedding ring, he'd have made a serious effort to take *a lot* more of her time. "Can I, ah, offer a cup of cvc'eese before you venture out in the cold?" he heard himself ask.

She blushed for a moment. "I'd really love that, Wilf," she said, and from the look her eyes, she meant it. "But, well," she continued, "I'm expected at a reception with my husband this evening. A command engagement, so I'd better be on my way."

"Too bad," Brim said. "Perhaps another time."

"I'd like that," she replied, then blushed again.

As they strolled back to the lobby, she unmindfully touched his arm. "I shall message your section tomorrow and tell them how much I enjoyed working with you, Wilf," she said. "You are an awfully good worker—far better than any of the Records Clerks they've sent in the past."

"Well, I thank you," Brim replied, feeling his own cheeks begin to burn. "B-but I, ah, doubt that they'll recognize me. I'm just another Records Clerk over there."

At the door, they paused awkwardly. "Good-bye, Marsha," he said, offering his hand. Hers was warm and soft. A gentle squeeze that lasted just a little longer than it might have, then the spell was broken.

"Good-bye, Wilf," she said, then quickly turned and hurried back into the lobby.

During the next week or so, Brim found it quite difficult to drive thoughts of his daughter *or* Marsha Browning from his mind. But he had a great deal of help. The day following his visit to the Embassy, Borodov and Ursis bundled him into another Roshov limousine skimmer and headed along snow-covered highways to the huge Budenny Spaceport on the opposite side of Gromcow. The guards had clearly been notified of their imminent arrival, for they were waved through the gates with only a cursory glance at their identification. Their final destination: a secret laboratory deep within the Sodeskayan star system where Brim would have his first flight in one of the new ZBL-4 killer ships.

Traveling to Sodeskaya by liner during his past visits, Brim had seldom been inside the great Budenny complex with its c'lenyts of heated takeoff runs on nearby lakes and Becton tubes for use on days when even those were frozen by the dreaded Rasputitisa storms.

Historically, Sodeskayans were space travelers only by necessity. Naturally nearsighted, these huge creatures much preferred building power plants and starships for others to purchase and fly. Nevertheless, it was a known fact that the Sodeskayan Fleet included many squadrons of military starships, including numbers of giant TB-3 battleships that could lumber all the way across the Galaxy to deliver colossal firepower against enemy forces.

Yet for all the imposing Sodeskayan weaponry, Imperial Fleet tacticians had long warned their friends in Gromcow about the vulnerability of these huge machines in actual combat. Not only were the great starships getting old (both in years and in technology), but recent development of killer ships like the Empire's now-famous Sherrington Starfury or the League's Gantheisser 262 had seemingly changed the rules of fighting forever.

Now, unless they could be provided with long-range killer-ship escorts, even the most powerful of battleships might be overwhelmed when venturing deep into enemy starspace. Certainly the principle had been proved out in the recent Battle of Avalon, when a six-month-long Leaguer attempt to take the Imperial capital planets had been hurled back at tremendous cost to both sides.

"You are silent, Wilf Ansor," Ursis said quietly as the limousine cruised past row after row of angular UC-3s floating on massive gravity pools.

Something about the craggy outlines of these giant ships awakened an almost racial memory in Brim, a primordial vision of death swooping down from the sky. Unfortunately, whatever power they might have projected twenty years previously was now all but sapped by the passage of time—and technology. "They're all antiques, Nik," he replied without turning from the window. "Leaguer Gantheissers will cut them to ribbons. I know. I spent six months of my life fighting those new Leaguer ships, and unless you've made some big improvements to the specs I've seen, your UC-3s'll be nothing but helpless practice targets for Hoth Orgoth's Military Space Arm."

"Yes," Borodov broke in, "but we have lots of them, eh?"

Brim heard Ursis guffaw. "Is like building widget for six credits, then selling for four—but making up loss in volume sales."

Brim shook his head and chuckled in spite of himself. "Not exactly a winning strategy," he said as they passed a large field of smaller gravity pools floating small, nimble destroyers that the Sodeskayans would almost certainly employ in the role of killer ships.

Like their battleship fleet, the inventory of smaller ships was also huge and largely obsolete. Most of the four thousand so-called frontline defensive warships were either J-153s—underpowered, undergunned starships built to fight a war that ended in an earlier age—or stubby J-16s, more modern and faster than their predecessors, but also no match for the powerful Gantheissers they would face during combat with the Leaguers.

Off some distance from the road, Brim could see a few squadrons of what appeared to be NJH-3s, a new class of Sodeskayan starships designed specifically for the killer-ship role, but they were known to be of a flawed design, unstable and lightly armed, although rumored to be extremely fast. From what Brim had learned, they would prove to be poor competitors in the swirling, wrenching space battles like those he'd experienced over the planets of Avalon.

As if reading his thoughts, Borodov reached across the passenger compartment and touched Brim's shoulder. "Situation is bad, I admit," he said, "but some hope gleams at our destination today."

Brim turned and nodded. "I'll count on that, Doctor," he said, "because there's nothing I've seen on *this* field that will stop the Leaguers I've run into so far."

"Only hope is they will serve to slow down invaders," Ursis said, "—at least until newer ships we will see today move up to frontline service."

Brim shook his head as they pulled to a stop beside one of the ubiquitous NJH-26 executive ships hovering at the launch end of a Becton tube. "They better move up in a hurry, good friends, or a lot of Sodeskayans are going to end up learning to speak Vertrucht."

"The lucky ones, in that eventuality," Borodov said, opening the door.

Brim knew what he meant by that. In the last war, Leaguers pronounced Bears to be "pelt beasts," and Bearskin hats and coats became quite fashionable throughout the League planets. In fact, Field Marshal Rodef *nov* Vobok was known as "The Hunter" because of the bear skins he had taken as an OverProvost in the previous war. He had been arraigned by a postwar tribunal as a war criminal, but powerful friends of the League made certain he never came to trial.

Some metacycles later, they were docked at a laboratory—one of several that made up the Sodeskayan Fleet's Central Design Ministry—orbiting a small, barren planet deep within the Sodeskayan star system. Various design bureaus from all over the Great Federation of Sodeskayan States brought their newest products to this colossal proving establishment, where they were run through their paces and either rejected or approved for further development and eventual production.

Today, Brim would fly the ultra-secret ZBL-4, an advanced killer ship powered by a brawny model of Krasni-Peych's Reflecting Drive. From advanced specifications Brim had seen in Avalon, he knew it ought to compare favorably with many models of the Sherrington Starfury and outmaneuver most of its Leaguer opponents.

It had even been rumored that the little ships were equipped with additional armaments, but at the time these were too secret for release in Avalon, and no sign of them had surfaced in the advanced simulators transhipped from Sodeskaya. Besides, he considered, there would be plenty of time to learn about the extras once he'd gained a better understanding of the basics.

The laboratory itself was shaped like a huge funnel constructed like a child's toy of six thick disks, with the largest—nearly a quarter-c'lenyt in diameter—at the "bottom," oriented toward the rocky surface of the planet. Around the outside of this huge disk were sixteen docking stations, each fully equipped to operate as an independent testing cell. The entire station was covered by transparent crystalline plates that reflected most of the dim blue light from the binary, and in doing so made the facility almost invisible from more than five c'lenyts away. It bristled with antennas, the largest of which—a fantastic KA'PPA broadcast tower—extended nearly a thousand irals beyond the top layer. Brim had been dazzled by the huge facility as soon as he spotted it in the distance. Now, inside, he found himself even more impressed as he walked with his two companions along the curving periphery toward test cell sixteen, where a ZBL-4 prototype and its crew waited for his arrival. Through the transparent walls and floor, he could see the little planet they orbited some four hundred c'lenyts below; off to his left, the pair of stars *it* orbited whirled furiously around a common center of gravity. His deep-blue Imperial battlesuit drew a number of curious stares from passing technicians who were clearly used to seeing only Bears in this most secure of test structures.

"Nervous?" Ursis asked.

"A little," Brim admitted. He always was, the first time he took up a new ship. And today he had a reputation riding on how well he handled the powerful little attack ship—the better he flew, the more cooperation he would get from the Bearish Helmsmen with whom he would come in contact during his extended mission in Sodeskaya.

"Is good," Ursis said, clapping him on the shoulder as they paused at the entrance to the brow. "Now go show these Bears how to fly."

Brim rolled his eyes and frowned. "Actually, I was planning to let *them* show *me* a thing or two this first ride, if that's all right with you, Nikolai Yanuarievich."

"Probably not a bad idea," Ursis said.

Both turned for a moment to look along the brow as it extended through the wall and ended at a sleek little starship, just slightly larger than a Sherrington Starfury. "They worked slowly and diligently on this beauty," Ursis said quietly. "It has undergone three extensive redesigns since development began nearly ten years ago."

"And believe me, Wilf Ansor," Borodov added, "this third-generation starship you see here at Design Ministry is considerably more sophisticated than first one."

Brim nodded, but kept his thoughts to himself. From what he could see, Sodeskayan ideas of quality control would have to change if their ships were to achieve their true potential. The fit and finish was somewhat below par and the hull-metal panels along the fuselage rippled in places. Otherwise, the ZBL-4 was an attractive-enough-looking starship—an intriguing, thirty-eight-thousand-milston blend of Imperial and Sodeskayan design philosophies. The single hull was nearly 250 irals in length, formed by two rounded, cone-shaped sections—the aft section only a third as long as the one forward.

The bridge was placed just forward—and faired flush to—the widest point of the hull. Channeled openings spaced equally around the aft cone vented four Krasni-Peych 91C Reflecting HyperDrive units, these powered by eight powerful Krasni-Peych K24000 plasma generators. Six superfocused, 388-mmi disruptors fired forward from a circle some fifty irals from the ship's nose; four others were mounted in turrets at the end of stubby sponsons protruding laterally from the hull beneath the bridge. Like the Imperial Starfury, she carried a small crew: one Helmsman, ten other officers, and forty-one ratings.

To Brim, somehow, the little ship looked, well, *capable*. She certainly no Starfury; but then, the original I.F.S. *Starfury*, as well as all the ships subsequently based on her design, were in a class by themselves, prodigious in elegant symmetry. He turned to his comrades. "Tell you all about her soon as I get back," he said, and pulled the heavy brow door open. Striding quickly along the mostly transparent tube—its narrow floor had been coated with an opaque substance for "rock lubbers," as spacemen everywhere referred to surface-bound individuals of any race—he soon reached the ship's boarding hatch, where he was met by a grinning Bear dressed in a bright crimson Sodeskayan battle suit adorned with the three stars of a Space Fleet Captain. Smaller than most—perhaps the size of Dr. Borodov, but clearly no more than a quarter of his age—he grinned and bowed slightly.

"Admiral Brim," he said in perfect Avalonian—still another reminder to Brim of his failure to learn another language.

"The same," Brim replied, extending his hand. Past the airlock, there was no saluting.

"I am known as Potyr," the Bear said, gripping Brim's hand. "Captain Potyr Simonovik. Welcome to my ship—I noticed you giving her the once-over from the ring deck."

Brim smiled as a rating closed the hatch after them. "I hear she's quite a ship," he said.

Simonovik grinned back. "A studied answer, Admiral," he said, "—and a fair one, considering you have never flown her." He laughed. "Certainly she cannot compare to exquisite lines of your trihulled Starfuries; but then, even I find it easy to admit they are most beautiful ships in known Universe. Nevertheless, G.S.S. *Probeyda*, here, has other qualities that Helmsman in you will almost certainly appreciate. Come," he said, motioning to a companionway before Brim had a chance to comment. "We will go to bridge so you can fly her."

Brim clapped the Bear on his shoulder. "Now you're talking," he said. "Lead the way."

Moments later, Simonovik had placed him in the left-hand Helmsman's console and had seated himself at the CoHelmsman's console directly to its right. "I have taken liberty to single up mooring beams, so . . . when you are ready, Admiral," he said.

Brim nodded and settled back in the deep recliner, so steeply reclined that when he placed his feet on the steering-engine controls, they were almost level with his shoulders. His hands reached up nearly an iral to touch the power and attitude controls. He looked down along the long nose at the six heavy disruptors—*fixed* instead of moveable—and the big machine suddenly felt very foreign. "I'm ready," he said, activating the seat restraints, "except for . . ."

"Except for what?" Simonovik asked.

"Well," Brim replied, "I can sense the trouble that would follow any dinging of this *very* important prototype."

"Admiral Brim," Simonovik said with a little grin, "I have followed your career since you first flew that little S-4 of Mark Valerian's during the second postwar race for the Mitchell Trophy." He grinned. "Most of us Bears would rather ride as passengers than fly these oversized skyrockets.

Eyesight, you know. So I'm not going to do a lot of worrying about the hull when you're flying."

Brim rolled his eyes. "We'd both better hope that trust isn't misplaced," he chuckled. Back home, he'd been given most of a day to memorize the Helmsman's station, so he ran through the main readouts and controls before giving the word to start. Clockwise from the left, a large red handle with Sodeskayan wording that probably meant "Panic Button" (it would shut down both Drive and gravity systems in case of a dire emergency); a timepiece calibrated in Standard Time Units—at least *that* was familiar; a velocity meter for HypoSpeed ("NEVER ENTER OXYGEN ATMOSPHERE ABOVE 9100 [6800 CPM] FOR LANDFALL"); graviton pressure (nobody in Avalon seemed to know what it was calibrated in—orpals of Logish Meem—but it didn't matter); Drive utilization in percent; gravity vector and pressure, a nicely conceived weapons-status panel with readouts that anyone could instantly understand under stress; four Drive-door indicators; and finally a proximity meter in some sort of Sodeskayan measure (the old-fashioned numeral "1," someone had explained, stood for 100 Sodeskayan cornoks, or about 328 Imperial irals—he'd decided to look out the Hyperscreens instead of attempting the conversion in his head). Despite the "foreign" markings, he felt pretty much at home.

However, below the main panels were a row of touch sensors that he'd had to memorize because the Sodeskayan characters made no sense at all. They controlled all sorts of things from electrical power to Hyperscreen brightness. There were also a number of warning indicators for the ship's power systems.

Other controls included a Helmsman's override on the main power bus, a steering-engine lock, and a sliding touch sensor to control the four Drive outlet doors. These remained closed while the LightSpeed-limited A-39 gravity generators propelled the ship. The hover trim, used to levitate the ship on the surface when it wasn't resting on a gravity pool or a Becton tube, was located to his left beside the communicator panel with its two global displays. Brim took a deep breath and glanced to his right, where Simonovik was watching with an amused expression.

"Something like me when first I fly Starfury," he chuckled. "Checked everything a hundred times."

"It all looks good to me," Brim said presently. "I'm ready."

Simonovik nodded. "I'll have generators connected with mains." He issued an order in Sodeskayan to a Bear in the next recliner, and almost immediately a rumble issued from beneath the deck. "Connected," he said presently. "Ship is yours."

Brim nodded, concentrating on what he'd learned about starting the gravity generators. Glancing at the power display panel, he gated power to the number three generator, pushed the graviton boost three times in succession, and activated START. The generators pulsed, caught almost rapidly, then died.

"With in-line generators like you are used to," Simonovik cautioned, "one is conditioned to release START immediately when generators catch. Big spin-gravs like these want START activated until generator is turning for few moments. Then you can release."

Brim nodded thanks and reset all the generator controls. Then he pushed START again and held it in until the generator was running more or less steadily. Once it had settled into the grumbly, belching rhythm he remembered from his simulator runs, he started the other three, then coupled them to the single thrust damper control near his left hand. His eyes met those of Simonovik, and the Bear nodded.

"Nice work for furless human," he quipped. "When you are ready, I'll switch us to internal gravity."

"Ready," Brim replied, bracing himself. For all the *years*

spent in space—and the thousands of cycles in and out of some ship's internal gravity—he had yet to overcome a queasy stomach at the moment of switchover. He watched the Bear issue a command into his communicator and clenched his teeth. A wave of nausea swept him while he desperately swallowed his gorge; then—quick as it started— the feeling passed.

"Everything is all right, Admiral?" Simonovik asked. He *knew*.

"Everything's fine," Brim replied with a wan smile. "Let's cast off."

Simonovik nodded, announcing something in Sodeskayan over the blower that silenced the flight bridge. Then he issued a command to another Bear in his display and moments later the mooring beams winked out one by one. Soon they were floating free.

Brim nudged the thrust damper; the gravs coughed before picking up. As he eased the ship away from the brow and headed for the run-up area, he began a final checklist with Simonovik. "Gravity?"

"Locked."

"Nav system?"

"Stable."

"Drive doors?"

"Ready: four green lights."

"Backup mains?"

"KA'PPA?"

"Energized and ready. . . ." Clearly, Simonovik had done his prework well, for the ship's systems checked quickly—a considerable feat for a prototype. "Shall I call for clearance?" he asked.

"Do it," Brim replied.

Simonovik spoke into his communicator for a moment, then nodded. "Cleared, Admiral," he said. "Vector of nine-teen by two-ten by thirty-seven."

Brim aligned the ship, made a last-moment systems check, then locked the steering engine and fed in power. The little killer ship bolted ahead with surprising acceleration. Grinning with approval, he pushed the thrust damper full forward and was rewarded by a tremendous surge of speed—and uproar. The ZBL's big generators could put out prodigious noise, too.

But acceleration was not the ship's only attribute. Because the spin-gravs were geared to turn at lower speeds than normal, they produced tremendous pulling power. For an experienced combat Helmsman, this could provide a definite edge in maneuverability; for a neophyte fresh from the training squadrons, it could be the difference between life and death.

The ship was, in fact, so easy to fly that Brim was immediately tempted to push it to the limits of its maneuvering envelope. However, he knew that most *old* Helmsmen were also *cautious* Helmsmen, so at first he prudently avoided much in the way of acrobatics and contented himself with basic maneuvers—steep turns and snap rolls—before he flew a mock approach to the orbiting laboratory, testing out the low end of the ship's speed range. The steering engine was extremely effective, and turns could be made at an incredibly abrupt rate, but despite its potentially vicious response rate, *this* ZBL-4, at least, was not what he could call twitchy. The ship did precisely what he told it to do—*when* he wanted it done. In spite of her less-than-perfect finish (and that would only affect atmospheric flight), she promised to be a potent little killer.

During the next three metacycles, Brim put the ship through every test and maneuver he could think of, plus a number of others the Sodeskayans suggested, until both he and, according to Simonovik, the crew were thoroughly tired. Only then did they set course for home. With the laboratory visible in the distance, he called for a clearance, picked up a vector of three-ninety degrees, pulled off the power, and blipped the gravity brakes—producing so much deceleration that a bit more power was necessary. Xaxtdamned good brakes! He moved the damper forward, but this time the gravs did nothing. Now they were heading directly for the surface with no power controls! Heart in his mouth, he glanced at Simonovik, who only smiled calmly and winked.

"No problem," the Bear assured him. "A-39 gravs always do that from deep retard." As he spoke, the generators grunted, coughed, then picked up again, leaving a great glowing cloud of gravitons aft.

When Brim started to breathe again, he glanced at the odd proximity meter, made a rough calculation in his head—to no avail—and eyeballed a landing place through the Hyperscreens. Working the steering engine, damper, and gravity brakes with great care, he turned head-on for the docking area and began his approach. He'd kept the velocity a little high at the first beacon to assure himself of maximum control, and predictably, the ZBL-4 tried to swing her bow, but he managed to hold the little ship on course with very little movement in either pitch or yaw. Amid enthusiastic cheering from the bridge crew, he floated to a near-perfect stop at the brow, where a deck crew connected her to the air lock. Then he switched the gravs to neutral and nodded to Simonovik. "Your ship," he said with a grin. He'd done a good job, and he knew it.

"The way you fly, you can borrow again anytime," Simonovik said, placing his hands before him in the universal gesture of giving.

Brim laughed and clicked off his seat restraints. "I may take you up on that sometime," he replied. "She's impressive—and I'm talking like a Helmsman, not a diplomat. I've rarely flown so maneuverable a ship."

"Next time, we try out the Drive," Simonovik promised. "You'll find she's just as impressive at HyperSpeeds."

"I'll look forward to that," Brim said. He meant it.

Ursis and Borodov met him at the lab end of the brow. Both had anxious looks on their faces. "So?" Ursis prompted. "How did it go?"

Brim grinned. "Went fine, Nik," he teased. "No problems at all."

Ursis rolled his eyes skyward. "No, no, Wilfooshka!" he said. "The *ship*. What did you think of the ship?"

"Clearly, your answer matters little to friend Ursis," Borodov quipped lightly, flashing a little smile. But a frown betrayed what lay behind his banter. Both Bears were deadly serious.

"Sorry," Brim said apologetically. "I know these ships are important to you."

"Not only to us," Ursis said with no little fervor in his voice, "—also to *Vorustia,* the Motherland."

Brim thought a moment. "The good news," he said presently, "is that the one I flew is a fine ship—a decent match for any Leaguer I've fought, and I've scrapped with a few in my day. It handled well . . . seemed to be extremely maneuverable—perhaps even more than the latest Starfury I flew . . . and I certainly liked the fixed disruptors in the bow. That's a great way to concentrate fire."

"Then you liked it."

"Of course I liked it," Brim said. "With a little more practice, I'd gladly take it into combat. But you've got to remember that the *real* proof you're looking for is not in words but in mixing it up with a sky full of Gorn-Hoffs—and that has to do with *crews* as much as with starships."

Ursis nodded. "Is true, Wilfooshka," he said, peering sightlessly at the deck while he thought. Then suddenly he straightened. "You said that was the *good* news, my friend—

which it was. After such endorsement, what bad news can there be?"

Brim took a deep breath and looked at Ursis, then Borodov. "Perhaps not *bad* news, but certainly substance for some serious concern."

"Go on," Borodov prompted.

Brim nodded, his mind groping for the proper words. "Good as she is," he said at length, "your new ZBL seems *no better* than the latest Starfury I flew, either. The fact is, Starfuries don't have all that much edge over their opponents from the League. The Battle of Avalon was really decided by a lot of factors: Helmsmen, production, quick repairs, bravery, stubbornness—and finally, by a lot of assistance from Lady Fortune."

"So?" Ursis broke in. "Our Helmsmen are excellently prepared, or certainly out to be. We copy *your* training techniques."

"And I have never encountered a cowardly Bear," Brim added. "Not only that, but Sodeskayan stubbornness is celebrated through the whole galaxy."

"On other hand," Borodov said with a frown, "our production of new ships is just beginning. One you flew is only prototype."

"And we must build a maintenance organization from the bottom up," added Ursis, "—though that can be done quickly enough by retraining maintenance crews from older ships."

"But, like you, we shall need a great deal of help from Lady Luck," Borodov said, "especially in the beginning—unless, of course, Nergol Triannic decides to wait five or so Standard Years before he orders *nov* Vobok to begin his attack."

"And crag wolves make lap pets," Borodov said, then frowned. "But, Wilf Ansor, I have feeling you have not said all you intend to say."

"I have not," Brim replied as the three started slowly toward an entrance to the laboratory proper. "And this is what worries me even more than the present lack of finished ships. Your excellent little ZBL-4 is presently at the same stage in its development as the *next* generation of ships from the League—and incidentally our own Imperial production facilities like the Sherrington works. When your production models begin their work at the various fronts, if they are not a generation behind their opponents, they soon will be."

Visibly moved by Brim's words, Ursis stepped in silence to a glowing tram-tube and punched in a destination on the wall-mounted hailer. Finally he sighed. "As is usual when you speak of starships, Wilf Ansor," he began, "you are correct. Technology has way of marching forward to nobody's beat but its own—which speeds up considerably during time of emergency like war." He shook his head as all three turned to peer down the tube for the next tram. "Unfortunately," he continued, "this situation—though we shall now worry about it—remains out of our control for at least the near future." He turned to look at Brim. "Had you missed so-called 'war games' we endured a short while ago, you could not appreciate the troubles we have endured just to produce our few prototypes and ready a small production facility. For now, ZBL is best we can do."

"It's a xaxtdamned good ship," Brim said defensively.

Borodov smiled. "We had faith that it was," he said, "although Nikolai Yanuarievich and I are engineers, not Helmsmen."

"Nevertheless, what Wilf Ansor says is true," Ursis added. "Good as they might be, the ships will soon be a generation behind, probably before they see much service at all." He was interrupted by an open tram that flashed around the curve and whirred to a halt in front of them. The bench seats that surrounded its cabin were empty. They boarded in silence and Ursis keyed in their destination at a small panel behind his seat. Moments later, their "station" had disappeared around the curve of the satellite and they were speeding toward a brow, where the NJH-26 waited to return them to Gromcow. Suddenly Ursis continued talking as if there had been no interruption. "Fortunately, Wilfooshka," he said, holding up a tutorial index finger, "new designs are already in development pipeline. Even now, prototypes of advanced types undergo testing deep within the Sodeskayan heartland, where they are safe from attack."

Brim frowned. Over the years, he'd heard of many prototype starships that promised greatly enhanced performance and firepower—most never made it to manufacture. And the few that did were extremely behind schedule. "Well," he said evenly, "I'll take your word for it, but you'd better keep those production facilities cranked up to turn out ZBL-4s, at least for the foreseeable future. Because I have a feeling that it won't be long until you'll have an opportunity to use everything you can build. Not long at all."

CHAPTER 3
Real Bears and Ro'stoviks

A week following Brim's visit to the orbiting laboratory, Count Orlovsky, youngest brother of Katerin, the Knezina, hosted his annual ball to commemorate the Sodeskayan holidays of *Oryol,* marking the dominion's attainment of faster-than-light flight—and subsequent entry into galactic civilization. According to Borodov, Orlovsky had been about to cancel the gigantic event because of the pending invasion but had changed his mind, believing that the capital needed something—anything—to lift at least some of the gloom that had settled as its citizens braced for the inevitable.

Barbousse held the huge invitation to a tall leaded-crystal casement window and shook his head. The old-fashioned parchment directive—one *did not* miss such occasions—was embossed with what appeared to be real gold. "When these Bears throw a party, Admiral," he mused, "they *really* throw a party. At the new Elizaveta Palace, no less."

Brim peered out over the small frozen lake that bordered

the spinward gardens of Borodov Hall. As the wintry afternoon drew to a close, peasants dressed in colorful winter costumes were leaving the smooth surface with their catches of fish trailing on strings behind them. He shivered in spite of the crackling fireplace behind him and the great ceramic stove that radiated heat into every cubic iral of his dressing room. Sodeskayan winters didn't seem to bother Bears as much as they did humans, probably because the latter didn't come equipped with natural fur coats—and wouldn't *dare* wear someone else's on any of the Sodeskayan planets. "I take it you've been there," he said absently.

"The Elizaveta Palace? You bet I have, Admiral." Barbousse chuckled, helping Brim into a service jacket that jingled with medals and decorations—tonight's soiree required parade dress, as usual. "It's one of the benefits of remainin' in the enlisted ranks. While you Admirals spend all your time doin' official functions, I've had a chance to see some of the city—an' it's worth seein', for all the nippy weather."

Brim smiled. Over the years, Barbousse had turned down countless promotions to the officer corps, choosing instead assignments with Brim because, in his own words, "no one else could provide so many great opportunities for getting into trouble." He was also the greatest finagler in the known Universe, who could produce virtually anything at any time under any conditions. A number of years ago, Emperor—then Prince—Onrad had "permanently" assigned Barbousse as Brim's aide on the reasonably well proven theory that it was the most damaging act against the League one could commit.

He stepped back to inspect himself in a mirror and groaned. The complex gold aiguillette fouling his right shoulder, the chestload of jingling medals, and the crimson sash across his chest displaying both of his Imperial Comet medals—the Empire's highest military decorations—all clashed with his most basic sensibilities about dress. Uniforms were to be smart but utilitarian—something one could fight in, should that become necessary. Right now, he felt like a cheap shop front on Avalon's Ealing Way during the holiday season. He shook his head. "I suppose I'll see a bit of it tonight," he said, "—at least some of the ballrooms."

Barbousse narrowed his eyes, straightened Brim's sash, then frowned. "Beggin' the Admiral's pardon," he said, "but m' guess is that you'll not have your mind much on the party tonight."

Brim shook his head. "Not with Rodef *nov* Vobok looking over my shoulder the way he is," he said. "That bloody zukeed could be starting his invasion at this very moment, for all we know." He'd actually given some thought to that possibility during the short Sodeskayan day, but his words were really only a ploy. What—indeed, *who*—had really been on his mind was Margot Effer'wyck, whose very existence was now in question. Through the years Brim had taken a number of magnificent lovers, but she had always been *the* one, and he never attended a ball or reception without thinking back to her.

He smiled wistfully as he watched the deepening gloom outside merge through nearly seventeen years to the night he met Her Serene Majesty, Princess of the Effer'wyck Dominions and first cousin to Onrad, the present Imperial ruler. It had been a routine wardroom party aboard Brim's first ship, the little destroyer I.F.S. *Truculent*. Margot was there as an ordinary Lieutenant—a hardworking one at that, he'd quickly discovered. And if the tall, amply built woman were not the most beautiful he'd ever encountered, she'd still appealed to him in a most fundamental manner. Even after all these years, he could picture her that night: artfully tousled golden curls and soft, expressive blue eyes, flashing with nimble intelligence. Skin almost painfully fair, brushed lightly with pink high in the cheeks. And when she smiled, her brow formed the most engaging frown he could imagine.

Moist lips, long, shapely legs, small breasts, and . . . He bit his lip.

They'd become lovers long after they'd fallen in love. She a princess of Effer'wyck, the Empire's most influential dominion—he a commoner from Carescria, the shabbiest sector imaginable. For a while, the desperate absurdity of galactic war had canceled that awesome gap in status. But reality intervened soon enough, forcing a political marriage between Brim's Princess and Rogan LaKarn, Baron of The Torond—a union designated to cement the bond between his massive palatinate and the Empire.

Afterward, the two star-crossed lovers continued as best they could, carrying on a tawdry affair filled with endless stretches of longing punctuated by brilliant flashes of their own special passion. For a while it had worked—even after ersatz peace forced a return to "normal" canons of class and status. But eventually distance, a child, and Margot's growing addiction to the Leaguers' devastating narcotic Time-Weed ate away their ties until only longing remained, buried deep within Brim's psyche to mask the pain it brought.

Now, less than a Standard Year after he was briefly shipwrecked in occupied Effer'wyck—and unknowingly stood close enough to reach out and touch her—once more Brim didn't know if she were even still alive. . . .

"Um, it's about time to go, Admiral," Barbousse said gently, holding Brim's great Fleet Cloak. "I believe I hear doctors Borodov and Ursis in the hall downstairs."

"Thanks," Brim said, turning while the big man placed the heavy cloak on his shoulders.

"An, um, Admiral . . ."

"Yes, Chief?"

"I know it's none of m' business, but . . . well, she's all right. I know she is."

Brim frowned. "Who's all right?" he damanded.

"Princess Effer'wyck, Admiral," Barbousse explained.

"What makes you think *she* was on my mind?" Brim demanded with a touch of irritation.

"Just a hunch, Admiral," Barbousse said evenly. "Over the years, I've helped you into your cape before a lot of affairs like this, an' no matter who you've been, shall we say, 'interested' in at the time, you've never failed to get that look on your face just before you go."

Brim was about to give his old friend a lecture on minding one's own business when suddenly he realized that Barbousse probably *did* know him better than anybody else in the Universe. "Interesting" women came and went with the years, but only Margot and Barbousse remained constant in his life—one a chimera, one real. "I guess you're right, old friend," he relented. "You know me pretty well." He shook his head. "And I thank you for believing in her. I know it's been hard—even I lost faith for a while."

Barbousse nodded soberly. "A lot of us lost faith in 'er over the years," he admitted. "She *did* certainly have problems after they sent 'er off to The Torond t' marry that zukeed Rogan LaKarn—you'll pardon my gutter Avalonian. An' I *still* believe she set you up to be killed that night in Fluvanna—but I don't think she was actin' under her own control, either." He shrugged. "In the end, she *did* save our skins at the Battle of Zarnathor. You know she did that for you, Admiral. It almost cost 'er life—and her kid's, too."

"Thanks, Chief," Brim said. "I don't know what to say. . . ."

"You don't have time to say anything." Barbousse chuckled. "It's time you were on the way. I think I can hear Dr. Borodov and General Ursis waitin' for you downstairs."

Brim strode through the door and clapped his old friend on his shoulder. "See you in the morning."

"Er . . . I put in for leave in the mornin', Admiral," he said. "I've got some important business to take care of."

"Is she pretty?" Brim demanded over his shoulder as he started down the staircase.

"Admiral, how could you?" Barbousse called.

Brim laughed. "Over the years, Chief, I've come to know *you* pretty well, too."

Elizaveta Palace was ablaze with lights when Borodov's private Roshov limousine skimmer arrived at the gate. The colossal building seemed to go on forever. Fifty windows, soaring ten stories in fantastically carved stone frames, marched from either side of its grand entrance—that itself would pass for a grand triumphal arch in any of the dozen large cities throughout the Galaxy. The three friends endured no less than four autonomous credential checks before the chauffeur glided them to a halt before the wide palace staircase flanked by its monumental pair of two-headed, crag-wolf statues.

Outside, in the glare of military spotlights, falling snow produced a sense of childlike enchantment, as if the winter-trimmed gardens had been turned into visions of make-believe. Through the windows of the limousine, Brim could see six ranks of Palace Grenadiers dressed in crimson parade uniforms, black boots, and tall woolen hats who flanked a wide runner of crimson carpeting. This led to a pair of high, ornately carved wooden doors that, according to Borodov, once adorned the very first Elizaveta Palace erected on this plot nearly fifteen hundred Standard Years in the past. Famed for their parade-ground precision, the Grenadiers stood at rigid attention, blast pikes at precisely the same angle, as if they, like the heroic crag wolves, were statues that might outlast even the famous doors. Brim smiled. He approved of formations like that, even though they harked back to military environments that were outmoded even before the first Bearish starships flew.

"Do we know how to overdo things, or what, Wilf

Ansor?" Ursis quipped as a giant Bearish page dressed in an ankle-length crimson coat with golden accents opened the limousine door and bowed deeply. "Grand Duke Borodov . . . General Ursis . . . Admiral Brim," he said slowly in Avalonian, clearly a singular honor for Brim, "Her Highness Katerin, the Knezina, commands me welcome you to Place Elizaveta." His gloves—now slightly soiled by touching the limousine's door openers—were otherwise so perfectly white that he must have changed them for each arrival.

Borodov, whose title of Grand Duke placed him in the highest social category, made the traditional answer for all three—again in Avalonian. "Please convey to Her Esteemed Highness the Knezina that we are honored by her invitation."

As least-ranking passenger, Brim exited the skimmer first, followed by Ursis and then Borodov. The moment they were clear, Borodov's chauffeur pulled silently away to make room for the next arrival—while the page bowed once more.

"You will please follow red carpet to reception area," the page said, again in Avalonian. This time his use of a foreign tongue was more practical than honorary. Brim would be required to lead the way into the castle, and although the words were meant for him, they were spoken to Borodov in deference for his seniority.

Inside the great doors—past a thin, vertical flow of warm, spice-scented air to seal out the winter cold—was the most ornate staircase—nay, *pair* of staircases—Brim had encountered anywhere in the Galaxy. Housed within a vaulted, five-stories-high anteroom, itself intricately tinted and decorated by hundreds of baroque mirrors and carved scrolls, this *most* grand double ascent occupied the entire far wall, its lavishly ballustraded, mirror-image flights leading to either side of a second-story balcony. Between the two magnificent staircases—and supporting the balcony itself—was an alcove in the shape of a great seashell that (according to Borodov) contained a heroic statue of twelfth-century Knez, Sergius the Nineteenth, astride Bazarov, the mythical ruler of all crag wolves.

Amid a hushed babble of excited voices, crimson-clad pages met each entering visitor on the gleaming expanse of marble that fronted this monumental staircase, trading numbered, solid-gold disks for wraps, then indicating one side or another of the staircase to keep a balanced flow arriving at the balcony and its four double doors that led to . . . whatever the next arriving station might turn out to be. Brim guessed it would be some sort of reception area, for through the hubbub of arriving guests he could hear a deep voice booming what sounded like Sodeskayan names from the doorway. Turning off the thermostat in his Fleet Cloak, he handed the heavy garment to a page, pocketed his token, then, when Ursis and Borodov were ready, started up the rightmost flight of stairs.

Each tread appeared to be carved from a single sheet of perfect Sodeskayan granite, as was the floor of the first landing, that was inlaid by a mosaic of the Great Sodeskayan Seal. The floor of the second landing held a mosaic representation of the Gromcow City Seal, and the balcony floor itself was decorated by what appeared to be a procession of ancient Bearish priests from the Kevian Dynasty, recognizable by their distinctive golden robes. To Brim, the effect was like treading on the contents of an art gallery, and it was almost a relief to turn and step through the four great double doors of the balcony, emerging between two graceful columns into the smoke-hazed, perfumed atmosphere of a ballroom that nearly defined description.

More than two hundred irals in length and almost half that in width, Elizaveta Palace's Smolny Ballroom richly deserved its fame, at least to Brim's way of thinking. Twenty massive alabaster columns lined both long blue-green walls, rising nearly fifty irals from the magnificent parqueted wood dance floor to a monumental fillet-and-fascia in pearl that circled the entire room and continued vertically another twenty-odd irals to meet the great arched ceiling. This, decorated around its rim by a most intricate system of mosaic patterns, contained trompe l'loeil renderings of woodland objects—leaves, cones, branches, and the like—endemic to those Sodeskayan planets warm enough to produce a "summer."

The curved extremities of the lozenge-shaped room were formed from eight tall arches enclosing lofty windows topped by rounded pediments whose thousands of crystal panes looked out on vast winter gardens with fantastic ice sculptures of allegorical scenes that could only come from the tremendous store of Sodeskayan folklore. Eight huge, four-tiered crystal chandeliers—these featured thousands of individual candles—hung in a row from the top of the arch, bathing the entire dance floor in warm light shimmering and sparkling from the dangling crystal reflectors behind them. The thousand-odd candles also further hazed the air and lent a subdued, yet somehow libidinous aura to the gay colors of the swirling dancers. Bears, humans, flighted A'zurnians, even a smattering of the quiet, semi-translucent Night Traders who had chosen only recently to do business with the galactic HyperLight civilization, circled the floor in time to the latest Avalonian "wave" music played by a large orchestra occupying a tiered stage at one end of the room.

Just inside the door, an elegantly uniformed Majordomo—clearly the one Brim had heard from the reception hall—bowed deeply and blew on a silver whistle announcing something in Sodeskayan that contained the words "Wilf Ansor Brim," "Nikolai Yanuarievich Ursis," and "Anastas Alexi Borodov." This produced a smattering of applause from those in the crowd near enough to hear him through the muffled din of pleasure: music, laughter, small talk in a dozen tongues. Then the three took their places at the end of a reception line. Craning his neck, Brim could see the ample figure of Katerin. In a snow-white gown sparkling with a thousand precious stones from all over the G.F.S.S., she was a most imposing Bearess, to say the least.

Ursis licked his lips facetiously. "Is only Katerin and damn fool reception line standing between us and oceans of superb Logish Meem," he said with a twinkle in his eye.

Brim grinned and nodded toward the gyrating dancers. "You mean you're not going to spend the evening dancing?" he asked jokingly.

"Aha!" Ursis exclaimed. "So that is what they're doing, eh?"

Brim placed a hand on Ursis's shoulder. "I'm not certain, old friend," he said nodding to the dance floor. "With some of the news steps from Avalon, I can't tell if they're good dancers or bad drunks out there."

Borodov laughed. "Looks like they're exercising everything except discretion."

"At these winter parties," Ursis pronounced, "discretion is often last thing on anyone's mind." He nodded his head. "Especially since this year most everyone has good chance of being war casualty before long. Does wonders for inhibitions. . . ."

A page dressed in a vermilion cutaway coat, gold vest, white knee breeches, and stockings introduced Brim to the first dignitary—a grizzled old Admiral of the Sodeskayan merchant fleet, who wrung Brim's hand until he almost gasped. His wife, a royal Bearess with bovine eyes, a gracious smile, and a decidedly gray muzzle, was as gentle as he was rough. Next came an Army General whom Brim had earlier met during the "maneuvers." Then three Dukes and Duchesses; then the Fluvannian, A'zurnian, Lixorian, and Effer'wyckean Ambassadors with their respective wives. By now they were closing in on the head of the line. The final Ambassador—closest of all to the Knezina, as befitted Sodeskaya's closest and most powerful ally—was the Avalonian Ambassador, S. Crellingham Browning, a most power-ful, politically important adjunct to Emperor Onrad's court. Tall and aristocratic with a thin mustache and proud eyes, the man looked down at Brim with a little smile. "Yes," he said with a slight curl of his lip, "I saw you at the Sodeskayan Army maneuvers, I think, Admiral. You're that Carescrian, aren't you?"

Brim bristled in spite of himself. Carescria was the poorest sector of the whole Empire, and he'd spent nearly his whole career fighting the prejudice it brought him. In recent years, however, the Emperor had come to rely more and more on the tremendous industrial might of the region—and the hard-working, tenacious people who, like Brim, were more and more manning the domain's bulwarks. "Right on both counts, Mr. Ambassador," he said, narrowing his eyes. "You indeed saw me on Vortuka—and yes, I am a Carescrian."

The Ambassador nodded contemplatively. "Quite proud to meet you, Admiral," he said at length. "I have followed that illustrious career of yours with some interest. Carescrians like you and your Admiral Calhoun do great service to the Empire and to your people."

Pleasantly surprised, Brim could only stammer, "Y-you honor me, Mr. Ambassador."

The man shook his head. "Truth is no special honor," he pronounced slowly, then turned to his right. "My dear," he said, "may I present Admiral Wilf Brim of our own Imperial Fleet—and quite a hero in the Battle of Avalon, if I'm accu-rately informed?"

His cheeks burning, Brim turned to confront a gorgeously dressed, statuesque woman—who presently had a *very* sur-prised look on her face. "Wilf Brim?" she gasped.

During that very instant, he recognized her, too. "Marsha Browning." He gulped, feeling his cheeks begin to burn. Why, oh, *why* had he allowed his little masquerade to con-tinue that day at the Embassy?

"I see you know each other," the Ambassador said.

"We . . . er, met at the Embassy some while ago," the woman answered, a deep blush indicating she was clearly at odds with herself.

"Good. Good," the Ambassador said perfunctorily, then turned to grip Ursis's hand as the line continued.

"Some Records Clerk *you* turn out to be, *Admiral*," she whispered, glancing in clear embarrassment at Brim's golden shoulder boards. Then her eyes flashed with anger. "You must have enjoyed your little joke a great deal."

"M-Marsha," Brim stammered, "please, let me explain."

A momentary smile passed the woman's lips and she nodded her head. "Yes," she said. "I think I do deserve an explanation. But later—when I've finished with this reception line."

"Perhaps I might, er, buy you that cup of cvc'eese?" he asked tentatively.

"You might make that a Logish Meem, since they're free," she pouted.

"*Two* Logish Meems," he said.

"I'll find you," she replied, then quickly turned to the regal-looking Bear next to her. "Baron Uilovski, may I present Admiral Wilf Brim of our Imperial Fleet . . . ?"

After Uilovski came the barons Tasnovish, Horogord, Kravinski, and Vorno, then Brim was shaking hands with Orlovsky himself.

"Ah, Admiral," the Count said in a high, affected voice, "a pleasure to meet you." His grip reminded Brim of a warm, but very dead sturgeon. He glanced toward Borodov. "Yass," he said, "you are Anastas Alexi's Imperial guest," he sniffed. "*Do* enjoy your stay here in Sodeskaya." Before Brim could utter a word, the Count was handing him off to the Knezina. "Your Highness," he oozed, "may I present Admiral Wilf Brim, one of Onrad's people?"

"Admiral," the Knezina said with a little smile, "how nice

you could attend." Up close, she assumed truly heroic proportions. Large as she was, she radiated a certain massive grace and dignity that was part and parcel of all Bears, yet somehow magnified. She fixed him with an abstract gaze. "Nikolai has mentioned you," she said soberly.

"I am honored, Your Majesty," Brim replied.

"Perhaps," she said, "it is we Sodeskayans who shall be honored before your visit is at an end." With a nod, she handed him off to another crimson-costumed Majordomo, who explained the location of refreshments, the bar, and other, more mundane accoutrements. Soon Ursis and Borodov joined him, and the three set off in search of meem.

Brim circulated through the glittering crowd with his two mentors, stopping here and there for introductions when Ursis or Borodov encountered individuals whom he should meet. Normally he liked meeting people; however, during the first metacycle and a half, he also endured two full sets of the more sedate dances, in spite of his most elaborate precautions (he often said he would rather singlehandedly face a dozen GH-262s). And difficult as he found dancing with human women, the same steps with Bears—some of whom stood nearly half again his size—were next to impossible. It was therefore a welcome break when his two friends became immersed in a long conversation with a Bearish historian, and he retired to one of the noisy refreshment alcoves to rest his feet. Pinching a just-vacated stool near the end of a long, crowded bar that bustled with revelers of all races and body types, he ordered a goblet of Logish Meem and relaxed, struggling to associate names with the seemingly million-odd faces he'd encountered since clearing the receiving line. Bears, humans, Lixorians. Maddeningly, the only face that managed to *stay* in his mind's eye was Marsha Browning's, and he wasn't certain he was looking forward to his next meeting with her at all. Staring at the inlaid surface of the bar, he felt a hand touch his arm.

"Are you going to buy me that drink?" asked the gentle voice of Marsha Browning.

He looked up and—at least she was smiling—nodded. "I've promised two," he said, slipping off the stool.

"Let's try *one* first," she replied, sliding gracefully onto the high seat. "I had two earlier, and you've already seen how easy it is to take advantage of me when I'm sober."

"Ouch," Brim said, motioning to the bartender. "I suppose I deserve that."

For the first time, Browning smiled. "Not so much as I have made you believe," she said with a little smile. "On reflection, I didn't give you much chance to contradict my error the other day."

"Not in the beginning, perhaps," Brim replied, enjoying—in spite of his best resolutions—the way the crowd was forcing him to stand so near this attractive woman. She was wearing the *most* seductive perfume. "But afterward, when I had plenty of time to say something, I didn't," he continued. "I guess by that time, I was enjoying your company so much that I didn't want the afternoon to end any sooner than necessary."

The bartender delivered Browning's drink, and she took a sip in silence, then set the goblet down and pursed her lips. "Funny," she said so quietly that Brim could hardly hear her in the noisy room, "I enjoyed myself that afternoon, too—so much that I stretched the work out a bit because I didn't want it to end, either."

Brim glanced at the woman's décolleté as she sipped her meem, and felt a certain thrill—albeit a guilty one. She *was* married, after all. "You didn't have to stretch the work much," he said in spite of himself. "We had so much to talk about that we didn't do all that much actual work anyway." He laughed. "A couple of malingerers, we were."

"I'd liked to have joined you for that cvc'eese you offered before we went home," she said, lowering her eyes, "but . . ." She gave a little shrug and drained her goblet.

Brim took a deep breath. His emotions were very quickly getting out of hand. He and this beautiful woman had *all* the right chemistry for each other. But as on the afternoon they met, he found himself quite reprehensibly unwilling to stop the flow of circumstances, and unless he missed his guess, she was feeling the same way. She looked up during the protracted silence and smiled. "I suppose I should let you get back to your politicking," she said.

"Can I order you a refill?" Brim heard himself ask. "I promised *two* meems, if I remember correctly."

She smiled and stared at her empty goblet. "I finished that quickly, didn't I?" she asked.

Brim looked at his own goblet, still half full—still his first. "Perhaps you were thirsty," he suggested.

"Perhaps," she replied. "And perhaps not. But I shall let you order a second goblet—if you promise not to take advantage of me."

She said the last with a careless little shrug and smile, but Brim was reasonably certain her words had carried a great deal more significance than their surface intent. "I guess it would be hard to take advantage of you in a crowd like this," he said, motioning to the bartender. "Besides, I'd certainly enjoy all of your company I can have." Then he frowned. "But won't the Ambassador, er . . ."

"He's too busy with his own politicking to be jealous," she said as the bartender placed the second goblet before her, "—if that's what you meant."

Brim made no reply, and for a moment, they said nothing. Then she looked up and smiled. "He's busy most of the time, and has been for years. I suppose if I ever *do* decide to be taken advantage of, it'll make things that much easier."

"I'm certain you've had, er, *numerous* opportunities," Brim said, more in truth than gallantry.

She looked him directly in the face. "I've had a few," she said, "mostly from visitors like yourself." She smiled wistfully. "On a planet where most females are Bears, I think I look a great deal more attractive than I actually am."

"Probably you ought to leave opinions like that to others who are more qualified," Brim said as the crowd pushed him against her. So close that he began to experience a certain compelling sensation in his loins and gently pushed himself away a step, just to be on the safe side.

"You didn't need to move back, Wilf," she said, taking another sip of meem. "I rather liked you touching me the way you were."

Brim could feel his breathing becoming labored. "I rather liked it myself," he replied, "but I'm afraid, well . . . Marsha, you're a damned exciting woman, and . . ."

"Thank you, Wilf," she said. "You're quite an exciting man." She looked seriously into his eyes. "Dammit," she said, shaking her head and grinning wryly. "Here I am comfortably drunk and snuggled against the first man in years with whom I'd cheat on my marriage, and—" She suddenly stopped, slipped from her chair, and looked him in the eye. "Before either of us regrets the remainder of this evening, I'd better trot off to the powder room and do something about what is soaking through my briefs. Then I'm going home—and the next time we meet, you will be 'Admiral' Brim again."

"M-Marsha," Brim stammered, "I'm terribly sorry if I have—"

"No, my dearest Wilf, you have done nothing," she said, touching his cheek. "It is I who am sorry because I have not been able to drive you from my mind since we met, and now . . . well, thanks for making me feel sexy for the first time in years."

Brim felt her hand press momentarily against his crotch.

"In the morning, I shall not forgive myself for doing that," she whispered, "but it's nice to know that I still have that effect on a man." Then she brushed his cheek with her lips and disappeared into the crowd.

Brim remembered only going through the motions of socializing for the remainder of the elaborate ball—that lasted until the planet's double star was well above the city skyline. Afterward, nearly a week passed before Marsha Browning's perfume completely departed his shirt—and until it did, Barbousse was forbidden to place it in the laundry.

Elsewhere in the Galaxy, the war continued unabated, with Avalon receiving almost daily raids in spite of the Leaguers' concentration on readying their Sodeskayan invasion. Forces from Grand Duke Rogan LaKarn's Torond, largest and most important ally of the League, pushed slowly through the Fluvannian star system, seeking to isolate Avalon from its last major supplier of Drive crystals. In the already occupied domains of Lamintir, Korbu, Gannat, A'zurn, and Effer'wyck, black-uniformed League Controllers held starving citizens in thrall, cruelly enforcing ironfisted surrender terms by any expedient means that came to mind.

Then, during the week following Orlovsky's ball, *nov* Vobok began testing the Sodeskayan frontiers. In small skirmishes involving no more than one or two planetary systems, his troops captured important population centers, held them until Sodeskayan reinforcements were dispatched, then fled, decimating whole populations, taking pelts, and leaving the cities for the most part in ruins.

"Will not be long now," Ursis growled to Brim and Borodov one snowy evening at the manor. "They make final rehearsals by raping poorly defended outer provinces." The three were seated before the huge fireplace, sipping meem and planning for their next in a series of meetings with the Knez's Minister of Production.

Suddenly Borodov's personal valet, Yakov Alksnis, appeared in the doorway. "A message for you, Admiral Brim," he announced.

"From whom, Yakov?" Brim asked.

"A Captain Potyr Simonovik," Alksnis replied. "He instructed me to remind you that you flew in his, er, ZBL-4 recently."

"Yes, of course," Brim said, looking around the room. "I'll take it in here."

"Very good, Admiral," Alksnis replied. Moments later, a small globular display on a nearby table materialized the head and shoulders of Potyr Simonovik.

"Good evening, Admiral," the starship commander said in Avalonian, then looked around the room. "Also good evening to you, Dr. Borodov and General Ursis." He nodded. "You will please pardon interruption, but is windfall-type opportunity for Admiral Brim to fly JM-2 Ro'stovik immediately."

"Immediately?" Borodov asked. "In middle of evening?"

"In middle of snowstorm?" Ursis added.

"According to Ro'stovik Helmsmen, is best time to test such starship," Simonovik replied soberly. "'Ice and snow please even the most venomous crag wolf pups,' as they say."

"I want to go!" Brim interjected. "Where is the ship, and how do I get there?"

Simonovik smiled. "Ro'stovik will come to you," he said. "Two friends passing through area in one will pick you up. Right away. Both speak Avalonian, more or less. You can be ready?"

"You bet I can be ready," Brim whooped. "But where? Tomoshenko Starport Budenny?"

"No. No," Simonovik said with a smile. "Just stay at Borodov Hall. Friends bring Ro'stovik there."

"They can't," Brim said with real concern. Everyone knew starships needed long stretches of water for liftoffs and land-falls—or lacking that, a Becton tube. The manor had only a pond. "They'll need to go to Budenny or Tomoshenko Memorial," he warned. "They'll kill themselves putting down here."

"Not in Ro'stoviks," Simonovik said with a little smile. "Just reasonably level field maybe quarter-c'lenyt long." He turned and spoke to someone out of range, then nodded. "Friends say manor house is already in sight—plenty room for landing in back. Other side of pond."

Suddenly the whole house shook as a great pealing roll of thunder cascaded down from above and gradually disappeared. Gravity generators made that kind of thrashing, pounding rumble. *Big* gravity generators.

"Ah," Simonovik said with a smile, "sound of gravs must be friends in Ro'stovik. Is saying good-bye for now." His eyebrows raised momentarily. "Oh, yes, Admiral," he added as if he had just remembered something. "I have not told friends of your exalted rank, so I leave it to you as to what you wear on battle suit. All right?"

Brim frowned. "All right," he said uncertainly.

"And, ah . . . Admiral Brim . . ."

This time Brim smiled. "Yes?" he asked.

"If you are as impressed with JM-2 as with ZBL-4 other day, then many of us count on you to lobby for its production, as well." He broke the connection before Brim could open his mouth to remonstrate.

Grabbing a Fleet Cloak that Barbousse was holding ready for him at the back door—how did the man *know*?—Brim rushed out into the driving blizzard, just in time to watch three beams of light materialize out of the snow-hazed sky perhaps a c'lenyt and a half distant. Scant moments later, the beams had turned into blinding starbursts and a great, mostly wedge-shaped object hurtled overhead with brilliant red and green clearance strobes marking its path. It was followed immediately by the paralyzing, tooth-rattling thunder Brim had heard inside—a couple of *big,* military-spec gravity generators pounding away up there, no doubt about it. And they were just *slightly* out of phase. Pulling the Fleet Cloak closer around his neck, he turned up the heat and watched the . . . whatever it was . . . circle around in a near-vertical bank at perilously low altitude. Roughly a c'lenyt downwind, its landing lights—once more almost lost in the swirling snow—rolled level and began to descend. Brim ground his teeth; he'd seen a number of crash-landings over the years— many from the helm. They weren't very pretty. Lower and lower came the lights, flooding the area in brilliance as the ship approached. Then it touched down in a cascade of snow and glittering proto-gravitons—but there was no sound of an impact, only the steady rumble of gravs, now retarded back to idle, as the angular form plunged ahead, then coasted to a stop on . . .

"Wheels!" Brim gasped. Big, fat wheels—one centered at the bow, one each on either side just abaft midships. *Those* were why it could land anywhere! The ancient devices would be at least twice as hard to control during both takeoffs and landings. But, by Voot, they *would* permit safe landfall on just about any reasonably level surface—at nearly any weight.

Someone in the flight bridge switched off the anti-collision strobes and began to taxi toward the manor, carefully skirting Borodov's pond. As the ship thundered toward them, Brim could see that it was modestly sized for a starship, at least compared to the Starfuries he flew—little more than a hundred fifty irals from bow to stern.

Then it turned directly toward the manor, its three landing lights carving painfully brilliant snow-streaked circles in the snowy darkness. Beyond these, the hull looked solid as a house-sized rock, and just as massive. Revving up the port grav in rumbling thunder, the Helmsman pivoted around the starboard wheel until the ship came to rest parallel to the manor house.

... And Brim's eyes had not deceived him during the recent off-planet maneuvers. JM-2 Ro'stoviks were indeed shaped like a simple wedge, with the sharp edge foreward and parallel to the ground. But there the simplicity ended. Both sides of the wedge took on a rounded quality about midships and ended in great flared graviton outlets at the stern. Clearly, gravity generators—and what promised to be prodigious energy chambers—were housed in these tremendous nacelles. A great cooling intake opened from the top side of the hull perhaps twenty irals back from the leading edge, marking the ship as one designed to spend a lot of its time in some kind of an atmosphere; space cooling radiators required completely different configurations. An angular series of Hyperscreen plates formed a flight bridge centered on the hull that rose from a position about a third of the way aft and faired back into the wedge some twenty-five irals from the stern, where it ended at a high, angular fin, more indication that this starship—if indeed it *was* a starship—spent minimum time among the stars.

Then the real reason for the great forward air scoop became apparent. Two preposterously large disruptors protruded from beneath the nose. Firing mechanisms for these monsters alone would require prodigious amounts of cooling—and when they were fired ... He grinned. Little doubt the Bears had brought off another of their engineering miracles. They'd produced what could really be called a flying crawler.

Four small turrets, two on top and two at the bottom near the stern, provided some protection from attackers aft, but the topmost were partially masked by the huge fin, and all four medium-displacement disruptors would accomplish little more than cause a Gantheisser Helmsman to be cautious executing a stern attack. However, Leaguers unfortunate enough to find themselves in *front* of this minuscule Sodeskayan brute would quickly find themselves rushing off to the far corners of the Universe in the form of subatomic particles.

As Brim peered up through the Hyperscreens into winking, colorful pinpoints of light from the flight bridge, a shadowy Helmsman, lighted from below by his readouts, reached above the raked-forward Hyperscreens and shut the gravs down in glittering clouds of proto-gravitons. Suddenly there was only the sound of howling wind and the pinging of cooling metal. Brim shook his head in utter awe as the wind carried the odor of hot logics equipment past his nose. JM-2s might be small as starships went, but up close on a stormy night, this one in particular looked bigger than a full-sized battleship—and just as deadly!

A few irals aft of the forward wheel, a hatch dropped open while a ladder slid to the ground. At the same time, Hyperscreen panels slid back on the flight bridge and a Bear dressed in a battlesuit leaned head and arm out and lifted his visor. "Hoy, gentlemens," he rumbled out in a gruff, deep voice, "we come take Mr. Breem ridink in Ro'stovik. Is allowed. Eh?"

"Is allowed . . . *yes!*" Brim answered excitedly. "Let me get into a battlesuit. Be right with you!"

"Got it in the study, Admiral," Barbousse said quietly. "I'll help you in."

"Thanks, Chief," Brim said, rushing back into the house. "How'd you *know* this was going to . . . ?"

"Keep m' ears open, Admiral," Barbousse replied.

"But *how?*" Brim asked, stepping into the boot shells and sealing the legs. "And," he said, glancing at his shoulders, "how'd you know to take off m' Admiral's stars?" The only insignia remaining on his battlesuit was his Helmsman's comet.

"Tell you when you get back, Admiral," Barbousse replied, holding the suit open at the shoulders while Brim slipped into the arms. "Besides, you wouldn't want to breach the 'Petty Officer's Network,' would you?"

Brim chuckled as he sealed the suit and slipped his belt and holster in place around his waist. "Not so long as it works as well as it does," he said.

"Have a good flight, Admiral," Barbousse said, handing Brim his helmet. "From what I can fathom, this one'll be new even to you."

Brim frowned for a moment while he jammed his service blaster into the holster and secured the flap. "What do you mean by that, Chief?" he asked, placing the helmet over his head and activating the seal with a quiet hiss.

"I don't rightly know, Admiral," Brim said. "Those are the words I got, so to speak, and there wasn't much of a chance to ask questions."

"Fair enough," Brim said. "And thanks, Chief. I appreciate the extra spadework." He headed for the door.

"I know, Admiral," Barbousse called after him with a grin. "That's why I do it."

Making for the ship at a run, Brim signed a brief "thumbs-up" to his friends, then dodged beneath the hull to where the ladder waited and climbed through a long, vertical tube to the flight deck. He waved to Urisis and Borodov below on the snow, then turned to his hosts. One was seated at the left helm, the other in a jump seat centered behind the two control stations.

"Dasha Poupychev," the Helmsman said, extending a hirsute hand. He pointed to the Bear behind him. "Co-Helmsman Mischka Bzhtva," he said.

By the dim light of the readouts, Brim saw the two Bears smile through huge mustaches of drooping black whiskers—

two of the redoubtable "Wild Ones" Sodeskayans often talked about, but people rarely saw.

"Is callink us Dashaa and Mischka," Poupychev said with a crushing handshake. "Otherwise, is spendink all night teachink pronunciations when what is wanted is flyink. All right, Mr. Breem?"

Brim returned the Bear's smile and shook hands—painfully—with Bzhtva. "All right," he said. "I'm Wilf."

"Good," Poupychev pronounced. "Sit in right seat, Weelf. Right in crag wolf's mouth." He flicked a set of switches, then nodded toward the starboard nacelle. "Is let me know when looks like energized, eh?"

Brim glanced out the side Hyperscreen and grimaced. The whole starboard side of the ship was suddenly alive with wicked-looking bolts of energy flickering over its surface.

"Energized," Bzhtva replied from the back.

Starting the big gravs was not a gentle process at all. A green light began to strobe inboard of the raised encabulator housing, then blurred. In the next moment, the whole starship shuddered while roiling, glowing clouds of proto-gravitons wreathed the half circle of open cooling hatches, then blew sternward in the wind. The grav clattered furiously, the graviton vent coughed, and Brim's heart leaped into his throat. Barbousse was right. He had *never* experienced anything like this before, even as a youth flying treacherous Carescrian ore barges.

"No radiation fires, either," Bzhtva added, his voice sounding as if he were somehow surprised.

Poupychev raised his eyebrows and nodded to Brim. "Always good sign!" he pronounced proudly.

Brim swallowed hard, then nodded encouragingly.

Moments later, the port grav was also running. In combination with the other shuddering, snorting grav, it was enough to jar one's spine out of kilter. Soon, however, they settled into a smooth, straightforward rumble, and without warning Poupychev switched to internal gravity. "Is bucked in, Weelf?" he asked.

Desperately swallowing his gorge, Brim suddenly recognized the seven-belt restraint system he'd seen aboard the crawler and hurriedly buckled himself to the seat, pulling the belts until they began to hurt. "I am now," he choked.

"Not bad for furless human," Poupychev commented. "You have done this before?"

"In a crawler," Brim replied, winning control over his stomach again.

The Bear grinned—several of his teeth were missing, but both fangs were inlaid with some sort of gems. "This not crawler," he said proudly. "This *killer* of crawlers." Then, without further comment, he released the brakes and taxied out toward the clearing on which he had landed, birches on either side of their track thrashing wildly in the storm of vented gravitons.

They pivoted into the wind and paused, tail out over an ancient stone fence that separated the manor from the tilled fields beyond. Poupychev tested the gravs one at a time, hands flying from one bank of controls to the other. "Ready?" he yelled.

Instinctively, Brim glanced for a moment at the readouts—a very basic panel, set up as if the readouts were placed at random. But something seemed wrong. On the power console, two graviton boost indicators looked big as a goblet of meem. Both read zero. "Hold it a moment," he said. "Are those boost gauges working?'

Poupychev glanced momentarily at the console. "All things workink," he said. "Boost don't show with wicks turned down like this."

Brim nodded meekly.

"Is doing takeoff myself," Poupychev said, settling himself in the seat. "Field lyttle short. . . ."

The Bear poured on the gravs and in spite of local gravity,

Brim could feel the seat back crowding his back. Scant moments later, the massive wedge of rushing sound and tonnage was airborne, rattling kitchens in the manor house below and anything else in their path all the way to Gromcow. As the wheels came up into their chambers with a succession of mysterious thuds and thumps, Poupychev raised both hands from the controls and turned to Brim. "Now!" he yelled over the hundering gravs.

Abruptly, Brim was flying a genuine JM-2 Ro'stovik, the craziest, noisiest, xaxtdamnedest starship he had ever encountered—anywhere. From the moment he got control, he knew Barbousse's warning was right on target. This was no Starfury, nor anything else he had ever flown. The controls had the firmness—not necessarily heaviness—he expected in a disruptor bus of its kind. But for all that, the massive little starship went where it was told, when it was told—and that quickly instilled its own kind of confidence. Moreover, the fierce storm through which they were climbing seemed to have no affect at all on their flight path.

"Is want try trouch-and-go?" Poupychev asked. "Bzhtva has clearance for special strip at Budenny."

Brim looked over his shoulder to see the smaller Bear talking rapidly into his helmet microphone and nodding encouragement. "You on proper downwind vector, Weelf," he said. "Just hold course, keep one-fifteen on clock—break out of soup just like that."

"I'm game," Brim said, drawing back the thrust dampers until airspeed read a perfect 115.

"Hold that speed," Poupychev said, his hands flying over the center console. "Lift modifiers comink down now . . . gear comink down. . . ." He peered into a display. "Nose wheel down . . . !"

"Is got a wheel port side—starboard side, too," Bzhtva announced from the rear as they broke out of the overcast into driving snow again. The lights of Gromcow glowed out the right window.

Brim spotted the landing vector almost immediately. He nudged the steering engine and the little ship turned sweetly onto final. A tall complex of buildings, each ringed in a thousand lights, slid by in the forward Hyperscreens. He looked down at the flight deck, where snow from his boots had hardly melted. No amenities on ships like this—if your battlesuit didn't have independent heat, you froze to death.

"Full lift enhancers comink in now. Hold one hundred."

No worse than a Starfury . . . lining it up. . . . He walked the big rudder—it was *alive*! Droop the starboard grav for a little crosswind . . . she just stayed where he put her. The team that drew this one up designed for stability *first*! "Flies great!" he whooped through a great smile.

"What you expect?"

Brim flared just a tad high, but the Ro'stovik forgave him, settling in easier on its wheels than a little NJH-26 on a Becton tube. Then Poupychev pushed in the thrust dampers and they went rumbling down the cleared strip and up into the storm again for a few more touch-and-go's.

While Poupychev adjusted the grav controls from their takeoff settings, Brim relaxed slightly and they climbed out into clear air at about thirty-one thousand irals, continuing out to the edge of space, where Brim glanced at Poupychev and raised an eyebrow.

The Bear grinned. "Whole ship is yours," he said. "Probably shouldn't fire disruptors so near Gromcow, but anything else you want is fine."

Brim leveled out and retarded the thrust dampers in a steep climb. He got a slight buffet, then the ship rolled left sharply and began to fall until he released the controls, at which point the nose came down quickly and recovery was almost instantaneous.

"She'll spin?" he asked.

Poupychev nodded. "But in atmosphere, wind pressure over level hull makes things difficult."

"What's 'difficult?'"

"Impossible to recover," Poupychev said matter-of-factly. "Everybody dead."

Brim nodded, deciding to avoid that. Instead, he banked into a tight turn and pulled to the limit. Then he barrel-rolled and looped. The little ship executed neither maneuver very elegantly, but it came through both with a stoic willingness that earned Brim's respect, if not his admiration. As it dived, wheeled, and soared under his hand, he got the feeling that somehow he was not making the heavy little ship do what its designers really meant for it. No nimble space fighter, this. Instead, he was at the controls of a flying crawler—and putting it through paces for which it had never been designed. The miracle was that it would do them at all. He glanced over at Poupychev and grinned. "All right, Dasha," he said, getting up and stepping aft, "I've had my go. You and Mischka show me what she'll really do."

As Brim and Bzhtva crowded by one another in the narrow flight bridge, Poupychev winked. "Not bad!" he said, "—for a human."

Brim sat in the jump seat glowing with pride.

Bzhtva took the helm, one hand easy on the controls. It was morning below; the tops of the clouds had taken on the glow of dawn. He laughed, shoved in the dampers, and dove vertically into the storm again, pulling out only a few irals above the treetops and streaking off across the dim, snowy fields.

"Hoy. That troika, down there?" Poupychev demanded, pointing out the side window.

"Is so," Bzhtva replied with a huge grin.

Brim peered out the side window. There in the distance ahead was a troika speeding through the snowy morning pulled by three loping droshkats. The *yamshchik* was standing high on the front of the sleigh while in the rear, two Bears were . . . "What in xaxt are they doing down there?" he asked.

Bzhtva roared. "Is called 'fucking' in Avalonian," he bellowed. "'All cubs and crag-wolf pups must come from somewhere,' as they say."

"Is why we call troikas 'love sleighs,'" Poupychev added. "Old Sodeskayan tradition calls for making love at highest speed droshkats can run." He laughed with glee. "Faster they go, stronger is love, or so story goes."

"Great fun!" Bzhtva put in, banking the Ro'stovik around in a tight turn. "You must try sometime—with human girl, of course. Much excitement!"

Brim grinned. "Sounds *WON*-der-ful," he mumbled to himself. Then he looked out the window again. "Hey!" he yelled over the thundering gravs. "What are you going to do?"

No one in the troika saw it or heard it coming. Flying just ahead of its sound waves, the Ro'stovik thundered over the lovemaking Bears no more than twenty irals off the ground. Then up into a tight turn and down, banking almost vertically over the snow-covered field. Brim looked out the Hyperscreens to see the two Bears in back jumping up and down and waving their fists while the driver struggled to regain control over the droshkats, that were clearly on their way to setting a new land speed record—in a direction of their own choosing.

Up front, Poupychev and Bzhtva were doubled over laughing. They waved out the window as they thundered over the troika again at some 250 c'lenyts per. The two Wild Ones were just hitting their stride now. They dropped Brim off at the manor house, then taxied out into the snow before he could even shout his thanks. Shivers of emotion raced along his spine as the big gravs built up their thunder. The Ro'stovik swung its tail out over the fence again, paused for a moment, then sprinted forward and rumbled aloft, drawing up its three wheels and returning to its wicked, deadly silhouette as it disappeared into the clouds.

As Barbousse and Borodov's servants ran sleepily from the manor house to meet him, Brim shook his head. He smiled. Today, he'd met some of the *real* Sodeskayans—the ones who were going to make Leaguers sorry they'd ever heard the word *Bear*.

CHAPTER 4
Hammer Strike

Two Standard Days later, in the early metacycles of 14 Tetrad, 52013 (Avalon Standard Time), Nergol Triannic's long-anticipated invasion—commanded by Marshal Rodef *nov* Vobok himself—exploded across a wide section of the G.F.S.S. frontier, capturing a number of border planets with little or no opposition. Within the metacycle, a huge armada of Sodeskayan transports hauling thousands of crawlers and superbly armed combat troops headed toward the battle zone, marking the developing battle as potentially one of the largest in galactic history. Early reports reaching Brim estimated that upward of 7,500 starships of all types had been mustered for the counterattack alone (centered on two tiny, fourth-class star systems named Bialystok and Lvov). There League forces of more than 1,800 starships, 570,000 combat troops, and 12,000 crawlers, plus another 1,500 support starships and transports, were engaged in a colossal offensive meant to drive a great, three-dimensional wedge through the Sodeskayan heartland. In terms of numerical strength alone, the League space fighters appeared to be fighting at a serious disadvantage.

The Sodeskayan numbers, however, were deceptive. By nearly any reasonable measurement of fighting strength, the Leaguers held a clear advantage in space, which in the recently revised rules of warfare promised to become even more of a key factor. And indeed, this appeared to be the actual case. At nightfall of the corresponding day in Gromcow, nearly thirty-five Sodeskayan planets had been occupied by the Leaguers and another fifty were under active siege.

Here and there, the Bears put up terrific defenses, but only on planetary surfaces, and when the Leaguers called in powerful ground-support ships like their famous GA 87-B Zachtwager "precision shooters" and GA 88-As, the Sodeskayan defenses were all too quickly annihilated. Moreover—as Brim had predicted—when the superannuated J-16s and J-153s of the Sodeskayan Fleet arrived to defend these pockets of resistance, they were quickly dispatched by swift, powerful GH 262-E killer ships that completely outclassed them. Even where the Sodeskayan Fleet might possibly have caused a difference by force of numbers alone, the Bearish chain of command got in the way. Most Sodeskayan starship elements were attached to—and took orders directly from—ground-based army commanders. The general aim of this paradigm had been to enhance cooperation between the two forces, but against the Leaguers' lightning-fast "thunderclap" stratagem, it resulted in nothing but a muddle. By nightfall of the second day in Gromcow, the Leaguers had turned their invasion into a Sodeskayan rout.

During the next Standard Month, Brim kept track of the Leaguers' progress as best he could from information supplied by Ursis and Borodov. However, even his advanced security clearances were not enough to get him firsthand information from the actual star systems under attack, so he relied on Barbousse's grapevine for much of the corroborating detail he included in his weekly reports. And in spite of a generally hopeful view of the future, these messages to Avalon were, in the main, descriptions of present disaster.

In the face of heroic, often virtually suicidal defenses by Sodeskayan ground and space forces, the pitiless Leaguers swallowed up star system after star system as they advanced inexorably through the great interstellar domain toward the capital planet of Sodeskaya itself. After their recent drubbing in the Battle of Avalon, these were glory days for the League's Deep Space Fleet. Hoth Orgoth's powerful squadrons of killer ships quickly built an overwhelming kill ratio of nearly eleven to one over their antique Sodeskayan opponents. Only four Standard Weeks after the original invasion, Eleventh Army forces (the Knez's Guards) on the crucial Ksnelomes star cluster surrendered, and the way to the star Ostra—as well as the city of Gromcow itself—lay open.

At least three times during that catastrophic period, Ursis and Borodov secured clearance for Brim to take observation excursions over some of the contested planets, but by the time preparations could be completed, Leaguers had overrun the target areas and the trips were canceled.

One evening—long after Ostra's twin stars had set behind Gromcow's turreted skyline—Brim arrived at the Embassy to file another grim report. Dog-tired after a day of rushing helter-skelter to Fleet planning sessions all over the capital, he collected his latest album of HoloGrams from Avalon (somehow, Hope had grown even cuter!), palmed a security scanner in the lobby, and started up the grand staircase.

On the second floor, he headed for the *third* gallery to his left, not the second that had mistakenly resulted in his meeting with Marsha Browning. And although he had not spoken to her in the weeks since Orlovsky's ball, she was *still* very much on his mind, especially during his trips to the Embassy. Try as he might to deny his feelings toward this mar-

ried woman, somehow he always hoped they would accidentally meet again.

Before he reached the second gallery, he sensed the sound
of woman's heels approaching along a marble floor, and
somehow *knew* who it would be. He stopped and waited until
she turned the corner and stopped in her tracks.

"Er . . . Admiral," she exclaimed, her cheeks reddening.
She was dressed in her usual severe business suit, but it did a
very poor job or concealing the seductive form beneath.

"Madame Browning," he returned with the same formality. "I am most pleased to meet you again."

She took a deep breath. "I suppose I should be pleased to
meet you also, Admiral," she said touching her hair nervously, "—had I not made such an utter fool of myself at
Count Orlovsky's ball."

"I'm sorry you're not pleased to see me," Brim replied,
"but I was totally unaware of your doing such a thing." He
feigned a frown. "Must have been *after* we talked."

A smile broke through the woman's obvious embarrassment. "You know very well what I mean, Admiral," she
murmured, "but it's terribly nice of you to try and spare me."

"I swear I have no idea what you are talking about," Brim
remonstrated. "But aren't we both a bit formal this afternoon,
madame?"

"A defense mechanism on my part," she explained.

"You don't need one," Brim assured her. "And it would be
awfully nice to hear my name pronounced 'Wilf' now and
then instead of 'Weelf.' "

"Well . . ."

"Come on, Marsha," he implored with farcically raised
eyebrows, "let's try to be friends, at least. Someday you may
need more help cataloging things—and now you know
where to find me."

"Wilf," she relented, "you are impossible."

"No," he corrected, "'Brim,' not 'Impossible.'" Then he

grinned. "I'll even extend my offer of a mug of cvc'eese tonight if you can wait till I transmit my weekly report."

She closed her eyes for a moment and shook her head. "I promised myself I wouldn't *do* this."

"You didn't promise *me*," he said.

For a long moment, she looked into his eyes. "As friends?" she asked.

"As friends," Brim assured her, with every good intention, even though down deep he *knew* he didn't mean it.

"I'll meet you, then," she said. "Half a metacycle—in the luncheonette. On level fourteen. It's still open."

"I won't be long," he replied with a strange, guilty sense of excitement. Then he strode off to the code room.

Ultimately, however, Ursis appeared in the luncheonette only cycles after Brim and Browning sat down to the mugs of cvc'eese.

"Wilf," the Bear said, bowing apologetically to Browning, "we are cleared for trip to front."

"What?" Brim demanded.

"*Front,* Wilf Ansor," Ursis said urgently. "We are cleared to leave."

"When?" Brim demanded.

"Now," Ursis replied. "Immediately. Two places reserved for us on transport—leaves in . . ." he consulted his time-piece, "little less than metacycle. Chief Barbousse packed your grip—is in staff skimmer outside."

"How'd you know I was here?" Brim asked.

Ursis smiled. "Except for lobby, is only place I am allowed in Embassy; everything else is off limits. So I came here."

Brim smiled wryly and glanced at Browning. "Wars are inconvenient at best," he grumbled. "Perhaps we might do this again?"

Browning grinned. "Next time, Admiral," she said as Ursis headed for the exit, "I shall even buy the cvc'eese."

"You've got a deal," Brim said, looking into her large brown eyes. "I'll be back for it." Then, in spite of himself, he touched her arm.

Browning glanced down to place her hand over his. She pressed his fingers for a moment, then looked up. "I'm counting on that, Wilf," she whispered.

He basked in the soft warmth of her hand before he nodded and pursed his lips. "So am I," he said. Then, grabbing his Fleet Cloak, he hurried after Ursis.

Less than a metacycle later—and only cycles from liftoff time—Brim and Ursis stood outside the forward brow of a huge Sodeskayan transport. Thunder from its idling gravs combined with repulsion generators in the gravity pool to form a nearly deafening rumble. Smells of ozone and hot metal filled the chill air with their own peculiar redolence. This was no normal departure for the huge ship. Palpable tension hung over the whole spaceport like a heavy cloak. On the way in, many of the roads had been clogged with wounded Bears back from the fighting. Sodeskayan foot soldiers were probably the greatest surface warriors in the known Universe and were clearly putting up a terrific fight. But in spite of their best efforts, they were steadily losing ground to the Leaguers and their overwhelming superiority in space.

Looking aft, he watched the last streams of crawlers moving rapidly through transparent brows leading into the starship's holds. Access roads to a another transport on a neighboring gravity pool were already filling with long columns of quick-stepping troops in dark-green battlesuits and full field packs—armed with the powerful Khalodni N-37 blast pikes that had been the hallmark of Sodeskayan surface forces for generations. How many of these brave

Bears would come back wounded like the poor wretches he had seen earlier? Or *never* return. He shook his head. The ground-loving Knez and his self-serving advisors would have a lot to answer at the end of *this* war—no matter who got final claim to the victory.

The pair showed their passes to a burly guard inside the boarding lobby who directed them ("Is hurrying, please!") to a special transport tube on the far wall. This sped them directly to the bridge, where they emerged among a small city of winking, flickering consoles at the rear of the navigator's station. There they were met by a tall, spare Sodeskayan dressed in the civilian uniform of *AkroKahn,* the official flag carrier of the G.F.S.S., who bowed deeply and smiled. "General Ursis, Admiral Brim," he said formally. "Is my pleasure to welcome you aboard bridge of S.S. *Maxim Chkalov.* I am known as Yakov Grigorovich—Executive Officer."

Ursis nodded in acknowledgement. "We thank you for your hospitality, Grigorovich," he said, "and my compliments to your Captain."

Grigorovich nodded to two huge helm consoles facing the massive Hyperscreens that occupied nearly the whole front end of the bridge. From the stripes on their battlesuit cuffs, both occupants were *senior* Helmsmen of the line. "Captain Pavel Rychagov—who is presently busy in left seat with last-moment checklist—has bid me direct you to observer seats," he said.

Observer seats! Brim felt his eyebrows rise. Even in a ship this size, observer seats on the bridge would seldom number more than ten, and with transport to the front drastically reduced, at least two high-ranking passengers would now be forced to ride somewhere in back. Old Borodov wielded tremendous political power to set up something like this.

Ursis clearly recognized the favor, too, for he bowed slightly. "Captain Rychagov honors us," he said. "You will please lead?"

Returning the bow, Grigorovich led them through what seemed like a quarter c'lenyt of consoles to a small area behind the helms where three rows of four comfortable-looking recliners occupied a small but valuable patch of flight-deck real estate.

In peacetime, Brim knew that seats like that would cost a planet's ransom in credits. In wartime, their price would be power. All were occupied by high-ranking Army officers save the starboard two in the first row—to which the Second Officer now led them.

"Please to activate seat restraints now," Grigorovich asked, indicating the two empty seats. "We lift ship immediately."

Just then, Brim saw the Captain touch his helm and begin to speak, his voice amplified by the ship's blower system. The words were Sodeskayan, but Brim needed no translation for the spaceman's traditional warning prior to liftoff. He braced himself . . . and shuddered as the gravity changed to local and his stomach tried to tie itself into a knot. He held his breath until the unpleasant sensation passed, then relaxed and activated the seat restraints. Presently the Captain made more announcements, then moved his hands over the helm. Soon the rumbling from below became distant thunder while the deck trembled beneath his boots.

"One assumes you need no translations, Wilf Ansor," Ursis intoned.

Brim chuckled. "Why, this my first trip aloft, General Ursis. Is dangerous?"

"Depends on Leaguers," Ursis replied in a mock tutorial manner. Then his face took on a serious look. "*Will* be dangerous, though," he added. "In fact, were it not so important you get firsthand look at fighting, I should be forbidden to risk taking you there."

"I've survived a few battles"—Brim chuckled grimly—"against some pretty grim odds."

Ursis nodded. "True," he remarked. "I have shared number of them with you—much to detriment of zukeed Leaguers. But *this* time, odds . . ." he shrugged, "maybe little worse." He frowned bleakly. "No choice, I suppose. Is all part of evil we call war."

In spite of himself, Brim felt a sense of foreboding. Never—in all the years he'd known the Bears—had Ursis seemed this apprehensive. The war must be going very poorly for Sodeskaya indeed, he mused—*much* worse than he had suspected.

While Brim pondered, the gravs once more increased in volume and the horizon slid wildly to port as *Maxim Chkalov* moved slowly from its gravity pad and swung starboard toward one of the gigantic Becton tubes he had spotted as they entered the base. Within cycles, the great starship was ponderously airborne, battling its way through stormy turbulence toward intergalactic space and the front.

Early that evening (Gromcow time), they rendezvoused with their convoy, taking position as the second ship in a column of six. Two other six-ship columns raced along in formation with them, one about a half c'lenyt directly to port, the other halfway between and perhaps a quarter-c'lenyt higher. At predetermined intervals, the whole formation abruptly jogged course in an attempt to throw off Hyper-Torps that might be fired from cloaked benders—starships capable of "bending" all forms of radiation around their hulls. But the price of invisibility ran high for these raiders. The energy required to hide their presence also severely limited their top speed, at least below the cruise rate of this particular high-velocity convoy.

In numbers, at least, the transports were heavily escorted, with squadrons of Karpov J-16s and J-153s—even a few of the newer Gurevich GIM-3s that flew constantly evolving patterns around them. But their beautifully executed maneuvering gave scant confidence to Brim. He knew only too well that stunting and formation flying made good practice for Helmsmen but provided little advantage in a dogfight against opponents flying superior hardware. Sometimes even raw courage and talent simply weren't enough.

Just after Morning Watch—as they were entering a more populated region of the giant domain—the first Leaguer scouting ships began to appear, showing up indistinctly on the escort's longest-range BKAEW indicators. At first they kept their distance, but as the ship's day—tagged to Avalonian Standard—wore on, more and more of them approached, attacking quickly, then retreating, as if they were *testing* the convoy's defenses. Finally, two metacycles into the Evening Watch, they all withdrew, almost as if they had been ordered to do so. After this, space became ominously quiet—and empty. . . .

The HyperTorps tore squarely into *Maxim Chkalov*'s massive hull as she was jogging to a new course at nearly full thrust; she was instantly doomed, as much by her own colossal power and velocity as by the enemy's fire. There were three slamming explosions on the port side about ninety irals from her bows, followed by the noise of ripping, tearing hullmetal—then the fateful sound of explosive decompression. An eruption of heat and shock from the stricken forward power chambers buckled the deck of the bridge, smashing out the Hyperscreens in clouds of splintered crystal and killing many of the command crew instantly. The huge starship lurched and rolled, then swerved wildly from her course—bringing even more damage to her shattered spaceframe and collapsing the giant guard rings that protected her Drive crystals. In moments, these disintegrated with catastrophic results, releasing tremendous free energy and turning the great starship into an inferno of expanding collapsiums—deadly radiation fires.

In scant moments the great spaceliner found herself without power to her interstellar Drive, ablaze in seven critical locations, and rapidly slowing through Sheldon's Great Velocity Constant to a drift rate just below the speed of light.

At the instant of disaster, Brim and Ursis were on their way to the ship's canteen, walking alongside a huge transformer in a small compartment aft of the bridge. The transformer's great mass saved them from the fate shared by many on the other side of the bulkhead.

The tremendous shocks coming through deck hit Brim like body blows, in spite of his Imperial battlesuit. At first he found it hard to believe they had been hit, but violent pulsing of the starship's local gravity and dimming lights could have only one meaning—aside from the grating tearing sounds the spaceframe was making.

There had been other noise, too—as horrible and paralyzing as any he could recall in a lifetime of warfare. It came from his helmet intercom: agonized, primordial howling that pierced to the most primitive layers of his brain and nearly drove him mad. It was the sound of those caught by the explosions which must have ripped open battlesuits and shattered bones by the hundreds. It was screaming by those burning to death in holocausts of uncontrolled radiation fire. It was desperate shouts for help. It was hammering on bulkheads. There was no help for any of them. The whole Universe seemed to have gone mad as he snapped the intercom to LOCAL and turned to Ursis, who also appeared to be unharmed, if somewhat dazed. "Visor *down*, Nik!" he yelled, and dashed for the bridge, slamming his own helmet shut and activating the seal.

He knew things were bad when he got there. The hatch was jammed shut, probably by atmospheric pressure from their own side of the sagging bulkhead.

"Not good, Wilf Ansor," the Bear said grimly. "No air on

other side." He shook his head soberly. " 'Death comes quietly across the ice,' as they say."

Brim ground his teeth; that explained the jammed hatch. "You're right," he whispered.

Standing on tiptoe, Ursis reached above the hatch to smash a glass plate and press a red button. Momentary hisses of escaping atmosphere died to silence; then the hatch swung slowly back to reveal a scene to rival the most daunting of the Galaxy's views of a hellish afterlife. The buckling deck had uprooted a number of control consoles, tossing them—and their unfortunate occupants—like so many toys throughout the huge, half-conoid chamber. Overhead, a great canopy of crystal Hyperscreens that once provided the illusion of normal vision above LightSpeed was now effectively gone. Only an arched framework remained, its empty segments filled by crimson stars and outlined with jagged crystal shards, now transparent, while the powerless starship inexorably slowed through LightSpeed into Hypospace. And brilliant little tongues of radiation fires glinted everywhere as the very hullmetal—a collapsium alloy—began to uncollapse.

Two bridge ratings who had survived the initial explosions were already using portable N-ray projectors to smother the dazzling tongues of released energy, but Brim knew it would take more than portables to fight this many fires. One glance at a systems console told him that there could be no N-ray pressure in the primary fire-fighting mains.

From a ripped battlesuit, the desiccated, lifeless body of Captain Rychagov gave "official," if silent, notification to Brim that command of the ship had transferred elsewhere. Unfortunately, nobody present was doing anything at all. Gathering his wits about him, he took charge. Turning to Ursis, he pointed to a dazed COMM rating. "Nik," he ordered, "tell that rating to call our escorts on the KA'PPA for help. Plain language. Send . . ." He glanced at a navigation console; interstellar charts looked the same in any language. Making a furious calculation in his head, he said, "Send, 'Torpedoed near coordinates,' er . . . 'TG dash twenty-eight minus . . . nineteen-nineteen.' Got that?"

Ursis nodded and began to speak rapidly in Sodeskayan.

Next, Brim grabbed Grigorovich, who also looked dazed but miraculously whole. "Have the crews preflight all the flyable launches on the hangar deck and update their nav systems with a position fix—but wait for my word before opening the outer doors."

"Aye, Admiral," Grigorovich replied, as if Brim had been inducted suddenly as an *AkroKahn* Captain—which, in a way, he had.

"Rating is only radio operator, Wilf Ansor," Ursis reported momentarily. "Says KA'PPA operator is dead."

"Tell him to try the KA'PPA set anyway," Brim retorted. "The thraggling things aren't that much different."

"He says he will try," Ursis reported momentarily.

"Sit with him, Nik. And tell him to call for a couple of heavy tugs, too," he added. "Just in case we can salvage this wreck."

"He will send, Wilf Ansor," the Bear promised.

Something large exploded below and the deck bounced violently. Outside, streams of gravitons from safety valves alongside the twisted KA'PPA mast momentarily blurred Brim's view aft.

"Surviving ship's launches are activated, but need position fix from maintenance console here on bridge for deep-space duty," Grigorovich reported in a voice tight with stress.

"Are there enough left to take off the whole crew?"

The Bear nodded. "Enough for survivors, anyway."

"Very well," Brim said. "Set up that console, then meet me over there," he ordered, pointing across the bridge. With that, he climbed over a smashed command station—beside which sprawled the twisted form of still another officer—and fought his way to the main systems console. There, one of the Engineers had miraculously survived; the others lolled brokenly against their seat restraints. He nodded toward the Bearess when Grigorovich arrived. "Ask her what shape we're in," he ordered.

Grigorovich asked a number of what sounded like rapid-fire questions, then frowned. "Says she cannot tell for certain, Captain," he stated grimly. "Evidently, most reporting stations are silent."

"What of the hull?" Brim demanded. "Sounded to me as if we took a lot of structural damage when we were hit."

Grigorovich again questioned the Bearess, then reported with a frown. "She thinks ship has broken keel," he said, "but that's not most important problem. Look . . ." He indicated a pattern of data flashing spasmodically near the center of her display. "Temperatures below decks have already surpassed melting point of plasma chambers that feed Drive."

"Sweet mother of Voot," Brim swore. *That* was serious. If the Bearess was correct—and he had no reason to doubt her word—*Maxim Chkalov* might soon blow itself to subatomic particles, along with anybody who remained aboard. "Ask her how long we've got."

"She says *maybe* one metacycle," Grigorovich reported presently.

Brim glanced at the Bearess, who held up a single finger.

Abruptly her eyes widened in horror as if she were staring at death itself.

"What's wrong?" Brim blurted out in Avalonian.

A moment later, he got his answer in spite of their language difference. The woman noisily vomited a glot of blood against her face mask, twitched spasmodically, then slumped lifeless against the display.

Grigorovich bowed his head. "Nothing more we can do here," he said grimly.

Brim took a deep breath and looked around the ruined

bridge. "No doubt about *that*," he growled, then shrugged. "Come on," he said, and picked his way through the blazing debris to Ursis and the COMM rating. "You two get through to anybody, Nik?" he asked.

Ursis grimaced. "Great communications," he said.

"Good!" Brim said. "They're sending help, then?"

"Did not say great *help*," Ursis growled. "Only great communications."

"I don't understand," Brim said with a feeling of dread.

"Got through to everybody," Ursis explained angrily. "Nobody is coming. All escorts are needed to protect convoy, Voot take it." Beside him, the COMM rating had a look of panic in his tear-flooded eyes.

"Nik, tell that Bear to get a grip on himself!" Brim growled. "Then have him set up to pipe a voice message to all stations. We've got to abandon ship—as soon as possible."

Ursis nodded and spoke to the frightened rating while Brim turned to Grigorovich. "You know the drill for abandoning ship?" he asked as calmly as possible.

Grigorovich nodded.

Brim raised an eyebrow at Ursis.

"Is set up," the Bear said, sliding from his seat.

"All right, Grigorovich," Brim ordered, pointing at the COMM station. "Get in there and go to it."

"I-immediately, Admiral," Grigorovich replied, seating himself beside the rating.

Brim nodded and turned to Ursis. "Nik," he said, "might as well tell that youngster to head for the hangar deck and board a launch. Won't hurt him to give him a bit of start."

Before Ursis could utter a word, however, the young Bear looked Brim in the face and directed a torrent of Sodeskayan at him with a horrified look.

"What was that all about, Nik?" Brim demanded.

"He wants to know if you think ship will blow up," Ursis replied.

"Tell him not with me on board." Brim chuckled grimly— hoping that his words were not *all* bravado.

Ursis spoke rapidly, indicating the aft bridge hatch with a wave of his hand.

Immediately, the young bear scurried aft and was gone.

Although his own insides were now churning with something that felt a lot like panic, Brim forced himself to stand calmly by the console while three times Grigorovich broadcast the *AkroKahn* version of "Abandon Ship" and the survivors of the bridge crew hurried aft toward the hangar deck. At last, the Second officer stood. "Is done," he said.

"We'd better go, then," Brim said, and the three started aft through the blazing wreckage, pausing again for a moment at the remains of Captain Rychagov.

"Hate to leave him here like this," Grigorovich whispered, his voice barely audible over the droning intercom. "We put a few c'lenyts in our wake over the years."

Brim nodded sympathetically. "However," he added, glancing around the blazing ruins, "I don't think the Captain would much mind, considering the circumstances."

Grigorovich stepped over the Admiral's body. "I guess that's the truth." He chuckled, hurrying aft as fast as the littered deck would permit. "Probably he'd be the first one to order us out, were he alive."

As they came to the aft companionway, Grigorovich stopped and grimaced. "Wait!" he swore under his breath. "No one has downloaded the nav fix into the launches," he growled.

"What do you mean?" Brim demanded. "I thought I sent you to set up the maintenance console."

"I did," Grigorovich said defensively.

"Then why aren't the launches updated?"

"Process needs nav console input also. I set up link for this, but . . ."

"But *what*?"

"I don't know how to operate nav console," he said.

"*WON*-der-ful," Brim growled. "Just thraggling won-der-ful. Without that data in the launches, we've got three choices: Find a habitable planet by accident, starve to death when our rations run out, or call for help and hope the League doesn't get to us first—which they will, because they've captured most of the territory around here." He shook his head. "Now what do we do?"

"Can you run nav console?" Grigorovich asked.

Brim frowned. "Yeah," he said presently, "I probably can, if they work anything like the ones on our ships."

"They should," Ursis said. "We import them from Avalon—much easier than developing same thing here."

"Which console did you link to?" Brim asked.

Grigorovich pointed into the blazing ruins. "There," he said, "second nav console from front. Explosion put most others out of business."

"What do I have to do?"

"Indicate area of star map for launches to remember," Grigorovich replied.

"That's all?"

"Once data is selected, download starts by itself. Is how I set things up."

Brim nodded. "All right," he said, "you two get started for the hangar deck. I'll follow as soon as I . . . figure what I have to do."

"We shall wait for you," Ursis protested.

"Don't," Brim said. "Get down there and make sure everybody is aboard some sort of launch. Then order them all a safe distance away in case this thing blows before I can find us a destination. No sense in all of going up in smoke. Right?"

"I cannot leave you to die," Ursis said.

"I'm not going to die," Brim protested. "Unless you stay here arguing with me until something bad happens." He put his hands on his hips and frowned at his old friend. "Nik," he said, "you're the highest ranking on this ship. Someone's got to direct the evacuation."

Ursis frowned. "But what about you?" he asked.

"If there's an empty launch left, I'll fly it out myself," Brim replied. "If not, then I'll signal you to bring the one you're in around to pick me up. All right?"

"Is not all right, but you point out my duty," the Bear admitted. "Just remember, Wilf Ansor," he said, "if you are killed doing this, I shall be angry with you for the rest of your life." With that, he turned and followed Grigorovich aft along the corridor.

Brim took one last look around what remained of the bridge. Clearly, the three of them had been the last living souls in this part of the ship. Moving to the wrecked navigation section, he found the workstation that Grigorovich indicated and dragged the corpse of its normal occupant to the buckled deck. Then he slid into its place before the console and breathed a sigh of relief—nothing here out of the ordinary at all.

As he scanned the familiar readouts, the deck beneath his boots began to shudder with the first tremors of what he instinctively knew must result in final collapse of the colossal power chambers lining the keel. He'd have to leave the bridge within mere *cycles*. Heat from the spreading radiation fires was already overwhelming the cooling unit of his battlesuit.

Calling a three-dimensional HoloMap of the galactic sector to a large central display, he bent to his work. Though he was no expert at transgalactic navigation (at least not since graduating from the Helmsman's Academy), years at a starship's helm had nevertheless kept him familiar with rudiments of the science—enough to get him where he was going, should he have to plot a course himself. Carefully, he engaged a SPHERE tool and scribed a lustrous globe around the tiny, flashing red icon that represented the ship's current location. With half an eye on his timepiece, he carefully enlarged the globe to a radius of some half a light-year, then commanded SELECT and waited. Moments later, the transfer began: first to the maintenance console and then—presumably—to the hangar deck and the waiting launches.

After this, he switched the cooling system of his Imperial battlesuit to EMERGENCY MAXIMUM and hurried aft through the flames. At the corridor, he dogged the hatch closed behind him only moments before a tremendous explosion came from the sealed-off bridge. Grinding his teeth, he ran aft as fast as he could over the dangerously buckled deck, but as he reached the gravity stairs, a tremendous flash came from behind him and a blast of raw energy nearly knocked him to the deck.

He spun around just as the bulkhead split asunder and a wall of radiation fire burst into the corridor from the bridge, flooding toward him like a blazing cataract. Fighting down impending panic, he desperately leaped onto the stairs, gliding rapidly to the next level down while the dazzling holocaust gained on him, its vanguard licking greedily at his boots as he ran. Ahead was one of the ship's security doors, placed at main bulkheads throughout the hull in anticipation of just this kind of crisis. From Universe knew where, he found a last reserve of energy and somehow increased his lead, reaching the massive hatch moments in front of the flames.

It was enough.

Smashing at the EMERGENCY CLOSE plate as he dove through the opening, he only just got himself to the other side before three massive blades dropped in place to bar the advance of the flames. As he gasped for breath, his mind's eye saw eight similar sets of blades that had fallen at the same instant on other levels of the doomed starship. He was now forever sealed off from the forward end of the ship. . . .

The machine room into which Brim had escaped was a dark shambles. Rows of huge generators lay toppled across what once were gleaming maintenance aisles. The big machines were sparking fitfully while their last charges of energy dissipated. Beside them, massive transformers glowed with the heat of their own destruction. Overhead, a tangle of shattered wave guides traded bolts of energy that flashed in the vast chamber like some wild electrical storm. And everywhere he looked, red, fitfully glimmering indicators screamed to dead operators that the distribution network had been brought to a total standstill—a scene from some Engineer's vision of hell. But at last there was no radiation fire here—for a while.

Fighting back his rising terror, he blundered through the dark wreckage, cursing wildly, tripping on downed cables, and struggling to maintain a course toward the aft end of the room, where he could pick up an emergency companionway running directly to the hangar deck. Somehow he made it, but one glance at his timepiece told him he was fast running out of time.

Desperately bounding down what seemed to be endless expanses of gravity stairs, he reached the hangar deck with only a single detour—around an unexploded enemy torpedo that had plowed through at least a hundred and fifty irals of starship to lodge itself astride a complex junction of wave guides. He knew its malevolent-looking warhead would be giving off enough radiation to crumble even an Imperial battlesuit, so he dodged off onto another gloomy deck, fortuitously stumbling on a nearby passage through the next two levels. The bypass cost him precious clicks of time, but miraculously he burst into the immense hangar deck while he and *Maxim Chkalov* were still miraculously in one piece.

Before him on the flight deck, only a single launch remained. Ursis waited at the hatch with his great old side-action blaster in his hand. The bodies of four clearly dead Bears lay crumpled at the boarding stairs.

"Nik," he shouted, running hard across the empty deck, "what happened?" As he spoke, the first characteristic rhythms of beta-temblors started to rattle the deck from below.

"Telling you all about it soon as you get us out of here," the Bear answered, climbing into the hatch of the little ship.

Brim followed him into the little ship's cockpit a click later, practically diving into the left-hand helm. While he buckled himself in at the helm with one hand, he moved GROUND POWER to the number one gravity generator and advanced its thrust damper to MINIMUM. A distinct thump came from aft as the unit coupled to the power mains. "Now, what the xaxt happened out there?" he demanded, nodding toward the empty hangar deck.

"You mean about bodies out there?"

"Yeah."

"Four ratings. Came from somewhere in Drive chamber after everyone else took off. Only one launch left, and they didn't want to wait for you. So . . ." He shrugged.

"Thanks, friend," Brim said, watching A/G BOOST rise swiftly until the indicator reached sustaining pressure at 3100. "What about the others?" he asked. "Why didn't they wait?"

"Big explosion forward," Ursis replied. "Everyone panicked and took off. . . . Damned civilians. No discipline when comes to emergency."

As Ursis spoke, The 1-RUN glowed flashing yellow, then changed to flashing green that steadied as the deck throbbed smoothly beneath his boots—in marked contrast to the awful jolting temblors from below—now already in distinctive gamma rhythms. "Looking good from here, Nik," he said reassuringly.

"Best news I have had maybe in whole life," the Bear growled. "Now, when we get xaxt out of here?"

"Right now," Brim said. He moved the GROUND POWER selector to NULL, then, switching the mains to ALL INTERNAL, watched a small utility analog speed across the deck and disappear beneath the launch. Cabin lights flickered momentarily as the exchange was made. Then, moments afterward, a fleeting sensation of dizziness indicated that the little ship was now on local gravity as well.

The analog reappeared a moment later with the disconnected power cable raised in the air. Brim waved it away. Cycles later—their extraordinary luck was still holding—he had all four gravs running, and the doomed starship was *still* in one piece. Overhead, the starry blackness of space beckoned like life itself from the flight deck's massive open doors.

A final check of the propulsion panel indicated the all systems were ready to fly. He shoved the thrust dampers to their forward stops—9100 on all four readouts. Retarding them back to 4500, he drew back on the flight controls and raised the nose toward the open doors and freedom. "Hang on, Nik," he said through clenched teeth. Moments later, heart in his mouth, he released both sets of gravity brakes and the launch surged upward, passing into free space precisely thirty clicks before *Maxim Chkalov* and all her cargo disappeared behind them in a roiling, blinding cataclysm of radiation fire and white-hot debris.

Instantly, a powerful energy wave overtook them, tossing the launch like a pebble in a millrace of molten lava—but their thirty-click head start was enough cushion in time and distance to save the launch, and within cycles, he had regained control. Fifteen c'lenyts distant, the convulsively glimmering puffball that marked the remains of a mighty starliner was already fading among the stars. Within the metacycle, it would be gone, as if it never existed.

Brim set the launch's KA'PPA burst transmitter on automatic—its randomly timed, nearly instantaneous broadcasts in code were designed to look like static blips on Leaguer KA'PPA receivers, but would act as position fixes for Sodeskayan rescue forces. Then he relaxed for the first time since the HyperTorps hit. So much, he considered bleakly, for his first visit to the front. . . .

As soon as the nav systems stabilized following the explosion, Brim and Ursis hurried aft to the launch's tiny nav console. Brim bit his lip as he slipped into the seat. Had *Maxim Chkalov*'s data system downloaded all the location information to the launch? There hadn't been time to check the results. And for that matter, was the launch's far-less-capable data system equipped with enough on-line storage capacity to cache all of it in the first place? Without that information, he and his friend were in deep, *deep* trouble, facing a decision to starve (or suffocate) or call for help in the clear rather than use the KA'PPA burst transmitters that stood a better chance of summoning Sodeskayan rescue ships instead of Leaguers. He activated the display, and slowly a large HoloGraphic globe materialized over the console. "Looks good so far, Nik," he said.

Ursis grinned. "Data would look better than empty display, furless friend," he said.

"You'll get no argument from me about that," Brim mumbled, while—heart in his mouth—he called up the available databases. Presently, an old-fashioned menu of symbolic characters appeared in the center of the globe; it offered eight choices:

CONTROL SYSTEM
ENVIRONMENTAL SYSTEM

MAINTENANCE
NAVIGATION SYSTEM
POWER SYSTEM
PROPULSION SYSTEM
WEAPONS SYSTEMS

• STAR MAP (D'LOAD)

"So far, so good," Brim mumbled, more to himself than to his old friend. Hardly daring to breathe, he grasped the control and selected STAR MAP (D'LOAD)—if nothing else, its inclusion as an extra list element proved that the data transfer had at least begun aboard *Maxim Chkalov*. Next, he commanded MANIFEST, then watched the global display fill with the same image he called up on the bridge before the big transport destroyed herself. The download *had* reached completion. "I did it!" he exclaimed with glee. "It's all here, Nik!" He gulped a draught of air, choking and laughing almost hysterically at the realization that he'd forgotten to breathe for a long time.

"Congratulations, Wilf Ansor," the Bear said slowly. "Now, my friend," he continued, "do we have anywhere to go? Just in case nobody hears KA'PPA burst transmissions right away. . . ."

"Good question," Brim replied looking up at his old friend with a frown. "We'll know *that* in a moment." Manipulating the controls with more care than they deserved, he homed in on the nearest stars, then commanded the system to search for those with human-habitable planets. Most of the pinpoints immediately dimmed—no habitable planets associated with those. Three, however, increased in brightness and began to pulse, the nearest orbiting a star no more than a Standard Week's travel from where they were.

"Looks like we've got at least one we can get to before the

air runs out," he said. "Let's see what it has to offer to a couple of castaways." When he touched the image with his logic pointer, an information box appeared in its place—in Sodeskayan. "You'll have to read this, Nik," he said, getting to his feet.

Ursis slid into the seat and peered at the globe. "Well," he began, "probably star won't burn out while we're there."

"Thraggling WON-der-ful." Brim chuckled. "Any more important information there?"

Ursis shook his head. "Worst part of this job," he said with sham melancholy, "—nobody takes me seriously."

Brim laughed. "I do, Nik," he said reassuringly. "It's just that I'm simply looking for more, shall we say, practical information at this time."

"Like what?" Ursis demanded.

"Well," Brim said, "for starters, what's its name?"

"Mmm," the Bear muttered. "Looks like star is called Kobrin. Very weak. Planet is . . . Zholvka." He looked up and grinned. "Speaking of practical information . . ."

"All right. All right." Brim conceded. "Who controls it right now?"

Ursis peered into the globe. "Looks like Leaguers, devil take it," he replied. "Captured two weeks ago."

"How about major population centers?"

"One supposes they have captured whole thing—population centers, farms, too," Ursis said absently.

"No, no." Brim chuckled. "I mean—does it have any?"

"Ah!" Ursis exclaimed, then consulted the globe again. "Two," he reported presently. "Both small. Not much down there. Bit of farming in short summer season. Lots of mining. No manufacturing to speak of." He raised his eyebrows. "Is famous as vacation planet for winter sports, especially hunting. Full of all manner of resorts. Sounds promising."

"That's promising?"

"Very," Ursis said. "Easy to get control of city populations—all crowded in together. Wide-open farms, park lands, and hunting lodges another story. Harder to find us there. And besides, not much vacationing these days, eh?"

Brim nodded. "Good thought," he said. "I'll try to bring us down in the open country, then."

"One possible flaw, Wilf Ansor," Ursis said.

"What's that?"

"Not much to eat in open country if rescuers take long time coming. Two week's rations aboard launch won't stretch much further than three—if we are lucky. Bitter cold means burning food energy fast. 'Breakfast of ice does little to calm wolf pups,' as they say."

"Well, we'll find a lodge or a farmhouse."

"You haven't spent much time on planets like that, have you?"

"You mean in the Sodeskayan hinterlands?"

"The same."

"No," Brim admitted. "I haven't."

"Wilf Ansor, my furless friend," Ursis said, suddenly becoming *very* solemn, "unless someone rescues us while we are still in space, we will need lot of luck to merely survive."

At the end of the eighth Standard Day—with no contact from Sodeskayan rescue forces at all—the atmosphere inside the little spacecraft had become positively foul, as had the two old friends themselves (including their tempers). Finally, after what seemed like a million Standard Years, the little planet had grown large in the windscreens, and soon it would be time for landfall.

Toward the end of the Afternoon Watch, Brim braked below orbital speed and began settling into the atmosphere— looking like a small meteor, he hoped, to any watching Leaguers. Actually, both he and Ursis had agreed that the ploy was probably a good one. On the surface the invaders would have had their hands full subduing the locals and probably were watching for anything but counterattacks from a mere launch.

Soon they were measuring altitude in irals instead of c'lenyts—or fractional light-years. They'd chosen the boreal hemisphere mainly because far fewer sources of radiation manifested themselves there—indicating fewer Leaguers, they hoped. Additionally, calculations showed their arrival in that hemisphere would be cloaked by the stormiest part of the year. And at least in this, they were clearly not to be disappointed.

Brim had just descended through a solid bank of clouds nearly as large as the continent it covered, and only a few hundred irals below he could pick out at least four more layers of dirty, gray-looking clouds—detritus of a frontal system moving slowly down from the icy polar regions of the planet.

It seemed strange not contacting some sort of planetary center for landing instructions—but the Leaguers now owned the lot of those, such as they would be on a planet this size.

He listened to the steady beat of the ship's four T56-A-7A spingravs thundering away in their dual housings on either side of the hull. No trouble there. He glanced beside him at Ursis. The Bear was straining his eyesight at the surface. "Anxious to get down, Nik?" he quipped.

Ursis smiled. "Anxious for fresh air," he said. He chuckled. "I believe I have learned new principle during this trip," he said.

"What's that?" Brim asked.

"Nobody suffocates when ship runs out of air. Probably death occurs much earlier from foul odors when filtration system uses up charge."

Brim chuckled. "I'm gonna save our lives, then," he said, setting the lift augmenters at four and feeding in ten degrees more power to take up the load. A series of slight bumps shook the deck as they descended through the first cloud layer; then things smoothed out again and he returned his attention to the controls. The atmospheric radiators were already in operation according to four graviton temperature gauges . . . and moments later his AutoHelm disconnected as the launch began to buck and twist through the increasing turbulence. Another layer of clouds was beginning to close in when he noted some lightning out to port and veered slightly to starboard, still losing altitude at about a thousand irals per cycle.

Increasing the lift augmenters to fourteen, he checked the nav switches and set the airspeed EPR bugs to just under one fifty—then altered course again while a powerful downdraft caught the ship from starboard and threw her on her side. "*WON*-der-ful," he grumped to himself. "Just thraggling *won*-der-ful. I've gone and picked the—" he grunted for a moment while he forced the ship upright, "worst weather in the thraggling Galaxy!"

"Hope you do not think you are making joke," Ursis said. "Probably *is* worst weather in Galaxy, xaxtdamned near."

The clouds broke for a moment to starboard, and he spied some sort of structure ringed by a stone wall. Otherwise, everything was snow—as far as the eye could see in the late-afternoon twilight. "Thraggling tropical paradise," he grumped.

"Only 'thraggling,'" Ursis corrected.

Overspeed warning horns sounded momentarily as the launch was once more swallowed up in dirty gray turbulent cloud. They squawked again moments later in another violent downdraft. Brim stoically kept to his course, losing altitude gradually. They'd come a long way in the little, LightSpeed-limited spaceship—no sense in wrecking her before he had to.

Abruptly they broke out from the last cloud layer. One moment they were wholly consumed by it, the next they were clear. Still indistinct in the failing light, he picked out lights from what could very well be a spacious lodge. Were there Leaguers in the area, they would be be there.

Then he was busy preparing for landfall. Sudden gusts of wind rolled them to port and he corrected, reminding himself to keep a light touch on the controls. Presently he was below a row of high hills that marched in parallel to what appeared to be a tremendous snow-covered forest, and the turbulence abated considerably. Only a hundred irals altitude now; the gravs were rumbling and bubbling just above idle; out to starboard, a frozen lake slid by in the snow-streaked side windows. There. He picked out a smooth run of level-looking snow. He'd do the least damage bringing her in on that. He walked the steering engine, lining her up for flare-out, then rolled slightly to starboard against a sudden crosswind. He checked his instruments a last time: descent, speed, pitch. All perfect. At about twenty irals, he pulled back all the way on the gravs and eased off the steering engines, slightly bow up to compensate for drift. He blipped the landing lights—all clear. Bow up a little more. . . . Just as the spaceship's hull began to rumble against the snow, he leveled the deck. Instantly, blinding cascades of powder shot into the air on either side of the hull, then subsided as the launch spun into a ground loop and bumped to a stop at the foot of a little hill on the edge of the forest.

Almost desperately, Brim unsealed the side window and slid it back—fresh cold air surged immediately into the flight deck. Leaning his left elbow on the sill, he thrust his head outside and breathed deeply, savoring once more that unmistakable smell of natural atmosphere. He took another deep breath . . . and another. It was a *fine* gray evening! He closed his eyes for a moment, listening to the spingravs pinging as they cooled, then relaxed at last in his recliner—he'd made it.

They were safely down—if not altogether safe.

CHAPTER 5

Crag Wolves and Benders

After a few moments, the two old comrades looked at one another in the dark cockpit. "Not bad," Ursis remarked with mock formality. "Probably I shall permit myself to fly with you again sometime."

"I am honored," Brim replied, with the same formality. It was already getting quite cold in the flight deck—and beginning to snow—so he slid his window shut and turned up the heat in his battlesuit. "Now, my furry friend," he asked, "as a taxpaying citizen of this domain, what do you suggest we do next?"

Ursis thought about that for a moment. "Well," he said, looking out the window at the falling snow. "Judging from the way it looks outside, weather will cover tracks we made when we landed. Unfortunately," he added a moment later, "will probably not cover launch, which is large enough to be seen if the Leaguers noticed our arrival."

Brim nodded. "Suppose we could drag enough underbrush out of the woods to make it look like something else?"

"Like what?" Ursis asked.

Brim shrugged. "A bush . . . a thicket, maybe. Something that doesn't look so . . . artificial."

"Hmm," Ursis muttered. "Not a bad idea. Shouldn't take much to cover six-place launch." He nodded. "Better we do it now," he added. "Will want as much snow on our camouflage as possible."

Out in what quickly became a howling blizzard, the two needed almost half the long night—that was constantly filled with howls of the two-headed killer beasts Sodeskayans called "crag wolves"—to complete their work. But by the beginnings of dawn, the wealth of branches and natural debris they had dragged from the forest and placed against the hull had considerably altered its appearance, at least to Brim's eye.

Unfortunately, the time spent out in the storm also had the effect of pointing out a glaring deficiency in Brim's standard-model Imperial battlesuit. Although it was supposed to be adequate in nearly all portions of the Galaxy officially designated habitable, its heating plant was clearly not up to the job of keeping humans alive on at least *this* planet of the Sodeskayan hinterland. At first Brim had tried to ignore his ever-increasing sense of chill; then, when he could no longer deny the discomfort he was feeling, he did his utmost to keep the problem from Ursis—at least until he could contribute his share of the camouflaging effort. And the strenuous work did help to keep him warm. But that same work also burned energy at a furious rate, and little more than a few day's rations remained—for both of them. Brim's make-believe pose came a cropper less than a metacycle after dawn when, in spite of the launch's cabin heater, he dissolved in a paroxysm of shivering that had him nearly unconscious on the cabin floor. When he finally had himself under some control, Ursis looked at him and rolled his eyes.

"Wilf Ansor," he said shaking his head, "you are an idiot."

Brim nodded agreement. "And probably not very smart,

either," he added. "But we did a pretty good job of covering this launch, if I do say so myself."

"You are also impossible," Ursis growled.

"Yeah," Brim answered, thinking of Marsha Brown's very words, "I've been told that before. Sorry, my friend."

The Bear sat slowly in one of the passenger seats and frowned. "I appreciate bravery—and help with camouflage—Wilf Ansor," he said. "But next time, skip heroics," he said. "Before this is over, we will need each other if we are to escape with our lives—and me with my fur."

"Sorry," Brim said lamely.

"No longer matters," the Bear said, placing a six-fingered hand on Brim's shoulder. "The object now is getting us off this planet—in something *other* than a Leaguer prison ship."

Brim nodded. "Yeah," he agreed. "They're not too polite with prisoners. I know from experience."

"Could kick myself about your battlesuit," Ursis said. "Plenty of cub-sized Sodeskayan suits that would have served you well for this trip." He grimaced. "Unfortunately, is impossible to turn back time below LightSpeed, so there is now a new first order of business."

"What's that?" Brim asked.

"Well," the Bear said, "according to systems panel up front, will be a close race between running out of food or launch running out of energy to heat cabin." He snorted. "Amounts to starving or—in your case—freezing to death. So getting you someplace warm, my unfortunately furless friend, is first order of business. Otherwise, I must carry you home in block of ice."

Brim laughed in spite of himself. "Wouldn't want you to do that," he said. "So what do you have in mind? I remember seeing some structures that looked like farmhouses as we came in—and there's that place back a couple of c'lenyts that looks like a big lodge."

Ursis nodded. "Those are what I have in mind," he said.

"Storm seems to have abated somewhat, so is time to search for shelter. 'Dark of moons is no time for cubs to slip on ice,' as they say."

"As they say," Brim agreed, reaching for his helmet. "All right. Let's be at it."

"Not *we*," Ursis said. "*I* shall search for shelter."

"But Nik!" Brim protested. "You can't go out there all alone. What about those wolves we heard last night?"

Ursis smiled as he reached for his helmet. "Should I find myself hungry enough, it is I who shall chase crag wolves," he said. "And you might hold me back. Do you understand? Inside this cabin, Wilf Ansor, your battlesuit will keep you warm. And besides—the KA'PPA burst transmitter is here in launch. Should rescue arrive while I am gone, you will tell them to search for me before they leave. Right?"

Brim settled back in his seat. "Yeah, you're right, Nik," he agreed grimly. "But for Voot's sake, take care of yourself."

"For *Ursis*'s sake, I shall take care of myself," the Bear chuckled. Then, planting his helmet on his head, he strode forward and opened the hatch. A blast of frigid air thundered into the cabin as he hopped through and slammed the panel shut again.

Involuntarily, Brim shuddered. During his many visits to Sodeskaya, he had never before encountered *real* Sodeskayan cold—and had clearly been unprepared for what he found. He wondered if perhaps the Leaguers were in for the same sort of surprise. He smiled for a moment. Perhaps the Sodeskayans' horrible weather might just be their saving grace. Time would tell . . .

The first Leaguer surveillance appeared some three meta-cycles following Ursis's departure when a scouting drone glided silently overhead. Brim would have missed it except for a momentary break in the clouds that projected its shadow directly over the launch. Probing in a negligent manner, it made one desultory pass around two large thickets some half-c'lenyt distant, flushed a small flock of odd-colored birds, then passed on rapidly to spinward. Evidently, Brim thought with relief—and a little pride as well—he and his Bearish friend had done a reasonably good job of camouflaging in the middle of the night. Of course, the fact that Lady Fortune had stopped the launch's landing slide at the edge of a forest *also* had something to do with his concealment. That and the obvious fact that the Leaguers hadn't been all that diligent about their search in the first place.

Still, he thought with a jab of apprehension, even disinterested searchers would make Ursis's job of finding shelter a thousand times more difficult and time-consuming—as well as dangerous. For a moment he idly wondered what the Leaguers were searching for, but lost the thought in the midst of other, more relevant concerns. He had been monitoring the radio channels—not the Sodeskayan ones he couldn't understand, but the Leaguers'. At least the ones that didn't broadcast in code. His Vertrucht was rusty after years of disuse, but he could understand enough to learn that someone of great importance was using the big lodge as a conference center during the lull in the fighting.

As Brim predicted, Ursis returned well after darkness had fallen amid the eerie howling of crag wolves. And even before he doffed his helmet, Brim knew things had not gone well at all.

"Rotten news out there, Wilf Ansor," the Bear said at length. "Lots open countryside, few places to go, and a worse-than-xaxtdamned surveillance drone buzzing overhead all day." He growled under his breath. "Kept me running for this or that cover almost all time. In Army battlesuit, I am walking target, Voot take it. And I accomplish practically nothing—except to locate that big lodge you spotted." He shook his head angrily. "Is full of Leaguers—officers, mostly. Bastards must be using it as a rest area or something. Going to be difficult getting food out of that place."

"Yeah," Brim agreed. "I've been listening to the radio all day. Somebody's holding a conference there, and whoever it is must be high-up brass. Code name for the big cheese is 'Stalker.' "

"Bad thraggling luck," Ursis growled. "But tomorrow is another day. Who knows? Maybe they pack up and go home, eh?"

"Maybe." Brim chuckled darkly, then smiled. "Thanks," he said, patting his old friend on the back. If you had to be in deep trouble, then Nik Ursis was the one to have with you.

The two shared a meager meal from the launch's fast-diminishing emergency rations; then Ursis headed quickly for a recliner. "Long day, Wilf Ansor," he said, easing himself down. "Sorry there is nothing more to say, but I am tired. And tomorrow I must be out again, for death is the penalty for both failure and not trying."

Brim placed his hand on the Bear's shoulder for a moment. "Please never think that I don't appreciate what you are doing," he said, "and the sacrifices you make. You are a good friend, Nik Ursis."

The Bear smiled tiredly. "When we get home, you owe me *beeg* goblet Logish Meem. Maybe even whole bottle. All right?"

"Nik," Brim said slowly, "you can count on it." But he wasn't sure his old friend heard a word of his answer. He'd passed into sleep almost instantly.

During the next day, Ursis achieved no more than he had on his first outing, and their remaining provisions dropped to near zero. Surveillance drones had been overhead at random intervals both days. Clearly, the Leaguers were looking for something, but were in no particular hurry to find whatever—or *whoever*—it was. And—in spite of Ursis's most optimistic hopes—the Leaguers' "conference" continued at the lodge, with most radio channels full of references to the mysterious Stalker.

Things were definitely *not* going the way they hoped . . .

On their third morning—*still* with no results from their KA'PPA-burst distress signals—Ursis was grimly preparing to make his foray into still another driving snowstorm when he glanced through the tiny window space they kept clear and stiffened. "Wilf," he whispered, "we *may* be able to receive some largesse from Lady Fortune. Whatever you do, don't come outside till I call you." With that, he bounded to the hatch and was gone in a flurry of blowing snow, shouting in Sodeskayan.

Brim ran to the window in time to see a ramshackle sledge pulled by a lone, shaggy droshkat, draw to a halt no more than two hundred irals away. Its sole occupant, a Bear dressed in several layers of woolly clothes that clearly had no internal heater, took one look at Ursis, then reached behind him and hefted what appeared to be an ancient slide-bolt blast pike. Aiming this at Ursis, he appeared to yell something in Sodeskayan; however, between the launch's insulation and the heavy snowstorm, Brim could hear little.

Ursis shouted an answer but made no attempt to stop, walking slowly through the blizzard toward the sledge—and the mammoth blast pike. Old as it was, the great, awkward weapon could clearly put a large hole in the launch, much less a Bear.

Brim held his breath. Once again, his old friend was risking life and limb on his account. In spite of clear danger, Ursis continued to walk slowly, deliberately, toward the leveled barrel of the blast pike, his footprints disappearing in the driving snow as soon as he made them. Finally, when no more than ten irals separated the two Bears, Ursis stopped and extended his hands, palm up, in the universal offer of friendship. As Brim watched, half in fear, half in fascination, the two Bears began to talk earnestly, gesturing with their hands. Then, abruptly as it had begun, the conversation stopped. For long moments, both stood still as granite statues. Only the old droshkat moved, casually turning to lick a spot on its flank that evidently required a quick cleanup. For long moments, the tension became almost palpable. Finally, after what seemed like a hundred thousand years, the native lowered his blast pike and jumped to the ground. In the next moment, Ursis stepped forward and the two embraced in a great Bear hug that looked to Brim as if it could crush hull-metal. Following that, a grinning Ursis scanned the skies, then turned and waved to him while the native rummaged in the bed of his sledge. Within cycles, both were laden with what appeared to be great, woolen garments, and running toward the launch.

"Wilf Ansor," Ursis boomed as he came through the foreward hatch in another blast of frigid air and flying snow, "is meeting new friend, Vikhino Perovo Yuzhnaya." He was followed by the native, whose face was now all smiles. Standing nearly an iral taller than Ursis, the huge Sodeskayan had small brown eyes that wore the hard, capable look of self-reliance, a short muzzle tipped by a great wet nose, and fangs that had never seen a gem and probably never would. He was dressed in what appeared to be a great, woolly overcoat, soft black boots that drooped just below the knees of his baggy trousers, mittens, and a floppy woolen cap that ended in a gray, furry tassel that matched the gray fur collar on his overcoat. From Sodeskayan lore Borodov had shared over the years, Brim recognized them as part of a crag wolf pelt—and the mark of adult Bearhood in these out-of-the-way provinces. Yuzhnaya spoke a few words, then bowed.

"He says welcome to Zholvka, Wilf Ansor," Ursis said. "He is proud to meet a human who joins us in our struggle to save the Mother Country."

Yuzhnaya added a few more words, and Ursis smiled. "He says he has seen pictures of humans before and is pleased to find you are not so ugly as one might expect."

Brim returned Yuzhnaya's smile. "Tell him I thraggling appreciate the xaxt out of that," he said to Ursis.

"I already told him that it would make you very happy." Ursis chuckled. "What will make you even happier," he continued, "is knowing that he has workable plan to get us to his farm where we fill stomachs for first time in maybe ten thousand years, it seems."

"At least ten thousand years," Brim replied. "But why did he point that pike at you the way he did?"

"Embarrassing question," Ursis said, his eyes clouding with anger. "Seems he has heard on KA'PPAed media from Gromcow that *some* Bears have thrown in lot with Leaguers. He would just as soon kill these turncoats."

"He's got a KA'PPA set?" Brim asked.

"No," Ursis said. "But some hidden KA'PPA sets still in hands of Sodeskayans, and they broadcast news locally whenever possible by radio." He looked bleakly at the cabin wall for a moment. "Brave Bears, those," he said. "Penalty for that, as I understand, is to become some Leaguer's fur coat."

"Voot's scabby beard," Brim whispered through clenched teeth.

"Speaking of fur coats, there's even more news," Ursis growled with a rare look of rage in his eyes. "This Stalker you have been hearing about on radio—Vikhino Perovo knows who he is."

"And?" Brim demanded.

"None other than our old friend Marshal Rodef *nov* Vobok," Ursis growled. "Your 'Stalker' is really the 'Hunter.'"

"Voot's greasy, flee-infested beard," Brim swore under his

breath. "No wonder the zukeed seemed so important! What d'you suppose he's doing here?"

"From what Vikhino Perovo has been able to learn, the Marshal is here for a little relaxation with his senior staff: tons of TimeWeed, a whole regiment of whores—both sexes—and a fancy lodge. Not a bad way to run a war, eh?"

"Did you learn what the conference is about?" Brim asked.

Ursis laughed cynically. "Some problem with Triannic," he said. "Seems as if the great Emperor is worried that they are advancing too rapidly and might outrun their supplies." He laughed wryly. "How I wish we Bears had such problems once in a while."

Brim frowned for a moment. "That's not enough to raise the anger I saw in your eyes a moment ago, my friend," he said. "Ordinarily, a situation like this would make you laugh at our predicament—whatever the danger."

The Bear fell silent for a moment. "You are correct, Wilf Ansor," he said presently. "Uncontrolled anger and sudden death go hand-in-hand during wartime. In the future, I shall be better controlled."

"But what set you off so, Nik?" Brim persisted.

Ursis ground his teeth. "You really want to know?" he asked.

"Yeah," Brim said. "I'm a big boy."

"Sorry, Wilfooshka," Ursis said apologetically. "Some things are simply too horrible to contemplate. According to Vikhino Perovo, Leaguers are also hunting 'pelt beasts' for coats."

Brim felt his hackles rise. "By 'pelt beasts,' you mean . . . ?"

"Bears," Ursis growled. "Prisoners of war. They release them. Then . . . " He fell silent.

"I don't know what to say, Nik." Brim groaned.

Ursis shrugged. "Say nothing, good friend," he said.

"Someday we will have victory. Then . . . " He stopped for a moment. "Will take mighty effort on *our* part to remain civilized." He shook his head as if to clear his mind, then clearly willed himself into a brighter countenance. "Enough of that, Wilf Ansor," he growled. "Importance is now—and efforts to escape death by starvation."

Forcing his own smile, Brim nodded. "I'm ready," he said.

"I hope so, Wilf Ansor," the Bear chuckled, his effort obviously taking effect.

"Hmm," Brim commented. "I've seen this look on your face before—just before I do something like step in a puddle."

"Ah, no, crag wolves take it," Ursis said. "Not half so much fun." He said something to Yuzhnaya, who immediately broke into gales of laughter. Bears could be moody, but as Brim knew, they were always ready to laugh, no matter what the circumstances. It seemed to be part of the domain's culture.

Brim put his hands on his hips. "What are you two potential miscreants cooking up, anyway?"

"Not to worry, Wilfooshka," Ursis said soothingly. "If we are to safely travel to Yuzhnaya's farm, we shall need to conceal you from surveillance drones. Luckily, friend Yuzhnaya just now returning from shopping trip to village with new clothes for family—and *you*, my furless friend, are perfect size for Bear cub." He pursed his lips and stepped back in mock consideration. "Little mangy, perhaps, with so much hair missing. But . . ." he glanced at Yuzhnaya again and the two dissolved in laughter, "ugly as you will be, he is willing to claim you as his own."

"As his *what*?" demanded Brim.

"Bear cub," Ursis replied, placing a hand over his mouth to stifle what looked a lot like a guffaw. "You are nowhere near big enough to disguise as a Bear."

"True," Brim acknowledged bleakly. "Besides, as you mentioned, it's better than starvation."

"Also true," Ursis said. "And there is positive aspect to this day of disguises."

"What's that?" Brim asked.

"Fact that I shall never be able to taunt you about your disguise."

"How come?"

"Because, Wilf Ansor," the Bear grumped, "I shall be dressed as your *mother*."

At this, Brim dissolved in laughter—joined promptly by Yuzhnaya, who clearly needed no knowledge of Avalonian to appreciate what Ursis must have just said.

Dressed in the woolly, layered clothing of a Bear cub, Brim checked the storm-filled sky for Leaguer drones, then stepped out into the driving snow. With the heat turned to MAXIMUM in his battlesuit, he felt comfortable for the first time since his arrival on the wintry planet. Behind him, Yuzhnaya stepped from the launch, followed by Ursis, who activated the security system and pocketed a remote alarm before slamming the hatch. When someone eventually found the launch and entered it, friend *or* foe would set off the alarm, signaling Brim and Ursis to activate their own short-range locator transmitters. With a bit of help from Dame Fortune, these would lead an Allied rescue team to them and not a squad of Leaguers. At any rate, it was the best idea either of them could devise. The Leaguers had yet to discover the purpose of these personal beacons . . . at least as of the day Brim and Ursis departed on their ill-starred trip.

On close inspection, Yuzhnaya's sledge turned out to be quite primitive, largely constructed from wood, although its parts were clearly fastened together by advanced-technology metals. Some twenty-five irals in length and perhaps nine in breadth, it consisted of a long open bed riding on four skilike runners. The rear skis were attached inboard directly to the frame. The front pair were attached to a crossbar that mounted to the box at its center via a swivel. Two long traces ran from the crossbar to a great, high hoop. Beneath this stood the droshkat, harnessed to the crossbars. A high platform provided an uncomfortable-looking driver's seat, on which Yuzhnaya had stacked several layers of cushions.

"Climb up on seat, Wilf Ansor," Ursis called to him. "Is sitting between us so we can hide your furless face." He laughed. " 'Even ugly cubs are seldom safe from ministrations of rock spiders,' as they say."

Brim nodded and climbed onto the high seat. Below, the big droshkat was now sitting in the snow, fastidiously licking its left paw. Moments later, the two Bears climbed aboard. Brim desperately stifled a guffaw as he glanced at his old friend. Ursis was now dressed as a Sodeskayan *arbatskaya*— a little grandmother—in a long, maroon coat decorated by flowered patterns at its hem and cuffs. He had wrapped a lacy shawl around his neck and wore the traditional crimson scarf covering his head and tying under his chin.

"If you ever breathe a word, Brim," the Bear grumbled as they got under way with a schussing of dry snow beneath the runners, "you will never again be safe in Sodeskaya—perhaps anywhere in Galaxy."

"Your secret is safe with me," Brim assured him. "My mouth is sealed. However," he added, "in my memoirs . . ."

Ursis rolled his eyes to the heavens, then stiffened. "Is surveillance drone," he warned, putting his arm around Brim's shoulders. "Is keeping down," he said, drawing Brim's head to his chest. "Hands covered, please."

Moments later, a ghostly winged shape glided overhead in the falling snow. Brim watched it bank gracefully, turn, and lose altitude as it headed back their way. This time, it passed with only a few irals clearance above their heads—terrifying the droshkat, which folded its tail between its legs and began to lope out of control, dragging its shaggy belly along the snow. The sledge nearly overturned before Yuzhnaya managed to bring the beast under control, and by that time the drone was back, skimming along beside them no more than an iral or so above the snow. This time, the droshkat took off at a right angle from its previous path, yanking the sledge around on its two port runners at such an angle that all three passengers had to grab for whatever handholds they could find. It took a supreme effort for Brim to keep his face to Ursis's chest while the panicked droshkat tried to escape, careening this way and that with the drone in easy pursuit. Only after most of the sledge's load was spilled did the drone's remote Helmsman appear to tire of his little game, and the drone silently banked away to spinward, disappearing moments later in the falling snow.

"Bastard Leaguer," Ursis growled as Yuzhnaya fought the winded droshkat to a halt. "*That* was done for the pure sport of the thing."

"Mmpff," Brim replied, struggling to free himself from the Bear's unconscious embrace.

"Oh, Sorry, Wilf Ansor," Ursis gasped. "I'd forgotten."

"It's all right," Brim sputtered. "Better a bit smothered than captured. I don't think I could have kept my face out of sight through all that."

Yuzhnaya vehemently bellowed out something that sounded a great deal like swearing, then pointed to the shivering droshkat, who had just lain down on the snow, its sides heaving.

"Says the poor droshkat's too old for this kind of abuse," Ursis grunted.

Brim looked at the shaggy beast and frowned. "Does Yuzhnaya think he'll make it all the way home?" he asked.

Ursis turned to him and shrugged. "Only droshkat knows for sure," he said. "But is seriously hoping so, because if I wait much longer for supper, droshkat is prime candidate—and he looks tough and stringy."

Brim chuckled. "Probably taste pretty good in a couple more metacycles," he joked. "By then, 'tough and stringy' won't much matter."

Ursis shared these words with Yuzhnaya, and the three of them were laughing vigorously when the sound of their mirth was suddenly overlaid by a bloodcurdling howl—more of a fevered snarling—so horrifying that hair stood up on the back of Brim's neck. He'd never heard anything like it at close range, but he instantly guessed what it was.

"Crag wolves," Ursis gasped, turning to face the noise. "Must have been attracted by drone, Voot take it."

Yuzhnaya dove for his blast pike while the droshkat made deep growling noises in his throat, ears back and tail bristling into a great *katsbat* that lashed nervously back and forth across his back.

Completely unarmed, Brim could only helplessly scan through the blizzard and wait.

Ursis drew his old side-action blaster and grimaced. "Used up much charge back in *Maxim Chkalov* 'reasoning' with bastards who tried to take launch away without you," he said, looking at the powerful weapon. "Hope they don't have revenge on us now."

When a second—obviously nearer—chorus of howls filled the still air, Yuzhnaya cracked his whip and spurred the terrified droshkat into action with words of urgent inflection. The old beast needed little persuasion, starting off through the snow as if he had shed half his years.

Twisted to face the rear, Ursis grinned in spite of the desperate state of affairs. "If nothing else," he said, glancing at Brim, "xaxtdamned wolves get us home to dinner that much faster." At this speed, the unsprung sledge transmitted every surface irregularity directly to the seat.

"Unless we become *their* dinner," Brim added.

"Won't be hungry anymore, then," the Bear replied pfleg-matically. "Always something to look forward to."

At that moment, the first crag wolf materialized through the billowing snow astern, barrel-chested, powerful, and *deadly* looking. Nearly half as tall as Brim, the ravening monster appeared to be fast as it was ugly—and gaining rapidly on the sledge. Both the brute's heads were straining forward as it ran, ears flattened and mouths open, revealing immense fangs visible even at a quarter-c'lenyt.

Carefully, Ursis made adjustments to his blaster, then leaned its barrel across his left arm, which rested atop the sledge's seat back. With utmost concern, he cocked the weapon, then relaxed, waiting. "Perhaps you should ready Yuzhnaya's blast pike, Wilf Ansor," he suggested in a voice icy with calm. "No telling how many more shots I have in blaster here." As he spoke, three more crag wolves material-ized out of the snow as the first drew ever nearer their sledge.

Brim gently took the blast pike from Yuzhnaya, who was now far too concerned with driving to fire at the wolves, and, turning to face the oncoming pack—now numbering seven—he rested the cumbersome barrel on the seat back and con-centrated on its controls. The sharp report of Ursis's first shot took him completely by surprise. He looked up in time to see the left-hand head of the lead wolf disappear in a small explosion of blood and brain fragments. The powerful bolt of energy peeled skin all the way back past the wolf's shoulder, but the beast continued to run, evidently controlled by the right-hand head. If nothing else, its speed was definitely im-paired, for the other six began to gain on it.

Yuzhnaya glanced to the rear and yelled something to Ursis.

"What's he say?" Brim demanded.

"Says got to hit *between* heads," Ursis replied, carefully drawing a bead for his second shot. "Heart there, he says.

Nothing else stops them." With that, he took another shot that kicked up a great glot of snow beside another of the wolves and nearly knocking it over, but did no appreciable damage. "Bad," the Bear grumbled to himself. "Now is no time for idle target practice, Nikolai Yanuarievich," he grumbled to himself. With that, he fired off a third bolt that smashed home precisely between the heads of his second target, clearly breaking both its necks with concussion and exploding the heart in a spray of blood. This time the wolf was stopped, falling in a great bloody tangle that rolled forward on momentum alone for nearly a hunded irals.

While Brim tried in vain to activate the old blast pike, Ursis took aim again, but this shot also went wild when the sledge bumped over a half-buried log just as he activated the trigger. Nevertheless, two wolves were out of the running—the first was clearly bleeding to death and had fallen back a considerable distance.

Once more, Ursis took careful aim and fired. Another close miss, but this shot at least broke its target's legs, for both heads of the ugly beast yelped in pain and it stumbled, falling in a cloud of snow.

Four more to go! But now the distance between wolves and their prey was *much* less. Brim glanced at the old droshkat, who was clearly flagging from the effort, even though Yuzhnaya urged him on with both voice and whip. "Nik," he shouted, "how in xaxt do I activate the trigger mechanism on this antique?"

Ursis glanced over at the old pike and shut his eyes for a moment. "The lever with *or' gutt* on it," he said. "Try to bring it back exactly three clicks, then push it sideways into the detent."

Brim found the lever in a recess and pried it back until it clicked three times—which lined it up with a small slot running sideways, then jogged forward at a right angle. He moved the lever into this position and suddenly two of the three green indicators lighted on the slide. "I think I've got it!"

"Then thraggling *shoot* it!" Ursis roared, firing at the lead wolf, that was no more than twenty irals from the rear of the sledge. The bolt of energy went slightly wide of its mark, burning a great rent in the wolf's hide but otherwise causing little harm. For his next shot, he hardly needed aim—the beast was only irals away now, both slathering mouths wide open, their tongues hanging to one side. His finger tightened on the trigger mechanism, but all that resulted was a shrill, piercing whistle from the energy pack—its charge was gone!

Desperately, Brim swung Yuzhnaya's clumsy pike into position, sighted down its long barrel—he couldn't miss—then thumbed the trigger. He was rewarded with an eruption of raw power that would make a disruptor blanch with envy. The traveling wave of raw energy caught the wolf square in its chest and instantly reduced the whole animal to what must have been its various atomic particles. A scant moment later, nothing but a glowing puffball remained, receding quickly in the distance as it collapsed on itself and dissolved into a dirty puff of smoke.

The sudden demise of their partner did little to discourage the last three wolves, who now appeared to be little more than trotting behind the sledge while they negotiated the spoils between them. Swinging the pike at the right-hand wolf, Brim again thumbed the trigger and was rewarded with the same eruption of power and resultant explosion where a moment before had been a large and hungry crag wolf.

Swinging the pike once more, he aimed at the closest wolf—who was clearly about to leap aboard the sledge—and thumbed the trigger, bracing himself for another great blast of energy. Instead, nothing happened at all. *Nothing! That* was what the green lights on the slide were about. Only two of the big weapon's charges remained when he got it. And now they were used up. "It's all over, Nik," he shouted. "The pike's discharged!"

"Not *all* over, friend Brim," the Bear said, drawing a huge knife from inside his overcoat. "I still have *this*." With that, he vaulted the seat back and started aft—just as both surviving crag wolves jumped, snarling, into the box, slathering and snapping in a paroxysm of maniacal rage.

"Nik!" Brim yelled, "you aren't wearing your battlesuit!"

Ursis paid no heed. Instead, he bellowed out a great Bearish roar that stopped the wolves in their tracks. Then, growling from somewhere in his stomach, he crouched and started aft over the wildly bucking floorboards, the knife in his right hand like a sword. As he approached, the hair on the wolves' four necks bristled and they tucked their tails, backing away from the growling monster that once had been their quarry. Suddenly the Bear leaped, grabbing the nearest wolf by its rightmost head and pricking his knife quickly into an eye socket. The head shrieked with pain while its partner instinctively turned the other way, momentarily exposing the soft spot between them. Ursis struck like lightning, driving the knife to its hilt in the beast's heart. Both heads gave a momentary howl of pain, then crumpled dead in a spray of blood while . . .

"Nik!" Brim shouted as the remaining wolf lunged for Ursis's neck, "Look out!" He started over the seat, swinging the expended blast pike like a club, but he was too late.

Ursis turned to confront this new danger, but didn't get even halfway around before the monster was on him, its momentum bringing both to the floorboards, with the Bear on the bottom.

Brim was about to jump into the melee when he was stunned by a blinding, crackling flash of light that blasted the wolf backward completely off the sledge and knocked Brim to the floorboards with concussion. As he fell, what looked like an open gate flashed by: then he landed in a heap against the side wall of the box, knocking himself nearly senseless. Moments later, he felt the sledge abruptly slow to a halt— while the head of a young Bear popped over the side above him, babbling excitedly in Sodeskayan. Grimacing from a growing lump on his head, he glanced across at Ursis, who was bleeding profusely from a badly ripped arm and lacerations across his muzzle that had come dangerously close to his eye. "Mother of Voot, Nik," Brim groaned, "you all right?"

Ursis propped himself up with his back against the crag wolf he had killed. "Just wonderful," he replied touching his arm with a grimace of pain. "Just thraggling wonderful." Then he peered at Brim. "Are *you* all right?" he asked.

"Yeah," Brim said, getting slowly to his feet while a dozen or so new stars swirled before his eyes. "B-but, where are we?"

Glancing around, the Bear managed a grin. "Seems we have made it to Yuzhnaya's place. Look," he said, nodding to a large female Bear standing atop the wall with a blast pike. "We have even more thanks to give—or at least *I* do." He turned and spoke to Yuzhnaya in Sodeskayan.

The native nodded energetically and said something in a pleased voice.

Ursis grinned. "Says lady Bear's name is Per'siki. Claims she's a crack shot—and I for one would never question," the Bear said.

Brim could only agree. "Her husband's no slouch at sledge driving, either," he said.

Ursis spoke a few more words to Yuzhnaya. The native smiled and made a pleased little bow. Then, gushing out a torrent of words, he pointed to the droshkat, which was cleaning a spot on its shoulder even though its tail was still bristled out to twice its normal size.

"Says old Chesnok—droshkat's name—is fine beast with great heart," Ursis said.

"I believe him," Brim said as a young Bear lead the shaggy beast off. "A *heroic* droshkat."

Ursis smiled for a moment. "Old Borodov will never own droshkat like that. Too much breeding ruins thoroughbreds every time." He winked. "Much like kings." By this time, Yuzhnaya's wife had reached the side of the sledge and was scolding him in an exasperated voice while pointing toward his arm. "Probably she is right," the Bear conceded, looking down at his slashed arm. "I should get this fixed—is making bloody mess in bed of sledge."

Brim rolled his eyes. "Yeah," he agreed, "you probably should."

While Ursis climbed down from the sledge, Brim had an opportunity to look around the compound. It was perhaps a hundred irals on a side, walled on three sides by a rough battlement made of carefully piled stones. Completing the enclosure was the farmhouse itself and a large outbuilding that looked like a barn and appeared to be the destination of their gallant droshkat. Beyond the wall, he could see a large metal tower that was probably the family reactor; no power lines would lead to this remote location. Perhaps two score of shaggy animals stood nervously off to one corner, still upset by the sledge's precipitous entry into their peaceful domain. Wool from these animals would be the source for much of the family's income. Three or four milk-givers—also somewhat ruffled-looking—huddled together near the barn entrance. A number of large, bare trees with black, twisting branches grew at random locations in the yard as if they had been there a lot longer than the wall.

From the house came the most colossally appealing aroma Brim could remember—the yeasty smell of fresh-baked bread! And there was Yuzhnaya, motioning him inside! Food, at last! He jumped to the ground and was scampering across the yard when—Voot's greasy, filthy, utterly disreputable beard!—the remote alarm went off in his pocket!

Someone had found their launch. He and Ursis would have to activate their personal locators almost immediately or risk missing the rescue ship—*if* indeed it was a rescue ship that had set off the alarm and not a Leaguer patrol.

He hesitated only a moment before he activated his own, then made off for Ursis at a dead run. Rescuers *or* Leaguers, the two of them would have to be a long way from the house in a very short time or risk implicating the brave peasants who were risking their very lives to help them.

Inside the house—one warm, comfortable, very large kitchen from which a number of passageways led in all directions—Ursis was lying on a huge divan before a roaring fireplace, munching what appeared to be a thick chunk of meat wrapped in two huge slices of bread, while Per'siki ministered to his savaged arm. "Nik," he said, nodding to accept a similar repast from one of the couple's colossal children, "the alarm's gone off."

Ursis stiffened—clearly not from discomfort in his arm. "We must be out of here immediately," he said. "Have you activated personal locator?"

"I have, Nik," Brim mumbled through a mouthful of the most delicious . . . whatever it was . . . he had ever eaten.

The Bear set down his meat and bread, then reached inside his woolly garments. "My locator is now activated as well," he said. Then he spoke gently to Yuzhnaya in Sodeskayan. The native nodded and immediately issued what could only be commands to three of his sons—who obediently disappeared along three of the passageways. After some discussion among the three adult Bears, Ursis faced Brim and frowned. "They will supply another sledge and a fresh droshkat," he explained while Per'siki completed wrapping his arm in some sort of medicated gauze. "At my insistence, they will drop us somewhere a safe distance away from the farm and return tonight after dark to be sure we have been picked up . . . by someone." He nodded to himself as if he were checking himself for details. "That way," he continued at length, "should nothing at all have happened to us, we have a chance of returning here rather than spending another night with packs of crag wolves."

Brim choked down the last of his food—actually, it was *very* tasty, tender, and magnificently seasoned—and nodded. "You'll be wearing your battlesuit again?" he asked with a grin.

Ursis nodded. "It may be after dark before something happens," he said. "Since we will either be rescued, captured, or brought back here, is no use trying to hide things anymore." Then he chuckled. "You, however, my furless friend, will still have to wear *both* battlesuit and cub clothing, lest I have to carry you on board rescue craft in block of ice."

Less than half a metacycle later, they were back in the sledge (now pulled by a small, brown-and-white-striped droshkat mare) while Luk, youngest son of the Yuzhnayas, drove through another worsening snowstorm. Wrapped in countless layers of woolens with his battlesuit turned up full, Brim promised himself that if he managed to stay alive through the war, he would eventually retire to someplace orbiting a slightly overactive star—with tropical heat throughout the entire year!

Luk dropped them off, along with a knapsack of food and two fully loaded blast pikes, at what appeared to be an ideal location for being rescued: a copse of trees standing out a short distance from the edge of a dense forest—at least ten c'lenyts from the Yuzhnaya farm. After proudly bidding good fortune to Brim in Avalonian, the hulking young Bear grasped Ursis's hand emotionally before he jumped back aboard the sledge and started home through still another howling blizzard.

Another freedom fighter to harry the xaxtdamned Leaguers, Brim thought with a smile. Bears were going to be *damned* hard to subdue. "Doesn't it *ever* stop snowing here?" he quipped as they trudged into the stand of trees and dodged behind a fallen log.

The Bear thought for a moment, taking a place behind the log also. "It must every once in a while." He chuckled, indicating the forest. "Otherwise, trees like this won't grow."

"Maybe they've been in deep freeze for the last million years," Brim suggested.

"You may have a point, there," Ursis considered. Suddenly his eyes narrowed and he peered off in the distance. "What in xaxt is *that*?" he whispered.

Brim followed Ursis's glance to an indistinct figure approaching them at a run through the snow.

"Sweet mother of Voot," Brim whispered. "Its a Bear . . . No, a Bearess—and she's wearing a *battlesuit*!"

In the next instant, the distant baying of hounds could be heard over the moaning wind, and another figure materialized behind the first, obviously in pursuit.

"That's a Leaguer chasing her!" Ursis exclaimed. "She's being *hunted*!" He rose to a crouch and tried to attract the Bearess's attention while Brim readied one of their old-fashioned blast pikes.

The Bearess never saw then. Instead, she glanced behind her and redoubled her speed, veering off toward the forest verge as fast as she could run.

At the same time, however, the Leaguer casually unslung a long, slim sporting blaster, took quick aim, and fired. His shot was superb, catching the Bearess square in the head; she was without a helmet. The burst of energy drove her body forward, head over heels, and she tumbled to a stop, twitching, then lifeless in a growing pool of blood no more than thirty irals from Brim and Ursis.

"Xaxtdamned *bloody* murderer," Ursis growled deep in his throat. He started over the log, but Brim yanked him back.

"No, Nik," he whispered. "There's nothing you can do for her now."

"Gorksroar," Ursis roared, grabbing for the second blast pike. He was about to swing its great barrel over the tree trunk when Brim grabbed it and shoved it to the ground.

"Xaxtdammit, Nik," he said hotly. "You heard the hounds out there. That Leaguer's not alone. His friends will catch up in a moment, and if they find him dead, they'll spend the next year hunting us down. It'll make our rescue a hundred times more difficult, and it won't help her at all. Does that make sense?"

The Bear ground his teeth for a long moment. Finally he closed his eyes. "Makes sense, Wilf Ansor," he admitted. "Sorry."

Brim was proved right only moments later, when two other Leaguers armed with sporting blasters drove up in a small, open vehicle that must have been part of the hunting lodge's equipment. All three strolled casually to the dead Bearess.

Brim kept a weather eye on Ursis, who was still breathing hard with an all-consuming rage.

"Is all right, Wilfooshka," he whispered. "I am in control again."

Standing over the dead Bearess, the three Leaguers doffed their battlesuit helmets and drank a little toast after touching what appeared to be silver flasks they produced from pockets in their battlesuits.

Brim glanced down to check the pikes when Ursis suddenly made a sharp intake of breath.

"By the Great Crag Wolf," he swore under his breath, "do you see who that is?"

Brim looked up, narrowed his eyes, and gasped. "Thundering Universe, Nik," he whispered. "It looks like Rodef *nov* Vobok himself."

"Not just *looks* like him," the Bear said. "*Is* him."

"So it is," Brim agreed, only now noticing the tiny circle of five stars at the man's left breast, "or somebody who's soon to be arrested for impersonating a Field Marshal." The Leaguer was tall and powerfully built, even without the bulk of his ebony battlesuit. Below painstakingly coifed hair, his face was narrow, as was his slender, patrician nose. His eyes were small and close-set, and he wore a wisp of a mustache above thin, nearly colorless lips. Brim had seen HoloGraphs of him countless times. There could be no mistake. Both of his companions wore the three stars of OverGalite'ers on their chests, but their faces were not familiar.

Nov Vobok abruptly knelt to unlatch the collar of the Bearess's battlesuit, then ripped it open to the crotch. Next he grabbed her head while his two companions peeled the suit down over her legs.

Ursis emitted a deep, primordial growl as the Leaguer drew a sturdy knife from a leg pocket and plunged it deep into the Bearess's abdomen, then drew it all the way to the neck with both hands.

"He's . . . he's going to . . ." Brim whispered, but he never completed his thought.

With a great roar, Ursis leaped over the log and charged out of the copse, covering the distance to the Leaguers in a few bounds.

Stunned, Brim watched the three Leaguers scatter from the howling apparition, fumbling for their sporting blasters, but before they had a chance to react, Ursis grabbed *nov* Vobok around the head and snapped his neck with a report that sounded like the crack of a whip.

Brim aimed the old blast pike at one of the Galitie'ers, but the next moment, a tremendous, rolling thunder assaulted his ears, coming from everywhere . . . and nowhere.

It was all too much for the Galitie'ers. Clearly dumbfounded, they turned in panic and began to run, but Ursis seemed immune to the sound. Swinging the Field Marshal's body by the feet as if it were some limp bludgeon, he took off after the two fleeing Galitie'ers, smashing them senseless before they could get out of his way.

At that moment, what appeared to be a whole platoon of Leaguers approached at a run through the driving snow, following three civilians who were dressed in winter gear and struggling to control six huge Leaguer Gratz Hounds, straining at their leashes. It took the soldiers no more than a click to realize that something had gone terribly wrong, and they struggled to unsling their powerful Zspandu .50s. Brim picked the frontmost and squeezed the trigger of his old blast pike, carrying him and two soldiers nearby off in a tremendous explosion that momentarily startled the others—and possibly saved Ursis's life.

While the Leaguers were recovering from this latest, unexpected shock, part of the sky opened—*literally* opened—like a window through which a small disruptor poked into the open and began to fire away with tremendous accuracy. Its first discharge blew a crater under the civilians and their Gratz Hounds, blasting all eight like rag dolls two hundred irals in the air atop at least half a millston's weight of loose dirt and debris.

"Wilf! Nik! Last ship for Gromcow. Hurry!" a woman's oddly familiar voice called out over some sort of invisible amplification system.

Invisible . . . Suddenly Brim recognized the noise. A bender! And a *friendly* one—evidently someone aboard knew his name!

"Wilf!" the Bear roared, glancing around him, heedless of the noise. "Where are you?"

"I'm here, Nik!" Brim yelled over the rumble of powerful gravs. He pointed to a hatch that appeared to be opening out of thin air. "Look!" he shouted. "It's a BENDER! One of ours. Go for it!"

As the disruptor fired again, blowing the remaining Leaguers to the seven corners of the Universe, Ursis seemed to regain his senses and set out for the hatch at a run.

Brim followed, lugging both blast pikes while the knapsack bounced painfully against his back. He watched Ursis reach the hatch and bound aboard, helped by at least four pairs of arms—one of whom belonged to Chief Barbousse. And it was at that moment he saw who had come to their rescue—none other than his onetime second-in-command aboard I.F.S. *Starfury*, Nadia Tissuard!

"Com'on, Skipper," she yelled with a look of utter urgency. "We've got to get out of here! Somethin' *big*'s happened close by, and every Leaguer within a light-year is on his way."

Brim dove through the opening, helped—actually dragged—by Barbousse and three other burly ratings dressed in Imperial Fleet Cloaks. He'd never been so happy to see anyone in his life. "Thanks, Chief," he gasped as others slammed the hatch shut.

Barbousse looked serious as he lifted the knapsack from Brim's back. "Glad to oblige, Admiral," he said. "But it's Captain Tissuard you need to thank for the rescue. She's the one who figured you'd head for this planet." He shook his head appreciatively. "We've been snooping around these blasted Leaguers for days now."

Close by, Ursis and Tissuard were conversing urgently, and the latter nodded emphatically. "Through that hatchway, General," she said. "I know it's important, but please *hurry*."

Ursis nodded and patted her on the shoulder. "Quickly as possible," he said. "Leaguers must *not* have her skin." He disappeared through a door in the forward bulkhead of the tiny boarding chamber.

Brim glanced at Tissuard and nodded silent appreciation.

"Thank me later, Skipper," she said, moving to Brim's side with a little smile. "I've got to get this ship on the road quickly—before more Leaguers stop for a chat." Tiny and prematurely gray, her round face, laughing eyes, pug nose, and full, sensuous lips endowed her face with the look of a true pixie. She had a compact figure with largish hands and feet—and a prominent bosom that rarely failed to attract male attention, even when mostly concealed by a Fleet Cloak. Years ago, as Brim's First Lieutenant aboard I.F.S. *Starfury* during a prewar tour of duty, she had proven herself to be an exceptional Helmsman who could carry out a myriad of duties with the cheerful willingness of a GradyGroat saint. She was also utterly frank and—off duty—quite extraordinarily sensual. A personal bond had formed between her and Brim, and on more than one occasion they had been at pains to remain on the safe side of professionalism. Following her reassignment as captain of the bender I.F.S. *Nord,* however, their friendship had gradually changed to one of a more intimate nature, though Dame Fortune had yet to provide them with opportunity for anything but a few hurried gropings.

After a few moments, the ship quivered momentarily as a disruptor fired once, then fell silent. Moments later, Ursis returned through the hatch.

"Thank you, Captain," he said, looking more tired than Brim could remember.

Evidently, Tissuard noticed the same thing. "No thanks needed, General Ursis," she said. "If anything like that ever happens to me, I hope someone like you is around to care." She turned to one of the ratings. "Take the General to my cabin," she ordered. "We'll work out permanent arrangements later."

When Ursis was gone, she turned to Brim. "By the by," she added with studied indifference, "I'd say you owe me at least a couple of meems for this little pickup. What do you think?"

Brim smiled. "*Logish* Meems, Number One," he said. "A lakefull of Sodeskaya's finest, if you're going to be in town. Otherwise, I'll send it."

"We'll be reprovisioning for about a day in Gromcow," she said. "Drag yourself away from your job for a few metacycles, I'll take you up on that." She grinned. "Maybe not a lakefull, but a couple of cases for the crew. . . ."

"You've got a deal, lady," Brim said, hoping no one noticed the blush that was warming his cheeks. "Just let me know where to find you."

She nodded. "I'll leave a message at the Embassy desk," she said. "Now come along to the bridge so I can get us out of here." Ushering Brim into a narrow companionway, she led the way to a cramped flight bridge whose meager Hyperscreen array was mostly covered by the sensing/projecting panels that cloaked the ship. Indicating a jump seat, she held his glance long enough to send a private—provocative—wink, then moved quickly to the Cloaking Officer's station. There she studied the myriad of multicolored data flowing over his display, nodded, and slipped into the left-hand helm and set the restraints. Beside her, the Co-Helmsman, a gorgeous redhead with clearly nonregulation shoulder-length hair, made a quick report, then the two began what sounded like a *very* abbreviated liftoff checklist.

They were airborne almost immediately, bumping gingerly upward in the turbulence of another storm toward the ultimate concealment of space. Through a narrow opening in the Hyperscreen cover beside him, Brim momentarily spotted the Yuzhnaya farm through driving snow and broken clouds. He smiled, recalling the doughty Bears he had met there and the aroma of baking bread that filled their warm, comfortable kitchen. It all appeared so peaceful down there. He even thought he caught sight of Chesnok, the plucky old droshkat. Suddenly he was swept by an immense surge of exultation— Sodeskayans like these *never* would be conquered!

In the next moments, *Nord* was swallowed by clouds, and the next prospect to appear was the starry endlessness of outer space. Four days later, they were back in Gromcow, and Brim had yet to see the fighting firsthand on this new and important front.

CHAPTER 6
A Puzzling Hiatus

That evening, after collecting Tissuard's promised message from the desk—and a lovely note from Marsha Brown, that he answered on the spot—Brim KA'PPAed his report to Avalon. Aside from a brief, personal recap of *nov* Vobok's demise, this latest submission contained little new data. In spite of his recent adventures in enemy territory, he had yet to reach the front lines.

This, however, would be the last communiqué he mostly compiled from the reports of others. Only metacycles after debarking from *Nord* that morning—and proving to a military hospital he was still in good health—he had convinced both Borodov and Ursis that the only way he was going to experience the war well enough to report on it was to actually join the fighting. The Bears had been resistant at first, but had finally given in and Borodov had arranged everything before teatime. In two days hence, Brim would report to a remote training station where he would become combat rated in a ZBL-4. Then, when he visited a battle zone, he would be able to *experience* the way the war was going, not merely observe.

Tissuard was waiting outside the Embassy that evening. As usual in Gromcow, it was snowing, and had been for more than a metacycle. Streets and buildings were already covered in a gentle blanket of white, turning the tall trees lining Moloco Prospekt into fantastic sculptures of black and white. Returning the salutes of Marines ceremoniously guarding the Embassy, he strode down the wide, recently swept staircase—already covered by a new layer of snow—and looked around for a staff skimmer. Nadia Tissuard had a way of charming transportation officers—male as well as female—like no one else in the known Universe. However, no skimmer appeared to be stopped anywhere near the Embassy; only a graceful white troika waited at the curb. It was decorated by intricately carved scrollwork in gold leaf and drawn by three huge calico droshkats. The *yamshchik,* on a high seat at the forward end, wore a high woolen cap with the two coveted zavencock feathers protruding from its right side, a crimson greatcoat with gold frogs, and black, shiny boots. He waved his long, slender whip as Brim approached, pointing to the passenger compartment with a great, toothy smile.

Brim peered through the snow at what appeared to be a mountain of multicolored blankets, then burst out in a guffaw as he spotted Tissuard peering out at him from near the top of the pile. Her face wore a huge grin, as if she had just perpetrated the best joke in the Universe. "Come cuddle with me, Wilf Brim," she said. "It's the *only* way to keep warm!"

Matching her grin for grin, Brim climbed into the seat beside her and began to open the blankets when a hand emerged from the blankets and grasped his forearm.

"Not with your Fleet Cloak on, you big dunce." She chuckled darkly. "That *will* be cold."

Brim felt his eyebrows rise and he noticed Tissuard's Fleet

Cloak lying in a heap on the opposite seat. "It's *that* warm in there?" he asked.

"The only way you'll find out for certain is to take off that cloak of yours and try it." She giggled. "I'm certainly comfortable."

"Yeah," Brim said. "You look comfortable." In point of fact, she did, wrapped in what, on closer inspection, was a single huge quilt. He took off his cloak and laid it beside hers on the opposite seat; then, dressed only in his service uniform, he partially unwrapped Tissuard and climbed into the quilt beside her.

"Cozy," she said, licking her lips.

"Sure is," Brim agreed. He slipped his arm around her shoulders as he folded them inside.

"*Cozier* . . . " she said with a big grin.

"Now what?" Brim asked.

She looked at him and her eyes widened. "Not much more here in front of the Embassy—in the middle of Moloco Prospekt." She giggled again. "Especially with those Marine guards staring at us. Or, ah, are you a lot kinkier than I think you are?"

Brim laughed. "I don't know." He laughed. "Depends on how much kinky you have in mind."

"Wilf Brim!" She groaned in mock exasperation. "You are impossible!" She turned to the *yamshchik*. "All right, Mr. Savloskaya," she whooped, "let's have that tour of the city!"

"Yas, madame," the Bear said in broken Avalonian, and cracked his whip. The troika started smoothly and picked up speed rapidly until it was skimming at high velocity along the great thoroughfare, filling the snowy air with the rhythmic jingling of the droshkat's harness bells.

Brim found himself grinning like an idiot as the great lighted buildings of Moloco Prospekt—Gromcow's "Embassy Row"—rushed past on the nearly deserted street. Trees, hazed streetlights, even the occasional pedestrians all appeared softer and somehow friendlier through the gently falling snow that peppered his face and eyes with sharp wetness. As they careened off onto a darker street, he looked at the pixielike face before him and shook his head. Hard to believe that little more than four Standard Days previously, his view of the next dawn had been not at all a certain thing. Now here he sat. . . . Her mouth was slightly open and she was looking at him expectantly. Without closing his eyes, he drew her gently to him—brushed her lips with his. It was only the second time in their long relationship that they'd been like this; he felt his pulse quicken as she pressed her lips to his with a very sudden urgency and explored his mouth with her tongue. He remembered her breath from the last time they kissed, fresh and fragrant as a spring breeze. Then he closed his eyes while his mind went spinning off in a thousand directions, each more exciting than the last.

The two old friends spent considerable time making up for lost time and past disappointments. By the middle of the night, they had visited at least three taverns, sampled countless labels of the city's justly famous Gromcow meem, and were now skimming the darkened banks of the Gromcow River at high speed, c'lenyts from the city's glow. Having groped themselves pleasantly ready to consummate a number of long-standing promises, the two were giggling with total abandon at their fumbling attempts to find a posture that would work in a troika designed for Bears. Now completely in the buff beneath their quilt, both had long since given up on any of the more "common" positions, and Brim was presently slouching on the seat cushions, nose to nose with the pixielike Tissuard, who was balancing on her knees astride his lap. Desperately gripping his shoulder with her left hand, the tiny woman was laughing wildly as she tried to lower herself onto him while the troika swayed and bucked along the undulating path.

"How about I just tell him to stop?" Brim offered when a

sudden bounce nearly plunged him into the wrong opening—and resulted in a painful squeeze as Tissuard sought to steady herself on the somewhat precarious roost.

"Sorry about that," she said, giggling and bringing herself erect again. "But no way are we going to stop. Bears do it with the troika moving, and by Voot, that's the way we're going to do it, too. 'When in Avalon,' they say. . . ."

"But we're not in Avalon," Brim protested. "We're in Gromcow, and Bears do it a different way!" He attempted to tighten the quilt around them again.

"That's *it*!" Tissuard exclaimed with a sudden look of triumph. "We've been going about it all wrong!" She threw her arms arouns his neck, kissed him wetly, then shoved him to one side of the seat. "Get behind me," she ordered, kneeling beside him and leaning over the back of the troika. Then she giggled. "And mind where you're steering that!" she admonished.

Laughing, Brim balanced himself as the troika rounded a sharp curve and pulled the quilt over them for the ten thousandth time. With one arm just under her swaying breasts, he thrust himself forward into . . . Finally!

Tissuard gave a little gasp. "That did it!" she squealed in a tight voice. "Ooo!"

Suddenly Brim was blinded by a pair of headlights as a skimmer careened around the curve behind them. An instant later, red and green strobes began to flash and an amplified voice boomed out something in Sodeskayan that sounded very, *very* official. Startled, he felt himself shrink and wither free.

Tissuard screamed and placed her hands over her eyes, slipping quickly to the floor of the troika between Brim's legs while she reached outside the blanket for her Fleet Cloak. Brim dodged down beside her, pulling his own—COLD!—cloak around him, and blindly grabbed his trousers in the folds of the quilt.

"Secret Police!" the *yamshchik* yelled above oncoming footsteps crunching through the snow. "Is demanding to see identification."

"Tell 'em to stay where they are or they'll see a damned sight more than identification," Tissuard growled angrily.

The *yamshchik* said something in Sodeskayan and received a gruff answer. The crunching footsteps stopped.

"What in xaxt do they want with *us*?" Brim wondered out loud.

"Secret Police not usually communicative about things like that," the *yamshchik* replied cautiously. " 'Bear cubs on thin ice seldom call out welcome to crag wolves,' as they say."

"Bastard cops," Brim grumbled, climbing onto the rear seat to drag on his trousers. He glanced over his shoulder toward four hulking forms silhouetted against the night sky.

Across from him, Tissuard was now on the front seat, awkwardly wrestling a pair of crimson briefs over her boots. "Bastard cops," she seconded, pulling her skirt down and fastening her Fleet Cloak.

Brim donned his own Fleet Cloak and pulled on his boots. "Ready?" he asked.

Tissuard looked up and grimaced. "For what?" she growled.

"How about the Sodeskayan Secret Police?" Brim suggested carefully.

"Tell them to go away," she said caustically, combing her short hair with her fingers. "I only do it with humans."

"Maybe they just want to talk," Brim said, wrapping the quilt around her.

"*WON*-der-ful," Tissuard replied, sinking into the folds like a tortoise. "In that case, bring 'em on."

"Tell 'em we're ready, driver," Brim said.

The *yamshchik* shouted something in Sodeskayan, and moments later a huge female Bear appeared beside the troika. She was dressed in a severe black uniform with a high, beaked cap and a white belt that crossed diagonally from right shoulder to left hip. "Admiral Wilf Brim?" she asked as a second skimmer hummed to a halt behind the first.

"That's me," Brim grumped.

"May I see some identification, please?" she asked in perfect, unaccented Avalonian.

Brim produced a passport from his Fleet Cloak and handed it to the woman, who shined a flashlight on it, then passed it open to a second Bear who had joined her at the side of the troika. This individual—a male in basically the same black uniform—studied the passport under the light, then ran a handheld scanner over portions of it. Moments later, the device emitted a series of chirps and both Bears came to immediate attention, saluting rigidly. "Admiral Brim," the woman said. "We are to deliver you to the Winter Palace immediately."

Brim returned the salute without coming to his feet. "On whose orders?" he demanded; Avalonians weren't accustomed to such ministrations in the middle of the night.

"We have not been supplied with such information," the female replied.

"On what charges, then?" he asked.

"We have only been instructed to take you to the Winter Palace," the female said. "We know nothing else."

"Well, you'd better damned well know how to contact the Avalonian Embassy," Brim bluffed. "Or I'm not going anywhere with you." He turned to the *yamshchik*. "Take us back to Gromcow—where you picked me up," he demanded. "Now."

"Sadly, I cannot do that," the *yamshchik* replied.

"And why not?"

"These police would kill me."

"Is right," the male Bear assured Brim, nodding politely. "We would kill him."

"I see," Brim said—so much for *that* bluff. He glanced at Tissuard, who suddenly had a concerned look on her face. Then he returned his gaze to the female. "What is to become of my companion, here," he demanded, "—should I decide to accept this outrage without a fight, that is?"

The female shrugged. "Either way, Commander Tissuard is free to do as she pleases," she said. "The skimmer I have summoned will return her to *Nord* or wherever else she may want to be driven. Or, as she chooses, she may remain with the troika. It is only you, Admiral, who is summoned to the Winter Palace." She shrugged. " 'Crag wolves must slide on ice during full moon,' as they say."

Brim looked at Tissuard and relaxed slightly as a wave of relief swept him. "Sounds as if *you're* all right, anyway, Number One," he said. "They even know who you are. And they certainly can't be taking me in for anything too bad if they're offering free rides back to your ship. They haven't even pulled a blaster—at least one I can see."

Tissuard nodded. "Yeah, I caught that," she said. She glanced around the snowy landscape. "Weird place, this Sodeskaya," she sighed.

"To us, yeah," he agreed quietly. "But it's got a lot going for it, too. These are good people here. Their minds simply don't work exactly the way ours do. Besides that," he added, "it doesn't look as if I have much of a choice about things."

"I don't thraggling *believe* this," Tissuard grumbled after a pause. "Last time we got together, you were so damned tired I thought you were going to pitch over on your face. This time, it's the xaxtdamned Secret Police. What's next, I wonder, Skipper?"

"Maybe the real thing," Brim said, reaching inside the quilt to take her hand. "At least we got, er, *connected* tonight. Next time, maybe we'll get to finish."

She grinned. "I'll look forward to that, er, *connection,* Skipper," she laughed, "—taking care of myself afterward *is* getting a little old." Reaching into her kit bag, she brought out a roll of credits and peeled off a fat wad that she handed to the delighted *yamshchik.*

Brim watched the Bear's eyes light up and grinned. "I guess it you're going to take the Police up on their offer of a lift."

"Yeah," Tissuard said. "Somehow, without you in the back seat with me, that troika doesn't look even *half* so romantic."

"Nice to know that," Brim remarked. "Sorry about all this."

Tissuard smiled. "You shouldn't be," she said. "You don't seem to have much control over things at all."

"Probably we should be on our way," the officer interjected, politely looking off in the distance. "Not good idea to keep Palace people waiting."

"In a cycle," Brim said. He turned to Tissuard and grimaced. "Well . . ." he stumbled.

"Well," she answered, tilting her head with a little grin. "Next time, maybe we finish."

"No maybes about next time," Brim said as the *yamshchik* snapped his whip and the three big droshkats padded off in a flurry of miniature bells. He squeezed her hand. "Next time for sure," he said.

"Your turn to buy the troika ride, then." She chuckled.

"Next time, perhaps we ought to try something a little more solid," he suggested, "like a hotel." Then he smiled and took her in his arms. "Just in case it slips your mind," he whispered, bussing her soundly, "I've waited a long time for you."

"I'm not likely to forget, Wilf Brim," she assured him. "You're not the only one who's been waiting." With that, she stepped back. "Let me know what the thraggling Knez wants," she said. "I can't imagine he's the kind of Bear who gets his kicks from spoiling other people's fun."

Brim laughed, handing her into the back seat of the skimmer. "Somehow, I doubt if either one of us is *that* important," he said.

"Well," she said, "go find out."

"I'll do that," Brim assured her. "It's the first thing I'll ask." With that, he shut the door and stood back as the skimmer glided forward . . . then came to a sudden stop no more than twenty irals from where it had started. Brim watched the passenger window slide open into the roof.

"Next time for *sure,* Skipper!" Tissuard shouted, leaning halfway out into the cold air.

Brim waved. "For *sure,* Number One," he shouted. Then, moments later, she was gone, and he was on his way to the Great Winter Palace.

Little more than half a metacycle later, Brim's skimmer paused for identification at a riverfront tradesman's gate—he was clearly expected—then glided onto the grounds of the Winter Palace and came to a halt beneath a portico sheltering what appeared to be an entrance to the Royal kitchens. An Army limousine skimmer also hovered at the curb nearby. Instantly, two huge guards with crimson uniforms, tall, woolly hats—and absolutely massive-looking versions of the famous Sodeskayan Khalodni N-37 blast pikes—opened his passenger compartment door with a veritable storm of cold air and blown snow. "Admiral Brim," one requested with a polite bow, "this way, please."

Brim—who by now had time to reflect on all he had just missed with Tissuard—was about to vent his spleen when he shook his head. These soldiers had nothing to do with it. "All right," he said, resigned to whatever Lady Fate had in store. "Lead on."

Ursis was waiting inside the foyer, looking very confused.

"Hmm" Brim said. "Somehow I *thought* you might be tied up in all of this."

"Not this time, Wilfooshka," the Bear protested. "I know nothing about anything." He frowned. "*Especially* when you visit with Captain Tissuard, old friend. You need all . . . shall we say . . . relaxation you can find on planet of mostly Bears."

Brim relented. "Sorry, old friend," he said. "I guess I'm a bit . . . well . . ."

Ursis was about to reply when a servant grandly dressed in the crimson-and-gold uniform of a Palace Majordomo appeared at one of the doors. "General Ursis, Admiral Brim, you will please follow me," he said with a deep bow.

Brim glanced at Ursis and shrugged, then turned and followed the servant into a long, narrow hallway of ancient-looking plaster scraped and scarred by an eon of passing delivery carts. Escorted by still another crimson-uniformed guard behind them—his Khalodni at the ready—they marched rapidly along a row of noisy kitchens until the corridor widened into a sort of heated gallery, filled with the spicy odors of cooking food. Turning to the right, they passed hosts of cooks drenched by runnels of sweat, butchers in blood-soaked aprons (one who was clearly in an advanced state of pregnancy), and what looked like a whole army of menials wearing the costumes of at least a dozen different guilds. At length, they came to a flight of narrow stone steps that curved upward through a rounded stone archway.

"This way, please," the Majordomo directed, and led the way upward until they reached a small landing that faced a massive double door. The Majordomo gestured for them to stop, then touched a glowing red panel on the wall. "A moment," he whispered sotto voce.

"What's in there?" Brim demanded.

"Sh-h-h," the Majordomo hissed. At that moment, the touch panel changed from red to green and he nodded to himself. "Please to stand clear," he said, pressing an Auto-Latch panel beside the doorframe. Slowly, almost majestically, the massive doors opened inward on silent hinges to reveal a chamber bathed in soft light. As the four stepped from their Spartan servant's passage, Brim noticed first an odor of fresh carpeting—then flowers! There were vases of flowers everywhere. In the center of the large, oblong room, two lavishly outfitted Bears were standing at a flower-bedecked table, their backs to the door. Above them, a giant, glowing fresco glorified the existence of some legendary Sodeskayan who, by the look of his clothing, must have lived in the *very* early days of spaceflight. The spacious canopy was divided into sections by simulated paint and plaster architecture that merged almost imperceptibly onto a colossal trompe l'oeil portrait of an unbounded firmament, viewed from below. Winged, Bearlike beings with a few humans thrown in roamed the allegorical skyscape, some appearing to spill dramatically over a rimming cornice, where they continued as sculpted figures. As Brim stepped into the room, both occupants turned to face the doorway: Grand Duke Borodov and his older brother, Nikolai the Twenty-first, Knez of all the Sodeskayas and Supreme Marshal of the Grand Federation of Sodeskayan States. Ursis and the escorts immediately knelt on one knee as the two approached. Brim stood his ground, waiting. . . .

The Knez said something in a casual tone while lackadaisically inspecting a fingernail.

Instantly, the guard and Majordomo lit out through the doors as if death stalked their every move. At the same time, Ursis rose watchfully to his feet.

After a moment the Knez nodded. "Welcome to Our modest study," he said in perfect unaccented Avalonian. "I trust We have not inconvenienced you too much this evening—although, Admiral Brim, I suspect . . ." he pursed his lips and opened his hands, "the Police may have interrupted *you* at a delicate moment."

Brim thought quickly. "When in Sodeskaya, one is never too busy for the Knez," he replied, swallowing a quick up-rush of anger.

"An excellent answer, Admiral," the Knez said with a lit-tle smile. "We shall remember that generosity and attempt to make amends." He nodded in the direction of a servant standing almost invisibly at the far end of the room, then winked at Borodov. "Perhaps we should sit," he said, mov-ing toward an ornate, marble-topped table decorated by a squat vase of exquisite flowers. "Anastas Alexi here feels that the two of you may have some insight on the present state of our war."

As they walked across the room, Brim noticed an athletic, almost nervous spring in the Bear's stride—here was a ruler who kept himself in trim. He chuckled to himself. Consider-ing the number of lavish state suppers a Knez could expect to attend during the year, a great deal of strenuous exercise would be a necessary part of life!

Nikolai took his place at a large, high-backed chair on one side of the table while Borodov, Ursis, and Brim sat opposite in smaller but very comfortable copies of the original.

Borodov broke the silence. "Nikolai Yanuarievich," he began soberly to Ursis, "Knez Nikolai Borovitskaya desires to hear results of our discussions on war." He stopped for a moment, as if considering his next words. "And, Wilf Ansor," he continued at length, "our conversations will be in Avalonian, so you can be part of them. Later, it will help if you share some of the weekly confidences you KA'PPA to General Drummond and Emperor Onrad—although you must suit yourself on *that* matter. What Knez most urgently desires is to learn why we are . . . er . . . *not winning* this war."

"Especially when our Sodeskayan Ground Army appears to be the best-equipped and -trained in the known Universe," the Knez added dryly, peering directly at Ursis. "Brother

Anastas Alexi has demanded that We ask your opinion, so We shall. Why do We not seem to be winning this war?"

Brim watched Ursis and Borodov exchange glances; the latter gave a little nod. Ursis took a deep breath and closed his eyes as if considering a life-or-death decision—which, on consideration, it probably was. "You are *not* winning this war, Your majesty," Ursis said. "You are, in fact, rapidly *losing* it."

"Treason!" the Knez exclaimed, hair standing erect on the nape of his neck.

"Brother Nikolai Kakhovskaya," Borodov interposed in a calm voice, "you will please keep in mind these persons are *my* guests—and therefore guests of your personal family. They speak the truth as they see it—and believe me, they have seen the truth."

The Knez tapped the toe of his boot noisily. "Very well," he relented. "Tell Us, then, General Ursis, how can we be losing when we have the best-equipped and trained Army in the known Universe? Especially since you have conveniently done away with the League's most talented commander."

"Our armies probably *are* the best equipped and trained in known Universe, Your Highness," Ursis said, leaning forward in his chair. "And yes, Marshal *nov* Vobok is dead, but he is only *recently* dead, and his policies are still in effect as if he were alive." He paused to think. "Only time will tell if our stroke of fortune will bear fruit. Nergol Triannic has many other talented officers from which to select a replacement. And who knows, the next may prove to be even *better* than his predecessor. But . . ."

"But *why are we losing presently,* General?" the Knez demanded sharply. "Our most trusted advisors tell Us that nothing is so important as our Army." He crossed his arms over his chest. "And," he added, "Our own training at the famed Sodeskayan Military Academy lends credence to this."

Ursis thought for another long moment. "What evidence do these advisors give you to prove such an idea, Your Majesty?" he asked.

"Evidence?" the Knez demanded in a reproving voice.

"Yes, Your Majesty. Surely they have provided you with recorded reports from front that show their . . . ah . . . theories in action." Ursis replied.

"They have," the Knez said with a frown. "They *do*. We personally see three and four HoloGrams a week boasting of great victories in the field—armies of Sodeskayan crawlers smashing the demon Leaguers and taking them prisoners." He threw up his hands angrily. "Yet brother Anastas Alexi tells me we lose new planets and star systems each day. How can this be?"

"Only, Your Majesty, when our armies are destroyed in the field," Ursis said.

"They are *not* destroyed!" the Knez protested. "We look at *all* the reports We get, and We see only victories." He frowned angrily. " 'Only most witless of Bear cubs bite crag wolves on tail,' as they say."

"Clearly, Your Majesty," Ursis said placatingly. "But perhaps these advisors of yours are something less than truthful. . . ."

"Anastas Alexi," the Knez warned, "your guest will speak respectfully when he mentions the members of Our Inner Court. They would never lie to us. They are lifelong friends—from the Academy."

"Brother Nikolai Borovitskaya," Borodov said quietly. "General Ursis did *not* use the word *lie*—you did. And perhaps the word *lie* is too strong. Perhaps . . ." He shrugged and waved a hand. "Let us not at this juncture spend too much time defining *truth*. For now, permit General Ursis to continue."

The Knez continued to glower angrily, but nodded assent.

"Thank you, Your Majesty," Ursis said in a somehow steady voice.

Brim wondered how steady his friend felt inside.

"I must beg Your Majesty's indulgence for a moment," Ursis continued, settling back into his chair. "Answer this, if you will. What kind of logic permits armies to win surface battles while losing planets and whole star systems?"

"Only Our troublesome brother tells me we are losing planets and star systems," the Knez grumbled.

"But for the moment, you will consider it as . . . a *theory*, perhaps?" interjected Borodov. " 'Not winning' is not all that far from 'losing,' is it?"

The Knez considered this in silence, then nodded his head almost angrily. "All right," he said. "For the moment, it is not."

Ursis nodded. "Once again, then, what kind of logic permits armies to win surface battles and yet lose planets and whole star systms?"

"Under those circumstances, no kind of logic," the Knez allowed. "Yet even military assessors in Avalon have called our armies invincible on the ground." He glanced for a moment at Brim. "Is that not so?" he demanded.

"It is, Your Majesty," Brim assured him, "but—"

The Knez interrupted as if Brim had suddenly exited the room. "There, General Ursis," he said. "Is *his* a word that you trust?"

"Yes, Your Majesty," Ursis said, clearly wrestling his own temper now. He glanced again at Borodov, who rolled his eyes toward the baroque ceiling. Suddenly he seemed to have an idea. "One would think, Your majesty," he began, "that if we were 'not losing' this war, then things would be in a stalemated condition and reports from the 'front' would be arriving from more or less the same distances away. Is that not so?"

The Knez considered only a moment. "That makes sense," he said.

"Good," Ursis replied. "Then I shall leave it to Your Majesty to check the planetary coordinates included with the reports you have received so far—you may be surprised where they come from." He paused a moment in thought, then nodded. "After that," he continued, "assuming that Your Majesty may become concerned as we are about the progress of the war, you may wish to consider what it might be that would prevent a normally invincible Army from winning victories."

The Knez frowned, obviously displeased with the way things were going, but nodded anyway—with ill-concealed discomfort. "Yes," he conceded, "We *might* wish to consider such an *academic* subject, were We concerned."

"Thank you, Your Majesty," Ursis said with just a hint of relief in his gruff voice. "In that case," he said turning to Brim, "I shall ask the Admiral here to provide your explanation."

Instantly—and *unexpectedly*—galvanized, Brim looked at Ursis, then swallowed a huge lump that had mysteriously appeared in his throat. "Ah . . ." he stammered, "what would prevent a normally . . ."

". . . invincible Army from winning victories?" the Knez finished for him. "You are the space expert. Go on. . . ."

Well, Brim considered, wryly, that *was,* after all, what his assignment was all about. Taking a deep breath, he looked up to confront the Knez's stony gaze. "It's all pretty simple, Your Majesty," he began. "No matter how well equipped or brave your armies may be, neither Bear nor land crawler alone can stall the League ground forces when they fight in concert with Hoth Orgoth's superb Deep Space Fleet. Your soldiers must have protection—as well as fire support—from space to be effective. Only a combination of forces can win, and higher priority must be given to both the production *and* application of offensive space forces. I saw a good example during the maneuvers in Vorkuta that you yourself attended only a few weeks ago. . . ."

Brim held center floor for nearly half a metacycle before the Knez appeared to run out of questions.

"Enough for today, Admiral," he said, holding up his bejeweled hand after a period of thoughtful silence. "You have given Us much to think about." He turned his baleful gaze to Ursis. "Do you have anything to add, General?" he demanded—almost petulantly, as if the Bear had caused him great personal trouble.

"Only to thank Your Highness for giving ear to this *most* critical matter," Ursis declared, bravely matching his Monarch's steely grin with his own.

The Knez nodded, then suddenly turned to Borodov. "So , Anastas Alexi," he growled, "this is why you have been plaguing Our hours for the past year?"

"*More* than year, Nikolai Borovitskaya," Borodov corrected.

"Yes. Yes. You need not remind us," the Knez growled. "And General Ursis—you feel as if we are not winning this war. Correct?"

"No, Your Majesty," Ursis said soberly. "I stated emphatically that we are *losing* this war. And," he added, "should we continue on this trend, some predictions indicate that League forces could be at gates of Gromcow, so to speak, within a Standard Year."

The Knez clenched the arms of his chair again, clearly struggling with Ursis's words. He growled something in Sodeskayan with a menacing voice.

"You will please remember your promise to speak only in Avalonian, Nikolai Borovitskaya," Borodov said.

"We said that your friend General Ursis has little trouble speaking his mind," the Knez grumbled, glowering.

"Is not literal translation," Borodov explained to Brim, "but much nicer than original."

Again the room lapsed into silence as the Knez rested his chin on a six-fingered hand and pondered, staring at the perfectly lacquered surface of the table. At last he looked up and looked grimly at each of his three visitors. "You have not made Us happy this morning," he growled.

"We had no intention of making you happy, Nikolai Borovitskaya," Borodov replied.

"You will allow Us to finish, Anastas Alexi," the Knez said reprovingly.

Borodov kept his silence, but made no apology.

"As We stated," the Knez continued, "none of you has much pleased Us this morning. In fact, you have raised great ire." He paused, staring idly at the baroque ceiling. "But," he continued at length, "if nothing else, We commend you on your audacity—even *you,* brother Alexi Anastas. Generally, it is difficult for one with such power as We possess to feel certain he is hearing truth. Often We suspect We are hearing what people think We *want* to hear." He chuckled darkly. "We have no such suspicions with you three." Pursing his lips, he thought for another moment or two, then sat back and opened his hands. "The audience is finished."

"Thank you, Nikolai Borovitskaya," Borodov said, getting to his feet. He and Ursis bowed while Brim saluted.

Immediately, their crimson-uniformed Majordomo appeared at the table.

"You will escort these two back the way you brought them," the Knez ordered, nodding to Brim and Ursis.

Borodov laughed. "Brother Nikolai Borovitskaya is not showing either of you discourtesy," he explained. "Is for your own good. Many in Court would, shall we say, *intrigue* against you, if they knew of your presence here. I assume you understand."

Ursis nodded and turned to Brim. "As I mentioned," he

whispered, "*perceived* enemies of certain Court members have ... disappeared, shall we say?"

"You mentioned something like that." Brim replied with a shudder. "Kitchen doors are fine with me."

At that moment, the Knez's voice boomed out. "One moment, gentlemen," he commanded.

Brim turned to observe that the Bear was now standing before the table.

"*Spasee'bah*," he said simply, then turned and strode through the front door.

Brim glanced at Borodov, who was now standing with an astounded look on his face. So was Ursis.

"By all crag wolves," the older Bear whispered.

"By *all* crag wolves and stone spiders," Ursis added. "Did I hear that correctly?"

Borodov nodded and smiled as he turned to leave. "You did, my friend," he said. "That is one for the records. . . ."

Shaking his head in wonder, Ursis signaled the Majordomo to lead, then motioned Brim to follow.

"What'd he *say*?" Brim asked as the three wound their way down the stone staricase.

"Oh, yes." Ursis chuckled. "I was so surprised—no, *astounded*—I completely forgot about you. Sorry."

"It's all right," Brim replied. "But what was it he said that so surprised you?"

"He said, 'Thank you,' " Ursis replied—almost as if he still didn't believe his own words. "The Knez said, 'Thank you.' "

"What's so strange about that?" Brim asked. His own Emperor Onrad V would certainly have said something like that at the end of such a meeting.

"Such words are not in the vocabulary of a Knez," Ursis explained. "I for one have *never* heard the words used by either of the Knez who have reigned in my lifetime. And clearly, neither had Anastas Alexi—who is the Knez's *brother*."

"Looks as if we got through to him, then," Brim suggested.

"It is to be hoped." Ursis sighed as they started down the long hallway with its eternal odors of cooking. "Otherwise, I fear that these basements will witness a great deal more slaughter than ever envisioned—and much of the killing will be for *pelts*."

That evening, as the three friends relaxed before a roaring fire in Borodov's manor house, Barbousse appeared at the study door with a folded slip of plastic in his hand and pointed to Brim.

It was a message form, and from its green color, Brim could tell it had come through military channels with no classification attached. "I'll take it here," he said.

"Thought you'd want to read this yourself," the big rating said with a little smile. "Came through military channels, but it was marked personal."

As Ursis and Borodov continued their discussion of the previous events, Brim opened the form and began to read:

TA-SAKMN;0975098 JR WER821 197/52013
[UNCLASSIFIED]

FROM:
N. TISSUARD, COMMANDER, I.F.
I.F.S. NORD, UNDER WAY

TO:
W.A. BRIM, ADMIRAL, I.F.
IMPERIAL EMBASSY, BROMCOW, G.F.S.S

<09538-3085>

SUBJECT:

PERSONAL TRANSMISSION

(1) GREAT PLEASURE CONFERRING WITH YOU
LAST EVENING. LOOK FORWARD TO NEXT
CONFERENCE SOONEST.
(2) AM STILL UNDECIDED IF ANGRY OR SIMPLY
INCREDULOUS. DISAPPOINTMENT VERIFIED.
(3) PLEASE EXTEND PERSONAL THANKS TO
KNEZ NIKOLAI (THE TWENTY-FIRST, KNEZ OF
ALL THE SODESKAYAS AND SUPREME
MARSHAL OF THE GRAND FEDERATION OF
SODESKAYAN STATES, ETC., ETC.) FOR
GORGEOUS BOUQUET OF FRESH-CUT FLOWERS
DELIVERED BY FAST STARSHIP SHORTLY
AFTER NORD UNDER WAY.
(4) SOONER OR LATER!

SIGNED:
"NUMBER ONE"

[END OF UNCLASSIFIED]
TA-SAKMN;0975098 JR WER821

In the course of the next four Standard Weeks, Brim—
wearing no military rank on his Imperial battlesuit—suffered
endless metacycles in a remote space-combat school training
for a war he had been fighting more than three years. Only a
spirited exchange of short KA'PPA messages with Marsha
Browning made time pass with even a semblance of its normal regularity. At last, however, he "graduated" from the
preliminary portions of the course, having passed the various
systems examinations close to the top of his class, and
moved on.

However, more than half a Standard Year had passed since
he had flown a starship in any kind of combat situation, and
he soon discovered how rapidly one could become rusty.

Fortunately, for the flying phase he and three other "students" were assigned to Captain Fili Kievskaya, a gentle and unassuming Bear who could fly beautifully and went to great lengths to foster a spirit with his pupils. Busy as he was, Kievskaya could always find time to explain a tricky point. When he and Brim strode across the brow at the end of a period of dual instruction, he would retrace the pattern of the flight and make certain that various lessons on the ZBL-4's idiosyncrasies—"features," he laughingly called them—were driven home.

After at least ten million years, the day finally arrived when Brim got to fly one of the little ships with no one but the crew and a graduating student in the right seat who could more or less make herself understood in Avalonian. As usual, Kievskaya sat with him at the checkout console while he guided an analog on an exterior inspection of the ship, drab in its war coat of matte black. Afterward, the Bear stood at the end of the brow to render assurance. "Somehow," he said, "I have this feeling that you could teach *me* a thing or two about flying starships."

Brim clapped him on the shoulder, knowing the instructor's frustration at the way the war was going for him personally. Students came and went, but the instructors remained, training batch after batch of beginners with little hope of ever seeing real action. Some of the sharper politicians among them eventually pestered their way to combat operations, but not many—and the better instructors remained anchored firmly in place. "Perhaps with a little practice, I *could* teach you about Starfuries," he replied, "but not this beauty. Here, you are the master."

"Thank you, my friend," the Sodeskayan said, "now go fly without me. Like mother bird, I push you from nest. Don't forget to trim ship *before* you leave the dock; otherwise, you make fool out of yourself—and me as instructor." He grinned. "Good luck!" With that, he ambled off down the brow with a nonchalant air, but Brim knew he would watch both the undocking and the docking with an instructor's critical eye.

Only eight days after his solo, Brim broke all records for graduating in a short length of time. During those few days, however, he spent all his time drilling in the maneuverable little ships, but was never given an opportunity to fire the fixed disruptors in the nose. This would come later, he was told—if time remained for advanced training. The first squadrons of ZBL-4s were just beginning to reach the battle front, and—depending on the availability of crews—even raw graduates could find useful employment around the clock. During Brim's abbreviated stay at school, the war had again turned worse for the Sodeskayan cause—if that were possible—and able-bodied Helmsmen were desperately needed at the front, along with every modern deep-space warship that would fly.

Shortly after Brim received his duly signed, official "Combat Certification" (he had to trust what was printed on the certificate; he couldn't read a word), he was temporarily assigned as a relief Helmsman to Regiment 31 of the 19th Space Division defending portions of the Novogireyevo star cluster. This time, he traveled to the front in one of Sodeskaya's swift new QF-2 light bombardment starships, arriving at his destination, the mining planet Govgod, safely and even a few metacycles ahead of schedule. It had been a long while since he'd crossed swords with a Leaguer Helmsman, and after reading a few reports from occupied Sodeskayan planets, he was fairly spoiling for a fight. Less than two days later, he got his wish.

He flew his first combat mission as replacement for a ZBL-4 Helmsman who had fractured her leg the previous evening at the local officer's mess—clear indication of frontline meem consumption. Rousted out before dawn, Brim reported to the flight line of "Govgod Station," a row of some forty-odd buoys tossing on a nearby lake kept ice-free by braces of hardworking portable reactors. The starship, an older "B" model, had just come off the maintenance list and appeared to be in excellent condition, although a number of odd-shaped patches on her hull indicated she had seen serious action since arriving at the battle zone two weeks previously. Gunnery Officer for the mission was a smallish Bear named Kalinin from the distant Krasniye Vorota star cluster; the Communications Officer, an ex-farmer named Nakhimovsky from Begovaya in the Filevsky Sector. The remainder of the fifty officers and ratings were the usual odd lot one would expect in a killer ship, but averaged some twenty-five missions each. The ship herself had accounted for three Gorn-Hoff 270-A killer ships—confirmed. Brim smiled as he completed his external inspection and garaged the analog. It proved his point: given a modicum of decent equipment, Bears were at least the equal of Leaguers in space.

Two metacycles later, they were patrolling with five other ZBL-4s below LightSpeed off the embattled planet Konkovo when a dozen GH-262s angled in out of the brilliance of a nearby star and were almost within firing range before someone spotted them. Shaped in the form of a double chevron, these Leaguer ships were heavily armed with fourteen super-focused disruptors and extremely dangerous. A voice shouted over the short-range radio, "*Ploschad! Ploschad!*"

"Means 'Break!' Weelf," Kalinin warned in a calm voice.

Brim grinned. He'd picked up a scattering of necessary words in Sodeskayan and was already reefing the ZBL into a tight spiral. After two turns, he was satisfied that no Gorn-Hoff was clinging to their tail and he eased out of the turn. However, immediately ahead of them—little more than a few c'lenyts distant—three of the angular Gorn-Hoffs were tracking on converging paths as if they were being hauled along the sides of a pyramid. At the apex was the exposed belly of a solitary ZBL flying straight and level, and Nakhinovsky was yelling to him from the rear of the flight bridge: *"Ploschad! Ploschad! Ploschad!"*

The message never got through, at least not in time to do any good. In the next instant, the combined fire of the Gorn-Hoffs smashed into the little starship, ripping through the hull like saws through a plank. The aft portion drifted into the ship's wake while the forward half went into a vicious power spin, then exploded in a great roiling puffball of radiation fire and white-hot debris.

The Gorn-Hoffs stayed to fight, and nearby space suddenly became a maelstrom of spinning, jinking starships. It was a dangerous place to be alone, and in the initial break, Brim found himself alone in space. He continued turning, always looking around for the nearest section of ZBLs he could join forces with. Abruptly, a Gorn-Hoff arced up in the Hyperscreens, then rolled onto a reciprocal course. Brim was very close to him and could see the sharp angles of the "wing" tips and the outboard control emitter for the steering engines. Large black daggers were painted on the dirty, gray-black camouflage, and there were orange markings immediately aft of the flight bridge. Brim swung his ZBL to get behind him and grinned in spite of himself. For the millionth time, he heard the words of Baxter Calhoun: "Cut and run—nail him and get out. But CLEAR YOUR TAIL FIRST!"

Nothing but empty space back there. Brim was quickly line astern of the Leaguer and hit him behind the bridge with all six of the big .388 disruptors fixed in the ZBL's nose, blasting debris onto the slipstream and exploding the enemy's Hyperscreens in a whitish stream of atmosphere. As the range closed, he sprayed the Gorn-Hoff with three more short bursts until its Helmsman half rolled onto his back and released a number of LifeGlobes. But the ship was still maneuvering, so somebody remained inside. Brim hammered the ship again and moments later, a last LifeGlobe popped into the ship's wake, just before the stricken ship began to tumble out of control and broke into several pieces, then bloomed into a giant explosion as its power chambers exploded. With the flight crew erupting in gleeful cheers, Brim drove the ZBL around a steep turn and checked his tail again. The combat had perhaps lasted all of several clicks; a great deal could have happened in that very brief time, and even the best proximity warning device could be blinded by one's own Drive plume. Nevertheless, nearby space appeared to have become empty of starships, and it stayed that way for the remainder of his patrol. Eventually he set course for Govgod, making landfall within the metacycle. Several other crews at the station had seen his Gorn-Hoff explode, so his first kill as a Sodeskayan was easily confirmed.

The resulting celebration for the "Furless Imperial" who had destroyed a Gorn-Hoff on his first mission lasted well into the next morning, and Brim set off on his second sortie with a headache that would stop even a Bear. He didn't score again until his third mission—after which the war took an abrupt and totally unexpected turn.

Aloft on his forth sortie, Brim cautiously led a flight of eight ZBLs into one of the most hotly contested sectors of the battle zone—only to find the whole area puzzlingly empty, at least of Leaguers looking for a scrap. Where were they? A quick overflight of the nearest enemy bases proved that Hoth Orgoth's powerful Deep Space Fleet was still present in force. The ZBLs were greeted by a tremendous barrage of defensive, ground-based fire—and were immediately attacked by what appeared to be a whole squadron of Gorn-Hoffs patrolling nearby space. But none of the Leaguers gave chase any farther than a few hundred thousand c'lenyts from the planets they protected.

Nor were Leaguer ground forces much in evidence at the

battle zones. Speeding to three of the most fiercely contested planets—where armies had clashed violently on the previous day—Brim found only confused Sodeskayans waving from the ground as the eight ZBLs swept overhead. Ordering Nakhimovsky to call up the latest battle reports, he learned that the Leaguers had simply abandoned every planet that was not yet subdued. The evacuations had gone so smoothly, it was almost certain that plans had been under way for Standard Weeks at least.

More probes of a few planets the Leaguers had formerly secured resulted in the same vigorous defensive activity, with great numbers of Gorn-Hoff and Gantheisser killer ships patrolling the new territories. If nothing else, *they* made it abundantly clear that the Leaguers had no immediate plans to go home. When Brim finally led his little flight back to Govgod Station, he made landfall in total bemusement, taxiing up to a buoy and mooring the ship while his mind flitted among a thousand possibilities, each more outlandish than the last. Whatever else was going on in the Universe, it looked very much as if Nergol Triannic had just brought his war to a halt.

While Brim was debriefing in the Operations building, a rickety shed left over from some long-played-out mine, a KA'PPA message arrived for him. It was of sufficient priority to silence even a Sodeskayan Intelligence Officer.

JK86QWH5F3257CH157 Q75FN1I 105 247/52013
[TOP SECRET]

FROM:
J.G. NELSON, ASSISTANT AMBASSADOR
IMPERIAL EMBASSY, GROMCOW, G.F.S.S.

TO:
W.A. BRIM, ADMIRAL, I.F.
GOVGOD STATION, GOVGOD, G.F.S.S

<N2375N348VNR>

SUBJECT:
MESSAGE FROM GENERAL URSIS

(1) N.Y. URSIS, COLONEL-GENERAL, G.F.S.S.
ENGINEERS, REQUESTS FORWARDING THIS
MESSAGE BY IMPERIAL COMM BECAUSE OF
CLASSIFICATION/TRANSLATION PROBLEMS
WITH SODESKAYAN MEANS
(2) IMPERIAL SHIP WILL ARRIVE GOVGOD
STATION NEXT SIX METACYCLES RETURN YOU
PLUS LATEST INTELLIGENCE TO GROMCOW.
(3) BE PREPARED TO BRIEF ABOUT WHAT YOU
HAVE SEEN FIRSTHAND.
(4) CONGRATULATIONS ON GORN-HOFF!

SIGNED:
"NIK"

[END OF TOP SECRET]
JK86QWH5F3257CH157 Q75N1I 105

Somehow the message came as no surprise. Since his arrival in Sodeskaya, he'd rarely unpacked his bags for more than a few days—and at least for the present could see no promise for change at all. Little more than six metacycles later, he'd KA'PPAed off a short note to Marsha Browning's office and was on his way back to Gromcow in what was rapidly shaping up as the damndest war in history.

CHAPTER 7
Marshal of the G.F.S.S.

Both Ursis and Borodov—with a small detachment of well-armed guards—were waiting outside Tomoshenko's Military Arrivals Terminal as Brim's packet coasted to a stop above a Becton tube, then taxied to a gravity pad on the short-term parking ramp. Its hull was still pinging from the heat of reentry when Brim saluted a hurried good-bye to his Helmsman, then hurried down the boarding stairs, snowflakes biting his face. "Voot's beard, Nik," he said, grasping the Bears' outthrust hands, "does it ever stop snowing in these parts?"

"Rarely snows in summer," Borodov said with mock defensiveness.

"True," Ursis observed. "Unfortunately, last year, I slept late one morning and missed whole season." He winked at Brim. "One needs much fur to *really* appreciate Sodeskayan climate."

"You brought intelligence data?" Borodov asked.

"In the passenger cabin," Brim said. "I got the base commander to send out a recon ship right after your message came. Everything's in the orange box."

Ursis nodded to one of the guards, who bounded inside the little starship and returned a moment later lugging a bright orange diplomatic pouch. "You know where to take it," he said to the guard, who saluted, then marched off surrounded by his eight companions.

"All right, friends," Brim said as they walked through the snow to Borodov's great Roshov limousine, "you Sodeskayans have the best intelligence capability in the known Universe, so just what's going on with the Leaguers?" He laughed. "You think maybe *nov* Vobok's untimely demise spooked Triannic, or something?"

Borodov frowned as his chauffeur opened the passenger compartment. "Our intelligence is *never* capable enough," he said with a dark chuckle. "But sufficiently expert to make few educated guesses, and—surprisingly enough—we think Nikolai Yanuarievich's little temper tantrum may *well* have borne unexpected results."

"You're serious?" Brim asked.

"Completely," Borodov answered. "*Nov* Vobok was a *very* influential man in the League High Command. Much power!"

"So what's the story?" Brim demanded. "How come everything's stopped out there?"

Once the doors were shut, Ursis settled back in the deeply cushioned seat and pursed his lips. "Where to start, Wilfooshka?" he mused with a frown. "What we hear stretches credibility long way."

"Yeah," Brim agreed, "what I *saw* did some serious credibility stretching, too. What's behind it all?"

"From what we can piece together," Ursis said presently, "Nergol Triannic *himself* is the main force behind the whole thing."

"Triannic?"

Borodov nodded. "He acts over strong vocal protests of High Command," he added. "Hoth Orgoth, Admiral Kabul Anak, Zoguard Groberman, even Hanna Notrom—all dead set against delay in war, but he overrode. He *is* Supreme Commander, after all."

"But for Voot's sake, why would he want to do a thing like that?" Brim demanded. "Triannic's no fool."

"Title of Emperor does not guarantee reliable brain at *all* times," Ursis interjected.

"Is true." Borodov chuckled. "He *did* have reasons, right or wrong."

"And?" Brim prompted.

"And," Borodov replied with a shrug, "it seems as if he has been getting cold feet since just after campaign began. No matter how well things seem to be going for him, this invasion of Sodeskaya is biggest project he's ever attempted. He *knows* what will happen if he loses." He drew a finger slowly across his neck. "Voof. . . ."

"According to our sources," Ursis continued—returning the salute of a guard at Tomoshenko's huge main gate— "about two weeks ago, he started demanding they consolidate their flanks and send additional forces to beef up the occupation." He laughed darkly as the Roshov glided forward again and onto the wintry expressway that led to the Gromcow city center. "Marshal *nov* Vobok was only one on General Staff with guts enough to disagree and make it stick." He shrugged phlegmatically. "Now he is dead—killed by the merest chance," he said, staring for a moment at his hands. "Sometimes it seems as if the Universe watches out for Bears and other fools. Sodeskaya must make the most of this blessing."

Brim nodded. "May be a good time to move some new equipment to the front—if it's available. We did a lot of damage out there when we had the right weapons to fight with—like the ZBL I was flying. Get a few squadrons of

those and some JM-2 Ro'stoviks in action, and the Leaguers'll soon know what kind of a mistake they made."

Borodov nodded. "Is so, Wilfooshka," he agreed. "And we
shall do such things—believe me; processes are already
under way. . . . Before he could continue, however he was interrupted by the footman, who began rapping on the glass
that separated the passenger compartment from the Roshov's
driving compartment.

Borodov's eyebrows momentarily rose. Clearly, such im-
position was rare among the manor's entourage. With a
frown, the Grand Duke touched a small glowing panel set in
the rich, wooden window frame, then nodded.

Immediately the footman began a rapid discussion in
Sodeskayan, his face a study in anxiety. At the same time, the
chauffeur accelerated their massive Roshov to a tremendous
speed, maneuvering in and out of traffic with deceptive agility.

Soon it was Borodov—then Ursis—who wore looks of
concern. When the servant was finished, the older Bear
touched the glowing panel again, then glanced at Brim.
"Wilf Ansor," he said with a serious look, "you will probably be greatly affected by whatever the outcome of this mo-
mentous news."

Brim felt a pang of apprehension. What could have occurred that unnerved such normally unflappable Bears? "I'm
all ears," he said.

"Whole High Command," Borodov began, still clearly be-
mused, "—they have *all* been dismissed—*personally,* by
Knez. Looks like greatest purge of military in recent history.
And now Nikolai Yanuarievich has just been summoned to
Winter Palace—immediately."

Brim frowned, only half aware of the snow-covered fields,
dachas, and farm-related outbuildings passing by at a terrific
rate. "What do you suppose *that's* all about?" he mused aloud.

"I have no idea," Ursis said in a calm, flat voice as he absently drew a great Zempa pipe from his cape and began to

puff. After a few moments, he turned and grinned impassively at Borodov. "Well, Anastas Alexi," he said, "I may *now* have cause to regret presenting so much painful truth to your brother."

Borodov frowned as Ursis's Zempa pipe plunged the air-conditioning system into overdrive. "I *had* thought about that," he mused.

"Too late to do much about it now," Ursis mused, again staring out the window.

"You will not go in alone, Nikolai Yanuarievich," Borodov growled in a low voice. "We have confronted danger together for . . . what? . . . thirty Standard Years now?"

"More than that, old friend," Ursis replied. "But I am adult Bear and able to face consequences of my own actions." He grinned and thumped Borodov on the arm. "Who knows? Perhaps he is about to promote me."

"Promotion or something not so nice as promotion," Borodov rumbled. "I go along with you, and no amount of complaining will sway me to do otherwise."

"Pigheaded aristocrat," Ursis grumbled.

"Stubborn militarist," Borodov answered back with a grin. He looked at Brim. "Wilf, will you wait for us, or shall I have chauffeur take you to manor?"

"I'll wait," Brim said without hesitation. "How could I do anything else? But perhaps I should make a call to Barbousse about this. He often has information that's impossible to get elsewhere."

Borodov turned. "Barbousse?" he roared. "Who do you think sent message to our footman in the first place? Knez has no idea where to find us at present time. . . ."

Dog tired from his long return trip to Gromcow, Brim was fast asleep in the waiting Roshov when Borodov returned—alone. Shaking his head to ward off the debilitating weakness of half-finished sleep, he sat bolt upright, shivering from the blast of cold air that entered along with the limousine's owner. "Where's Nik?" he demanded.

Borodov shook his head and plopped into the seat as if he were a thousand years old. "You will never believe," he mumbled, looking bleakly at his hands as if he had only just become aware of their existence.

"Believe *what*?" Brim demanded, suddenly fearful for his old friend Ursis. "What's happened? Is Nik all right?"

Borodov adjusted his spectacles for a moment, then looked at Brim and smiled. "Physically," he began, "Nikolai Yanuarievich is 'all right,' as you put it. . . ."

"*But?*"

"After what has happened to him, I am not certain that *he* thinks so."

"Dr. Borodov," Brim demanded in exasperation, "what's *happened* to him?"

"He has been promoted," Borodov said as if he still did not believe his own words.

"Promoted?" Brim gasped.

"Just as he facetiously suggested," the old Bear said with a laugh. "Little did he know."

"Promoted," Brim echoed in amazement.

"To Marshal of the G.F.S.S., no less," Borodov continued. "He is now in charge of all defensive forces."

"He's thraggling *what*?"

"Marshal of the G.F.S.S.," Borodov repeated in a dazed whisper. "Knez has put him in charge of repulsing whole Leaguer invasion."

"Sweet mother of Voot," Brim swore under his breath. "Unless he turns things around quickly, it's nothing more than a thraggling death sentence."

Borodov made a grim little laugh. "Nikolai Yanuarievich noticed same thing," he said.

The two comrades sat in silence for a few moments as the

Roshov idled before the Palace. "Where is he?" Brim asked at length. "And when will we see him again?"

"He is inside, changing to new uniform," Borodov replied. "And—" he peered out the window, "we will see him immediately. Here he comes now."

Sure enough, the great crystal doors of the palace were swinging slowly open while the regiment of Guards outside came to quivering attention. Presently, a familiar figure emerged, now dressed in the emblematic "Knez Green" uniform of a Sodeskayan Marshal, with heavy gold embroidery on the collars and cuffs of his tunic. "Nik," Brim whispered to himself, "a Marshal."

Moments later, Borodov's footman opened the passenger compartment again, and the new Marshal climbed in, plumping himself heavily on the cushions. When the door was again shut, his tired eyes glanced first at Brim, then at Borodov, and without moving his head, he said, "I wish to spend this tumultuous evening before your fire, my good friend Anastas Alexi. You, Wilf Ansor, and I have much to discuss."

"I did not strive for this position—nor did I particularly want it," Ursis grumbled after supper. The lustrous, knee-high riding boots he wore from the Palace were replaced by the droopy, soft-leather footwear that matched the colorful native costume he always preferred when at his ease. "*Nor* do I particularly want it now," he added grumpily. Borodov's study was hazy from the smoke of two Zempa pipes, and Brim's ability to smell anything had long before gone completely numb.

"But," Borodov said, interrupting his old friend's soliloquy, "job is yours, and you must now carry it out successfully—not only to save your own life but also life of Mother Planets themselves."

"Yes," Ursis said, sipping his meem, "I know that also.

All too well." He turned to Brim. "Well, Wilf Ansor," he said, "now you can see how much trouble I have managed to get myself into."

Relaxed in a huge, Bear-sized chair with his stockinged feet near the fire, Brim nodded. "Except it's no joke, Nik. I don't know anything about this death-penalty business, but I'm pretty certain that if anybody can turn the tide of this war, you can."

"Not alone, my furless friend, can I do anything," Ursis said. "Luckily, some of my colleagues in upper echelons quietly resisted Revisionists and survived by pretending to fawn like the others. You met a few of them at maneuvers—many more were simply not invited. They will form kernel around which I can build a new General Staff, near-term. But even more fortunate is collection of younger officers—renegade Colonels and Brigadiers—who completely reject the out-of-date Tactics Masters and their teachings. They are my hope for long-term future—and they have largely survived present slaughter because Revisionists refused to send them to war zone."

"Damned decent of Revisionists, I'd say." Borodov chuckled in his deep voice.

"What about the Fleet, Nik?" Brim asked. "I didn't hear you mention Captains and Admirals among your young renegades. Has anyone survived the slaughter in space to run your Fleet?"

Ursis smiled and glanced at Borodov. "That," he said with conspicuous pride in his voice, "is one of the few areas in which Anastas Alexi and I have been able to quietly put some advanced plans into action. *And*," he added with a great smile from which fang gems sparkled in the firelight, "they are all trained in your homeland of Carescria."

Brim felt his eyebrows lift in surprise. "But of course," he said after a moment. "Onrad's Production Minister, Zolton Jaiswall, has transferred all sorts of programs to Carescria—

including much of the spaceflight training. I remember a lot of Bears on my last visit."

"Additionally," Ursis continued with a smile, "I shall depend on *you*, Wilfooshka, to help me plan first few victories, eh?"

"That would be a great honor, Nik," Brim replied.

"Much more than great honor," Ursis said. "Also fulfilling direct orders of Knez."

"I don't understand," Brim replied.

"Easy," Ursis explained. "One reason I was chosen for job was relationship with you." He chuckled. "You have tendency to downplay achievements of last few years, but seems like every battle you are involved with turns out to be big victory—largely through your efforts."

"Gorksroar," Brim remonstrated. "I certainly appreciate the semtiments, but—"

"Call it what you like, Wilf Ansor, but your deeds speak volumes that you cannot deny. Besides," he added, "other political factors come into play, also."

Brim frowned. "Like what, Nik?" he asked.

"Oh, *minutiae*, shall we say . . . like close friendship between you and Emperor Onrad," Ursis replied. "Do not think that his temporary adoption of your infant daughter, Hope, has escaped view of Sodeskayan intelligence—as if that were only manifestation." He shrugged, " 'On mountaintops, moon shines no brighter than in valleys,' as they say."

"Hmm," Brim mused with a frown.

"I assume you understand neither Anastas Alexi or I had anything to do with passing *that* information," Ursis interjected.

"Yeah," Brim conceded. "There aren't too many people in the Galaxy I trust as much as you two." He laughed. "And Sodeskayan Intelligence is *thorough*. Everybody knows that."

"So you will help?"

"As I said before, I shall be *honored* to help, Nik," Brim assured him.

"Thank you, Wilf Ansor," Ursis said, recrossing his feet by the fire. "That takes care of everything—except equipment." He puffed contendedly on his Zempa pipe for another few moments, then made another broad smile. "Is where you—my Grand Duke Anastas Alexi—enter picture."

"Me?" Borodov asked, placing a hand on his chest in obvious surprise. "What role can old man like me play in galactic war?"

A deep laugh escaped Ursis's throat. "Minister of Production for Fleet Vehicles," he said. "No one I can think of would be so effective in such a job."

"Mother of Voot," Borodov whispered, glancing at Brim as if he had somehow just stolen the Avalonian profanity. "What makes you think that?"

"Anastas Alexi," Ursis chuckled, "surely you do not think that your part in temporarily financing Sherrington and Krasni-Peych went entirely unnoticed. After all, it did permit the Starfury prototype to be completed after only two additional donations."

"Nikolai Yanuarievich," Borodov gasped with raised eyebrows, "where did you hear such a . . . a . . . a *prevarication*?"

"Prevarication, my booted foot," Ursis laughed, refilling his goblet from a nearby decanter. "It is widely known that both ZBL-4 and JM-2 development efforts were *also* partially financed and, shall we say, *vigorously* shepherded by anonymous 'benefactor.' "

Borodov sank back in his chair and shook his head. "Nikolai Yanuarievich!" he protested. "How can you . . . ?"

"Be comforted, old friend," Ursis said, rising from his chair to place a reassuring hand on the Grand Duke's shoulder. "Your privacy will never be publicly breached. But

those of us who know doubly appreciate your past efforts—
and desperately require that they continue."

Borodov closed his eyes. "Nikolai Yanuarievich," he
said, "even if I *were* willing to admit such clandestine activ-
ities—which I am not, mind you—what makes you think
that I could function as well before the glaring eye of the
media? Does it occur to you that some of us are simply
bashful? Or, more specifically, perhaps have had our fill of
being the Knez's brother—and greatly prefer privacy to
fame?"

Brim watched breathlessly as Ursis stood silently by his
old friend's easy chair. Finally he pursed his lips and nodded, as if he had made an important decision. "Anastas
Alexi," he began, continuing to speak in Avalonian, despite
what clearly was a highly emotional moment, "no one in
Galaxy respects your privacy more than I. And," he added,
"few have known you so well and so long as to understand
how much that privacy means to you." He paused. "But time
has come, old friend, when all of us must put aside our own
lives for much larger cause. As we did when we served
aboard ship many years ago during first war with Leaguers.
You understand, Anastas Alexi? Is time to put lives on line
again. Otherwise, we lose Sodeskaya herself."

In the flame-lit dusk of his study, Borodov seemed to sink
deeper into the great high-backed chair while he clearly
fought something deep within himself. After a long time, he
stirred, then slowly pulled himself to his feet, turning to
stand muzzle-to-muzzle with Ursis. "You are right, Nikolai
Yanuarievich," he said at length with a firm, youthful timbre
that Brim had not heard in years. "Sometimes excess of comfort makes one forget that such never comes without inevitable cost." He nodded. "Count on me, Nikolai
Yanuarievich," he said, raising his glass. Then he looked at
Brim. "Come toast with us, Wilf Ansor," he said.

"Yes," Ursis urged. "Toast with us, Wilf Ansor, for much of the fate of Sodeskaya rests on our shoulders from tonight."

Caught up in the emotion of the moment, Brim stood and touched his goblet with the other two.

"To ice! To snow! To Sodeskaya we go!" they repeated solemnly.

"Now," Ursis said in a quiet voice, "I can finally begin to believe that I may not lose my life."

Five Standard days later, on 10 Heptad, 52013, Nergol Triannic promoted OverGalite'er Naire'dug Znieh to Marshal of the League and placed him in charge of the Sodeskayan campaign as *nov* Vobok's replacement. One week later, the League Armies—now rested and literally overflowing with provisions—returned to their onslaught while the Sodeskayans resumed their slow, grudging retreat.

During the next Standard Month (by his own reckoning), Brim—with the indispensible Barbousse—spent most of his waking moments in endless conferences and tactical sessions at military centers prudently dispersed throughout Gromcow. In spite of feelings of regret, he had time for only two conversations with Marsha Browning—and even they were abbreviated by his ridiculous schedule. Each evening, he, Ursis, and Borodov further conferred in private at an underground headquarters to check progress and frame a cohesive strategy that—for the first time—would thoroughly integrate Sodeskayan space and ground forces. Production of new war machines was rising sharply, especially ZBL-4s and JM-2s that were arriving in a nearly constant stream from giant factories erected far beyond the range of even the most advanced Leaguer attack ships.

One early evening—after two long, harrowing sessions with a number of high-ranking, stubborn Army officers—Brim was on his way to still another conference when Barbousse stopped him in a corridor. "Admiral," the big rating said, nodding at a suit bag folded over his arm, "if you don't change right now, you'll be late."

Brim shook his head in confusion as he attempted to cut through a billion or so military details and remember his own confused schedule. "Late for what, Chief?" he asked presently, squeezing the bridge of his nose. "I'm sorry. I've simply forgotten."

"Count Orlovsky's again, Admiral," Barbousse said. "Another big bash—with the Kncz himself as guest of honor. Can't miss this one, Skipper. Besides, both Marshal Ursis and Grand Duke Borodov will be there—they have no choice, either."

Nor does Marsha Browning, a voice pronounced in Brim's head. He ignored it. "I've got a meeting to attend . . . somewhere," he protested.

"I know where it is," Barbousse said. "I'll give your official regrets *and* take notes. You need a couple of hours off, Admiral—badly."

Brim shook his head. "What I *really* need, Chief," he said, "is some time to myself." But it wasn't the truth, and he knew it. He badly needed the kind of relaxation only a woman . . .

"I hear the meem's top grade, beggin' the Admiral's pardon," Barbousse rebutted.

"Yeah," Brim relented. "If nothing else, Orlovsky's got a lot of *good* Logish Meem." And Marsha Browning's closeness at the bar. . . . She'd be there, he knew it. He bit his lip—she was *married*, xaxtdammit. He should *never* have carried through with their xaxtdamned KA'PPA correspondence!

"Come on, Admiral," Barbousse urged, "give me that grip. I've got your best dress uniform all ready to go in this bag an' . . . ." he pointed to a nearby doorway, "you can change in that empty office. I'll pick up what you're wearin' now when I leave."

Brim felt his chin. He'd been working steadily since early morning, and the day in Gromcow was nearly half again as long as a Standard Day in Avalon. "I'm kind of grubby for a formal ball," he protested helplessly.

"Your kit's in the bag with the uniform," Barbousse replied impassively, "an' the head's six doors down the hall on your left—shower an' all."

"Sounds like you've got it all figured out, Chief," Brim said resignedly. After all, nothing was going to happen between himself and Marsha Browning. They were simply friends. And even if they *did* decide to do something, where could they go? Nowhere. Besides, she was *married*.

"I've even got a staff car waitin' at the curb outside the front door," Barbousse added, breaking into Brim's thoughts again. "Start code's set for your Fleet serial number. Do yourself a favor, Admiral," he entreated. "Do *all* of us a favor."

"I take it I've been a bit short, of late?" he asked, catching Barbousse's meaning only at the last moment.

"You'll never hear anything like that from *me*, Admiral," Barbousse said, rolling his eyes to the ceiling.

Brim handed over his grip. "All right, Chief," he acquiesced. "You've got me."

"You won't regret it, Admiral," Barbousse said, proferring the suit bag. "Six doors down the hall on your left."

"Aye aye, Chief," Brim said, saluting the Petty Officer with a wry grin.

"Bad business, Admiral," Barbousse returned, a twinkle in his eye. "You know it's against regulations to salute ratings."

"Here's to the thraggling regulations," Brim said, extending his hand. Somehow, Browning's face passed before his eyes when he said it.

Barbousse grinned, pressing Brim's hand in his large, callused grasp. "See you in the morning, Admiral," he said.

"See you in the morning, Chief."

"The *late* morning, Admiral?"

"We'll see about *that*. . . ."

If anything, the Palace's grand Smolny Ballroom looked even grander than Brim remembered. Tonight, as he passed along the reception line, the great columns appeared more remarkable in size and the smoky, spice-laden atmosphere seemed to have truly electrified, although a promised appearance by the Knez might have helped the latter along. True, the dancers moved more traditionally, as did the music— probably because most of the junior officers were now at the front lines, many permanently. Nevertheless, now that the Leaguers' war had finally come, the dauntless members of Gromcow's wellborn society were bearing up in their usual Bearish manner, amid grandiose pomp and splendor, even though all might be reduced to dimly glowing debris at any time.

In spite of having utterly rid himself of all thoughts concerning Marsha Browning, she'd passed in and out of his imagination a dozen times since the staff car dropped him off at the Palace door. Now, as he moved through the reception line with frustrating lack of speed, he felt a sudden, uncontrollable rush of excitement—one that he fought back with very little success. Only a few more dignitaries separated him from . . . He bolstered his resolve. No more flirting with married women, and that was *that*.

After Brim's very official introduction to the new Marshal Nikolai Yanuarievich Ursis ("Nik," he whispered, "you've finally made the big time!"), he paused for a moment with the Ambassador from occupied A'zurn and his wife. They immediately remembered his rare A'zurnian decoration, awarded years ago for bravery during his first tour of duty, and bid warm welcome before passing him, in turn, to the Ambassador from Lixor and his wife. These two represented an undeviatingly neutral domain that for a thousand Standard

Years had grown fat on credits earned from selling weapons to *both* sides of any conflict happening to come their way. Brim always translated the word *neutral* to *avaricious* when referring to Lixorians, but he had also learned to smile diplomatically, and so passed quickly on to the Ambassador for occupied Effer'wyck. As he did so, he glanced in the direction of the next couple for his first glimpse of Marsha Browning, and . . . *she wasn't there*! Nor was her husband, Crellingham. Quickly paying respects to the representatives of what was once the most important Imperial ally of all—now reduced to an occupied territory of the League—he found himself passed into the hands of one Stephanie Tate, *Assistant* Ambassador from Avalon. After the usual formalities, he inquired about Browning himself and learned that the Ambassador had been suddenly recalled to Avalon the day before.

During what seemed like the next five hundred Standard Years, he was further presented to three more barons and one Bearish Archbishop of the Gradgroat-Norchelite church before he was again presented to Knezina Katerin. This time, she was dressed in a splendid amber gown that accented her dazzling chestnut coat. On her noble head was a tiara clearly worth the price of a small star. She smiled. "Well, Admiral," she asked, "are you surprised to be so involved with the Sodeskayan High Command? I hear we have kept you *quite* busy."

"One does what he can, Your Majesty," Brim said. "And work goes much easier when one believes in its outcome."

"In Sodeskaya?"

"In Sodeskaya, in the Empire, in civilization, Your Majesty. Eventually we must return freedom to those who have lost it."

Katerin looked down at him. "Strange, Admiral," she said, "I actually think you believe those words."

Brim frowned. "I do, Your Majesty," he said, "—or I should have not spoken them."

"That," Katerin said, "is why we believe so much in you, Admiral." She smiled and turned to a Majordomo. "Klaus," she said, "you will make certain the Admiral has access to all he desires?"

From the Majordomo, Brim proceeded into the swirling crowd to join Borodov, who had arrived somewhat earlier and was beckoning to him from the dance floor. The elderly Bear had his eye on an upcoming industrialist and was about to corner him for an extended browbeating session that centered on low production rates at two of his factories. Winking, Brim declined the old Bear's invitation to join in the "fun" and pushed his way through the glittering throng to the nearest refreshment alcove.

Not that he was *that* disappointed at missing Marsha Browning, he reassured himself. She was, after all, a married woman. Still, he mused half guiltily, they *were* friends, and she was a most *attractive* one, at that. A lot like the woman talking to a huge gray Bear in a Grenadiers uniform. . .

"Marsha" he exclaimed as she glanced his way, "I didn't expect to find you here tonight."

Dressed in a dark blue low-cut gown that clung to her ample figure in a way that must have driven every Bearess mad with envy, she hesitated for a moment, then made a little smile and motioned for him to join her. "I didn't plan to be here myself until the last minute," she whispered with a blush, then turned to the trio with her. "Colonel Tulsko Dobrenin, Assistant Secretary Marston, Curator Kittnoczek—may I present my countryman, Rear Admiral Wilf Ansor Brim?"

Dobrenin quickly extended his hand. "Ah, Admiral Breem, but I have heard of you," he said, adjusting an ebony-rimmed monocle. "You are friend of recent Marshal Ursis, are you not?"

"I am, Colonel," Brim said. "The Marshal and I go back a number of years."

The Bear smiled. "Then perhaps we shall meet again soon, Admiral," he said. "My crews arrive only this morning from training in your homeland of Carescria. During next few days, we take possession of new JM-2B Roshovs and receive further tactical training here in Gromcow. Your name has been mentioned numerous times."

"You honor me, Colonel," Brim said in turn, shaking hands with Lydia Marston, a leggy blonde (with the eyes of a trained killer) on temporary duty from Avalon, then Boris Yaltii Kittnoczek, a tall, well-dressed dealer in rare manuscripts.

As the five passed pleasantries, Dobrenin was captured by two stylishly dressed Bearish socialites, while Marston and Kittnoczek drifted away by themselves, hinting about subjects that led Brim to believe the "manuscript shop" probably displayed little in the way of real manuscripts. "I'll bet your Sodeskayan-Imperial Cultural Exchange doesn't do much business with Kittnoczek and Company," Brim mused when he and Browning were finally alone.

Browning chuckled. "No," she agreed, "although I can't imagine why. Perhaps I don't have the proper kind of manuscripts for him."

"Marsha," Brim said with a smile, "I think you can count on that."

"Ah, well." She sighed. "Life has its little disappointments." She peered at the empty goblet in her hand. "Like this." She pouted theatrically. "Can you help?"

"I can easily deal with *that* kind of disappointment," Brim said, signaling the bartender while steering her toward a small table that had just been vacated nearby. Moments later, he returned with the most gloriously hued Logish Meem he could recall. His first sip proved the old adage that "the more Logish the Meem, the fairer the hue." He touched the rim of her goblet with his. "Here's to Count Orlovsky," he toasted.

"May he live longer than either of us and serve meem such as this to his dying day!"

"To Count Orlovsky," Browning agreed, raising her goblet in salute, "and his long life!" She sipped for a moment, then smiled. "Wilf Brim," she whispered with a little blush, "I . . . well, I hoped you'd be here—in spite of myself."

Brim met her eyes. "Thanks, Marsha," he replied, a little self-consciously, "—for a lot of things, including all those wonderful notes you KA'PPAed. They more or less kept me sane during several very trying weeks." He grinned bashfully. "I hoped you'd be here, too—you are beautiful tonight."

She lowered her eyes. "I don't know whether those words are true or not, Wilf Brim," she said, "but I wouldn't trade them for a million credits right now."

He smiled. "You won't get your million credits with those words," he said seriously. "Nothing that obvious is worth a million." After that, they made small talk about a number of unimportant subjects before both seemed to run out of conversation at the same time and sat back listening to clamorous music coming from the ballroom while a whole galaxy of glittering creatures swirled noisily around the nearby bar. Suddenly Brown's eyes narrowed and a mischievous little smile stole her countenance. "I don't *really* have to be here tonight, you know," she said in a conspiratorial voice. "Do you?"

Brim frowned. "No," he replied with a raised eyebrow. "Actually, I'd forgotten all about it until Chief Barbousse reminded me it was on."

"Barbousse?" she asked with raised eyebrows. "He isn't that huge, absolutely adorable noncom from Avalon, is he?"

Brim thought for a moment. Probably in all Sodeskaya there wasn't anybody else who looked like Barbousse. "Completely bald?" he asked.

"Yes—completely."

"It's got to be the Chief," Brim stated flatly. "Where did you run into him?"

"He came into the office the other day," Browning said with a little frown, "to drop off some sort of notice . . . about tonight's ball, if I'm not mistaken. Left it with my secretary. I just happened to notice as he went out the door and asked. He's *big*." She frowned. "Wonder why he was passing those around."

Brim stifled a groan and shook his head. "I wonder," he said evasively—but he could make an excellent guess.

"In any event," Browning continued, unconcerned, "I'd like to be out of this noisy zoo. Do you have a skimmer?"

Brim smiled. "Just so happens I do," he said. "But I hope you aren't going to desert me now that I'm glad I came."

"Not unless you want to be deserted," she said. "I know a perfectly wonderful little tavern on the way home, where the meem isn't quite as good as here at Orlovsky's—and it's certainly not free, either—but we could drink it *and* hear each other talk." She gave a little laugh. "I'd even treat . . . and, well, nobody will be there to, er, ask why we're spending so much time together." She took a deep breath. "Gromcow has the greatest rumor mill in the whole Galaxy."

"How do you know?" Brim joshed. "Could be all kinds of places on League planets with better rumor mills. I'll bet you've not been to *all* of them."

"You are impossible, Wilf Brim," she said. "But you know what I mean. And I really would like a chance to get to know you."

Brim smiled. "You've got a deal, Marsha Browning," he said. "How are we going to carry off this clandestine mission?"

She laughed. "I shall send the limousine along, and you will—eventually—take me home. How does that sound?"

"Sounds like a plan to me," Brim said. "I'll get your coat

and meet you at the top of the staircase." Within half a meta-cycle, they were on their way.

Grand, tree-lined boulevards and dazzling estates of Gromcow's Monarchical Sector near the Winter Palace soon gave way to the commercial heart of the city—pennant-be-decked Shamray Prospekt, bordered by great, imposing mercantile buildings, their peacetime lights blacked out because of the all too real threat of assault from space. While Brim drove, Browning navigated the early-morning streets with a relaxed confidence born of years in exotic cities throughout the Galaxy. She was dressed in a fitted woolen overcoat and a tiny pillbox hat that reminded Brim of a disruptor turret without its disruptors. Even mostly covered, she was a fine-looking woman. "Turn right there at that building with the golden spire," she said, pointing through the snow-flecked windshield, "then left onto the ramp to Bersov Promenade."

Brim smiled to himself. He guessed that following behind an up-and-coming diplomat-husband throughout the far-flung Empire had provided this extremely cosmopolitan woman the ability to feel at home almost anywhere. "Let me know when we reach the Avalon city limits," he joked.

She laughed. "You're a pretty speedy driver," she said. "I don't even remember going through LightSpeed."

"Smooth driving," Brim explained, swinging onto the Bersov ramp. "Fools you every time."

"You'll want to take the Turchik exit," she warned. "It's easy to miss." On both sides of the roadway—now shrunken from twelve to four lanes and covered with new snow—huge, spiraling towers rose into the hazy darkness, connected to one another by what appeared to be heavy, drooping pipes and softly glowing cables.

"Where now?" Brim asked as the skimmer glided across the half dozen glimmering guide tubes controlling what must have been a major ground transit line. Their surroundings had quickly turned residential, mostly two- and three-story town houses with steep, pitched roofs, carved balconies, and elaborate balustrades that lined streets flanked by ranks of small, snow-bearded trees. He glanced at Browning, who was squinting ahead through the snow.

"Go slow," she cautioned. "Without street lighting it's tricky, but we should be coming to a little tract of shops and . . . yes, at the next intersection turn left and park anywhere you can."

As Brim swung around the corner, the little neighborhood gave way to a narrow street of shops—all closed at this hour—in ancient-looking black stone buildings that rose no more than four or five stories from the sidewalks, each delicate feature of their carved facades punctuated in white. For all the closed shops, however, both curbs were largely filled by parked skimmers of every kind.

"There's an opening," Browning exclaimed, pointing through the windshield. "Better get it."

Brim peered down the street, dimly lighted by their running lights that glowed only enough to warn pedestrians out of the way. "Good spotting," he said.

"We're lucky," she said. "This place is popular—with people as well as with Bears." They had no sooner maneuvered beside the curb than three more skimmers appeared out of nowhere, shrouded headlights glowing like slitted eyes in the darkness. "See?" she asked.

Brim nodded, looking at her in the darkness as the warmth of the skimmer's heater dissipated in the Sodeskayan chill. She even had a beautiful silhouette.

She glanced his way for a moment, then turned full face and stared at him for long, silent moments. "A credit for your thoughts," she said.

"I'd probably be more than a credit's worth embarrassed if I let you in on those," Brim admitted, feeling his cheeks burn.

"Come here," she said, suddenly putting her arms around his neck and kissing him squarely on the mouth. "There," she said softly, her nose touching his, "would that earn me a credit?"

"Mmm," Brim whispered, "I think so—but maybe we ought to try again." With that, he drew her to him, covering her opened lips with his own. After a few moments, he drew back slightly. "Perhaps we ought to, ah, check out the tavern," he said. "Before I, ah . . ."

She took a deep breath and sat up in the seat and straightened her hat. "I—I think so," she replied, her voice sounding a little shaken.

Already the windshield of the skimmer was covered with snow, and when Brim stepped out, he found the new snowfall was already over his ankles, although the street had clearly been plowed within the metacycle. Hurrying around the front of the car, he waited until a maintenance worker passed with a power shovel, then helped her out onto the sidewalk and they hastened toward an entrance beneath a hanging sign that proclaimed something in old-fashioned Sodeskayan symbols.

As he opened the heavy door, they were greeted by a blast of warmth that carried the rich aromas of meem, Hogge'poa, mu'occo cigarettes, perfume, and spices of all kinds. The inner door opened into a bustling, candlelit room with a low, beamed ceiling and smoke-darkened walls, filled with sounds of animated conversation and the tinkle of crystalware—all overlaid by the pensive, half-melancholy sounds of Sodeskayan folk music played on three towering stringed instruments Bears called *akialalabs*. A huge russet Bear dressed in black except for a white starched shirt and a natty red ribbon at his neck bowed low and smiled warmly. "Welcome to Grovnik Tavern," he said in Avalonian. He glanced around the room, then consulted a greasy display in his battered-looking rostrum. "I have only single booth to offer," he said, "but would give me great pleasure could I seat you there."

Brim was about to answer when Browning nodded and replied for them in the Bear's own language, bringing a great smile to the headwaiter's face. Immediately he took her hand and kissed it, then bowed to Brim again, and after signaling to a waiter, led them into the smoky twilight to a tiny wooden booth beside a painted wall decorated with Sodeskayan peasant art that looked authentic enough to be the real thing. In the next booth, two of the mysterious Night Traders held hands over goblets of deep red meem. At the table beside them, four young Bears wearing costumes of some local guild quietly toasted something *very* important— at least to them. Many nearby tables were taken by humans who seemed much too busy to notice two more of their race attired more for hobnobbing with royalty than having a drink in a local tavern—even one so polyglot as the Grovnik.

"I didn't know you spoke the language," Brim commented as he helped her from her coat, then draped it over her bare shoulders as she sat.

"Oh, not very well," Browning replied, her face coloring slightly. "It's sort of a hobby with me. I've tried to learn at least a little of the language wherever we've been stationed."

Brim ordered a bottle of a favored Logish Meem and slipped into the seat opposite her. "I think that's a pretty wonderful hobby," he said. "I've only managed to learn the Leaguers' Vertrucht—and I did that because it helped me put bread on the table when I was a kid."

She laughed a little. "Ironic, isn't it?" she observed. "Especially since you seem to have spent most of your life fighting them."

"I've had occasion to think of that more than once," Brim agreed wryly as a waiter in white apron and tall cook's hat served their meem. "They're a mean lot." He frowned as he sampled the excellent vintage. "And I don't imagine they've done much to endear themselves to you and the Ambassador," he added, toasting her with his goblet.

She sipped her meem. "Actually, they've provided some wonderful postings," she said with a smile. "If the Leaguers hadn't been so awfully troublesome, the Foreign Service would be much smaller than it is and . . ." She gave a little shrug.

"And what?" Brim asked.

"Oh," she said after a moment, "I suppose I shouldn't have seen so much of the Galaxy as I have . . . nor learned so many languages."

"How many do you know?" Brim asked, fascinated by this modest woman who was clearly as intelligent as she was beautiful.

She thought a moment and smiled. "I haven't really kept track, but there must be . . ."

With Brim's beguiled urging, Browning managed to recall twelve languages and dialects—including his own Carescrian Avalonian, which to most Imperials sounded like a completely foreign tongue. And during the next metacycle, he found he'd not lost the ability to relax at all; he'd only temporarily forgotten how. Feeling *very* comfortable by now, he finished the first bottle of meem by pouring the last drops into her goblet.

"Wilf Brim," she protested with a little smile. "If I didn't know better, I'd think you were planning to take advantage of me."

"Not with those few drops." He laughed. "In fact, if you're not in any hurry to be home, I was planning to order a second bottle."

"Oh." she laughed. "Then you *are* planning to take advantage of me."

"Hmm," Brim responded, wondering idly if she was feeling the meem as much as he was. "Never," he said with theatrical finality. "Death before dishonor—or however that goes."

"But do you *really* mean that, Admiral Brim?" she demanded with sham suspicion. "Had I suspected you of other than honorable intentions, I should never have permitted you to drive me home."

Brim pinched the bridge of his nose in mock concentration. "How can I prove this to you?" he asked.

"Hmm," she mused, then frowned melodramatically. "I don't suppose we'll ever know unless . . ."

"Unless we order the meem?" Brim asked.

"That's about it," she said.

Brim signaled the waiter. "I guess we'd better find out," he said.

They sipped the next bottle much more slowly while the bustle of the tavern seemed to diffuse in the smoky atmosphere. And as they became more familiar, their dialogue shifted toward the intimate. Somehow, Margot Effer'wyck, first—and most famous—of Brim's loves, had become the subject of conversation.

"And she actually saved your life at the Battle of Zonga'ar?" Browning asked. "She must have loved you very much to take such a risk."

Brim could only nod. "Once I think she did," he said. "Unfortunately, the Leaguers' TimeWeed took it away—almost as if it had killed her. I've got some hope she's licked it, but . . ."

"I've seen HoloGrams of her a number of times," Browning said, looking into his eyes. "She was—*is,* I suppose—very beautiful."

Brim nodded. "Yes," he said, hoping to change the subject, "she, er, *is* . . . I hope. But, well, you are a very beautiful woman yourself."

"You said that earlier," Browning remarked almost in a whisper. "I hope I am, at least to you."

"Believe it," Brim replied. Over the course of the evening, the coat that he had placed over her shoulders had opened considerably, revealing what seemed to be vast acres of creamy skin. During the last few cycles, he had been at pains not to stare. She took that moment to shift on her seat, and before he could stop himself, his glance strayed to the small, firm-looking breasts pushing over her décolleté. He felt his cheeks burn as he quickly looked up and met her eyes. Apprehended!

She smiled. "Why, Admiral Brim," she cooed with a twinkle in her eyes. "I think I caught you peeking."

"Sorry," Brim mumbled bashfully. Somehow this extremely seductive woman could also make him feel like a little boy.

"I'm not," she said.

"Not what?" he asked, feeling even more nonplussed.

"Not *sorry*," she said. "I can't imagine why I'd wear this kind of a gown if I didn't want people to notice." She gave a quick little lift to her shoulders that revealed considerably more creamy skin. "I wonder," she said with a twinkle in her eye, "are my breasts as pretty as Margot Effer'wyck's?"

Brim felt his breathing start to labor again. "Hmm," he murmured, this time taking a long look with no pretense, "I imagine they might be—what I can see of them. . . ."

"That sounded like a leading statement," Browning murmured, color rising in her cheeks.

"Only an incomplete observation," Brim replied slowly. "I can't really make a comparison."

"Would it help if you could see the rest of mine?" she asked, looking him directly in the eye.

Brim thought for a long moment. This was treacherous ground indeed. "Of course," he answered in a joking tone. "But here?"

Taking a glance around the room, she made a little smile. "This is the reason I seldom drink much in public," she said, reaching behind her to make a little zipping noise, "and Crellingham simply hates it when I want to do this. But sometimes I absolutely *love* to show off where I shouldn't." Slowly pulling her coat forward like a shield, she drew the top of her gown well below two small, slightly pendent breasts that would have made a woman half her age jealous. "Now," she demanded in a triumphant little giggle, "tell me how these compare to Margot Effer'wyck's."

Embarrassed for a moment, Brim glanced around the room, then quickly discovered that he was the only one who could see anything but her outthrust coat.

"Well?" she asked, gently massaging one enormous nipple to a dark, brownish pink.

Brim felt an extremely compelling sensation begin in his loins. "You really want to know?" he asked, staring in fascination at the network of tiny blue veins surrounding her great, knobby aureoles.

"Really," she assured him. "I want to know."

"Well," he answered, feeling his cheeks burn, "you're bigger and . . . *rounder*, I guess. Margot's are . . . well . . ."

"I won't ask whose you prefer," she said, slipping her gown back in place.

"I—I don't think I could tell you right now," Brim stumbled. "But Mother of Voot, Marsha, you are one *magnificent* woman."

"You haven't even seen the rest of me," she said. "Would you like to?"

Brim smiled. "Here?" he asked jokingly.

Browning giggled and thought for a moment. "That would be a real challenge," she said. "Especially in this long gown." She looked into his eyes. "Wilf," she said after a moment, "it's pretty clear that I've decided I want to . . . well, *break the rules* tonight. I've wanted you since we first met, and I can't seem to get it out of my system. Will you pleasure a married woman?" Then she smiled. "Somewhere a little less public, of course."

Brim felt a suspiciously moist sensation in his crotch. "You won't be the first married woman I've loved," he said. "And Universe knows I want you, too. I have for a long time now—as I'm sure you've noticed."

"I've hoped," she said, fumbling in her purse. "Some of my friends have a little apartment they share for times like this. I . . . er . . . borrowed the key tonight, for some reason. . . ."

"I've got to ask," Brim said, grinding his teeth. "What about, er, the Ambassador?"

"Thanks," she said with a serious little smile. "I hoped you'd be man enough to ask." She folded her hands for a moment, then looked into Brim's face. "Oh, Crellingham might mind, all right—he used to, at any rate. But right now he's probably got himself skewered in one of the young Ambassador's assistants who travel with him. He's been, well, 'sampling' for years. I suppose it's my own doing, anyway," she added with a little hesitation. "I did some 'sampling' myself, soon after we married. An old flame. Crellingham found us one afternoon. . . ." She closed her eyes for a moment.

"Ouch," Brim said.

"It's not that bad," she said. "We've been together a number of years now; we're comfortable. In his own way, he loves me—I'm quite useful. And in my own way, I love him. Besides, he'll never leave me—or my family's wealth." She shrugged and pursed her lips. "Oh, Wilf Brim, if you can accept all that, as I guess *I* can, well . . . I'm at least very much in *lust* with you tonight." She smiled. "Maybe even in love. Right now it's awfully hard to tell."

"I'm content with love *or* lust," Brim said in a quiet voice. "I haven't been able to get you from my thoughts for a month now. . . ."

"Come on, then," she said with a *very* serious look. "My briefs have long been soaked through, and I want to feel you inside me *now*."

"Let's find that apartment of yours," Brim said, taken by a sudden feeling of great urgency.

Browning showed him "the rest" only moments after the skimmer's heater became active.

CHAPTER 8
Home Is Where . . .

During the next Sodeskayan Week (Gromcow-local time), the frantic pace of Ursis's strategy meetings continued apace, and the Bear's initial battle plans finally began to gel. By the beginning of the following week, a high-level consensus had been finalized: The only alternative that could slow the Leaguers sufficiently to save Gromcow was a Sodeskayan *counterattack*, somewhere among the numerous planetary systems that made up the "front."

It was a simple enough plan—deemed "obvious" by many of the High Command officers who had survived the Knez's purge. But in reality, the decision hinged primarily on whether adequate resources had yet been acquired for such an attack. The basic problem: Not just *any* resources would do. If "Vylyit," the code name assigned to Ursis's new plan, were to have any chance at all of overcoming the Leaguers' tremendous advantage in space, only marks like the new ZBL-4 killer ships and PE-3 Petyakov attack craft—along with the wild new JM-2 Ro'stoviks that didn't seem to fit any established category—would do at all. Otherwise the offensive would result in little more than a disastrous continuation of the long, slow Sodeskayan retreat that had continued since the earliest metacycles of the war.

Space planning had been Brim's major contribution to the brutal strategy sessions. It was not enough that Ursis himself believed their only chance lay in strengthening the space arm. He was famed as both a master tactician and a scholar—but he could argue space matters only from the viewpoint of a Drive-chamber Engineer. Brim alone had the experience of actively fighting Leaguers in space—and most important of all, *leading* the fight against Leaguers in space. He had faced Ursis's most stubborn Bearish adversaries, and he had prevailed—not just forcing them into yielding to his friend's new power, but patiently arguing his case over and over until the Bears were convinced that spacepower actually *was* critical to their survival—and eventual victory.

In the end, however, as much responsibility for success would accrue to old Borodov as to Ursis and his whole General Staff. If there was magic in the plan, the Grand Duke would act as magician. Ultimately, his job was fixing priorities and allocating resources to plants and factories spread across nearly a sixth of the Galaxy. He would ensure that on the fateful moment designated for attack, the doughty Sodeskayans would fight *at least* as well equipped as their Leaguer foes.

"Even then we may not have enough," the old Bear said late one evening as he puffed thoughtfully on an ornate Zempa pipe before the fireplace in his beloved study. "These production forecasts of mine permit very little to go wrong—and we know how trouble-prone new processes are, even in best of cases." He, Brim, and Ursis had gathered in secret at the great manor house for a few metacycles of relaxation prior to issuing the orders that would begin preparations on a large scale.

"After all is said and done," Ursis mused, peering into a

huge goblet of Logish Meem, "we will do our best—perhaps a little better than our best. Then will be matter for Lady Fate to decide."

"Is true," Borodov said. "But until we have done all we can do, we leave things in hands of Leaguers." He paused a moment. " 'Only winged stone spiders can hope to reach the moons,' as they say."

Boots resting on a great, padded hassock, Brim had been primarily listening to the Bears, only now and then taking part in the conversation. At last he reached a decision and sat his goblet on the rich carpet beside his chair. "Perhaps now is the time for us to look for additional help elsewhere," he suggested.

"There is nowhere else," Borodov said grimly. "This effort will absorb everything in Sodeskaya—even smallest facilities that grind our parts, much less major fabricators." He pursed his lips. "Our Bearish civilization will suffer before we bring this one off."

"I didn't mean here in Sodeskaya," Brim said. "I meant back in Avalon." He shook his head dourly. "There's not much to be had there, either—not after the pounding we took last year stopping Operation Death's Head. But now that the Leaguers are dedicating much of their energies to you, it seems to me that we might be able to come up with something to help. And right now, *anything* is better than nothing."

"Is true," Ursis growled. "But Sodeskayans do not beg. Not like doormats from Effer'wyck, who begged for your Starfuries and soldiers even after they had given up the fight."

Brim nodded. "Yes," he agreed, "they did. And in truth, that fact will make things a lot harder for me. Especially since Vylyit is planned primarily as a holding effort to save Gromcow. But it's worth a try."

"What would you ask for?" Borodov demanded. "You Imperials don't make ZBLs or Ro'stoviks."

"Not yet," Brim said. "But, well, Starfuries, for example. What if I could get a couple squadrons of them?"

"Greatest killers in known Universe, Wilf Ansor," Ursis said. "But without Imperial crews, they would never be ready for the offensive. Takes time to learn a starship—as you have always told me."

Brim frowned. "Yeah," he mused. "They'd certainly have to be manned by experienced Imperials—at least at first."

"I cannot imagine Emperor Onrad willingly sacrificing both men and their starships to a losing cause."

"Wouldn't be a sacrifice," Brim replied. "War is war, after all; losses are going to happen no matter what. Onrad's a realist. Every strike against the Leaguers—no matter *where* it's made—is important. Eventually they'll add up to some sort of victory."

Ursis nodded soberly. "You will speak for us?" he asked.

"That's what I had in mind," Brim said. "Thanks to your efforts, I've finally managed to see a little of this war from a Sodeskayan point of view. For the present, I think I've done all I can do here. Now it's time to go home and bring some of my colleagues up to date on the situation. The Chief will be glad for a little sunshine, too. It's springtime there, if I haven't forgotten."

"You both will be sorely missed, Wilfooshka," Borodov observed, pouring himself another half goblet of meem.

"I don't plan that we'll be there long at all," Brim replied. "Only a few weeks—enough to drum up some help for the coming campaign." He smiled a little. "The Chief's 'special friend' lives there, and perhaps I'll spend a little time catching up with my daughter. From our HoloGrams I'm sent, she seems to have grown considerably."

"Like cubs all over Universe," Ursis said, settling back in his chair, "you miss single day and lifetime passes." He shook his head for a moment, then came upright again with a start. "Voot's greasy beard," he exclaimed, "how swiftly things change! Only little while ago, we sat before the same fireplace wondering when war would start. Now seems Knez has given it to us *personally*."

"I, for one, would be glad to return it," Borodov growled wryly. "*If* it were really brother Nikolai's war to take back."

"Unfortunately," Brim said, "the *real* owners seem to be everywhere. Not just Nergol Triannic—or his worse-than-xaxtdamned lackeys. Our hoary old Empire is full of them: CIGAs and all the rest of the human filth who gave the Leaguers their chance to rebuild after the last war while systematically destroying our own Fleet. All in the name of a self-serving 'peace' that existed only in their own timid minds." He peered into his goblet for a moment. "And I guess you Bears don't exactly get off unblemished either."

"Don't we know," Ursis growled. "Like self-serving 'Antiquarians' from Sodeskayan Military Academy who made certain that their power with Knez was intact—at expense of Space Fleet." He smashed a fist into his open hand. "I have purged most of them by now, but damage they did cannot be undone for years."

Borodov nodded sagely. "Had *all* of our allied domains shown some collective backbone early on, is good chance Triannic might never have returned to establish this second evil sovereignty at the outset."

"*If only*," Ursis growled with disdain. "Words with no meaning. What has happened in past can be undone only in present and future. And," he added, "such undoing is usually expensive." He looked at Brim. "Wilfooshka," he continued, "is very important thing you do, going to Avalon. No question that we need help desperately, and although I have little hope you will bring back more than token force, that will at least indicate to our people that we are not alone in the war."

"And pave the way for more assistance, should we need it

in future," Borodov added. He laughed without humor. "Perhaps that will not be necessary," he said. "Perhaps we will help *you*. But whatever future outcome, my guess is that we will need each other before this Leaguer evil is finally driven from Universe."

"When will you leave, Wilf Ansor?" Borodov asked.

"Soon as I can," Brim replied. "Onrad has ordered General Drummond to lay on transportation home whenever I request."

"Hmm," Ursis observed with a smile, "direct orders from Emperor ought to give you *some* priority, one supposes."

Brim nodded. "One supposes," he said, returning the Marshal's grin. "Now that I know it's all right with you two, I'll have Barbousse set things up immediately."

The next day, he was aboard one of the Empire's astonishing little DH-98 starships, streaking toward the center of the Galaxy—and Avalon.

Little more than three Standard Days later, brilliance from the shining trinary star called Asturious was streaming through automatically dimmed forward Hyperscreens and Commander Terry Rido, the Helmsman, was slowing past Sheldon's Great Velocity Constant into normal Hypospace. From his place in a jump seat abaft the single helm, Brim watched the view change from "normal," as translated by the Hyperscreen logic, through a confusion of angry red photons (the Dyla-Perif Transition Effort) to natural vision as the ship made its transition. Jeremy Lockheart, the Cohelmsman, had just gone aft for a cup of cvc'eese when Rido looked over his shoulder and grinned. "Like to take her in, Admiral?" he asked. "Lockheart won't mind."

Brim felt himself break into a hopeless grin. "I'm pretty low time in the type," he said, giving the man a way out of his offer.

Rido turned in his seat and shrugged. "She's a little skittish at low speeds," he said, "but I've flown Starfuries and she's not *too* much worse near the ground than they are." He nodded thoughtfully. "Just keep half an eye on the V meter and you'll be fine. Besides," he added, "the way I figure, I'd have to live a couple hundred years to fly as many approaches to Avalon as you have."

"None of 'em in one of these beauties," Brim replied. "But as long as it's all right with Lockheart, I'll gladly give it a whirl." Moments later, he was in the Cohelmsman's seat, setting up the restrainer beams. As always, Brim's view changed the moment he was at a helm. Helmsmen's seats were unlike anything else in the Universe—views from only a few irals away paled in comparison. Possibly it was all psychological; once or twice he'd even tried to convince himself of it. But . . . here in the flight bridge of the DH-98, everything became wonderfully different again.

He glanced around him. Unlike the long-nosed Starfuries he'd flown during the last few years, this ship had almost unlimited vision forward. To either side, however, everything from the "horizon" down was completely blanked by two enormous, more or less teardrop-shaped nacelles jammed with twelve A876 gravity generators, twice the number used to power the Starfury—in a starship less than half again as large with a crew of only thirty. Little prior inquiry had been necessary to determine that the Imperial Fleet's newest addition was rapidly gaining reputation as a Helmsman's ship. He'd watched Rido during the takeoff at Tomoshenko, and the man acted a great deal more wary than normal for a Helmsman of his age and rank.

He picked up the first orbiting buoy approximately twenty cycles later, off to port, winking steadily against the moderating glare. Below, Avalon, the planet, imperceptibly rotated its night terminator toward Avalon, the city, whose tangled, willy-nilly web of streets and byways would soon emerge from the trailing edge of a large weather system. "Looks like they've had a bit of cleaning today," Brim observed.

"Never wash off all that dirt in a million years." Rido laughed, pointing a small crystal spike at the buoy.

Presently, a section of Brim's readout panel filled with a shimmering menu of weather targets. He chose AVALON, and the menu was replaced by old-fashioned symbolic characters:

AVALON / LAKE MERSIN SURFACE
CONDITIONS AT 2147 AVALON STANDARD
TIME: 6000 SCATTERED, 21000 SCATTERED,
VISIBILITY 10, TEMPERATURE 101, DEW
POINT 67, WIND CALM, ALTIMETER 2992,
LANDING VECTOR 18 RIGHT 17 LEFT VISUAL
APPROACHES IN PROGRESS.

A Controller from a distant satellite appeared in a globular display by Brim's right elbow. "Orbital Control to Imperial W4050," he said, "you are cleared direct to Avalon Primary-Nine. Continue present descent vector until flight level two-fifty and three hundred velocity."

Rido nodded, and Brim continued the litany, glancing at four graceful, trihulled Starfuries that came hurtling out of the darkness to make a visual inspection, flashed a quick salute, then banked and were gone as if they never existed. "All right," he said, "Imperial W4050 cleared direct Avalon Primary-Nine arrival to flight level two-fifty at three hundred."

Within moments, the little starship began its fiery reentry through the planet's atmosphere while Brim carefully applied the gravity brakes. Soon the hullmetal was glowing white hot, and even the slightest distortion in the airstream caused a wake of free ions that merged into a long comet's tail several hundred irals behind the ship.

At just below 150 c'lenyts altitude, Brim sighted the huge

mass of an orbiting killer-ship base in the distance. FleetPort 30. He'd kept his eye out for its awkward and terribly familiar shape all the way down. During the Battle of Avalon, it had been his home—and awesome responsibility to command. A lifetime of the most savage battle memories orbited there—some good . . . heroic, even. Most were appalling. Once he'd spied its bulk, he returned to flying and never looked back. No more than a quarter metacycle later, he leveled the ship above a high bank of scattered clouds at an altitude of precisely 25,000 irals—and an airspeed pegged on 300 c'lenyts.

"Avalon Primary-Nine to Imperial W4050," announced a second Controller—this one based somewhere on the surface, by the cut of her handsome uniform, "checking you in at flight level two-fifty and three hundred velocity. Descend and maintain flight level two-forty."

"Thank you, AP-9," Brim replied, "Imperial W4050 will continue to flight level two-forty."

"Looks like they had a bit of weather through here not long ago," Rido commented from the left seat. "Look, there's lightning coming out of that big one to the left."

Brim glanced off to starboard. "Glad it's on the way to somebody else," he said bleakly, remembering how he almost lost I.F.S. *Defiant* in such a thunderstorm when lightning struck its uninsulated KA'PPA mast and shorted out the big ship's gravity controls.

"Imperial W4050: contact Avalon Center on channel two-seventy-six," the controller ordered presently.

"Imperial W4050: channel two-seventy-six. Thanks for the help, AP-9."

"You're welcome, sir. Good day . . . "

Below, where the cloud bank had already passed, the surface appeared to be swathed in a billion shades and hues of springtime *GREEN*! Beautiful beyond belief. Brim felt himself breaking into still another outrageous grin. For weeks—

Sodeskayan weeks, at that—he'd been too busy to notice how deathly sated he'd become with the whole concept of snowy whiteness. "Wonderful," he whispered, more to himself than to anyone else.

"Admiral?" Rido asked from the left seat.

Brim began to reply, but was interrupted by a third Controller. "Avalon Center to Imperial W4050. . . . "

"Avalon Center, this is Imperial W4050 with you out of twenty-four and a half for twenty-four."

"W4050: Thanks."

"No snow," Brim finished to Rido.

"Say again, Imperial W4050. Snow?" Avalon Center asked.

"Sorry, Center," Brim said, feeling his face redden. Sometimes voice pickups on VRG-104 instrument sets failed to shut down quickly enough. "Open mike," he explained self-consciously.

"Avalon Center," the controller acknowledged.

Ahead, the city itself was still mostly covered by clouds, but the overcast was quickly breaking up as it passed. "Imperial W4050: Turn new heading of five zero two five zero to join the Covingdon-32 radial inbound. Descend and maintain ten thousand at velocity of two-fifty; the altimeter two nine nine one."

"Imperial turning to five zero two five zero and descending to ten thousand at two-fifty."

"What's the lift-enhancer value here?" Brim asked, smoothly banking the little ship to its new heading.

"I, er, use about four here," Rido replied.

"Set 'em," Brim ordered.

"Warning panel?"

"Check."

"Altimeters?"

"Three check and agree."

"Cabin gravity restraints?"

"Set . . . now."

"Hullmetal ought to have cooled enough, too," Brim commented. "Lets get the landing lights uncovered while we're at it."

"Uncovered, and . . . on."

A polite chiming filled the flight bridge. "AutoHelm's disconnected, Wilf."

Brim nodded. "Got it," he said, feeling the controls come alive beneath his fingertips. Now came the *good* part. "Avalon Regional Approach: This is Imperial W4050 coming through eleven with you from Orbital Control."

"Good evening, Imperial W4050," the Controller replied. "Fly new heading two-thirty-five and . . . descend to seven thousand."

"Imperial W4050 out of eleven for seven."

By now the colossal city occupied most of the horizon, a study in sparkling crystal towers and hoary monuments to antiquity; beyond, Lake Mersin was a foreshortened expanse of gray. A chill of excitement raced along Brim's spine. Home!

"Imperial W4050," Regional called, "radio check."

"Loud and clear," Brim answered through a broad grin. Their vector was going to bring them right over the city! Ahead, Locarno Square and the massive stone buildings of the Imperial Admiralty were already slipping beneath the nose.

"Imperial 4050: Turn left ten degrees and reduce speed to one-eighty c'lenyts."

"Imperial 4050 acknowledges," Brim replied. The slight course correction lined them up perfectly on the lake. "How about more lift enhancer?" he asked.

"Dialing in twelve degrees," Rido answered.

The clearing storm left rough air in its wake; Brim gently countered it with aplomb won in a thousand similar approaches over the years, keeping the little ship steadily on course as if she were a battleship five times her mass. "Let's start the approach check, Terry," he said.

"With you, Admiral," Rido said. "Continuous boost?"

Brim scanned the grav panels. "On," he said as the ship bounced in the cloudy turbulence.

"Radio nav switches?"

"Set on RADIOS."

"Auto flight panels?"

"Imperial W4050," Regional interrupted, "soon as your speed is reduced, descend to five thousand."

"Imperial W4050 at one-eighty out of seven for five," Brim answered, retarding the thrust dampers. "Terry, was that 'auto flight panels?' "

"Auto flight panels."

"Checked." Off to starboard, the Imperial Palace—where his infant daughter lived as ward of the Emperor himself—was sliding rapidly out of sight behind the right nacelle. He wondered if she'd grown as much as the HoloGrams showed. . . . "Let's get everybody down now," he said.

"Aye, Admiral," Rido said. Moments later, his voice was on the blower: "All hands to landfall stations. Hands to landfall stations. All hands man your stations for landfall. Secure from Hyperspace operations. . . . "

"Nav radios?"

Brim focused on the COMM panel. "Manual."

"Altimeter, flight, and nav instruments?"

"You tell me," Brim said as a gust blasted them off course.

"Ah, set and cross-checked," Rido replied. "Sorry. You couldn't have known the cross-check sequence."

They were rapidly approaching the Grand Achtite Canal that bisected the city and emptied into Lake Mersin. Nearly a year ago—during one of the worst raids on the city—Brim had crash-landed a crippled Starfury in that canal. His eyes followed it to a small turning basin where a great sooty blemish still blackened the retaining walls and loading plaza.

The wreckage had long since been removed—and largely re-cycled, he supposed—but the smudges left by the radiation fires would endure for centuries. It had been a *bad* night.

"Airspeed EPR bugs?"

Brim realized that Rido was repeating his question. "Er, sorry, Terry," he replied with a glance at the flight instruments. I've got 'em at one thirty-nine—and cross-checked." Moments later, they were bumping and juddering over the tree-filled parks of the ancient Beardsmore Section now. Brim picked out graceful old Kimber Castle. How many times he'd passed that on his way to the Admiralty. And, he thought, looking through the forward Hyperscreens, it WASN'T snowing!

"Speed brake levers?"

"These?"

"Yeah."

"Locked."

"Imperial W4050: Reduce speed to one five zero, contact Fleet Tower one two six five five."

"One two six five five," Brim acknowledged. "Thank you, Region; we've appreciated the help." He reset the radio. "Imperial Tower, W4050 requests landing vector."

"Imperial W4050 cleared vector one seven left; wind zero three five at two five, gusts to seven five."

Brim grinned as he parried the turbulence. "Probably didn't need to tell us it's windy," he joked.

"Y-yeah," Rido said in a suddenly awestricken voice.

Too busy to wonder about that, Brim went on with the landing. They were crossing the ten million lanes of Verecker Boulevard now and soon were out over the heaving lake, Grand Imperial Terminal at the end of its causeway some distance off to the left. "Let's finish that landing check, Terry," he said.

"Er . . . vertical gravs?" Rido asked.

"Verticals on. Three green."

"Lift enhancers and extras?"

"Thirty-three, thirty-three, green light."

"That does it," Rido declared.

"Here we go, then," Brim said, now totally concentrated on his task. Ahead, a solid ruby light flashed out of the distance. Sudden gusts of wind pushed him to port and the light began to separate into horizontal lines. As he slipped to starboard, the light shimmered into vertical lines. One last correction and it coalesced again. Off to starboard, a forest of great loading cranes and goods houses slid by the rain-streaked Hyperscreens.

Only a hundred irals altitude now. He walked the steering engines carefully—the little ship was slippery, but she lined up and mostly stayed where he put her despite the stiff crosswind gusts. Ahead, the ruby vector was flopping back and forth between vertical and horizontal, Brim was now concentrating on the ranks of waves marching at a slight angle to the ship's track. They'd make things a little harder . . . but not *that* much. He checked the instruments once more: descent rate . . . speed . . . pitch. None perfect, but close enough in this kind of turbulence. He called up a little more thrust and eased off the steering engines. The little ship's bow swung to windward, then he slanted the deck a little for drift. Nose up ever so slightly. Judging the wave troughs, he held her off . . . deftly leveling the deck only an instant before cascades of gray lake water shot skyward in the side Hyperscreens, diminished as they slid through a trough, then shot skyward once more and stayed that way as Brim plastered the ship's gravity foot to the surface. They sliced through two more of the big waves before he gently pulsed the gravity brakes, sending long, triple streams of gravitons out ahead that flattened the waves while they slowed the ship. Moments alter, they were stopped, rolling wildly above the foot their gravity system punched in the surface of the storm-roiled lake. Exhilarated, Brim relaxed. "Your ship," he said, turning to Rido. "And *thanks*."

Rido took the controls—with a look of utter amazement on his face. "Sweet Mother of Voot," he whispered in an awestruck voice, "How'd you *do* that?"

"Do what?" Brim asked, now turning enough in his seat to check Lockheart. He also looked shocked. . . .

"Imperial W4050," the Tower broke in, "contact Surface Control one eight one nine. Traffic on a c'lenyt and a half final behind you."

"Imperial W4050, thank you, Tower," Rido replied, and switched the radios. "Imperial W4050 with you from Tower; request gravity pool assignment."

Brim glanced across to Rido again. "What'd I *do*?" he demanded.

"You, ah, landed it, Admiral," Rido replied. Still looking a little nonplussed, he continued to taxi toward the odd agglomeration of low buildings and repair sheds that made up the main Fleet complex.

"What do you mean, I 'landed it'?" Brim demanded. "What was I supposed to do—thraggling leave it up there?"

Rido laughed. "Sorry, Admiral," he said. "I think we do owe you a bit of an explanation."

Brim relaxed as Rido got instructions from Surface Control. When they had their gravity pool assigned, he looked over at the Commander and frowned. "Now, what's all this about my landing?" he demanded. "Did I screw it up, or something?"

Rido blushed visibly and glanced back at Lockheart. "Er, no, Admiral," he said. "You definitely didn't screw up the landing."

"Actually . . . it was an *excellent* landing," Lockheart added.

"Then how come you both looked as if I'd just broken all the laws of thermodynamics?" Brim demanded.

"Well, Admiral," Rido explained after a slight pause, "the thing is . . . this little DH-98 is *really* considered to be a Helmsman's ship."

"As in 'difficult to fly,'" Lockheart added in a quiet voice. "I know it's a handful of starship for me."

"Yeah, a handful for me, too," Rido added. "But *you.* Wilf Brim, flew like you've been driving the type for years. How the xaxt do you do it? Did they have you flying the prototype, or something?"

"No," Brim protested in surprise. "This trip makes only the second time I've even *seen* one of these buses."

Rido looked up from a globular display filled by the visage of a mustachioed controller. "We know," he said. "We checked by radio." He shook his head and chuckled. "You must be damned near as good as they say you are. We figured you'd be beggin' us for help before we got halfway through the atmosphere."

"Yeah," Lockheart added. "Instead, we were both takin' notes about how it *ought* to be done—'cept you made it look so damned easy I didn't learn a thing."

Brim laughed. "I don't know what you're talking about," he protested.

Rido shook his head. "That's the trouble with you xaxtdamned 'naturals,'" he grumbled amiably. "You make things look so easy."

"I still don't understand," Brim said, feeling a little irritation.

"Admiral," Rido explained at length, "only the best Helmsman ever get to fly these little beauties—and then only after a lot of practice. They're tricky . . . touchy. You just walked aboard and pulled off a perfect landing without even so much as a metacycle in the simulators. That's pretty impressive."

Brim felt his cheeks burn. He'd spent so much time at a helm during his lifetime, the very act of flying seemed as natural as walking—especially after recently "graduating" from the Sodeskayan combat flying school. "Er, thanks," he stammered trading seats with Lockheart again. As the maxim went: A little practice never hurt anybody. . . .

Less than a metacycle later the DH-98 was temporarily moored on a gravity pool in the transients' section of the base, and Brim was leading his tote bag down the brow to see if he could get surface transportation for himself and Barbousse. At the bottom, he happily gulped the moist, perfumed air of late spring (along with some of Avalon's perpetual pollution), then headed for a bank of public Holo-Phones to call the base's Transportation Section. He'd taken no more than a dozen steps when a rating stopped him and saluted energetically. The young man was dressed in a *summer-weight* Fleet Cloak. "Admiral Brim?" he asked, glancing at a tiny electronic notebook in his hand.

"That's me, mister," Brim replied, staring at the first summer uniform he'd seen in a million years. "Can I help you?"

The chauffeur looked confused for a moment, then smiled. "Aye, Admiral," he said, "I'm ordered to take you directly to the Admiralty."

"Sounds like a good idea to me," Brim said. "Especially since I was just about to see if I could cadge the same sort of transportation myself." He grinned. "Who sent you?" he asked.

"Don't know for certain, Admiral," the rating answered. "I was just next in line at the dispatcher's window."

"Whatever's fair," Brim replied with a grin. "Hang on a moment for Chief Barbousse," he said. "He'll be headed in the same direction."

"Chief *Barbousse*, Admiral?" the rating asked, his eyes going wide. "You don't mean *the* Chief Barbousse—highest-ranking Petty Officer in the Fleet—do you?"

"That's the man," Brim said with a chuckle. Here in

Avalon, the young starsailor probably drove Admirals around all day. But the highest-ranking Petty Officer in the Fleet—now, *there* was someone worth having as a passenger.

Moments later, Barbousse appeared at the entrance to the brow, nodded, then hurried over, his tote bag bobbing along in his wake. "You get your ride, Admiral?" he asked.

"Right to the Admiralty," Brim replied, throwing his own tote bag in the baggage compartment. "Somebody sent a staff skimmer for me." Suddenly he frowned. "Right," he said. "I *think* I just discovered who set up my ride . . . *Chief.*"

"Thought you probably wouldn't be in the mood for waitin' once we got here," Barbousse said with an embarrassed grin. "Not after that greaser of a landing, beggin' the Admiral's pardon."

Brim shook his head and smiled. "Somehow you're always a couple of steps ahead of me, Chief," he said.

"That's m' job, the way I see things, Admiral," Barbousse said. He turned to the by now totally awestruck rating. "You'll take good care of the Admiral, starsailor," he ordered.

"I—I will, Chief Barbousse," the rating replied. "I promise."

"Good," Barbousse said, and turned to Brim. "I'll be on m' way, then, Admiral."

"You're not going to the Admiralty?" Brim asked.

"I've got a few errands to run, unless you'll need me right away," Barbousse replied.

Brim knew from years of experience that Barbousse never went anywhere that wasn't important in some way or another. "Catch up when you get a chance," Brim said. "Somehow I've got the feeling that you'll know where I am better than I do."

Babousse saluted smartly. "I'll be checkin' in, Admiral."

Moments later, Brim and a thoroughly starstruck young

rating departed the military complex bound for the Admiralty.

The staff car wasn't even halfway through town before Brim got a good idea of what he would be facing when he campaigned his Empire for Sodeskayan aid. The city's war damage had been evident from the Hyperscreens of a DH-98, but somehow not very real as they slipped beneath the nose. At street level, however, the view provided details that woke memories his mind had long before tried to erase. Some of the damage looked quite new—clearly, the Leaguers had not given up their obsession of making the lives of Avalonians as miserable as they could.

He glanced around at the familiar panorama, recalling the same streets nearly two years ago, before the actual attacks started. In those days, it was impossible to drive anywhere wearing a uniform without howling, spittle-drenched assaults by League-funded CIGAs fixated by peace at any price—including their own freedom. For a number of years, they'd held sway under the leadership of Brim's old shipmate. Puvis Amherst, nibbling away at the military's capabilities and weakening the Fleet to near extinction. "Contemplate Galactic Peace" was their chief catch phrase—and a number of the zukeeds had been given their chance to do just that—while watching their homes blasted to smithereens by squadrons of League attack ships.

He laughed mirthlessly; the irony wasn't so much funny as tragic. Since the Leaguers began their execrable campaign against Avalon, the CIGA dimbulbs had become *very* scarce. Especially after a number of them were beaten bloody by the very citizens who supported their misguided peace efforts in the first place. Only Puvis Amherst himself continued his failed program with any sort of resolve, and few but the most dead-headed holdouts paid attention to his empty declamations anymore. Perhaps for Amherst, that was the worst punishment of all. . . .

Brim smiled as his skimmer was swallowed up by the familiar traffic of Locarno Square and careened around the statue of Gondor Bemis—back to the business at hand. Any immediate aid to Sodeskaya he might manage to cadge on this trip would literally be carved out of the Empire's primary effort to merely survive. And it didn't take much more than the simple act of peering around to understand that there wouldn't much in the way of resources left over for sharing.

Somehow, Brim's driver managed to survive the wild traffic and pulled to a stop in front of the Admiralty after only three wild circuits of Locarno Square—Brim had been a passenger on more than one occasion when *six* revolutions of the square had been necessary to reach the curb. Striding up the broad staircase (while carefully avoiding the "traditional" pidwing droppings that had fouled the marble treads for centuries), he returned salutes from ceremonial guards dressed in parade uniform and marched through the front entrance doors without breaking step. Inside the majestic domed lobby, he made his way to the directory—half a year's absence was enough time for everyone in the building to have traded offices at least twice. Midway across the inlaid marble floor, however, he felt a hand on his shoulder.

"Ane assumes you are tryin' to warm up back here in Avalon, Wilf Brim," a voice said.

Brim turned to confront the handsome visage of Grand Admiral Baxter Calhoun, Commander-in-Chief of the entire Imperial Fleet. "Cal!" he exclaimed, grinning with real pleasure. Shrewd, cunning, and utterly patriotic, Calhoun was one of the few individuals in the Universe Brim completely trusted—in everything.

"I think I know why you're here, Wilf," Calhoun said, his gray eyes boring into Brim's soul.

"The Sodeskayans need help," Brim said, gripping Calhoun's large, smooth hand in his own. "I've come to see what I can mooch for them."

Calhoun laughed. "Weel, weel," he said. "It's good to know that your tour in Sodeskaya ha'n't made you any less direct."

"I figure you don't have any more time to waste than they do, Cal," Brim replied with a grin, thinking how fresh it was to hear a Carescrian accent again. He'd been listening to a *lot* of Bear recently.

"You're right," Calhoun said. "An' I take it you feel this is very important."

"*Very* important," Brim acknowledged.

Calhoun nodded. "We ha' but little to share wi' onyone right noo, Wilf," he said. "At least for the next year or so, we'll be lucky to save our own skins. But then you know tha', don't you? You could na' ha' missed it on your way through the city from the Lake. The zukeed Leaguers still mount daily raids across the 'Wyckean Void from Effer'wyck."

"I know," Brim admitted. "But it won't always be this way—not if we expect to win this war eventually."

"I understand," Calhoun said. He considered for a moment while a whole Universe of military workers and feather merchants swirled around them on the vast floor. He nodded. "You need at least some help *now*, tho', don't you?" he asked.

"Immediately," Brim replied. "Their first offensive is coming up right away."

Calhoun grinned. "Sounds like our auld friend Ursis," he said. "Those Bears have needed to gat on the offensive for a long time. To xaxtdamened bad the Knez didna use his brains a wee sooner."

"Can't turn back time," Brim said with a wry smile, "much as I'd like to sometimes."

"Don't I know," Calhoun said. He thought for another moment, then fixed Brim with a steely glance. "For the nonce, the best we'll be able to provide is a token," he said thoughtfully. "Somethin' t'show 'em we'll do better later, when we're more able. Can you make do wi' somethin' like maybe twa squadrons of Starfuries an' their crews?"

"How about three?" Brim said. "They've got to have hope for the future. Otherwise . . . "

The two friends strolled slowly across the floor. "You really believe in those Bears, don't you?" Calhoun asked.

"Yeah, Cal," Brim said quietly, "I do. They're tough—great fighters. And there are *a lot* of them. All they've needed is the right equipment. Thanks to old Dr. Borodov, that's starting to come through, but it'll be a while until they can hold their own in space."

"'Tis settled, then," Calhoun said. "Three squadrons plus crews an' support. We'll hae to make it luik as if you've had to fight hard for what you want. There's many o' the High Command who wull question the wisdom of 'wastin' precious resources to prop up a government that appears to be loosin' its struggle wi' the League."

Brim nodded agreement. "I remember when Effer'wyck was on the same slippery slope—right before she surrendered. If we'd sent the Starfuries they wanted at the time—and lost 'em—we might not have won the battle of Avalon."

"Don't worry, Wilf," Calhoun said, "in the end you'll get your token. Onrad and I wull take care of that." He frowned. "What will be a lot tougher, though, will be gettin' follow-on support. Our friends the Bears will somehow have to improve their image as warriors capable of dealing with the League. People like your old friend General Hagbut simply *hate* sending equipment off anywhere except where Imperials can play with it."

Hagbut! What a flood of memories *that* name brought with it. "I guess he's got his reasons," Brim said. "We lost a lot of equipment—and troops—trying to save Effer'wyck.

And he took the heat when the politicos were sniffing out a scapegoat."

Calhoun nodded. "I assume *you* are willin' to stick your neck out for the Bears." He smiled humorlessly. "You know, *you'd* be one o' the prime scapegoats if we lose a lot o' people an' equipment over there.'

Brim shrugged. "Cal," he said emphatically, "I wouldn't have to worry, even if the possibility bothered me in the first place. Those Bears are unbeatable on the surface. They simply lack a space force. Once they've built that back, they'll be damned hard to stop. Especially when they're fighting for their homes."

"You know that an' I know that," Calhoun said. "But a lot of people won't want to believe it." He shrugged. "That big fight's still in the future. For the nonce, you've got your 'token,' although you won't be able to tell anybody until after every politician in town's had a chance to make a speech about it." He glanced at the huge clock in the center of the lobby. "We'll start things when you *officially* contact me at . . . say, Brightness and one. All right? That ought to give you time for a short visit to the Palace. The Emperor's anxious to talk to you—as are Harry Drummond and Bos Gallsworthy, among others."

Brim nodded. "I'll be glad to see all of them," he said. "Sodeskaya's a great place, but you sure see a lot of Bears there."

"Strange, that." Calhoun chuckled. "I've noticed it myself, on occasion." Then he glanced at the great lobby clock again. "I'm due at a meeting now. You've been assigned a skimmer and driver while you're here—it'll save us all time in the long run. In the courtyard by the carport; the driver will recognize you." He started in the direction of the lifts. "Tenth floor," he called over his shoulder. "They'll recognize you there, too."

"Thanks, Cal," Brim said as his old friend—and now one

of the most powerful individuals in the Empire—strode quietly through the bustling crowd and disappeared into a lift. Head swimming, he glanced at his timepiece and laughed to himself. His trip would probably last two or three Standard Weeks, excluding travel time. But except for the political showmanship, he had already achieved his objective—within two metacycle of his touchdown on Lake Mersin. Welcome back to the real world, Wilf Brim, he chuckled to himself. Welcome home.

Barbousse and the stunning redhead Cosa Tutti were waiting when Brim arrived at the Imperial Palace. Both looked tired and more than a little dreamy, as if they had recently been making love after a long, lonely time apart. Tutti was holding a tiny, bright-eyed girl in her arms who, at the tender age of one, had already grown a mane of sable hair that promised someday to rival that of her late mother. The child was dressed as if she were royalty, which—as the personal ward of Emperor Onrad V, Grand Galactic Emperor, Prince of the Reggio Star Cluster, and Rightful Protector of the Heavens—she clearly was, in spirit if not in actual fact.

She smiled and reached toward Brim with both hands.

"Who is that, Hope?" Tutti prompted.

"Daddy Wilf," Hope said.

"Daddy Wilf?" Brim asked, taking the little girl in his arms. "Honey," he protested with a smile, "nobody's supposed to know you're my daughter. What're we going to do about that?"

"Not to worry, Admiral," Tutti replied. "Aside from her official 'Father Mustafa Eyren,'—who *does* come to see her now and then, by the way—she also has her 'Daddy Onrad' as well as her 'Daddy Cal.' And today we've added 'Daddy Utrillo' and 'Daddy Wilf.' So there's little chance of her real patrimony getting out, at least for a while."

Brim looked into the little girl's laughing face. She would

be a beauty someday—she already had her mother's almond-shaped eyes. For most of her short life, he'd seen her only in HoloGrams, a tenuous relationship at best. But here in his arms, a whole year of tenderness came flooding into his very soul, and he pressed her to him while gentle tears coursed along his cheeks. "Hope," he whispered. "Hope. Hope. Hope. . . . "

He was very nearly late for his appointment with Calhoun that afternoon, but his chauffeur, a sober-looking Petty Officer named Quinner Twist, drove as if Nergol Triannic himself were chasing him. As a result, Brim dashed into Calhoun's office-suite lobby with barely a cycle to spare.

"You must be Admiral Brim," declared a leggy civilian secretary who was bending provocatively over a display panel.

Brim nodded. "I think I've got an appointment with Cal just about now," he said.

The woman smiled knowingly. "You do, Admiral," she said, pointing to a closed door. "Just walk in."

"Thanks," Brim said. He knocked once, then activated the latch and . . . stopped in his tracks.

Inside the office—intersanctum of the Empire's whole military effort—Emperor Onrad V, Grand Galactic Emperor, Prince of the Reggio Star Cluster, and Rightful Protector of the Heavens, sat backward on a chair facing Calhoun's desk, concentrating on a handful of Cre'el playing cards. To his right miniscule Admiral Bosphorous Gallsworthy, Chief of Defense Command, frowned at his cards with a look of genuine concern; to his left, General Harry Drummond stared at the ceiling in rapt conversation. "Come in, Brim," Calhoun said from behind the desk, then turned to Onrad. "I'll see your five and raise you ten." Before him was a substantial accumulation of credits—much larger than those of his three compatriots.

Onrad, a handsome, heavy set man with a goatee, turned

and winked at Brim, then shook his head. "I'm out, Cal," he said, pushing a large portion of his credits toward Calhoun.

"So'm I, dammit," Gallsworthy grumbled, pushing a slightly smaller heap of credits Calhoun's way. "Brim," he growled, "this must be your fault. I'm normally a tremendous Cre'el player."

"Can't be anybody else's fault," the broad-shouldered Drummond said with a glower. "Wilf, you always were a troublemaker."

Onrad pulled a chair to the desk from a nearby table. "Come join us, Wilf," he said. "We have these top-level planning sessions every week. Cal's, er, *technique* keeps us in practice for dealing with Nergol Triannic the rest of the week."

Calhoun fluttered a hand over his heart. "Your Majesty," he said. "How could you so impugn my gentle brand o'gamin'?"

Onrad placed a much-diminished stack of credits in his wallet. "I have always been known as a truthful Emperor," he sniffed with great dignity.

As Brim took his seat, the four men turned to him and smiled. "Wilf," the Emperor said, "it's good to have you back among us. Tell us how things are in Sodeskaya."

Brim thought for a moment. "They've been worse, Your Majesty," he replied. "Have any of you seen my reports to Cal?"

Drummond guffawed. "They're among the few KA'PPAs from the theater I bother to look at."

"Yeah," Gallsworthy added with a chuckle. "You' keep 'em short enough to read." He frowned. "In all seriousness, you're the only one who sends in reports without adding a bunch of political claptrap."

Onrad nodded. "I think we all appreciate that." He chuckled. "But what's this business about Marshal *nov* Vobok? Did Nik really kill the zukeed?"

"Oh he *did*," Brim assured the Emperor. "I watched him break *nov* Vobok's neck, then use the corpse as a club on two or three more Leaguer bigwigs." He frowned. "I never did find out what happened to them, but they weren't moving when I climbed aboard Tissuard's *Nord*. And after that, we left in a big hurry."

"I shouldn't wonder about *that*." Drummond chuckled.

"Brim," Onrad said, shaking his head in wonder, "I have never met anybody with so xaxtdamned many close calls— or friends who are willing to risk their necks for you. How in Voot's name do you manage it?"

"I'm only a simple Helmsman," Brim replied.

"Oh, r-r-r-ight." Calhoun chuckled, collecting the colorful Cre'el cards and replacing them in a handsome, inlaid wooden box. "Well, wh'ever you are, you may well ha' wit-ness'd the most important single event o' the war so far—at least for the Sodeskayans. Our sources tell us tha' *nov* Vobok's death is almost wholly responsible for Triannic's decision to hold up the war an' bring in reinforcements."

"Then the zukeed's demise couldn't have come at a better time," Brim stated flatly. "This so-called 'lull' is providing Ursis with the opening he needs to move extra forces in place."

"And speaking of extra forces," Gallsworthy interjected, "tell us about these squadrons we're going to send back to Bearland with you. From what I understand, all three are coming out of my hide."

Brim smiled. He'd rehearsed answers to that question for days now—and they knew it. "Well, for starters," he said, "I'll want Starfuries out there. Probably the new 5-Bs, be-cause the Leaguers are using their latest equipment against the Bears." He paused for a moment. "We'll need spares, too," he added with a nod, "—some way to maintain those ships so far away from home. They'll be in the thick of the combat all the time. And because they're different, they'll attract all the wrong attention."

"Are we sending a sacrifice?" Gallsworthy asked. "Clearly, we're always going to have casualties and losses, but I really can't condone pure sacrifices. What's your take, Wilf?"

"I'm not sure there's a simple answer to that, Bos," he said finally. "First, what's your definition of a sacrifice?"

Gallsworthy frowned. "I guess," he said after some deliberation, "a sacrifice in my book would be sending those ships and crews off to be lost in battles we know the Bears are going to lose."

Brim nodded. "Well," he conceded, "in the course of this campaign, most of the Starfuries probably *will* be lost—and nobody can be certain that this first offensive will permanently recapture anything. So in *those* terms, we may have a sacrifice."

"You look as if you're about to say 'but,' " Gallsworthy said. What makes this different?"

"When we fought the Battle of Avalon," Brim continued, "our killer ships had—what?—an average lifetime of eleven missions, or something like that. We didn't call *them* sacrifices."

"But we won that battle," Gallsworthy interjected.

"I understand," Brim said. "It's an important point you make. But keep in mind that winning and losing always have a time context, one we haven't figured into the Sodeskayan campaign because the 'battle' isn't over *there*."

"Wait a moment!" Gallsworthy demanded. "What does time have to do with anything?"

"So far as the three squadrons are concerned," Brim explained, "ships *and* crews, a time continuum is actually critical when deciding if their losses are counted as a sacrifice or simply casualties."

"Time, eh?" the Emperor said. "Brim, you're way outside *my* sphere of understanding."

"I doubt that, Your Majesty," Brim replied firmly. "Think about the loss of my own Starfury last year. In the context of the day it was lost—and indeed nearly that whole month—it was a needless sacrifice, because at the time, we appeared to be losing—badly."

"But in the context of the whole five-month battle," Onrad said with a nod, "it was simply a loss. I understand what you're getting at. How about you, Bos?"

Gallsworthy nodded. "Of course I understand, Your Majesty," he said. "I just didn't want to send three squadrons out to be immediately ground up for nothing."

"Well," Brim added, "nobody's going to guarantee how much of a contribution the Sodeskayans will see from any individual ship. If one of those Starfuries flies in front of a Gorn-Hoff on its first sortie, it will *definitely* be ground up for nothing, but—"

"But it won't have been sacrificed to a hopeless situation," Calhoun finished for him.

"The Sodeskayan situation is *anything* but hopeless," Brim said. "Nik and Dr. Borodov plan to throw almost everything they've got into it, although eventually they'll have to pull back when they begin to run out of resources."

"I guess that's another thing I'm talking about, then," Drummond said. "During that pullout, some forces will have to be left behind to cover the retreat. I'd like to make certain that our people aren't part of that. At least not by plan."

Brim nodded. "I see your point," he acknowledged. "I'll have that promise from Ursis before I take those squadrons to Sodeskaya."

"What else will you need?" Calhoun asked.

"Well," Brim said, "I'd hoped I might be able to get Toby Moulding to lead them. What's the possibility of something like that?"

Onrad put his chin on his arms and nodded. "I was afraid you'd ask for Moulding," he said. "He's clearly the man for the job—especially the way you two have worked so well together in the past."

"I think I hear another 'but' coming, Your Majesty," Brim prompted.

"You guessed it," Onrad said with a wry grin. "Moulding's one request we won't be able to fill." He shrugged. "Sometimes even Emperors have to give in to politics—and this, unfortunately, is one of those times. Ever hear of Sir Cecil DeBrugh?" he asked.

Brim thought for a moment. The name was familiar. "Isn't he that Member of Parliament who owns all those hullmetal fabrication mills off Vega-31?"

"The same," Onrad said with a distinct manner of distaste. "And those mills are damned important to the war effort." He shook his head. "I could take 'em over, but everybody knows what happens when government tries to run something like a factory. Anyway," he continued, "seems he's got a son, Basil, who's Commander of 91 Wing out at FleetPort 93, orbiting Protius—three squadrons flying brand-new Starfury 5-Bs. And Dad's got his heart set on Captain Basil becoming a hero."

"How does Captain Basil feel about all this?" Brim asked.

"Aflame with ambition." Onrad chuckled. "A chip off the old block if ever there was one."

"Aside from that, Your Majesty," Brim asked, "is he any good at what he does?"

"That may be his one saving grace," Gallsworthy said. "He's known as a pretty good Starfury driver who takes care of his crews. Aside from that, unfortunately, he's also somewhat of a noisome blockhead, and he doesn't like taking orders."

"Oh, they're going to *love* him in Sodeskaya."

Onrad smiled. "That's one of your *two* challenges, Brim,"

he said. "If he can't be loved, it'll be up to you to make him useful at least."

Brim closed his eyes. *WON*-der-ful, he thought, just thraggling wonderful. Then he frowned. "That's only *one* challenge, Your Majesty."

"The other may be harder still," Onrad replied with a very serious countenance.

"Your majesty?" Brim asked with a raised eyebrow.

"Also," Onrad answered, "you've got to keep the smart-assed zukeed alive. . . . "

CHAPTER 9
Ksnaymed

Just short of three Standard Weeks later—following what seemed to be at least thirty-five years worth of irrelevant haggling and pompous oration by some of the Empire's most useless politicians—the Imperial foray to Sodeskaya was on. Now, with Basil DeBrugh and his three squadrons "chosen" for the mission, Brim and Barbousse were presently passengers aboard a shuttle in the process of docking at FleetPort 93, an orbiting killer-ship base protecting a large research complex on the planet of Protius.

During the approach, Brim could see from a distance that this FleetPort was one of the originals, built in preparation for a war fought and won more than a hundred Standard Years earlier. As such, it was also one of the most elegant of the orbiting bases, designed for a long-disappeared Fleet whose officer corps was made up exclusively of scions from the Empire's wealthy, influential families. Losses from the most recent war finally put paid to that custom, but prejudice against "commoners" died slowly, as Brim was still occasionally reminded.

DeBrugh was waiting outside the air lock as Brim and Barbousse stepped from the brow. The man had done his homework, for he saluted Brim immediately. "Admiral," he snapped. "Welcome to Defense Command's Ninety-one Wing, home of Nine-fourteen, Twenty-eight, and Fifty-six Squadrons."

Brim returned his best Helmsman's Academy salute, then extended his hand. "Glad to meet you, Captain," he said— only a modest prevarication. "This is Master Chief Petty officer Utrillo Barbousse, who's scheduled to meet with some of your enlisted people to help set up details of the mission to Sodeskaya."

"Delighted to meet both of you," DeBrugh replied. "I understand you've spent some time there recently." He laughed. "I'll wager you're glad to get back to some human civilization."

Brim smiled good-naturedly. "Actually, the Bears completely spoil me," he said. "I don't suppose I've ever felt more welcome—anywhere."

"That so?" DeBrugh said with something that sounded like surprise in his voice. "How about you, Chief? What did you think of the place?"

"The Bears couldn't have been more neighborly, Cap'm," Barbousse replied. "I always look forward to goin' there."

"Well, I should think they would try to make you feel at home," DeBrugh said out of the side of his mouth. "You must be like gods to them—I mean . . . they're only animals, after all. Everyone's heard about their *special* sleigh rides and the like," he said, laughing salaciously.

Brim felt his cheeks burn. After his adventure with Tissuard, he kind of liked the idea. . . .

"But enough of that," DeBrugh continued breezily. "We shall teach them how to live and fight—our human burden, I suppose. Come, Admiral, let me show you around our meager accommodations. They're old, but acceptably elegant.

And afterward, we're putting on a bit of a celebratory banquet for the officers. It will be a fine opportunity to become acquainted."

Frowning, Brim decided to ignore the man's worrisome talk about a 'human burden'—for the present. He'd have ample time to handle that kind of problem once he discovered how much—and what kind of—education or discipline would be most effective. His present task was to learn as much as possible about . . . everything. "Good," he said decisively. "I'm anxious to meet everyone involved—especially the people who will actually be going to Sodeskaya."

For more than a metacycle, DeBrugh led Brim through every nook and cranny of the huge old satellite. Everywhere they went, one thing was immediately clear: DeBrugh's officers held him in high esteem, although it was not clear to what extent the rank and file shared this opinion. It was also quite apparent that DeBrugh kept his base in absolutely pristine condition—a lot more pristine than Brim remembered any of the other orbiting Defense Command stations he had visited—or commanded. The century-old hangar bays, for example, looked as if they had been constructed only a few Standard Months previously. And although Brim was no expert on starship maintenance, over the years he'd learned enough to appreciate gleaming new gear that was obviously the high-end equivalent of less attractive but serviceable government-issue equipment. It didn't take a rocket scientist to guess where the outlandish funds for tools like *those* came from.

The same was true about the Wing's Starfuries: three squadrons of twenty pristine killer ships each, looking fresh from the builder's yards. With two huge 565-mmi disruptors supplanting eight of the ship's normal fourteen superfocused 425s, the new Starfury 5-Bs represented a potent upgrade to the already legendary performance figures of the original Sherrington design. At the end of his tour, Brim found himself tremendously impressed with the station itself—while not a little troubled by its flagrant disregard for standards.

The uprated tools gave him the most worry. They produced the same results as those that were issued through normal channels, of course. But he knew from experience that they often operated in different ways—some subtle and some not so subtle. What would happen if the mechanics and crew chiefs suddenly found themselves with only standard gear to use? Could they immediately perform their jobs as well, or would they find themselves in a very poorly timed learning curve?

Clearly, one way or another, young DeBrugh had cadged permission to operate in this manner. Political clout could justify nearly anything at any time, but it mostly lost its power in the stress of battle. Brim made a note to warn Onrad and his "Poker Staff" about the situation, but he had little hope that even the Emperor would be able to do anything about it, at least before the scheduled departure for Sodeskaya.

That evening at the Officers' Mess Hall, Brim and DeBrugh—dressed in formal uniforms—sat centered at a counter that headed three long banquet tables, each identified by a massive squadron number in carved ice: "904," "76," and "25." On three sides of these tables, nearly one hundred spirited men and women were dining from the most elegant tableware Brim had seen since his last visit to the Imperial Palace. At least forty ratings shuttled to and from the kitchens, bringing and removing course after course of delicacies and refilling crystal goblets with rare old Logish Meems. Brim ate quietly, feeling somewhat discomfited by the banquet itself—it would have pleased the Knez—while making polite conversation on either side and busily sniffing out the flavor of DeBrugh's working organization.

For his part, DeBrugh himself kept their talk centered

mostly on starships and flying—subjects clearly dear to his heart. To Brim's right, however, Lieutenant Commander Susanna Kehler, a glorious blonde with flowing, shoulder-length hair, lazy, deep blue eyes, and a positively lascivious mouth in a heart-shaped face, spoke softly of financial accomplishments in a voice so mellow that her dreary subject almost sounded interesting. The galaxy-famous décolleté of her Imperial Dress Uniform revealed acres of creamy skin—accentuated by the woman's endearing habit of bending close when they spoke—and revealing even more. In the moments before he assisted her into a chair, Brim had been aware of long, sturdy legs and a tiny waist. She looked enough like Margot Effer'wyck that the two women could have been sisters—this one younger and more immature, but nearly as beautiful. He'd laughed to himself. DeBrugh had done *a lot* of homework for the visit.

Before the main course, one of the officers stood, raised his goblet, and said in a loud, clear voice, "Long live the Emperor!"

Instantly, each occupant of the room stood and raised a goblet, reciting the age-old toast, "Long live our glorious Emperor, long live our gracious Emperor, Universe preserve the Emperor."

Before the echoed words died out, a second officer raised her glass and proclaimed "Three cheers for Admiral Brim," then led the room in three rousing cheers while Brim stood helplessly, feeling his cheeks burn.

Before a third toast could begin, Brim raised his goblet and quickly put in, "Three cheers for Ninety-one Wing and Sodeskaya!"

After this, the room went wild with applause, which somehow redoubled when Brim and DeBrugh touched goblets, then raised them to the cheering officers themselves.

After a number of further toasts—and much more cheering—the officers took their places and the banquet began.

From the first appetizer to the last of multiple desserts, Brim could only describe the banquet as magnificent, yet somehow tasteful. Unlike the Knez, DeBrugh recognized subtle differences between sumptuous and extravagant entertaining. Moreover, for all his postured fixations, young DeBrugh was truly a fascinating conversationalist. And, of course, Kehler's amazing resemblance to Margot Effer'wyck lent an almost magic ambiance to the whole affair.

As the last dessert plates were cleared away and the officers sipped rare cordials or lit up mu'occo cigarettes, DeBrugh, stood and once more toasted Emperor Onrad—to a much subdued room full of officers—then abruptly turned to Brim. "Fellow officers of the Fleet's Ninety-first Wing," he began, "I know that all of you have craved more information about our next assignment. Therefore, I give you Admiral Brim, who has been monitoring the situation since long before the Leaguer invasion of Sodeskaya began."

Surprised—and a little put out—Brim got to his feet amid renewed applause, locked eyes momentarily with the smiling DeBrugh, then nodded to the officers and raised a hand for silence, his mind working at top speed. "Thank you, Captain DeBrugh," he said with a smile he didn't mean. "I'm happy for this opportunity to share a few observations about your fascinating new duty station—and about the Bears whose domain you will be helping to save. You're in the vanguard of an operation that may one day be looked upon as one of the war's major accomplishments. . . . "

For the next half metacycle, he recounted his view of the Sodeskayan campaign to date, the Bears' strengths as well as their weaknesses, and what peculiarities could be expected from area Leaguers. At the end, he looked around the old satellite's banquet room—now considerably quieter and more sober than when he started—and frowned. "It's a different war out there," he said in summary. "So far, a defensive effort," he added, "but not like the one you're used to here at FleetPort Ninety-three. Sodeskaya's *big*. Over the years I'd visited their capital a number of times, but never had a clue as to how big the domain itself actually is." He glanced at the serious faces around the room. "Probably I still don't have an accurate grasp of how big it is, but I'm getting there. And for the most part, that bigness is unpopulated: you won't find yourself stationed in a palace like this, orbiting within metacycles of one of the grandest cities in the known Universe. Sodeskaya has its urban centers, all right— many rivaling Avalon herself. But more than likely you'll find yourself on some out-of-the-way planet that's not only barren, but frozen as well. It's an ugly war out there—a lot uglier than any war most of you have yet encountered, even those of you who fought with me in the Battle of Avalon."

When he finished, his listeners remained in silence for a moment more, then burst out once more in resounding applause—not the whistle-punctuated, whooping accolade he'd received earlier. This was a real token of appreciation. As he settled into his seat, he glanced at DeBrugh, who was staring at him with what could only be described as surprised admiration. *My point,* he thought a little sadly—and hoped that the young Wing Commander beside him would dedicate as much of the same kind of energy into fighting Leaguers as he had trying out his new—and very temporary—commander. Soon enough, the man would be reporting to a Sodeskayan.

During the following reception, Brim answered what seemed to be a million often disturbing questions about Sodeskaya and Sodeskayans themselves. Did Bears eat their enemies after they killed them? Might they be prone to attacking their allies in the heat of battle? Did they use normal sanitary facilities? Were the males attracted to human women, especially when the women were "in season"?

Brim often found himself grinding his teeth as he talked. The whole Galaxy owed much of its HyperDrive technology to the Bears' skill at engineering, yet here was a whole group of highly educated, highly talented starship drivers who thought of them as mere animals—savages at best. He shook his head. At least part of the problem had to do with the kind of war they were waging here at FleetPort 93. Bears had been an integral part of Brim's own life from his first day aboard an Imperial warship. In those days, Avalon had yet to suffer its first direct attack, so he waged his first war out in the Galaxy in ships crewed by representatives of every race of the Empire.

In the present sequel to the same conflict, however, Nergol Triannic and his Leaguers brought combat to Avalon's very doorstep. As a result, these Imperials had been wholly engaged just defending the five stars that made up their own capital and therefore got little chance to interface with anyone outside their very homogeneous group—including allies.

Now that the Fleet was making a first, hesitant step to take the war beyond its immediate boundaries, starsailors at all levels would have to relearn a number of new talents—ones that had little to do with the warriors' primary duty of "killing and breaking things." They would soon have to begin practicing the skills of tolerating and cooperating—often the most difficult of all to master.

As the evening progressed, Brim often found Kehler at his side while he circulated among the officers, clasping hands and answering their often witless questions. By the time the crowd had thinned noticeably—and the meem began to have its inevitable effect—he found the differences between Margot Effer'wyck and Susanna Kehler were fading rapidly. When, as he expected, she ultimately suggested that they withdraw to her room, he was hard-put to turn her down. "Susanna," he said as gently as he could, "I feel really honored by that invitation." He glanced down at her creamy bosom and took her hand. "Believe me, I would *love* to help you out of that uniform," he said regretfully, "but I think perhaps we ought to get to know one another a little better first. Don't you?"

She frowned. "I don't understand," she said. "You mean you don't want to?"

"I mean that under any other circumstances, I'd have carried you off to *my* room at least half a metacycle ago—and maybe will sometime in the future. But if and when you and I share a bed, it'll be by *your* choice and not your Commander's. You're too nice to be used that way."

Kehler's cheeks colored and she looked down at the floor. "Was I that transparent?" she asked in obvious humiliation.

Gently, Brim put a finger beneath her chin and raised her head until she was looking him in the eye. "No," he said. "*DeBrugh* was that obvious." He chuckled. "Susanna—with looks like yours, you could entertain a different stud every night if you wanted to. A knockout like you doesn't go jumping into bed with a middle-aged man like me unless he first *charms* her out of her pants—and I haven't had time to do anything like that. Right?"

Kehler smiled. "You're doing quite a job on me now, Admiral," she said.

"Probably we need to reach a point where you call me something more endearing than 'Admiral' before that happens," Brim added with a smile. "Now," he said after a moment of silence, "since we've got all that past us, is this going to put you in trouble with DeBrugh?"

She shook her head. "I don't think so, Admiral," she said quietly. "He simply wanted me to, er . . . " her voice trailed off.

"Just what *did* he want?" Brim asked.

Kehler looked frightened for a moment. "Admiral, couldn't we just drop the whole thing right now?"

"I'd really like to know what he said to you," Brim stated firmly. "I'll take no action unless you want me to."

"You promise?" she asked. "I've worked a long time for this assignment."

Brim nodded—he understood *that*, all right. "I promise," he said.

"Basil DeBrugh didn't actually *order* me to do anything," she said, blushing. "He just suggested that I make myself available, so to speak—for your, er, entertainment. I guess that I look a lot like a princess you used to see. Margot Effer'wyck?"

Brim fumed. "How in xaxt does he get off thinking he can ask something like that of an Imperial Officer?" he demanded hotly. "That's *terrible*. Does he treat everybody here that way?"

"No," Kehler said. "Not everybody. It's just that at Fleet-Port Ninety-three, everything and everyone exists for the flight crews." She looked him in the eye. "And Admiral," she continued, "it's not all that *terrible*, either. Those crews get sent out every day in all sorts of gravity conditions to risk their lives, while we support types go our way in relative safety." She smiled. "Maybe I did resent DeBrugh's asking me to do a little whoring for him. But I *am* pretty good-looking—and if spending a couple of metacycles on my back rutting with a rather attractive Admiral can help make their lives a little easier, it's time well spent in my book. Wouldn't you agree?"

"You're quite a lady, Susanna Kehler," Brim said. He meant it.

"You're quite a man, Admiral," Kehler replied. "It's nice to know that you had too much class for DeBrugh's little ploy to work." For a moment she got a smile on her face. "Except . . . " she said.

"Except what?" Brim asked.

Kehler looked at him, moving her tongue slowly over her lips. "Except . . . " she said after a few moments, "maybe you've *already* charmed me out of my pants, as you put it. I think I'd enjoy spending some time on my back with you sometime—when DeBrugh doesn't have anything to do with it."

"I'll be around," Brim said noncommittally. "Let's see what we can work out."

That very night, he was awakened from a sound sleep by an extremely attractive blond visitor tapping at his door. "Hey, Wilf Brim," she whispered languidly, stepping from her fatigues, "charm me out of *these*." All she had on was a pair of briefs. . . .

A Royal Page in scarlet livery was waiting at the foot of the brow when Brim and Barbousse returned to the capital. Tall and slim, with a largish nose, the woman reminded Brim of the great herons he had encountered years ago on one of the watery planets of Naftar. Her demeanor matched her looks. "Admiral Brim?" she inquired loftily.

"The same," Brim said, producing his military identity disk with a frown. Why would someone send him a message from the Palace? Had something happened to Hope? Dismissing *that* worry immediately—really bad news came by KA'PPA—he glanced at Barbousse, who only shrugged. If *he* didn't know, then the woman really had a secret. He waited impatiently while she ran his ID through every test imaginable in the authenticator at her side. When finally she appeared to be satisfied that he was at least not Nergol Triannic, she reached inside her pouch and withdrew a purple folder. "Personal from the Emperor," she said. "It will destruct the second time you press the Royal Seal."

Brim nodded; it wasn't the first Royal folder he'd received—nor was it likely to be the last. "Thank you, ma'am," he said, signing her authenticator with the prints of three fingers. The woman nodded curtly, then disappeared into the crowded military terminal at great speed.

While Barbousse picked up their skimmer, Brim retired to

a quiet corner of the terminal and pressed the Royal Seal embossed in the upper-left corner of the folder. After a moment, the enclosure opened to reveal a letter from Onrad himself:

BRIM: THOUGHT YOU OUGHT TO SEE THIS
REPORT BEFORE IT GETS TO YOU THROUGH
OTHER CHANNELS. NOBODY I TALK TO SEEMS
WILLING TO PREDICT WHAT'S IN STORE FOR
COUSIN MARGOT, BUT AT LEAST IT'S SOME
NEWS ABOUT HER. I'LL KEEP YOU POSTED AS
MORE GETS TO ME—ONRAD.

Unwilling to uncover the message in the terminal itself, Brim closed the folder and paced impatiently until Barbousse drove up in their staff skimmer. At last, in the privacy of the backseat, he distractedly touched the PAGE icon to dissolve Onrad's note, then began to read the HoloGraph itself: a partial report compiled by covert Imperial agents stationed somewhere within the League. Censors had deleted message headers and all other clues to the message's ultimate source.

<BEGINNING OF EXCERPT>

ITEM 15

AFTER PROCLAIMING HIMSELF ONCE AND FOR
ALL DIVORCED FROM HIS "TRAITOROUS" WIFE
(HER SERENE MAJESTY, PRINCESS MARGOT OF
THE EFFER'WYCK DOMINIONS), ROGAN
LAKARN, GRAND BARON OF THE TOROND,
PERSONALLY LED THREE BRIGADES OF THE
LEAGUE'S SPECIAL CONTROLLER COMMANDOS
AGAINST A RESISTANCE ENCLAVE ON THE OC-
CUPIED EFFER'WYCKEAN PLANET OF BRA'VE.
EARLY REPORTS INDICATE THE RAID NETTED

ALMOST TOTAL DESTRUCTION OF THE CON-
CEALED BASE, ESTABLISHED MORE THAN A
YEAR AGO BY PRINCESS MARGOT, AT THE
TIME ALSO GRAND BARONESS OF THE
TOROND.

ALL OCCUPANTS OF THE FOREST CAMP WERE
IMMEDIATELY PUT TO DEATH, EXCEPT
10-YEAR-OLD RODYARD GREYFFIN LAKARN,
ONLY ISSUE FROM LAKARN'S MARRIAGE TO
PRINCESS MARGOT. YOUNG LAKARN WAS
LAST OBSERVED BOARDING A STARSHIP FOR
THE TOROND.

AT THE TIME THIS REPORT WAS COMPILED,
THE PRINCESS HERSELF HAD SO FAR ELUDED
CAPTURE BY VIRTUE OF AN ALMOST
PROVIDENTIAL ABSENCE FROM THE CAMP
WHEN THE LEAGUE FORCES BEGAN THEIR
ASSAULT.

ON-SITE INFORMANTS REPORT THAT IF THE
PRINCESS CAN BE CAPTURED, LAKARN WILL
PERSONALLY DIRECT HER PUBLIC EXECUTION
IN EMOR-RUDOLPHO, CAPITAL OF THE TOROND,
LATER THIS YEAR DURING CELEBRATIONS
MARKING THE THIRD ANNIVERSARY OF THE
TREATY BINDING THE TOROND AND THE
LEAGUE IN MILITARY ALLIANCE.

IF THE PRINCESS'S ESCAPE PROVES
PERMANENT, CONTINGENCY PLANS CALL FOR
LAKARN (AND, IF POSSIBLE, HIS SON) TO
BEGIN A MEDIA-CENTERED CAMPAIGN OF
SLANDER DENOUNCING HER AS A TRAITOR TO
THE DOMAIN THAT "ADOPTED" HER. HE WILL

ALSO OFFER A SUBSTANTIAL PRICE FOR HER
HEAD.

<END OF EXCERPT>

Shaking his head, Brim pressed the Royal Seal a second
time. The folder disappeared in a small cloud of odorless
smoke. "It was about Margot," he said at some length.

In the front seat, Barbousse nodded without turning
around. "I heard when I picked up the skimmer, Admiral,"
he said, weaving through Avalon's chaotic early evening
traffic. "Bad news, I'm afraid. How do you read it?"

Brim stared out the window without seeing. "I don't know,
Chief," he replied at some length. "Every moment she's free
gives her a better chance of escape—we've clearly planted
agents on Bra've who can help." He sat back in the seat and
stared at his hands. "It wouldn't be the first time she's come
through odds that would utterly demolish anyone else."

"Like when the space fort at Zonga'ar blew up right on top
of her," Barbousse added. "She lived through that."

"I thought you said things looked bad," Brim remarked.

"I said 'bad news,' beggin' the Admiral's pardon," Barbousse amended. "And it is. But Princess Margot's tougher
than both of us, I think. She'll come out on top, just like she
always has before. I'd bet on it."

"Only a fool would take that bet," Brim said.

"Like Rogan LaKarn," Barbousse said thoughtfully.

"Yeah," Brim agreed. "Like Rogan LaKarn. . . . "

With Standard Year 52013 fast drawing to a close, De-
Brugh and his 91 Wing reached the Sodeskayan front on 19
Decad. They were immediately assigned to the Grivna Sector
close by some of the fiercest combat zones of the day. In
spite of the most primitive conditions imaginable at Zemsky,
their lakeside—rather *ice*-side—base on Veche, third planet

of the star Yarlyk, Imperial maintenance teams reconverted the first squadron of Starfuries from ferry configuration within three Standard Days and had the whole wing ready for combat a week later, including reserves.

During their year-long assignment to FleetPort 93, De-Brugh and his Helmsmen routinely jousted with some of the League's finest; now they were more than ready to continue as soon as ships were available. Accordingly, from the first missions on, the three squadrons of superb starships tore into their Leaguer opponents with gratifying results.

Brim himself took an active part in the fray almost from the first. Requiring little time to familiarize himself with the powerful new Sherrington killer ships, he led combat flights whenever his duties as liaison to the Sodeskayans permitted and scored two victories within his first five missions. After all their easy kills against inferior ships and inexperienced crews, Orgoth's minions had clearly permitted themselves to become soft; they now paid dearly for their arrogance.

With adequate support from space, Local Sodeskayan ground forces began to reverse the Leaguers' once unstoppable advance almost immediately, and only a few Standard Weeks following the Imperials' Year's End holiday (celebrated during a day-long battle including the loss of three Starfuries) they had driven the invaders from nearly a dozen planetary systems. Soon their efforts began to change—if ever so slightly—the very shape of the front itself. On the surface, it was a small episode in a large war—almost an anomaly. But for those whose job it was to plan the future, the small, remote operation composed an utterly significant event. It was soon the subject of intense study by *both* sides of the war.

With the Imperial squadrons off to a very solid beginning, Brim decided to see how well the Imperials would perform when dealing directly with Sodeskayans. Since the haughty young DeBrugh's racism first surfaced outside FleetPort 93, he had voiced no further words of contempt—nor had any of his officers. But Brim had been careful to buffer all direct exchanges of commands between the Sodeskayan commanders they actually served and the proud Imperial officers of 91 Wing. Now, leaving Barbousse at Zemsky to monitor the situation, he returned to Gromcow—and a *very* pleased Nikolai Yanuarievich Ursis. Both he and Dr. Borodov were waiting at Tomoshenko Spaceport.

"Imperials have fought gloriously, Wilfooshka," the Marshal said after an almost painful exchange of Bear hugs, "as we hoped they would. Throughout your Grivna Sector—small as it might be—Leaguers are actually retreating from planets for first time in their accursed campaign."

"Thanks, Nik," Brim said, seating himself in a limousine skimmer for the trip to Borodov Manor. "If anyone had doubts about Sodeskayans beating the Leaguers, this ought to reassure them once and for all. With any kind of decent support from space, you Bears are absolutely invincible on the ground."

"Unfortunately," Borodov added, "effective as your three squadrons of Starfuries might be *locally* in Grivna Sector, they can have only minimal effect on rest of campaign. Thrice-damned Leaguers continue invasion with all-too-obvious impunity."

Brim nodded. He'd kept up with developments elsewhere. Less than a year following his arrival in the G.F.S.S., advance Leaguer units were already in control of numerous Sodeskayan planets of the Ksnaymed star cluster, only one hundred fifty light-years from Ostra herself—and Gromcow. "How are things going in the city?" he asked.

"No outright panic yet—at least overtly," Ursis replied, "but fear is everywhere—and who can blame? To Leaguers, we are 'pelt beasts.' You saw yourself when we were stranded on Zholvka. Had it not been for friend Tissuard, my own skin would now be curing to provide warm coat for some xaxtdamned Leaguer. Is enough to frighten even crag wolf."

"What are you going to do?" Brim asked as the big limousine ghosted silently past picturesque neighborhoods on the far spinward side of the city. Old homes, narrow, tree-lined streets, and quaint shops: all were apparently deserted. As Marsha Browning warned him in the latest of the short notes they infrequently exchanged, Gromcow's residents were quietly evacuating the city.

"Only one thing we *can* do," Ursis replied. He glanced at Borodov. "With help of friend Anastas Alexi here, we have somehow—perhaps miraculously—amassed sufficient resources to begin reasonable counteroffensive at Ksnaymed star cluster almost immediately."

"Thank the Universe," Brim said. "That'll take a lot of pressure off the city. When does the attack begin?"

"If all goes well," Ursis said, "midday tomorrow, Gromcow time. Your Captain DeBrugh and his squadrons were under way for Ksnaymed day after you departed." He laughed. "They won't like where they're going. It's a new, advanced base called Fomett on J19-C. *Awful* planet, I hear. Leaguers just evacuated it."

Brim grimaced. "I should be there!" he exclaimed.

"You should be *here*, Wilfooshka," Ursis rejoindered with a gentle smile. "Chief Barbousse is with Ninety-one Wing in case anything goes *badly* wrong. One week from now, Gromcow time, we have brand-new ZBL-4 for you to fly to front. Then you can trade for Starfury and zap Leaguers to heart's content."

"What's wrong with tomorrow?" Brim demanded. "Or right now?"

"Well, Wilfooshka," Ursis said. "Next few days is good time to see if Imperials *really* can fight beside Sodeskayans without people like you to act as buffers."

270 / BILL BALDWIN

"I don't understand," Brim said, but he already had a good idea. DeBrugh!

"Is nice of you to try and protect us from reality of intolerance," Ursis said, "but seems to be part and parcel of modern life. Years ago, when three of us first met in I.F.S. *Truculent,* Bears were invariably destined for engineering duty if they wished to serve aboard Imperial starships—Grand Dukes included."

"I never let it be known who I was," Borodov protested.

"Gorksroar," Ursis admonished him. "One needn't skirt subject with human kinsman. Prejudice exists in all societies—ours included—and more homogeneous society is, worse prejudice gets. Even your brother is prejudiced in many ways—look how he treated Wilf Ansor that day. And I am certain two of us have similar defects."

Borodov nodded soberly. "True," he conceded, "but in this war, we will either learn to forget these prejudices—all of us—or we will surely perish at the hands of greatest bigots of all, Nergol Triannic's Leaguers."

"What happened that alerted you to DeBrugh's attitude?" Brim asked. "I thought I'd somehow put a lid on it before we got here. He even fooled Barbousse."

"Very worst kind of prejudice is often subtle," Ursis replied, "especially to those who have little. We were fooled as well. It only surfaced when we sent representatives to your maintenance organization with information concerning how to re-calibrate Sodeskayan test equipment so it can be used with Imperial power buses."

"And DeBrugh's people weren't interested?" Brim asked.

"Not much," Ursis answered, "at least according to our maintenance people."

Brim considered a moment. "Well, DeBrugh *did* bring along a lot of his own equipment," he said. "Maybe he feels he won't need to use any of yours."

"This DeBrugh expects no battle losses to ground equipment?" Ursis asked in amazement. "He must have great confidence in prowess of defense."

"Or great stupidity," Brim added.

"Hmm," Ursis mused politely. "Perhaps he is unaware of certain, shall we say, 'quirks' in Sodeskayan equipment that—someday—he may have to use."

Brim nodded. "I see," he said. "And DeBrugh's not exactly pounding on the door to learn anything about it, eh?"

Ursis shrugged. "One does not know about DeBrugh, himself," he said, "but his maintenance organization recently made it *very* clear that they were not interested in taking advice from Bears—on the subject of Starfury maintenance or, we understand, much of anything else."

"I see," Brim said, pursing his lips. *Here* was a problem. "I'm terribly sorry. You should have told me about it right away."

"Not critical issue yet," the Bear replied. "Perhaps DeBrugh's close proximity with brave Sodeskayans who fly killer ships in same class as Starfuries can cure issue with no further action. Same-side combat often makes close brothers of otherwise belligerent creatures. Besides," he added with a wry grin, "as we agreed earlier, Imperials and their Starfuries are doing splendid job shooting Leaguers."

"I guess there are worse situations," Brim acquiesced. Clearly, a lesson learned by experience was much better than a lesson forced down one's throat. Still, he thought as the limousine skimmer came to a halt beneath the manor's great portico, it would be a *real* pleasure sometimes to simply pop a few miscreants on the nose.

As he hoped, Brim found a note from Marsha Browning when he checked in late that afternoon at the—very busy—Imperial Embassy. The Ambassador would be tied up all night for conferences, and she had arranged for a late supper at the Golden Cockerel, a place she described as a small, out-of-the-way bistro on the banks of the Gromcow River. She had even sketched a tiny map.

In truth, Brim found Marsha Browning on his mind considerably, of late. For quite some time now, Gromcow had been in danger of imminent assault by the Leaguers. The fact that her husband had neglected to send her home *months* ago was a matter Brim found to be beyond understanding. It did, however, serve to assuage certain pangs of guilt owing to a considerable yearning for her company.

In the Embassy lobby, he admired the latest HoloGrams of Hope sent from Avalon, placed them in his pocket, and bounded up the staircase to KA'PPA his final summary to the "Poker Council" before Ursis launched his offensive in the morning. His report was, he reflected, exiting the code room, considerably different than the first briefs he'd sent prior to Ursis's promotion. It was nice to report a few victories among the dreary succession of losses the Sodeskayans were still experiencing outside the Grivna Sector. And unless he missed his guess, he would have a considerably more good news in the days to come—at least until the Sodeskayan offensive began to run out of resources. It would go a long way toward convincing people like General Hagbut that Sodeskayan aid was a sound investment. He smiled, Marsha Browning once more on his mind. By that time—if everything went well—the city of Gromcow would have a new, although still temporary, lease on life. And so would she. . . .

On this eve of the new offensive, the Embassy was rife with activity. As Brim descended the staircase to the lobby, he noticed a tall, distinguished-looking man and a slim redhead, young enough to be his daughter, dart across the lobby through the crowd. Familiar-looking man. . . . He narrowed his eyes. It was *Browning*—who didn't even have a daughter! When the two disappeared along a side corridor, he followed, pushing his way into the hallway just in time to see them sidestep—now arm in arm—through a pair of doors marked DORMITORY WING. He stopped short of the doorway and smiled to himself. So much for *those* feelings of guilt. Retracing his steps to the lobby, he retrieved his staff skimmer and set off for the Golden Cockerel, whistling tunelessly to himself.

Quite late that evening, in a corner of a murky dining room, Marsha Browning finished her third goblet of meem, closed her eyes for a moment, and puffed a mu'occo cigarette to life. "That was a wonderful supper, Wilf," she said, settling back in the booth and breathing spice-laden jets of smoke from her nostrils. "So wonderful that I feel absolutely evil."

"You couldn't be evil," Brim returned, suddenly very much aware of the woman's compelling charm and ample sexuality. "You're far too beautiful to be evil."

"Thanks, Wilf," she replied. "I love to be beautiful for you—especially when you look at me that way." She appeared to consider that for a moment, then peered furtively about the room. "Hmm," she mused, sinking deeper into her seat and licking her lips. "About this looking business," she whispered with a mysterious little smile, "—drop something on the floor."

Brim frowned. "What?" he asked.

She pointed to his cup of cvc'eese. "Drop something like your spoon on the floor," she said, "—under the table. Then pick it up. All right?"

"I don't understand," Brim said. "Drop my spoon?"

"Yes," she said with a little smile. "You've seen what meem does to me. It makes me want to . . . well, show off. You know."

"You mean, like the last time we were out?" he asked, with a little rush of titillation. His reaction to her surreptitiously bared breasts in the crowded dining room had surprised him—he'd found himself thinking about it at the oddest times, with strong feelings of arousal.

"Uh-huh," Browning murmured. "I've got the urge again—especially now with a shorter skirt." She laughed. "Don't worry, I haven't been caught yet."

"Oh, I'm not worried about that," Brim replied, "but are you sure you wouldn't like to go somewhere more private?"

"You don't understand," Browning said, running her tongue over her lips, "Doing . . . 'things' . . . in public when nobody can see turns me on—a little fetish I've enjoyed since I was a girl." She widened her eyes in mock astonishment. "It was a real surprise when I discovered how much better things got with a boy watching."

"Well," Brim said with a smile, "I'm your 'boy'—a couple of years too late, of course, but willing nonetheless."

Browning giggled. "You'll do," she replied, "believe me. Now drop your spoon under the table and pick it up. All right?"

Grinning, Brim ceremoniously dropped his spoon, then bent under the table. Voot's Beard, but she did have *extraordinary* legs!

As he watched in fascination, she opened her knees, then drew the skirt well above an ample pair of startlingly white thighs. Even in the dusky light beneath the table, it was quite evident that, beneath, she wore only dark, silken briefs, that she slowly drew aside.

"Like what you see?" she asked a little breathlessly.

"B-beautiful," Brim replied in a shaky voice. "Just beautiful." He continued to search for quite a long time before he found his wayward spoon.

Afterward, they retired to a small apartment in an old but fashionable part of the city. That night—while she knelt astride his hips, sucking her lower lip and wildly grinding herself against him—Brim momentary pondered why anyone would prefer a skinny redheaded kid. He watched a rivulet of sweat run down one swaying breast and drop from its large, swollen nipple; then, with a suddenly runaway compulsion, he became *much* too consumed by the moment for metaphysical thoughts of any kind. . . .

The following afternoon (Gromcow time), Ursis launched Vylyit, his first counteroffensive, at a sorry little twelve-star cluster called Ksnaymed, lost among the burned-out space holes and asteroid shoals midway between Gromcow's star Ostra and the ancient constellation Imperials called Morzik Minor. He'd chosen the relatively unimportant area because, as the Leaguers' farthest penetration into Sodeskayan territory, it was already mostly globed by Sodeskayan forces.

On 22 Unad, 5204 at precisely Dawn:2:70, Gromcow time—concurrently on all twelve habitable Ksnaymed planets—Leaguer troops of the Second and Tenth Army Groups found themselves under a coordinated attack lead by a greatly altered Bearish Fleet. The Sodeskayan starships—emblazoned with fierce legends such as VENGEANCE! and DEATH TO LEAGUERS!—flew in large, perfectly orchestrated formations, the likes of which Leaguers in the area had never yet experienced.

First came squadron upon squadron of deadly ZBL-4s, whose mission it was to clear the sky of Leaguer killer ships. They accomplished their grisly task with astonishing efficiency, to the utter confusion of the Leaguers, who for months had grown lax and soft dealing with second-rate opponents. Behind the ZBLs came powerful attack craft like QF-4s and UV-2s to hammer orbiting Leaguer starbases and land-based supply depots. Last came the surface-attack starships—distinctively Sodeskayan JM-2 Ro'stoviks, angular in shape and heavily plated with armor. From cruising altitudes of less than 2,500 feet, these brutes singled out crawlers, supply skimmers, columns of troops—anything that moved—

and sprayed the ground with murderous disruptor fire, hurling wreckage, bodies, and debris in every direction. Then they dived abruptly and came in closer to their prey, some to altitudes of fifty irals or lower. The Ro'stovik Helmsmen—many of them Wild Ones from the Kvass region, like Poupychev and Bzhtva—had a bewildering repertory of tactics they'd developed while training in far-off Carescria, Brim's homeland. One was a fearsome maneuver known as the "orbit of death," in which they circled around a cluster of enemy crawlers in groups of four, six, or eight, delivering blasts from their prodigious disruptors that literally "burned holes in Leaguer armor," as one Bearish Helmsman boasted later in a report Brim watched that night in Gromcow. Barely one metacycle after the arrival of the Ro'stoviks over the Controllers' 9th Crawler Division on planet Zacrith-19, seventy Leaguer crawlers were in flames.

Elsewhere in the sector, other leaguers met similar fates. On the planet Bylina-19, the Leaguers' 3rd Crawler Division lost 270 of its 300 armored vehicles to the pitiless Ro'stoviks. And a corresponding fate occurred to their 17th Crawler Division that lost 240 of its 300 armored vehicles in only four metacycles of desperate combat against the Bears.

As the campaign progressed, Brim followed KA'PPAed reports in Gromcow with awe. Captured League officers appeared to be thunderstruck by the onslaught. "The Bears have used starships of such numbers and excellence as we have never yet seen in Sodeskaya," one Galite'er was quoted. The woman spoke shortly before her execution—she'd been captured wearing a Bearskin coat. . . .

"The Sodeskayans are puncturing our whole operation," another stunned League prisoner was heard to say. No official record of comparative losses was available during those first few days, but a very tired DeBrugh reported that more than six hundred Leaguer starships had been destroyed against about two hundred for the Sodeskayans (and so far, three of his Starfuries). More important—at least to Brim—the toll of League crawlers and mobile disruptors numbered into the thousands, while Leaguer dead and wounded numbered in the *tens* of thousands. Toward the middle of the second day (Gromcow time), the Sodeskayans managed to link up and form a huge globe around the trapped Leaguers that fairly bristled with disruptors—all pointing inward.

On 2 Diad, precisely one week following Vylyit's onset, Ursis kept his promise when he assigned Brim a brand-new ZBL-4 to be ferried to Ksnaymed, then *personally* chauffeured him to Tomoshenko. As the Bear piloted his great Roshov limousine along the convoy-jammed right-of-way, he kept his silence for a long time, clearly bothered by something. Finally he turned to Brim and frowned. "Funny stuff going on there in Ksnaymed," he said, "having nothing at all to do with humor."

"What's happening?" Brim asked. He hadn't heard of any problems with the new campaign, except perhaps that some supplies were already beginning to grow scarce.

"Don't know yet," Ursis replied, "but . . . if you were Nergol Triannic, what would you do if you suddenly found some hundred thousand of your best troops—with all their equipment—nearly globed by enemy forces?"

Brim didn't need a lot of time to think about *that* question. "I'd order their commander to break out and link up with friendly forces at once. No excuse for casualties when they don't do any good."

Ursis braked around a large mobile disruptor that had wandered partially out into his lane, then nodded. "My thoughts exactly," he said. "Even bloody Leaguers have some sense of avoiding downright waste—at least of their own forces."

"So?" Brim prompted. The base's main entrance was already in sight ahead.

"So," Ursis said impassively, "both of us agree retreat

what Leaguers *ought* to be doing; so does General Staff. Only trouble is, Leaguers aren't doing that. Numbers of their field commanders requested permission to withdraw—we picked up their transmissions. But they were all turned down, direct from Tarrott." He braked to a stop at the gate and presented his ID disk to a guard whose eyes grew large as saucers when he glanced at Ursis's five stars. Smiling reassuringly, he returned the young Bear's astonished salute, then continued into the base through streams of convoys departing for Ksnaymed—and arriving casualties. "Looks like Triannic's personal work again," he continued. "No military professional would permit such a debacle."

"You mean that he's actually trying to hang on to Ksnaymed?" Brim asked in amazement. "I'd pretty well gotten an impression that the place doesn't have much to offer in the way of military significance."

"It doesn't," Ursis said. "Miserable star system wouldn't even support a decent penal colony. We know—tried to put one there nearly century ago. Closed five years later."

Brim shook his head. "If it's true that Triannic's doing this on his own, it'll be the second time he's crossed his High Command this year," he mused. "He's either the greatest military strategist in the Universe or the greatest fool."

"Unless he knows something about Ksnaymed that we don't, is looking very much like latter," Ursis growled. "'Winds and rain ruffle fur of Bears and crag wolves alike,' as they say."

"Maybe he's *really* on our side," Brim suggested with a wild look.

Ursis rumbled a deep belly laugh. "That is possible, too," he said, turning from the main right-of-way toward a section of gravity pools that appeared to be occupied by brand-new ZBL-4s. "But I think there is a more *basic* reason for this stupidity."

"And?"

"Much as I feel constrained to downplay my lucky encounter with Rodef *nov* Vobok on Zholvka, I cannot ignore the fact that the Marshal would have been first to sound retreat—and make his decision stick with Triannic."

"Why wouldn't *Triannic* want to do the same thing?" Brim demanded. "He's not a complete fool."

Ursis nodded thoughtfully. "Intuition tells me that he is a bigot—another kind of fool—and cannot abide the thought of being beaten by mere 'pelt beasts,' as he calls us." He peered over his spectacles. "Whatever cause, thanks to *someone's* stupidity, is beginning to look as if many, many Leaguers are heading for either destruction or captivity. War takes much in way of resources. Those globed Leaguers will swiftly run low of essentials." He chuckled and made a tremendous grin. "Something we Bears will simply hate, of course."

"Unless . . . " Brim interrupted thoughtfully.

"Unless what?" Ursis said, glancing with a frown at the numbers on the gravity pools they passed.

"Unless the Leaguers could be supplied from space," Brim replied.

"They are supplied from space already," Ursis remonstrated with a laugh. "*Everybody* supplied from space. Us, too."

"But supplies normally come in freighters," Brim replied, "that normally travel in *friendly* space, or at least out in the real interstellar voids." He thought for a moment, then nodded to himself. "Right now there's no friendly space anywhere *near* Ksnaymed, and freighters don't do so well in active war zones." He looked at his old friend. "Xaxt, Nik, they don't even do very well in the interstellar void. If anybody knows about transport losses, it's the two of us."

"So," Ursis replied, "you are agreeing with me, then, that the cursed Leaguers will starve?"

"Damned good chance of that, Nik," Brim replied, "*unless*

they tie up most of their fleet attempting to *punch* those transports through. I mean, protection like they gave their attack ships during our Battle of Avalon."

"Voof!" the Bear exclaimed, glancing back at Brim. "What a cost! Tying up that many attack ships would be felt throughout whole war zone." For a moment he fell silent, thoughtfully rubbing his chin. "They'd need to ferry at least thirty milstons of supplies a day to *each* of the twelve planets if their troops are even to survive, much less protect themselves," he said presently. "And way I calculate, *that* would take upward of hundred and a half serviceable transports."

"Hmm," Brim considered. "If I remember correctly, their order of battle only calls for half that number for the whole campaign."

"Is correct," Ursis said, pulling to a halt at a gravity pool where a great crowd appeared to have gathered. "To do it, they would have to draw on other fronts and even drain homeland of available ships." He turned and smiled. "Is interesting situation to which you travel, Wilf Ansor. Keep me informed. All right?"

"A couple times a day, when it's necessary, Nik," Brim promised. Then he frowned. "Who are all the brass?" he asked, peering at a number of crimson-clothed guards who had suddenly come to rigid attention. "Looks like the Knez is here."

"Good reason for that," Ursis replied, opening the door.

Brim turned and raised an eyebrow.

"Knez *is* here," Ursis replied, "in specially constructed stateroom, waiting for you to fly him to Ksnaymed."

"Me?" Brim gasped.

"Your name is Brim, is it not?"

"Universe. . . . "

"Not to worry, Wilf Ansor," the Bear said with a little smile. "Knez will not bother you too much this trip."

"Why?"

"New courtesan on board with him—just come into season. Probably won't leave stateroom until you make planetfall."

"Why's he going?" Brim asked. "It's got to be dangerous out there."

"Is duty of Knez to appear among troops in dangerous situations now and then," Ursis explained. "Something like your Onrad visiting that BKAEW satellite last year, when we *all* nearly got killed," he explained with a chuckle.

"How do the troops feel about him, with all the losses you Bears have borne lately?" Brim asked.

Ursis peered over his glasses. "Knez may not be perfect," he said, "by a long shot. But with all his . . . what you call 'warts' . . . he does best he can, and soldiers know it. Except for one disastrous oversight with Fleet, he has done much in interest of domain." For a moment he shook his head. "However," he added, "neither history nor Sodeskayan people— including me, if I survive—will ever quite forgive him for *that* blunder. . . . "

CHAPTER 10
Partners!

When Brim made landfall at a small planet named Tazi, about 150 light-years short of the Ksnaymed pocket, the Knez was still "occupied" in his stateroom—as had been the case since Tomoshenko. Expressing personal regrets—and his need for haste—to a number of ministers, Brim immediately set out to cadge a ride to DeBrugh's tiny Imperial base on the planet of Budanova, some eighty light-years farther on, toward the front.

Just short of the Operations shack, he sensed, rather than heard, familiar thunder high above the clouds that started whole floods of memories. A Starfury: Nothing else in the Universe sounded like that! Both ZBL-4s and Starfury 5s were powered in HyperSpace by twin Wizard-E8 Reflecting Drives designed by the Sodeskayan firm of Krasni-Peych. Below LightSpeed, however, only Starfuries flew on big A876 Admiralty gravs, and the bass thunder they made was unique in the Galaxy. The sound grew louder; moments later, his ears picked up the characteristic, high-pitched whistle of air passing across three cooling intakes just forward of the portside "trouser." Looking up, he spotted the ship just as she broke through the gloomy overcast—a handsome sculpture; more art than mere practical form. Trihulled, as were many of Mark Valarian's finest designs, the starship's main fuselage was complemented on either side with "pontoons" attached slightly below the centerline by stubby, winglike "trousers." A raked, low-set bridge/deckhouse protruded some third of the way back from her sharply tapered bow, and, except for streamlined blisters housing the main battery, constituted her principal slipstream disturbance anywhere.

Losing altitude quickly, the ship rolled into a vertical bank and thundered across the base, silhouetted against the clouds like three slim needles. She was low enough when she passed overhead that Brim could see her single Helmsman in silhouette through the raked bridge Hyperscreens. The ground shook to the deafening beat of its six Admiralty gravs, and he watched with enchantment until the ship turned sharply again and glided to a perfect landing on one of the base's portable Becton tubes.

"Magnificent," commented a half-familiar voice behind him.

"She is that," Brim replied absently, watching the ship leave the tube at a high-speed exit and taxi toward the Operations shack. Grinning, he turned to see whose taste in starships ran so closely to his and . . . "Your Majesty!" he gulped, coming face-to-face with the Knez. "I—I thought you were still aboard the ship."

The Knez smiled. "Until moments ago we were, Admiral," he said. "But we decided to take advantage of this opportunity for a few words before you fly off to battle. Much depends on what you *personally* see and report in the next few weeks."

"Your Majesty?"

"Brim," the Knez said, "you know as well as we do that after the next few weeks—should you survive them, of course—you will most assuredly be called upon for your views of continued Imperial support for our struggle with the cursed Leaguers." He closed his eyes for a moment and paused. "Much responsibility will then rest on your shoulders—a great deal of it caused by my own personal misjudgment."

Brim felt his eyebrows raise. This was the Bear who never even said "Thank you."

"Puzzlement shows in your face, Admiral," the Knez continued with a sad little smile. "As Knez, We are not permitted normal emotions available to Our subjects, especially shame and embarrassment. But the fact is that beneath the layers of pomp and tradition that cloak Us, We are no more than fur and bones Ourselves. In the end, *We*," he said, placing a hand at his chest, "are only a Bear." He frowned for a moment. "Perhaps you know that better than most," he added. "You have a long-standing—and *rare*—friendship with your own Emperor, Onrad V."

Brim considered that. Somehow the words came as both a realization *and* a shock.

"At any rate," the Knez continued, propelling Brim's attention rapidly back to the present, "it is as a Bear that We speak to you at this moment, not as a monarch. Soon We must personally beseech the leaders of your entire civilization to overlook Our personal blunders and aid the Sodeskayan people—who richly deserve that help. Once they can stand on their own two feet again, they will prove to be your greatest allies in the coming struggle with the hordes of Nergol Triannic."

Brim took a deep breath and looked the Knez in the face. "That aid has already started, Your Majesty," he said as the Starfury swung onto a nearby gravity pad and shut down its generators in a great shimmering cloud of gravitons. "*There* is a small beginning," he said, nodding toward the graceful starship.

"An appreciated beginning," the Knez acknowledged. "But, as you say, a *beginning* only. We Sodeskayans shall require truly massive aid in the coming years if the damage caused by Our personal mistakes is to be overcome."

Brim started to speak, but the Knez held up a hand.

"You need not remind Us what we Sodeskayans must prove to you Imperials and your Emperor," he said. "We are well aware of your real mission here, and have been since you arrived." He smiled. "That is not to say that We look upon such a mission with enmity; in fact, We regard it as necessary due diligence and would do the same thing were the circumstances of our domains reversed."

This time Brim made no attempt to interject his thoughts; besides, his attention had been supplanted momentarily by the sight of Utrillo Barbousse and a highly decorated Sodeskayan Helmsman striding toward him at a fast clip, clearly unaware of the Knez's presence. Four crimson-clad guards halted them some distance away.

Nikolai glanced toward two figures and smiled. "It is time both of us attend our tasks," he said. "But before We go, We have a message for you, Admiral—also your Emperor and his 'Cre'el Staff,' as he calls that marvelous band of hoodlums with whom he surrounds himself." He looked off into nowhere for a moment. "They—as well as you, Admiral—are his best protection from mistakes like the ones We made. At one time or another, each of you has pronounced three words for him that We are only now beginning to hear, thanks chiefly to Our vexing brother and *your* old friend Ursis."

"What words are those, Your Majesty?" Brim asked before he could stop himself.

"'*You are wrong,*'" The Knez quoted, "—words whose value We learned far too late, but appreciate all the more for it now." He laughed sardonically, then became very serious and took Brim's arm. "The message We would send to all in the Imperial High Command is this," he said: "Base your decisions concerning the long-term certainty of Sodeskayan military success on the *people* of Sodeskaya—the actual warriors—and what *they* demonstrate, not on their Knez, who is almost solely responsible for the difficulties in which they presently find themselves." He stood for a moment in silence, then frowned. "Any questions, Admiral?" he asked.

Deeply moved, Brim came to attention and saluted. "Count on me, Your Majesty," he said simply. "I have long known the excellence of the Sodeskayan people. Now I have seen the greatness of their Knez, as well."

Silently, the Knez saluted, then, without another word, turned and strode off to a group of high-ranking Sodeskayan officers who appeared to be waiting for him.

Once into HyperSpace, Brim checked the Starfury's proximity alarm—nothing registered—then cleared the ship visually through the Hyperscreens. Again nothing. He relaxed—as much as any Helmsman could relax in contested space—and set the AutoHelm on course for J19-C, only a few light-years outside the Ksnaymed Sector. "All right, Chief," he said to an image of Barbousse in a globular display, "bring me up to date."

Barbousse thought for a moment. "Hard to know where to start, Admiral," he said. "We left for Fomett Base the day after we got the movement orders. There was a bit of trouble over that. The crew chiefs and mechanics were expectin' a shipment o' their special tools, which hadn't arrived yet, an' Captain DeBrugh wanted to wait for 'em. The Sodeskayans needed him out immediately, an' in the end, they yelled loudest. But it took one of their Generals to do the trick, an' DeBrugh was mighty angry." He laughed. "So were his mechanics—they had to take along a lot of standard tools instead of the fancy ones they were used to, an' it took 'em a while to learn how to use them."

"Maintenance is all right now?" Brim asked.

"Seems to be," Barbousse answered. "The Starfuries don't spend much time in sick bay, so to speak."

"How about everything else?" Brim asked. "I've tried to keep track from Gromcow, but . . . "

"We've done passing well, Admiral," Barbousse said. "As I'm certain you know, we've lost three ships so far, two from Nine-fourteen Squadron, one from Twenty-eight. But we've also knocked down or damaged nearly twenty of the League's ships—including a couple of really big transports just yesterday. I watch the figures all the time."

"Good man, Chief," Brim said. "And how are DeBrugh and his people getting along with the Sodeskayans now?"

Barbousse frowned. "Tolerably," he said at some length. "You can tell there's still a bit of a problem; the Captain has his little snits now and then. But the Sodeskayans mostly pay him no mind. What they're interested in is killing Leaguers, and since DeBrugh represents a way to kill *lots* of Leaguers, they're willing to put up with a lot."

"So there's no improvement?" Brim asked.

"No," Barbousse replied. "I wouldn't exactly say that. Little by little, DeBrugh's people are learning how good Sodeskayans are at things." He frowned. "Like engineering and that sort of stuff. The Bears are so *terribly* good that our maintenance people have actually started a number of friendships with them. Of course, they're mostly ratings, like m'self, and not so highfalutin as officers are—present company excluded, o'course."

Brim laughed. "Thanks, Chief," he said. "I take it that the officers haven't been getting along so well?"

"Well," Barbousse said with a wince, "they weren't at first, anyway. Most of the ZBL-4 crews were fresh from trainin' while DeBrugh's people had been poppin' after Leaguers for better 'n a year. But as the Bears rack up combat experience, they're turnin' out to be pretty fine space warriors—a lot better 'n any of DeBrugh's people thought they'd be."

"So you think maybe things will work out by themselves?" Brim asked.

Barbousse nodded. "Not sayin' that somebody's *never* going to push some Bear over the edge with 'is or 'er nastiness. Probably someone will—an' that person's going to get the livin' daylights slammed out of 'im. But the Sodeskayans seem to be basically patient people, and our Imperials are mellowing." He smiled. "The way I see it, Admiral, some things you can't legislate—like respect. They come only with time. Just like you, beggin' your pardon. But you've spoken about it lots of times. Years ago, when you joined the Fleet, Carescrians like yourself were really considered to be low-life people. Now look at you. Admiral Calhoun's head of all Armed Forces, and you're the Emperor's right hand in Sodeskaya. Things do change."

Smiling, Brim visually checked the ship's tail, then glanced at the proximity alarm—all quiet. "Chief," he said, "I don't believe I've ever heard you make that long of a speech before."

"I don't, normally," Barbousse replied.

"You feel pretty strongly about this, don't you?"

Barbousse nodded. "I do, Admiral," he said.

"Thanks, friend," Brim said. "I appreciate it."

Barbousse nodded, and the display winked out. Little more than a metacycle later, they landed at the dusty, half-finished base of Fomett, set into as barren a landscape as Brim had encountered anywhere.

DeBrugh was waiting by a dust-covered gravity pad when Brim taxied in from the Becton tube and shut down his gravs in a cloud of gravitons. Taking his hands from his ears, the young Wing Commander waved amiably; he was dressed in a battlesuit that looked as if he had only recently made landfall himself. With him were a number of other officers, including the Wing's three squadron leaders and Susanna Kehler. Brim had formed an occasional, somewhat bawdy friendship with the latter that had so far completely escaped DeBrugh's detection.

Brim waved back, then turned the ship's systems over to the Engineering Officer and powered off the helm. Winking to Barbousse, who was shutting down the master weapons console, he made his way aft to the flight-bridge companionway. Moments later, he was at the foot of the brow, where two Imperial commandos, whose eyes were visible under a crust of dirt and sweat, helped him jump to the ground. In spite of noticeably weak gravity, he sank in it up to his ankles.

"Welcome to Fomett," DeBrugh said, saluting, then extending his hand. "It's a dusty, filthy wilderness of a place," he explained, "but it's warm and its ours—at least until somebody wants it back . . . which," he added with a grin, "I can't imagine."

Brim saluted and grasped the man's hand. "You're right," he said, looking around him. "But look. There's no snow!" It was the first Sodeskayan planet he'd visited that wasn't frozen; no wonder the Leaguers hadn't wanted to leave. The base itself was located to one side of what appeared to be a large, shallow crater completely ringed by disruptor batteries pointing skyward. For nearly a c'lenyt out from the six Becton tubes, arranged in two parallel trios forming a narrow X, the terrain was completely flat and barren. Beyond, to spinward, a craggy upwelling of equally barren-looking mountains invaded the gray horizon. As far as his eye could see, nothing grew anywhere—a totally wasted atmosphere. "Not much to recommend it as a vacation spa," he remarked with a raised eyebrow.

The officers laughed, each of them saluting and shaking

his hand. Kehler turned her head to include a surreptitious wink with her greeting.

DeBrugh nodded when the little ceremony was finished. "J19-C was one of the first planets the Bears recaptured from the Leaguers," he said. "They'd only just secured this part of it and plunked down the Becton tubes when we arrived, so you won't want to stray far from the base perimeter or do much walking in the areas between the tubes. In fact, when you're out, you probably oughtn't to touch anything. And, ah"—he pointed to a nearby area marked off by cloth strips waving in the considerable breeze—"don't go *near* areas marked like that; they're still mined. We lost three people in the last two days to the Leaguers' xaxtdamned mines. And if that weren't enough, one of our mechanics was just wounded by a League sniper hiding somewhere in that rocky belt who had long-range sights. We got that one, but there *may* be more."

"Sounds just thraggling wonderful," Brim said bleakly. He'd been in worse places, he was certain. But he couldn't remember where, for the life of him.

After a bleak supper of field rations and a miraculous bottle of Logish Meem, Brim and DeBrugh retired to the latter's tiny office in a buried Operations module to discuss the campaign's progress so far. The young Wing Leader was in an expansive mood after claiming two Gorn-Hoff 262-Es destroyed during his previous sortie, and was anxious to share his thoughts.

"It's been quite a good scrap," he observed while an orderly served mugs of steaming hot cvc'eese. "We've had a few losses; I'm certain you've already heard about those. And we've taken a bit of damage, Voot knows. All in all, though, we've made the Leaguers pay with eighteen—now twenty—of their finest attack craft and two utterly huge supply ships, just since we arrived here." He frowned. "Come to think of it, we've seen whole gangs of freighters around here in the last few days—heading in *and* out of the Ksnaymed area. And the Leaguers send enough escorts with them to protect a planet. Do you suppose they're trying to evacuate those people?"

Brim shrugged—just as Ursis described. "It may be the other way around," he said. "The Bears in Gromcow see strong indications that the Leaguers intend to hold on to Ksnaymed at all costs."

"But they're totally globed in there," DeBrugh said. "The only way they'll be able to hold on is . . ." He paused. "So *that's* their plan, is it? They're going to supply those trapped forces by punching freighters through the Bears' blockade." He shook his head. "Mother of Voot," he swore in amazement. "That will require their biggest freighters—and enough escorts to seriously hamper operations everywhere else along the front."

Brim sipped his cvc'eese—clearly the finest that Imperial credits would purchase. "That seems to be the plan, though," he said.

"But it's pure folly," DeBrugh said. "There isn't anything in Ksnaymed worth the risk, or do they know something that I don't know?"

"Not according to the Bears," Brim replied. "To them it's worthless territory, too—except for some small-time mining operations."

"Then *why*?" DeBrugh asked rhetorically.

"The Bears think it has something to do with Nergol Triannic's ego," Brim replied.

"What in xaxt could there be about Ksnaymed that would stoke Triannic's ego?"

"Maybe nothing about Ksnaymed itself, Basil," Brim said. "But think about egos for a moment. Consider someone so completely prejudiced against Bears that he can't accept the possibility of them winning *anything*—even when the Bears have clearly superior forces."

"That would be absolutely crazy," DeBrugh said.

"So is bigotry," Brim said, finishing his cvc'eese. "It exacts a terrible toll."

After staring into his own cup of cvc'eese, DeBrugh met Brim's glance and he nodded. "Yes," he said presently. "I think I see just what you mean. . . ."

Following more conversation, Brim bid DeBrugh a good evening and headed for his room—an austere but roomy (Bear-sized) officer's cubicle in one of six buried, portable barracks modules designed for use by the Sodeskayan Army. Outside, darkness had fallen, but he had not the first clue what *local* time it was. As he hoped, Kehler arrived soon after he did and, following a long, soothing interlude of persuasion, declared herself once again "charmed."

Afterward, Brim relaxed on the bed while the beautiful blonde snored softly in the crook of his arm. If indeed one had to find himself in a combat zone, he thought, *this* was the way to do it. He was just falling off to sleep himself when he heard the rumble of starships overhead, but they didn't sound familiar at all. Their gravs were unsynchronized and . . . Leaguers! Low, too! He stirred, accidentally waking Kehler.

"It's all right," she said sleepily. "If they were Leaguers, our disruptors would have already opened fire."

She had scarcely finished speaking when a tremendous series of explosions shook the building with enough force to land them both on the floor. "Voot's greasy beard!" she exclaimed as emergency lights shone dimly through the darkness. "That was close. We've got to get out of here before we're buried!" Picking herself off the canted floor, she threw open the door and was met with a burning gust of air. "C'mon, Wilf," she yelled, struggling into a jumpsuit.

Brim needed no encouragement. Tugging on his trousers, he followed her into the suddenly crowded hallway.

The moment they stepped outside, every disruptor on the base seemed to open fire, and the sky above them turned into a swaying mass of 155-mmi energy beams. Instantly it was light as day. Brim grabbed Kehler and followed a number of others who dove beneath the great bulk of a Sodeskayan lorry. As a second salvo of Leaguer fire began to explode around them, a parked Starfury caught fire and the flames drew the attackers like insects. Dust and debris fell thick as rain all around them, rocks and jagged chunks of wreckage. The explosions began to come thick and fast now. One hit so close that the impact threw Brim in the air and gave him a painful bump against the lorry's frame. Two disruptors less than thirty irals distant were firing away in deafening series of bursts. The barking discharges pierced his eardrums, but at least spared him the screaming of others trapped beneath the big machine. Battered and half sick, he and Kehler could only wait out their ordeal, shivering with consternation.

Probably less than a metacycle later—a period of time that seemed like years—there came a lull. Brim sprinted across to see what remained of the barracks and to look for survivors, but the structure had been destroyed totally. Had he and Kehler remained in his room, they would now be dead. Grinding his teeth, he wondered how many casualties the raid had actually caused, but quickly put the question from his mind. He'd have an answer all too soon in the morning.

When he got back to the lorry, other ex-occupants of the ruined barracks were crawling out from other hiding places, dusting themselves and swearing. DeBrugh had evidently weathered the raid in a nearby storage shed with a number of his favorite Helmsmen—few of them women. Nine-fourteen Squadron had departed on a raid of its own earlier in the evening, so its crews would not figure in the casualty reports—from the Leaguer raid, at least.

The all-clear sounded nearly a metacycle later. Haggard, grimy, and dusty, Brim stumbled with Kehler to her room in another module, where the two of them immediately went to sleep, only to be awakened little more than a metacycle later by a knock on the door. Springing from the bed alertly—despite her lack of sleep—Kehler slipped on a robe and opened the door a crack, then stood back with a surprised smile. "Good morning, Chief," she said. "What can I do for you?"

Brim quickly drew the covers over himself.

"Good morning, Commander," Barbousse's quiet voice said, still outside the door. "I, er, dropped by to leave Admiral Brim a fresh uniform and a toilet kit. His clean gear was blown to bits in last night's raid, an', well, I noticed you were good enough to take him in after the raid."

Kehler paused for a moment, and her cheeks reddened. Then she got a great, worldly smile on her face. "Why, thank you, Chief," she said. "I know the Admiral will be *very* glad to get them. Everything he wore is, er, rumpled, to say the least."

"Yes, ma'am," Barbousse's voice agreed.

Quietly Kehler stepped outside in the hall.

"Commander!" Barbousse's voice gasped with surprise. "Er . . . t-thank you."

Moments later, Kehler stepped back into the room carrying both an overnight bag and an ear-to-ear grin. "Oh, he's *so* cute," she giggled when she'd closed the door.

"What did you do to him?" Brim demanded, catching her infectious grin. "I've never heard the Chief at a loss for words."

"I didn't say anything," she laughed with a fraudulent pout. "I kissed him—right on the cheek."

"Why, Commander," Brim chided with a playful grin, "that sort of fraternization with the enlisted ranks is against all sorts of regulations."

"That kiss had nothing to do with ranks, or even soldiering," she said thoughtfully. "It was about friendship and dedication, the kind that man has for you. It makes him pretty special, in my book—and well worth an 'illegal' kiss on the cheek."

"Thanks, Susanna," Brim said. "The Chief is a pretty special person."

She laughed. "You think the regulations might just allow fraternization of that sort with enlisted men, then?

"My regulations do," Brim declared. "So none of the others matter, anyway."

"How about fraternizations with officers?" she asked with a little smile.

"What kind of fraternization did you have in mind?" Brim asked.

"This kind," she said, opening her robe. "Can I talk you into a short demonstration before breakfast?"

Ever vigilant for opportunities to further his knowledge in all fields of endeavor, Brim readily agreed. . . .

Some time later, he arrived alone at the Officer's Mess and ate his breakfast with two of DeBrugh's Helmsmen, discussing deflection angles and the Starfury's sighting systems. Kehler arrived nearly half a metacycle afterward with two friends wearing Operations flashes on their battlesuits. When DeBrugh appeared moments later with rings around his eyes, it was soon clear from his conversation that he still had no idea the night's "entertainment" he once planned had blossomed into such a friendship. Brim smiled. Probably, he considered, it was better for everyone that way.

Next afternoon, Brim flew his first Sodeskayan mission in a Starfury, amazed for the ten millionth time how light the little starships were on the controls, responding to the slightest passage of his fingers over the sensors. A masterpiece! He'd specially volunteered for the difficult sortie because he'd logged more time in low-level fighting than anyone else in 91 Wing. DeBrugh had immediately insisted that Brim *lead* the raiders—then volunteered to fly as his wing.

With the wealthy young Wing Leader tucked close behind his left pontoon, Brim was now leading twenty-four Starfuries from both 914 and 28 Squadrons on a hunt for a huge Leaguer starship. An ultra-fast cargo transport of some 100,000 milstons displacement, the *Leumond-szegnis* had loaded a precious cargo of foodstuffs and weaponry two days previously and was moving toward the area with a huge escort of killer ships. The day before, she had been damaged by twenty-four ZBL-4s, but her large escort had set up an escape and she had subsequently disappeared in extremely unsettled gravitological conditions.

Rediscovered only metacycles ago at a League-held port on the planet Tserb-9, the ship appeared ready to be discharged from the repair facilities and continue on her mission. Five of the League's curious but lethal disruptor barges, each equipped with twenty-one twin-mount .189-mmi disruptors, were reported to be moored at a hover nearby, and sizable concentrations of killer ships cruised in stationary orbit overhead. Local gravity conditions were getting worse from the sudden eruption of three cyclical space holes in the area, and the surface weather was decaying rapidly with rain, fog, and low cloud. A great day for a visit! And if that were not enough, the repair yard itself was heavily defended by at least two hundred rapid-firing disruptors that had been rushed to the site.

Forty-two of the Sodeskayans' fast, nimble Petyakov PE-3 attack ships—specially equipped for such missions with .796-mmi super disruptors—were to force entry to the repair yard and try to finish off the *Leumond-szegnis,* or at least destroy her important cargo. The job assigned to Brim's Starfuries was escorting the PE-3s to their targets, drawing some of the barges' fire as they did so, and covering the operation against the Leaguer killer ships.

Brim separated his two squadrons into six flights of four ships each. He designated two flights as combat space patrol; the remaining four—numbered Red through Green—would fly the actual ground-level attack, silencing disruptor barges during the few moments necessary for passage of the PE-3s. After that, any survivors were to go after League killer ships drawn by the fracas. Even the most audacious of DeBrugh's Helmsmen considered the mission decidedly precarious— and Brim heard *many* remarks to the effect that when the Sodeskayans had a really difficult job, the poor bloody Imperials were called in to clear up the mess. This time, he quietly conceded their point. This *was* a tough trip, and no doubt about it. But there was also a war to win, after all. And in the process of breaking things and killing people, warriors ran a good chance of having themselves broken as well—or killed.

On the way to the rendezvous, they passed five Imperial-built Defiants painted with the Sodeskayans' crimson eight-pointed star insignia and fairly bristling with strange antennae. These ships would be headed off to take up station where their jamming gear could hamper the Leaguers' long-range BKAEW spotting gear. That jamming, combined with the gravity storms that were already causing a violent ride, poor surface visibility at the target, and massive blessings from Dame Fortune *might* just allow them to accomplish their dangerous mission.

Leading as Red One, Brim picked up the Petyakovs while skimming the fiery surface of a star known only as Mogor-938. Immediately they all set off obliquely across the void for Tserb through increasingly violent gravity storms that often hid the stars from their Hyperscreens and threw the starships around like toys. In spite of their enormous disruptors, the Petyakovs were setting a good pace and the lighter, storm-tossed Starfuries had their work cut out keeping up.

At Daylight:2:15, they slowed through HyperSpeed halfway between Tserb and its ninth planet—a dangerous maneuver, but necessary if they were to achieve any surprise at all. By now their own BKAEW systems were inoperable—and, a priori, the Leaguers' as well—thanks to the jamming efforts of the three Defiants. But there was always the possibility of meeting a chance Leaguer picket ship, so they dove at much higher speed than normal. In moments, the ships were blazing through ever-thickening atmosphere like meteors—heating rapidly to temperatures just short of explosively diffusing the hull metal collapsium that formed their hulls. Simultaneously, they were decelerating near the very cushioning limits of their internal gravity systems. At these insane velocities, even the best Helmsmen found themselves greatly challenged, for the ships twitched nervously as they passed through changing atmosphere pressures—and the slightest swerve could crumple their hulls. At the far edge of his vision, Brim watched one of the PE-3s suddenly come in half, then explode like a puffball. Everything forward, including the great disruptor, flew off to one side; the aft section with its heavy power chambers and Drive crystals went on falling like a great comet, while debris followed in every direction. Brim bit his lip—too bad about the Bears. But more importantly, at least to the mission, their target was still considerably around the horizon, so the Leaguers may not have seen what was coming.

Down he led them toward shapeless, smoothed-over cloud banks that quickly became moving, grayish masses fringed with color, hurtling toward them at truly frightening speeds. The flight bridge was tomb-silent—all he could hear on the intercom was breathing and an occasional gasp. He chuckled to himself, wondering how many of the crew were frightened as he was. At only a few hundred irals above the first cloud layers, he *carefully* nursed the steering engines and pulled out of the perilous dive with the spaceframe groaning and creaking. A glance in the rear viewers verified that the remainder of his flock had not only come through safely but was still in some semblance of formation. Now came the difficult part.

They entered the undercast abruptly, bumping and jolting in the stormy atmosphere while the ships made their final deceleration (he hoped) to the Petykakov's optimum ground-attack speed. By some miracle, they came out through the bottom in reasonably unaltered formation. Ahead, a dense fog bank loomed like a great solid wall, obscuring the planet's horizon like some great mountain range. Dropping to 150 irals altitude above the rolling surface of what appeared to be a vast lake, they flew through a few gray wisps of haze. Then the mist quickly thickened and rain began to pelt their Hyperscreens, boiling to vapor on contact with the white-hot crystal surfaces. Instinctively, the Helmsmen closed up to maintain visual contact. Any radiating source, even a proximity alarm, would give precious moments of warning to the Leaguer gunners below.

Suddenly a deep voice with a strong Sodeskayan accent broke the radio silence: "Target straight ahead in thirty-five clicks."

Bracing himself for whatever might come next, Brim strained his eyes to see anything through the soupy mist. "Enable weapons systems," he ordered. "Fire at will."

"Disruptors enabled," the Fire Control Officer acknowledged. "Full plasma charges at main batteries."

"Look out, Red Section, disruptor barge, bearing Red, Red-Orange," someone radioed.

Now directly Before Brim's speeding Starfury was an ugly gray mass in the rolling mist, a squat bridge, raised barbettes with twin-disruptor arrays, a KA'PPA mast bristling with communication gear. "Red One attacking on Red Red bearing!" he announced, instinctively lowering his head and nestling down behind the narrow flight bridge's scant forward armor.

Clusters of green and red disruptor beams started up from

every direction. Brim splashed through the spray from a burst that only just missed them; for long instants, water blurred his Hyperscreens. Suddenly his main battery fired a long, continuous burst, too low at first, exploding the water in soaring geysers of steam. Then the strobing beams rose toward the barge itself as it hovered motionless above the surface. Rising again, the beams exploded against the black-and-white-striped hull, then rose higher still to the first row of barbettes. An antenna crashed down; a tongue of flame spurted from somewhere. Seventy-five irals away, two Leaguers in black battlesuits hurled themselves flat on their faces. Fifty irals, the two ugly barrels protruding from a disruptor barbette swung to point straight at the nose of his Starfury. Brim's disruptors fired first, exploding all around the Leaguer barbette. Nearby, another Leaguer sprinted across the deck with two rounded tanks in his arms. Abruptly he toppled overboard, his legs burned from beneath him.

The barbette's two disruptors fired back; Brim could feel the vibration of powerful energy bolts searing overhead as he dove. The sky went momentarily dark and the Starfury shook violently from graviton columns while they passed beneath the hovering barge, their KA'PPA mast nearly scraping another barbette mounted on the vast plated belly. Then they were on the other side, turrets indexing rapidly aft to continue their murderous fire. Brim drove on at speed, zigzagging between great waterspouts raised by the enemy fire.

A flight of eight Petyakovs thundered past to port with their huge disruptors blazing. They looked like a swarm of fiery wraiths.

Brim skidded in a vertical bank over some sort of fortification—an eyeless, bristling octagon whose entire surface appeared to be belching fire as the structure turned on some internal axis. The Starfury jinked from a sudden updraft, then suddenly they were out over an immense curving apron of gravity-pool quays muddled with Leaguer starships of all kinds and descriptions. This surrounded a veritable forest of shattered wrecks sticking from the grayish bay at odd angles. Everywhere the hellish scene was intercrossed with strobing disruptor beams, lit up with blinding flashes, dotted with black and white puffs of smoke that erupted into flames and showers of sparks. Brim could see the *Leumond-szegnis* girdled by explosions, flames, and debris, rising above the other starships like some great bloated slug bristling with derricks and odd-shaped appendages. Her thick KA'PPA mast stood clear above the smoke like an obscene monument to death. A cheer went up from the bridge crew as the structure abruptly shattered in three places and disappeared into the flame and smoke below.

The Petyakov attack was at its height now, with disruptor fire erupting like a single extended explosion across the whole area. Colossal bursts of flame and dark clouds of smoke shot up everywhere, darkening as they drifted away in the wind. A Petyakov dissolved in the flash of disruptor fire loosed by the starship immediately in its van. A whole row of the enormous shipyard cranes near the big transport toppled slowly into an inferno of dark flame and sparks.

"Red Leader—Patrol Leader calling! League killer ships are about. Look out!"

A brace of Petyakovs emerged from the smoke, and Brim's disruptors indexed toward them. "Wait!" he shouted to the Gunnery Officer as he put the Starfury into a steep climb. "They're ours!" With huge grav units mounted on either side of the fuselage, they *did* look a lot like League GH 270s.

"Break, Red One!" DeBrugh's voice shouted on the radio.

Brim swung hard to port, white plumes of moisture trailing each pontoon. Instantly a GH 262 flashed past his nose, firing its main battery. One of the beams flickered onto the Starfury's nose with a deafening clangor. Brim rolled onto his back to give the gunners a better shot and a second 262 loomed up in the forward Hyperscreens, head-on and nearly on top of him. Its big winglike hull seemed to fling itself at him, and every turret lit up as it opened fire. With a tremendous crash, Brim's armored Hyperscreen shattered and became nearly opaque—but miraculously remained in its frame. Stunned by the terrific shock—and blind directly forward—Brim grimly held his course and hoped the Leaguer could see well enough to avoid a collision. A split click later, it passed below—just as yellow caution indicators flashed all over the Starfury's power console.

"Plasma pressure falling in the power chambers," a Systems Officer reported. "We'll turn up the wick, but watch for overheat."

The sky was alive with starships and disruptor bursts. Before Brim could reply, every forward turret let fly with enormous bursts of energy at another 262—this time, hits exploded along the enemy ship's slightly raised bridge. As Brim watched through his quarter 'screen, the Leaguer slowly turned over and headed down vertically, making sparks and belching greenish yellow smoke from its starboard Drive doors.

"Good show, Red One! You got him!" DeBrugh shouted jubilantly from the radio—while the bridge filled with raucous cheering.

Moments later, nearly a quarter of the caution lights turned from yellow to red, and a temperature warning glowed fitfully in the power quadrant. "Recommend we depart at once for Fomett Base," the Systems Officer said in a tight voice. "We'll need space cooling immediately if we're going to make it all the way."

"Got you," Brim replied, easing the Starfury into a shallow climb. He looked back once more at the furious battle that was still raging on the surface, warned DeBrugh of his predicament, then grudgingly set course for star J19-C.

They only just made it to Fomett, sliding to a dead stop at

the end of a Becton tube with the plasma pressure hovering just a little above absolute zero, and white-hot power chambers ready to explode. On final, Brim had used his blaster to shoot out some of the shattered Hyperscreens so he could see land.

After the other ships returned, he limped stiffly to the Operations Room, where he learned that 914 Squadron lost two Starfuries with all hands and 28 Squadron lost one. Eight of the Sodeskayan Petyakovs had been destroyed—also with all hands—plus two more whose crews had ditched in space but later had been picked up by rescue ships.

The *Leumond-szegnis*, however, had only been further, if *much* more grievously, damaged. Reconnaissance starships racing over the burning harbor only metacycles after the raid reported that the big transport was still hovering across the three gravity pools whose repulsion generators had been combined to support her mass. She was afire in a number of places, but it was clear that these would be extinguished soon.

On the surface of things, it seemed initially as if the mission had been a failure. But even though the two would-be allies had sustained considerable losses without achieving their objective, they'd obtained a real victory that—had they known—would have frightened the Leaguers to the soles of their jackboots. In the combined raid, humans and Bears finally had learned to work with each other. . . .

Midway through the next Standard Day, a brand-new Petyakov thundered down on Fomett Base to deliver a dozen cases of the most sublime Logish Meem Brim could remember tasting. That evening, ten fast Sodeskayan transports landed at the base, crowded with the crews of the Petyakovs who had gone on the raid—and more Logish Meem. *Much* more. The grand, drunken party that ensued for nearly a full day afterward (protected by an entire Group of ZBL-4s orbiting the base) would be the basis for friendships that, in later days, were credited for much, *much* more than destroying great numbers of Leaguer transports during the next Standard Weeks.

After the raid, however, three full Standard Days were to pass before Brim could file a meaningful mission report to Avalon. Albeit seriously damaged and operating under only one-third power, the *Leumond-szegnis* miraculously succeeded in getting under way a day after the raid, limping slowly from star to star until she reached the little cluster known as Voseludd in the old 19th District. There she was caught in open space and destroyed by another squadron of Petyakovs—this one with sufficient killer ships to scatter her escorts.

As the weeks continued, Brim flew a number of missions against Leaguer transports attempting to run the Sodeskayan blockade of Ksnaymed. Each time, he found himself amazed at the tremendous resources the Leaguers were willing to squander toward retention of the twelve next-to-worthless planets. Communiqués from both Gromcow and Avalon reported that the League's advance elsewhere along the Sodeskayan front had ground to a standstill. Most important, the frontline ground troops had experienced a drastic reduction of supplies that were normally brought in by transport. Added to this was a sudden—devastating—lack of support from space when Leaguer Army units called for help during attacks by powerful Sodeskayan ground forces.

Slowly, but very surely, it became clear that the Sodeskayan Army had never lost its vaunted invulnerability. Instead, its leaders merely had been lulled into complacency by years of dependence on an Imperial Fleet that no longer could cover the whole Galaxy with its great, royal-blue umbrella of power. In turn, that very complacence enabled the self-serving courtiers who deluded the Knez and almost drove the final nails into the Sodeskayan military coffin.

All that was in the past and rectified. Now the most critical questions had to do with Sodeskayan staying power. When the Ksnaymed offensive drew to a close—as it *absolutely* would during the next few Standard Weeks—could the Bears hold on until their own fabrication yards churned out starships enough to win a war? And how much aid would her allies have to supply? Answers would be needed immediately, for in spite of the Sodeskayans' most valiant efforts, Hoth Orgoth's transports *were* getting through the blockade, and each one that managed to unload even part of its cargo reduced the number of Standard Days the Sodeskayans could retain control of the area.

Brim was in Gromcow on 36 Triad when Vylyit began to end. It came as no surprise. The Leaguers had completed their buildup in Ksnaymed toward the end of the twenty-eighth. During the succeeding days (Standard time), Sodeskayan transport brigades had been quietly preparing a retreat that would cost them least in the way of lives and resources. Shortly after Dawn Watch began on the thirty-sixth, he was awakened by quiet chiming from the HoloPhone in the other room—he'd half expected a call and had slept lightly. Gently extricating himself from the warmth of Browning's sleepy embrace, he padded to the 'Phone, switched off its outgoing video, and enabled the display.

Immediately an image of Barbousse appeared in a tiny globe. "Admiral Brim?" it asked.

"I'm here, Chief," Brim said, enabling a military scrambler/decoder he'd installed at the phone's input. "Where are you?"

Barbousse's image appeared to reach beyond its enclosing globe; then a quiet chime announced that he was also using a scrambler/decoder and that the two devices had recognized one another. "I'm at the Defense Ministry," he began in a calm voice, "and it looks as if the Leaguers have started their breakout."

Brim frowned. "When?" he asked.

"About three metacycles ago," Barbousse replied. "They started strong assaults in at least ten locations around the Ksnaymed globe perimeter."

"Where's Nik?"

"At the Ministry, Admiral. He got here about a metacycle after the thing started, took one look at the situation, and KA'PPAed DeBrugh to pull back immediately for the big base at Zemsky, Grivna Sector—Starfuries, crews, and no more equipment than they could quickly stuff in that little packet of theirs. Then he told me to let you . . . beggin' the Admiral's pardon . . . er, *enjoy* yourself as long as I could before I called—which I did just now because Cap'm DeBrugh's on the KA'PPA mad as a dried-out knarl'l, demandin' to message with you in real time. I told 'im that you were on your way."

Brim let it all sink in. Little Operation Vylyit *had* to end this way, he supposed, but nonetheless . . . "Thanks, Chief," he said presently. "I'll be there soon as I can. If DeBrugh gives you any trouble, just break the connection; we'll blame it on the KA'PPA set." As the HoloPhone went dark, he tip-toed back into the bedroom and retrieved his clothes. Over the years, so many romantic encounters had ended with a predawn call to duty that he'd long ago learned to stack his clothing all in one place. It saved *much* fumbling in the dark.

As he pulled on his boots, he felt a hand on his arm. "Leaving so soon?" she asked.

"Yeah," he said softly. "Big doings out Ksnaymed way."

"No time for a little more . . . ?"

"Not this morning, Marsha," he said. "Wish I could, though."

He watched her nod in the half-light streaming from the living room. She hadn't pushed down the bedclothes, so it was clear she understood his business was critical. "It may be a while before we can get together again," she said offhandedly.

Brim frowned. "Anything wrong?" he asked with a strange sense of concern.

She shook her head. "Oh, nothing—except that these wonderful Sodeskayan nights with you are, well, at an end, I'm afraid," she blurted out abruptly. "Crellingham's got a new assignment in Avalon, Wilf, one he's been shooting for all his life. And I guess I've got to go along."

"Marsha," Brim exclaimed. "How long have you known about this?"

"Weeks now, Wilf," she said. "I just didn't want to face ending this—and I hate good-byes. But there's no putting it off anymore; we leave tomorrow on the afternoon packet."

Surprised at the strength of his reaction, Brim forced himself to smile and took a deep breath. "I'm glad you kept it to yourself," he admitted. "I hate good-byes, too." He took her hand. "Will I see you again?" he asked.

"In *Avalon*?"

"If that's where you'll be."

"Will you *want* to see me again," she asked, "—when you've got a whole city of human women to choose from, most of them younger than me?"

He shook his head. "You never did understand how absolutely desirable you are, Marsha Browning," he said. "And I guess you never will. But if you'll oblige me once in a while when I'm in town, I'll consider it quite an honor to keep on doggedly trying to get the information across."

She put her arms out to him, and they embraced. "I'll only be as far as your HoloPhone," she said.

"You'll hear from me," he pledged, feeling her tears on his cheeks, "whenever I'm in town."

"Promise?"

"Promise."

They kissed for a long time; then he stood.

"Don't say good-bye," she warned quickly.

He struggled for a moment, searching for the right words. "Next time in Avalon," he whispered.

"Next time in Avalon. . . . "

He let himself out of the apartment and drove to the Sodeskayan War Ministry with the damnedest feeling of emptiness. And it simply *wouldn't* go away.

After the thirty-sixth, Sodeskayan ascendancy around Ksnaymed quickly began to erode as the League poured even more reinforcements into the area. At last, on 6 Tetrad, the breakout was complete, and from Tarrott, Nergol Triannic crowed of another great victory for Leaguer tenacity. Vowing on intragalactic media that he would never—under any circumstances—relinquish a planet once it had been "purchased with the sacred blood of our gallant Controllers," he struck a whole series of garish new decorations for the Ksnaymed veterans. In his exultation, he even forgave fat Hoth Orgoth his failure to subdue Avalon, promoting him to the rank of Marshal and bestowing the wide gold sash of a "League Paragon," one of Tarrott's loftiest honors.

And ominously, pundits on both sides of the war once more began to proclaim that the League's Deep Space Fleet was "invincible."

While Orgoth's specially borrowed starship units returned to normal assignments along the front, their Sodeskayan opponents, as always wanting of support in space, resumed the endless succession of reverses that seemingly characterized their lot. But even as their war reached new depths of affliction, forces of renewal were stirring throughout what remained of Sodeskaya's huge domain. From critical lessons learned at Ksnaymed, Ursis immediately began reshaping and reforming the whole Sodeskayan military establishment, while old Dr. Borodov aimed for quantum strides in production. These accomplishments were hardly noticed by the galactic media, whose focus was toward spectacular battles and close-ups of bloody defeats. But in the context of a final victory, the workmanlike deeds, while slowing the Leaguers' seemingly inexorable advances, were also laying considerable groundwork for dramatic reversals of fortunes—if the Sodeskayans could only hold out for a little while more.

If. . . .

It was to that end that Brim found himself standing with Nik Ursis, Dr. Borodov, and a two-hundred-Bear honor guard one early morning at Budenny Spaceport. Out on the heated lake, I.F.S. *Royal,* one of a new crop of Imperial battleships, had just thundered to a stop at the end of the active landing vector and was turning onto the buoy-lined taxiway, her deep footprint shouldering aside big, white-crested rollers in lofty sheets of spray.

Aboard were General Harry Drummond and General (The Hon.) Gastudgon Z' Hagbut, traveling from Avalon for a first-hand "orientation" to the Sodeskayan armed forces, or so their travel orders read. But from the moment they arrived, it was most clear that they were in Gromcow for one purpose only—to discover what they could about the Sodeskayan domain's chances for survival in the immediate future.

Gastudgon Hagbut—most conventional *and* conservative of all Imperial Generals—wasted no time before unblushingly questioning the wisdom ("xaxtdamned *non*wisdom," in his terms) of supplying the Sodeskayan theater with *anything*. The first morning of the talks, he suggested pulling DeBrugh's busy squadrons back to Avalon. All the numbers he had seen indicated the Leaguers were winning their campaign—and rather handily, at that.

In the days that followed, Brim was on hand to tell him otherwise; so were DeBrugh, Ursis, and Borodov. Analysis of reliable information coming out of Tarrott via UPGO, the Bears' matchless intelligence ministry, suggested that although the war seemed little altered on the surface, Ksnaymed operations may already have effected a fundamental change in the likely outcome of the whole war.

During the three days of briefings, two underlying facts supported predictions of a dark future emerging for the minions of Triannic, especially when results of Ursis's recent gamble were taken into consideration:

Fact: While the Sodeskayans had indeed lost nearly seventy percent of the killer ships with which they started the war, the Leaguers had suffered destruction of almost *sixty* percent of the whole space force available to them in the Sodeskayan theater during one short campaign. Comparatively speaking, fleet strength had been drained to a degree that could only have been alarming to their commanders.

Fact: Many of the Sodeskayan losses during Ksnaymed were odd lots of old and obsolete starships, while the League's were nearly all modern Gorn-Hoff 262s, Gantheisser GA 88-As, Kreisel 111s, and scores of heavy freighters. The latter, in wartime, were virtually irreplaceable. Worse for the Leaguers: Even after factoring in production start-up problems, Sodeskayan starship replacements—in the form of potent new models—were still arriving at the front at a rate greater than the Leaguer factories could match. As Borodov reminded often, Leaguer industry was *also* tasked to provide for continuing warfare against a steadily strengthening Galactic Empire, among others. By no stretch of the imagination could it serve the needs of all theaters simultaneously.

Bombarded for three more days with accurate—irrefutable—numbers, both generals eventually conceded that the Sodeskayan Domain had at least an even chance of survival—and probably better than that. After more conferences—plus uncounted interviews with Brim, DeBrugh, and the "Imperial Bears," as DeBrugh's three squadrons were now affectionately known—reports were made and forwarded by KA'PPA to Avalon. Before the eighth day of their trip, the two-man working party had received back the first draft of a new treaty written by Emperor Onrad himself. According to this highly unique document, the Knez would provide limited charters to Sodeskayan territory on which Imperials could construct advanced bases and mount long-range attacks on the Leaguers. In turn, Onrad would supply war materiel in excess of his own strategic needs—as soon as that materiel became available. The treaty was initialed by both sides on its fourth draft, and soon afterward, Brim found himself in a limousine with his old Bearish friends, seeing the two generals off to Avalon.

Nothing—absolutely nothing—was finished, of course. Implementation of the new treaty still faced ratification by the Imperial Parliament in Avalon and the Sodeskayan Court in Gromcow, but that was the dominion of politicians, not soldiers. Much of what Brim personally hoped to accomplish in Sodeskaya had come to pass. However, alliances and promises were only a small part of successfully waging war. His place was now at the front, getting on with the fighting. And it appeared a *lot* of that remained to be done. . . .

Epilogue: Off Again . . .

It was snowing at Budenny Base beneath a dark, lowering overcast. The dreaded season of Rasputitisa was nearly at hand, and it was predicted that late winter in Gromcow would soon grow even colder as terrific gravity and radiation damped the star Ostra herself. Sodeskayan and Imperial banners snapped in the blustery wind, causing the hefty Bearish flagbearers to visibly brace themselves against the storm. Above the line of limousines drawn up at a huge gravity pad loomed the colossal bulk of I.F.S. *Royal*, moving restlessly in the growing storm. Singled-up tractor beams flashed and blazed to their optical bollards as the powerful starship tested her moorings above the deafening rumble of thirty oversized repulsion generators.

With the ceremonies and speeches at an end, General Hagbut had already said his good-byes and gone aboard the big starship. Now, at the bottom of the 'midships brow, the Bears had stepped back to permit Brim and Drummond a few last words. The General smiled and grabbed his hat as it tried to escape in the wind. "You've done quite a job here,

Brim," he said. "Onrad's damned pleased; but I think you know that."

Brim laughed; in the cold, his lips were already getting stiff. "The Bears did it all," he said. "I just got lucky—again." He paused, lightly touching Drummond's arm. "Harry," he urged, "for Voot's sake, don't let Hagbut go home to tell people this is a done deal. It isn't. Both we and the Bears will have to work damned hard to make any of this come true. Nik's said it time and time again—he *could* lose before old Dr. Borodov can really fire up production enough to stop the Leaguers. And without somebody back home to keep bothering everybody in Avalon, *we* could easily forget about how badly the Bears need our help. This Sodeskayan thing—it's a job for *both* domains."

Drummond grinned, his cheeks cherry red in the frosty air. "I won't forget, Wilf," he promised. "You can count on that. And you can count on Onrad, too. He doesn't forget his promises."

"I'll count on both of you," Brim said, then stepped back and saluted. "Now," he said, "I'd better let you go. De-Brugh's pulling back from Zemsky Base, and I ought to be there to help. If nothing else, I can still handle a Starfury pretty well."

Drummond returned the salute. "You're right about letting me go—I'm thraggling *frozen* in this Voot-forsaken wind. But you're dead wrong if you think you're going back to the front." He chuckled. "At least the Sodeskayan front, that is."

Brim frowned. "I don't understand," he said.

"I'm sure you don't," Drummond agreed, taking a crimson folder from inside his Fleet Cloak. "This arrived at the Embassy in the diplomatic pouch only this morning. Its so secret, I'm the only one who's read it since it left Avalon." He smiled. "Enjoy," he said as he leaned against the wind. "It's probably a little warmer on Hador-Haelic, where you're going.

"Hador-Haelic?" Brim demanded.

"Read it," Drummond said with a grin, then stepped into the brow. "See you soon!" he called over his shoulder as the moving stairs carried him rapidly up into the ship.

Brim looked at the familiar sealed folder from the Bureau of Fleet Personnel. Atalanta: the grand old Fleet outpost on Hador-Haelic, where he'd spent much of his second duty tour. A throng of memories *there*! And in a war like this, more chances for danger than there were stars in the sky. He shook his head. "Here we go again," he chuckled to the wind. With a wry grin, he strode back to the waiting limousine skimmer and his friends, the Bears. Another adventure was waiting somewhere out among the stars, and—truth to tell—he was anxious to be on his way.